THE

COURT

OF

MORTALS

THE

COURT OF MORTALS

STARIEL: BOOK THREE

A.J. LANCASTER

Published by Camberion Press, Wellington, New Zealand

Printed by IngramSpark.

A CIP record for this book is available from the National Library of New Zealand

ISBN 978-0-473-49911-2 (paperback)
ISBN 978-0-473-49912-9 (eBook)

Cover design © Jennifer Zemanek / Seedlings Design Studio

ajlancaster.com

To Erin, who has chill when I have none.

1

LADY PHOEBE NEARLY HAS A CONVERSATION

"HETTA, DEAR, YOU know I'm very fond of Mr Tempest," her stepmother began ominously, hovering awkwardly on the edge of her seat in the study. Phoebe had invited herself in for tea a quarter of an hour ago and had been slowly working herself up to this conversation since. Now her hands fluttered awkwardly as she finally neared her point: "And I don't like to interfere, but you *are* the lord and—"

Hetta hastily swallowed the sip of coffee she'd just taken, in order to interrupt. "And I deeply appreciate your non-interference!" She put the now-empty cup aside and rose in what she hoped was an authoritative way. "Now I really must be going; I need to speak with Mr Brown today."

It wasn't truly a lie; she *had* arranged to speak to the man who ran the Home Farm today, though technically that appointment wasn't until somewhat later. She glanced out the window in that direction, though the vast copper beeches screened the Home Farm from view. Fragments of cold sunshine filtered between wisps of cloud, and her land-sense told her the wind would rise throughout the day, bringing rain after sundown.

Phoebe gave a small sigh and put her own cup aside, recalling Hetta's attention. "Oh. Yes, yes of course. But…perhaps we could speak about it later?"

Or perhaps we could speak about it never, since I know what you're going to say already, and it's none of your business! She had to bite her tongue from replying. Phoebe didn't deserve her wrath; she was, in her own misguided way, trying to help, so Hetta mastered her irritation and said tactfully, "I'll see you at dinner." She moved quickly to the study door and let herself out into the hallway before Phoebe could protest.

Stomping along the hallway wasn't a particularly mature approach to the situation, but it was better than snapping at her relatives or tenants, so she gave in to the urge as she made her way through the house. If only her family hadn't all seen Wyn kiss her last year! Before that they'd been perfectly unconcerned about what Stariel's lord got up to when alone with the steward. But ever since Wintersol, she'd been subjected to everything from condescending lectures about family honour and propriety from the likes of Aunt Sybil to Marius's thinly veiled excuses to chaperone her every waking moment before he'd gone down to university at the start of term. Her younger siblings' reactions had varied from disgust (Gregory), staunch support (Alexandra), to embarrassing curiosity (little Laurel).

How foolish of me to think being lord would gain me more freedom in that department rather than less. Being scandalous whilst far away and low in the family hierarchy hadn't exactly been acceptable, but it *had* been ignorable. Of all the adjustments she'd had to make when she'd returned to Stariel Estate after living in the great Southern capital for years, that was probably the hardest. There, she'd been anonymous, but here she had no such luxury, and sometimes it made her yearn to be back at the theatre with her company.

She paused to glare into Grandfather Marius's eyes at the top of the stairs down to the entrance hall, the painting serving as a proxy for every interfering family member over the last few months. The past lord simply continued to look down his long nose, aristocratically disapproving as ever. She huffed at him and carried on down the stairs. *Why do they all care so much about my personal affairs anyway? Haven't we got far greater concerns to worry about, between repairs and linesmen and bank loans?* Her family's disapproval also seemed particularly unfair given that between them and the needs of the estate, she and Wyn had had precious little time for impropriety in any case.

That thought pulled her up short, and she halted as she reached the front door. Halfway up its smooth length was a circle of slightly different coloured wood where the door had been repaired after a fireball had damaged it—Jack had been very provoking that day. She touched her hand to the spot and had a short, guilty debate with herself.

Even though she wasn't actually due to meet with Jack and Mr Brown until later, a responsible lord still ought to use her morning efficiently. Since she'd left the accounts books back in her study, she couldn't mull over the estate's finances as she'd originally intended—but there were any number of other things that could do with her attention. Such as, to pluck a random example from her list, detouring to the library to continue her reading about sheep breeding. The library where she knew Wyn did lessons with Alexandra on this day each week—a lesson that would probably be ending very shortly.

Hetta made a face at the door and admitted to herself that sheep were unlikely to make an appearance in this scenario. She turned back towards the entrance hall anyway, her heart growing lighter with anticipation. The estate could just cope with her being Hetta-the-woman and not Hetta-the-lord for a short while; she was determined that the latter wouldn't swallow the former whole.

"Hetta!" Her half-sister Alexandra's voice sounded from the landing, making Hetta look up in surprise; clearly she and Wyn had finished their anti-compulsion lesson earlier than usual, then.

"How did the lesson go?" Hetta asked, searching Alexandra's expression. Alexandra had insisted Wyn try to teach her to resist compulsion, ever since Aroset had used that fae magic on her a few months ago. She'd been having nightmares. Anything that made her feel less helpless had to be a good thing, even though the lessons never left either participant in a great mood. But Alexandra seemed even more agitated than usual this morning.

Alexandra jerked her head in a wholly ambivalent motion. "Okay, I suppose." She was holding a piece of paper, and she glanced down at it and bit her lip before hesitantly beginning to descend.

A black kitten abruptly raced down the stairs in front of her, and Alexandra had to stop rather hurriedly to avoid treading on it. The kitten skidded to a halt in the entry hall and meowed up at Hetta. Since this one had taken a particular shine to Wyn, she couldn't help scanning the upper landing for a sign of him. But Wyn didn't appear, and Alexandra finished her descent without further misadventure, holding the piece of paper out to Hetta.

"It's from Wyn. He received it a few minutes ago, in the library—a wyldfae delivered it." Alexandra shaped the word 'wyldfae' tentatively; all of them were still adjusting to the new realities of their world. "He asked me to bring it to you."

Hetta took the note curiously. On thick, expensive paper in red, glittering calligraphy were the words: *10 o'clock, Starshine.* Beneath those, a hastily scrawled addition in Wyn's handwriting.

This isn't your debt. Debrief at the Stones, after?

A chill went down her spine, her wistful plans vanishing in an instant, because it wasn't hard to work out what the red calligraphy meant, not when the paper smelled like cherries and beeswax. Fae magic had scents—signatures specific to the person responsible for it—but even if she hadn't recognised this signature as belonging to Wyn's ex-fiancée, Princess Sunnika was the only person he currently owed a debt to. The princess had absolved him of his promise to marry her, in return for a favour unspecified. Was she calling in that favour now?

She stared at the princess's words, smoothing her thumb over the velvety texture of the paper. Despite the physical object, the summons still seemed faintly unreal. Oh, she'd known, when she'd dragged Wyn back through the portal to Stariel months ago, that that wouldn't be the end of it, but it would've been nice to be wrong, and the quiet months since had lulled her into a false sense of security. *It's not fair*, she had the childish urge to say. Surely bank loans and her badgering relatives were trials enough for anyone without having to deal with fae politics as well?

Stariel surged up in query, and she reassured it. <It's all right. It's just a note. No one's in danger.> Except danger frequently followed on the heels of fae, in her experience. A cold stone lodged in her stomach. What did Princess Sunnika want with Wyn, anyway?

The kitten meowed again, blinking up at her expectantly, as if she would suddenly produce Wyn if it complained sufficiently. Alexandra bent down and picked it up, and it grumblingly accepted the substitute. Its purr was much too large for such a small creature, echoing in the entrance hall.

Hetta read Wyn's note again and had a sudden urge to shake the paper in lieu of him. *This isn't your debt*, he'd written. Him trying to keep her and Stariel out of anything involving Princess Sunnika was all very well and noble, but also completely foolish. Hadn't they agreed they were in this together now? At least he'd sensibly named a rendezvous location outside the house after his ill-thought-out meeting, so she could rail at him for his foolishness at length without being interrupted by helpful 'chaperones'.

She glanced at the clock in the entrance hall, which showed two minutes to the hour, and some of her irritation ebbed. It explained at least why he hadn't brought this to her in person. Even flying, it would be a stretch to reach the boundary at Starshine in time.

As she thought the location, her land-sense stretched automatically out of the house, unravelling across the lake and down the course of the River Starshine to where the water crossed the estate boundary, deep in the woods to the south-west. The cool shade under the trees and the trickle of the water seeped into her. Pine needles and the bright green of budding oak leaves swayed, and her senses filled with the small sounds of the forest.

A tall, winged figure landed with a thump on the banks of the river just inside the border. He looked different through Stariel's eyes, and not only because he was in his fae form, a bright blaze of foreign magic unconnected to the estate. His wings lit up in the sunshine, hundreds of overlapping jewels. They were blue now rather than white, though little flashes of iridescent purple, indigo, and even emerald caught the light as his feathers rustled in the slight breeze. Silver frosted each wing tip. It was the first time she'd 'seen' him in his fae form since their return from ThousandSpire, even though that had been several months ago now.

Stariel curled around him like a cat, as if it would scent-mark him if it could. Before ThousandSpire, the land had viewed him with suspicious jealousy, but those events had swung its attitude from one extreme to the other.

Wyn frowned and turned a slow circle, as if he knew he was being watched. He gave a small, wry smile, and said softly: "Tell Hetta I'll be careful."

"What does it mean, Hetta?"

Her sister's voice pulled her back to the entrance hall, and the world wobbled slightly as she found herself back within the limits of her own body again.

She swallowed to rid her mouth of the taste of pine needles, unsettled. Spying on people using her land-sense wasn't a path she wanted to go down, not after seeing where it had led King Aeros. But Stariel was so ready to zero in on Wyn with the slightest encouragement, these days. *Which is almost definitely my fault*, she reflected.

<Don't do that again unless I specifically ask,> she told the land sternly. <I know you've decided you like him now, but you mustn't keep drawing my attention to him, or keep interrupting us just because you can't bear to leave us alone for five minutes together!> The latter had been particularly trying, of late. She was pretty sure Stariel meant well, but there was nothing more deflating than the equivalent of a boisterous puppy lurking over your shoulder and egging you on.

"Hetta?" Alexandra repeated, this time with a trace of concern. "It's about fae things, isn't it?"

Hetta shook herself back to the present again. "Sorry, Stariel and I were having a conversation." She'd had to admit to this more than once over the last few months, to explain her moments of abstraction. Her father had never had this problem, that she remembered, but then again Stariel had undoubtedly not been as magical back then, before the Iron Law came down. Not for the first time, she wished faelands came with a manual.

Alexandra raised her eyebrows and looked at the note meaningfully. "Isn't it?" she repeated.

Hetta frowned down at it. "Yes. But not dangerous fae things, I don't think." *I hope.* Princess Sunnika had been relatively friendly, in the past, or at least what passed for it among the royalfae Hetta had met. But still, why did Wyn have to be so very *reckless* about his own safety?

At least if she went up to the Stones now, she could spend some of her anxiety in magic while she waited for him. Emotion made her pyromancy stronger, though it had the opposite effect on her illusion, which required a cool head and fine control to do well.

But before she could move, a knock sounded at the front door, and both she and Alexandra swivelled towards it. In theory, Hetta knew she shouldn't open her own front door. But there was no sign of the hall boy, and it was frankly ridiculous to leave someone to wait on the chilly stone steps because of that.

She opened the door. There was a pause.

"Apologies, my lord," said the man on the doorstep, doffing his hat after a moment of blinking confusion. Hetta recognised him as Mr Plimmer, the foreman in charge of the men currently repairing the Dower House. "I meant to ask to speak to the steward." He looked sheepishly around the foyer. "I see this wasn't the right door."

"Oh, come in," she said, trying to adjust to the sudden change from fantastical to mundane. "But Mr Tempest is currently unavailable. What do you wish to see him about?" She dragged a rough idea of the schedule from memory, though Wyn had had far more to do with the day-to-day work than her. Making the Dower House habitable so it could be rented out was, after all, a key part of securing more funds for Stariel's future. "How are the roof repairs going?"

The foreman shifted uneasily from foot to foot, looking extremely apprehensive. "That's the problem, my lord. They're not. There's, um, a bat problem."

"Bats," she repeated blankly, inwardly rather relieved. The foreman's expression had suggested something much worse.

"Yes, my lord. Bats. Problem is, they're in the roof. My crew can't work with them there."

Her mind tried to stray back to Wyn's location at the boundary, and she jerked it back. *No.* She was the lord; she needed to deal with this, even if household pests seemed quite beside the point right now.

"Well, I admit I've no idea how one goes about de-batting a roof, but surely this is a problem to which there exists a solution…" She was about to ask him what he'd suggest when an idea occurred to her. "Actually, now I think of it, I'll be of much more use to you than Mr Tempest."

After all, she *was* the lord of this faeland, wasn't she—and therefore connected to all the creatures in Stariel Estate? That ought to mean she could magically encourage bats to vacate a roof. Guiltily, she found herself becoming much more interested in the problem. One ought to care about mundane things just as much as magical ones, but the problem was that one did not. The fact that exerting her land-sense in such a way would be an excellent distraction from eavesdropping on a certain location at Stariel's border was merely happy coincidence.

The foreman's apprehension only deepened. "The thing is, my lord, that they're not normal bats. And I thought Mr Tempest might know…" He trailed off, flushing.

A funny jolt went through her as she realised what he was getting at, and why he might want Wyn specifically.

He steeled himself and confirmed her speculation with his next words. "They're…I think they're fae."

PRINCESS SUNNIKA

YN WAITED JUST inside the southern boundary of Stariel, alone but for the wildlife. The birdsong that had paused at his entrance had now recommenced, and fluting calls of spring trilled from tree to tree against the watery background of the Starshine. He stood so still that a blue squirrel scurrying along a low branch beside him didn't notice his presence until it stopped to contemplate a leap, rearing back in offended surprise before disappearing in a streak of fur.

And then he was no longer alone. He tensed as the presence of a greater fae blazed along the leylines, though the birds didn't appear to care as Princess Sunnika stepped out between two trees on the other side of Stariel's border. He didn't cross to greet her, even though she stood further than a comfortable speaking distance away. The greater fae of DuskRose weren't winged—unusual for the greater fae of Faerie—but the shadowcats had a very powerful talent that made up for that lack. Normally it only worked on line-of-sight, but Sunnika had shown herself unusually talented with that magic. If she touched him, she could take him miles away from Stariel in an instant.

"Princess," he said, inclining his head. She was dressed for a formal meeting, and he felt suddenly under-dressed, in mortal clothes and plain ones besides. Her long dress had wide sleeves, and jewels cut in glittering leaf-shapes adorned her long straight hair, black as ink at its roots and morphing to cherry-pink at the tips.

Her midnight eyes were unreadable, and her furred ears twitched, a slightly warmer black-brown than her hair. "Prince Hallowyn Tempestren."

His true name should not sound so strange nor make him so uneasy.

She looked pointedly at the distance between them. "I do not intend to harm you."

Would it make her angry if he refused to approach her? It was technically impolite to show such open distrust, and he was in her debt. But he *had* promised he'd be careful.

"Forgive me," he said, "but harm is very subjective, and I'd like some reassurances that you don't mean to teleport me away the moment I cross the border."

Her smile was darkly amused. "I will not."

He stretched out with his leysight, checking they were truly alone, and crossed the boundary with reluctance. There was no loss of magic, since he was not bound to Stariel as the Valstars were, but he felt more exposed nonetheless, and he pressed his wings tight against his spine.

Sunnika took in his new wing colour. "I see you sport new colours." Her tail curled into a question mark.

"I do," he acknowledged, flaring his wings slightly. Any more would be considered a challenge, though he didn't know if a DuskRose fae would know that. Best not to take the chance. "Stormdancers often change their plumage when they come into their powers. We call them blood feathers."

"And have you come into your power?"

He shrugged. "How does a tree know that it is finished?" Her flat expression didn't change, and she didn't remind him that he owed her more than levity, but he reined himself in nonetheless. "I went into the Maelstrom and lived to tell the tale," he said, trying to explain a thing he himself didn't fully understand. "It...affected me. And, as you know, my broken oath is repaired."

He had no plans to tell her his control of his new power was still a fledgling thing, easily overcome. Perhaps she wasn't an outright enemy anymore, but she wasn't a friend either. Still, she was the first tangible contact he'd had with Faerie in months, and he desperately wanted to ask her for news of ThousandSpire's succession. Rakken had said he and his twin Catsmere had some plan to ensure Aroset didn't inherit, but surely they ought to have prevailed by now? Was no news good news? What if it wasn't?

He'd attempted to summon his godparent for answers, but the only response had been a deep, resounding silence along their connection. That had never happened before. But Lamorkin was one of the oldest fae he knew—surely that meant they would weather this storm? It was difficult not to worry, regardless.

But he could not ask Sunnika directly to remedy his ignorance, not unless he wished to increase his debt to her. A sideways approach was in order. "I hope that you've been well, Princess, and that your aunt did not disapprove of your actions." She'd released him from his vow to marry her, at the time when he'd most needed the power that his broken oath had shattered; Queen Tayarenn might not have regarded that as a good thing, even if it left him owing Sunnika a personal favour.

Sunnika tilted her head to one side, dark hair smooth as water. "You truly do, don't you? Perhaps I made a poor decision, releasing one who cares so greatly for my welfare from his promises to me."

Probably she was only teasing him, though it was hard to tell from her cool expression, but it still felt like thin ice. "I do not think it's helpful to re-live the might-have-beens of this decision," he said mildly. "But in any case, I am grateful for my release. I owe you a favour."

"Yes," she said, her lips curving. "You do. Tell me, how is Lord Valstar?"

"She is well," he said as neutrally as possible, but apparently he was losing his ability to mask his emotions, for Sunnika's smile widened.

"Ah, and there is the reason I don't regret my decision, Prince Hallowyn. You truly love her, this mortal woman, don't you?" She said the word 'love' with a kind of amused fascination.

"Yes," he admitted, struggling with the reflex to deflect the conversation away from his vulnerabilities. But it served no purpose here; the fact that he loved Hetta was a truth as inarguable as gravity—and as much a secret now too.

"And I have no wish to play second fiddle to a mortal," she said matter-of-factly. "Nor to play a minor role in someone else's starcrossed romance. I hope Lord Valstar appreciates my magnanimity."

His eyes narrowed. Sunnika had said before that she wished the Court of Dusken Roses to be on good terms with Stariel, the reason obvious enough, since Stariel was the only faeland he knew of that was also part of the Mortal Realm—but it didn't mean he liked Sunnika trying to use *him* to influence Hetta, even less than he liked her musing on his love life.

"Why did you call me here today, Your Highness?"

"So abrupt," she chided. "But very well." She paused, and he could tell she was choosing her words with care. "Tell me what is happening in the Spires."

FAIRY BATS

ETTA AND THE foreman contemplated the Dower House. It was a smaller and more modern building than Stariel House, although of course that still made it about eighty years old. A previous Lord Valstar had built it to house his mother, who Hetta assumed he hadn't much liked, given that Stariel House possessed plenty of spare bedrooms and the fact that the Dower House was on the other side of the lake from it.

She didn't have long to admire the facade, because the front door opened as they approached, and a confused jumble of workmen spilled out amidst billowing smoke, coughing and shouting.

Alarmed, she reached instinctively for Stariel. Her awareness rushed over the gravel and into the house, up and down stairs and through walls, shivering through brick and mortar. For heartbeats, she *was* the house, every creak and cranny of it. Bitter smoke sank into her ageing drapes and curled lazily in the drafts from ill-maintained windows. But there was no fire in the house. The only point of burning heat travelled with the humans who'd fled her, her floorboards holding the echo of their footsteps.

Her awareness flowed back outside, down the steps, and found the smoking torch being messily beaten out on the gravel driveway. She curled hands around it and *pressed*. The already dying embers snuffed out.

It was done. She pulled back her land-sense, trying to become merely Hetta again. For a few moments, it was like trying to stuff spilled tea back into a teapot, rivulets of awareness threatening to slosh out from her feet. She focused on her heartbeat, on the in and out of her ribcage with each breath, the cold bite of the air despite the sunshine. *I am a woman, not a faeland.*

Digging her fingernails into her palms to ground herself, she let go of the intense *knowing* that always came with reaching out too deeply. Remembering the number and location of every beam in the house's interior—and moreover, what each one *felt* like—was a good way to give herself a headache.

When she'd fully settled back into herself, the foreman was already striding forward towards his men. She measured the shortness of the distance between them with relief—good, she hadn't lost time then. She hated it when that happened, and she always worried that one day she'd go so deep she wouldn't be able to find her way back.

"What's going on then? Is that a torch, Fletcher?" The foreman scowled around at his crew.

There was some sheepish mumbling, out of which Hetta pieced an explanation: they'd been trying to smoke out the bats.

"*Does* one smoke out bats, typically?" she asked, coming up beside the foreman. There was a chorus of 'my lords' and doffed hats from the crew.

"No, one does not," the foreman said, with a scowl at the man he'd named Fletcher. "What were you thinking?"

Fletcher shrugged and looked around at the other men for support. "We just wanted a closer look at them, didn't we, after what Davey saw?" He waved at a curly-haired man with skin the colour of the freshly turned earth, presumably Davey. "We thought the smoke would make 'em quiet. Works for bees." He grimaced. "But didn't work on the...bats." He shot a nervous glance at Hetta.

"What exactly did you see?" she asked, noting his pause. "And what sent you running out of the house?"

The sheepishness levels increased, which she had no difficulty interpreting. None of the men wanted to admit they'd been afraid. But afraid of *what*, exactly?

"They're not bats, my Star," Davey spoke up, a touch defensively. The address startled her—it was an old-fashioned address for the Lord of Stariel, but it was Wyn's preferred one. His presence had crossed the border some time past now, and she tried not to worry about what that meant. What if it was an ambush? It was hard not to dwell on the fact that Princess Sunnika could teleport Wyn miles away in a heartbeat, outside the safety of the bounds. But Wyn wouldn't have been foolish enough to step across, if he'd thought there was danger of that happening. Would he? If only they'd had more time to discuss it first!

Davey looked round at the others. "Well, they're not. One of them bit Wilson. Show the Star your hand, Wilson."

At this, presumably-Wilson held up a reluctant hand, displaying an inflamed bite about the size of a coin, from something with a lot of needle-sized teeth.

"And I know what I saw." Davey met Hetta's eyes and straightened. "Those weren't bats like the steward isn't a man."

The crew, as one, sucked in their breaths, waiting for her reaction.

"They may well be lowfae," she said calmly, though her heart beat rather fast. The news of Wyn's nature had spread like wildfire across the estate, but so far no one had directly confronted her about it. "But it's unfair to compare them to Mr Tempest, who is not."

The man blinked at her. "But—"

"Mr Tempest is greater fae, and they have about as much in

common with lowfae as humans do with cats," she continued without pause. "Now, will someone please take me to these 'bats', and I'll see about encouraging them to move out of this house so you can continue your work. Mr Wilson, you should get that hand seen to." She looked around expectantly. "Mr Plimmer?"

The foreman jerked into motion. "Uh, yes, my lord."

Hetta's heart continued to pound as she followed him into the house. It was a measure of Wyn's charisma that the general reaction to news of his nature had been fascination and wary acceptance rather than outright hostility, but she was too aware of how quickly that could change.

They passed rooms full of white-draped furniture; the house had been shut up since before her father died. The smell of wood shavings and mildew curled around them, creating a strange echo of memory from when she'd let her consciousness roll into the house before.

The foreman's pace slowed as they reached the upper storey, and it was with trepidation that he approached the ladder that led to the attic. Through the open trap door at the top of the ladder came a strange chittering sound, subtly unlike birds. She reached out with her land-sense, more cautiously this time. She didn't need to count the nails in the floorboards; she just wanted to know what manner of creature she was about to encounter.

Touching the several dozen tiny sparks of the 'bats' in the attic, she found it as she'd suspected: the bats were lowfae.

<What are you?> she asked them—and Stariel. Stariel's attitude to the estate's native lowfae was generally disinterest, and so was its answer now: a shrugging impression of caves and small wings. *Piskie*, came the name. Hetta knew it, from childhood fairy tales, accompanied by charming illustrations of small, adorable blue cherubs.

The lowfae vibrated in response to her touch, and the chittering increased, acknowledging her as their lord. Now *that* was a disconcerting thought, that she had some level of responsibility for these creatures. "Will some of you come out so I can see you, please?" she asked.

There were fluttering and scrabbling sounds. With extreme suspicion, a trio of creatures hopped down the ladder and perched on the topmost rung, clinging with both clawed hind feet and hands. The foreman gasped, and all three creatures flared out their wings and hissed at him, baring sharp, needle-like teeth.

"They might look like bats, but that ain't normal bat behaviour," he said.

Hetta gave him a surprised look, because they didn't look at all like bats to her—or like the innocent cherubs named piskies in children's books. They *did* have bat-like wings stretching from their arms, but otherwise, they were spindly insect-people with furry ears, bluish-grey skin, enormous dark eyes, and tufts of wildly messy white hair.

Glamour, she realised with a jolt. Ever since Stariel had chosen her, she'd been immune to glamour. Maybe the foreman really was seeing only normal bats. She wondered if the crewman who'd said they weren't bats had a touch of the Sight.

"No, they're clearly not normal bats," she agreed. She directed her next words at the piskies. "I'm sorry, but you can't live in this attic."

More chittering. It wasn't words, but Hetta got the gist of it through Stariel. They liked the attic. No one else had a claim on it, and that was a hard thing to find now, with more and more lowfae arriving with the ways to Mortal open once more. They'd been pushed out of their cave in the Indigoes by other wyldfae, but this attic was better than that old cave anyway. They would defend it against the men with their smoke-sticks!

More lowfae. Coming to Stariel—and presumably to the rest of the human world as well. Despite her land-sense, she suddenly felt very small and ill-equipped. Stariel brushed over her for a second, responding to her emotion, half a question in the air. Worryingly,

it sent her an image of tumbling pebbles and the shaking begin-
nings of a rockslide. It mirrored her own sense of looming changes
beyond her control, which might mean she'd given the worry to
Stariel in the first place. How much did her own emotions influence the faeland? She sent wordless reassurance along the bond, and
the faeland subsided. Now just what, exactly, was she supposed to
do with that ominous yet incredibly vague metaphor?

She pushed that worrying thought aside for the moment. That
was a problem too big for her to solve right now, but this one at least
she could do something about.

"Nevertheless, this is a human home, for humans, not lowfae,"
she said firmly. "You shall have to find somewhere else."

Immediately, they began to cry out, high-pitched and pleading.
She tried to harden her heart against them. The wider estate desperately needed more funds, funds that would make her people's lives
better in real, tangible ways, and making the Dower House habitable again was a small but key part of that. The bank had granted
them the first part of a loan on the understanding that the Dower
House rents would provide much-needed cashflow, proving that the
estate was a reliable investment before any more funds were released.

But Hetta couldn't help thinking of how the piskies had acknowledged her as their lord, and she cast about for somewhere to send
them. Somewhere high and vacant. With some trepidation, she said
to them, "The western tower of Stariel House has a tower room that
is unoccupied at present. You may occupy it *temporarily* while the
workmen are here." After that… Would whoever rented the Dower
House accept lowfae living in the attics?

The lowfae's chittering took on notes of excitement, and she got
the impression that Stariel House was a coveted location.

"*Temporarily*," she repeated as they hopped back into the attic,
disappearing from view.

They didn't respond. The high-pitched calls increased, and from
above came a leathery whir of many wings as the flock took flight.

She felt their sparks swarming out of the attic through the hole in the roof, streaming towards Stariel House. Had she done the right thing? *Well, at least they're out of the roof, and I can always order them out of the Tower Room if I have to,* she reflected philosophically.

She turned back to the foreman, who was staring at her with his mouth half-open. She gave him a bright smile. "Well, as you can see, the bats will no longer be a problem."

He shut his mouth. "Er…yes, my lord." He said something else, but she didn't hear it, distracted by the sudden knowledge springing to the front of her mind as Stariel tugged at her attention: Wyn had just crossed the border.

REFLECTIONS

Wᴀ YN ʀᴏʟʟᴇᴅ ʜɪs shoulderblades, feathers rustling with the motion. Somewhere out of sight along the river bank, a frog croaked. Well. That could have gone worse, he supposed. On the one hand, he still owed Sunnika, but on the other, she'd inadvertently given him new information about the Spires. Worrying information. He hugged his wings tightly against his body before unfurling them with a snap.

Magic rushed out with them, flexing alongside feather and bone. His mortal form had felt more and more like a prison of late, ever since the Maelstrom and ThousandSpire. How had he gone nearly ten years without taking his true form, before the fae found him? He wasn't sure he could have managed it if he'd had access to his full powers, but he hadn't known then what he was missing. Youth and a broken oath had made him a shadow of what he'd been meant to be.

He flexed his wings, examining that thought. What was he becoming? He'd been Mr Tempest, mild-mannered butler, for so long. Who was Prince Hallowyn? Did he even *want* to be him?

He took flight in a rush of air magic. *But everyone knows what*

I am, now, he thought as he flew low over the woods and then swooped up above the lake. It didn't stop him from wrapping himself in glamour to make himself invisible to anyone chancing to look up. Glamour warped people's perceptions, but it had no effect on the physical world, so his blurry reflection arrowed across the lake below, an unfamiliar streak of silver and blue.

To his surprise, he reached the Stones before Hetta did, landing inside the stone circle with a commendable imitation of grace thanks to the lack of wind. He hadn't taken this form enough to regain the flying skill of his youth, and landings remained tricky.

It was peaceful up here, with only the distant sounds of sheep, and he turned in a slow circle, grounding himself in the familiar greens and browns of this mortal landscape. Despite the snow still dusting the foothills, the air had changed, holding a tantalising, earthy promise of rebirth. He smiled; he'd always liked spring here.

Inevitably, his gaze sketched higher, catching on the jagged peaks of the Indigoes, where King Aeros's bones lay deep in the earth, where Stariel had swallowed him. Wyn hadn't been up there since. The smile slipped from his face, and he turned back to face the Stones.

He'd built a portal here to ThousandSpire last year—where Hetta had saved him, hauling him back to Stariel before the Spires could claim him. Sometimes he woke, feeling the Spires' claws closing around him, digging into his soul. Other times he relived the moment the Maelstrom had snapped his wingbones. He'd never forget the sound of them breaking, felt rather than heard.

Suddenly cold in a way that had nothing to do with temperature, he changed back to his mortal form. It felt a little like stepping from a wide, wild vista into a small, tidy room. Known. Domesticated. Safe.

Smoothing down his hair, he extracted the rest of his outer garments from the bag he'd snatched up before his flight from the house. *But does this count as donning a costume or removing one?* he wondered as he twisted his bowtie into place.

The gentle crush of footsteps drew his attention, and he turned towards the sound and met Hetta's eyes just as she crested the hill. Her cheeks were pink with cold and exertion, and strands of flyaway auburn hair had escaped from beneath her hat.

A dizzying, soaring happiness bubbled up in him. "Hetta," he said, drawn to her as helplessly as iron to a lodestone. She was in his arms the next moment, eyes grey as stormclouds.

"I'm annoyed with you," she said absently as she twined her hands around his neck and tugged him down. "Just so you're aware."

He made a wordless, urgent sound of agreement as she kissed him. Heat arced between them, magic and desire both.

Kissing Hetta had become an exquisite torture over the past few months. Familiarity had only intensified it. Now he knew the intimate curve of her mouth, the way her breath would hitch when he kissed his way along her jawline. He knew the shape of her body, and the small, helpless sound she made if he ran his knuckles very lightly over her curves.

Fae politics could be damned.

Stariel hit him with the force of an enthusiastic wolfhound, and he reeled back. "Stormwinds-cursed faelands!" Magic fizzled under his skin, a frustrated crescendo.

Hetta grimaced, and the faeland's affectionate nuzzling abruptly subsided. "Sorry. You're still it's new favourite toy. It's because of me, isn't it? My emotions."

"Maybe," he admitted. "Though I cannot be sorry for…stirring your emotions." She looked even more kissable now than before, with her pupils blown wide and colour brightening her lips. He gave a very heartfelt sigh.

She chuckled and sat down on one of the long-fallen stones, and her gaze went distant in the way that meant she was prodding at her land-sense. "I feel like Stariel's trying to tell me something with all these antics, but the gods only know what."

"It could be the season," he suggested. "Springtime is traditional for...antics."

"I'm not a bird," she said crossly, drumming her fingers on the stone. "Tell me about Princess Sunnika. What did she want?"

Ah, right. Thoughts of fae politics came rushing back, almost as effective for cooling ardour as an ice bath. He sat down next to Hetta on the stone, leaving a careful inch of space between them.

"She wanted information." He gave a hollow laugh. "Information I did not have to give. Someone has closed the borders to ThousandSpire; no one has gone in or out since...we were last there, including DuskRose's spies."

Hetta frowned. "You've always said ThousandSpire had powerful wards against translocation."

"Even if they survived my Father's death, there have always been passage points, heavily monitored though they might be." It was fiendishly difficult—though not technically impossible—to make spells that would outlast the death of the caster. Had his father gone to such lengths? He hadn't thought King Aeros would acknowledge in even so tacit a fashion that his rule might one day end. "But all the ways have been sealed. Even the overland borders." It explained why he'd heard nothing, and why his godparent hadn't answered any of his summons in the last few months.

Hetta's expression shadowed. "What or who could close the borders like that?"

He looked towards the lake, where on the far horizon the distant peaks of the Saltcaps rose to mark the other side of the wide valley, outside Stariel's territory. "I don't know. It would take extremely powerful magic—or someone very gifted with portal magic, specifically."

Did Aroset have the power to do that? She'd shown an uncanny ability with portals, the last time he'd seen her. It might be possible. His heart squeezed. If she'd closed the borders, what did that mean for his other siblings?

"Aroset," Hetta guessed, echoing his own thoughts. She put a hand on his arm. "Would you know, if she were Queen of ThousandSpire now?"

"I'd know if the others were dead." He'd feel the shockwaves of his siblings' deaths through his bloodline, even in the Mortal Realm.

Hetta's hand slid down to his, interlacing their fingers in silent comfort. It felt impossibly selfish, to be here, to have this, when who knew what chaos reigned in his home court. Again, his gaze fell on the stones where the portal had formed, and he remembered the heady relief he'd felt when Hetta had dragged him away from ThousandSpire.

A needle of guilt wriggled towards the surface. If he'd let the Spires take him…but he pushed that thought down. Why should ThousandSpire's fate rest on his shoulders? Even discounting Aroset, he had four other older siblings all eager to take on responsibility for it.

Well, maybe not Koi, he amended. The High King knew what Wyn's oldest brother's desires were, but Irokoi had never been ambitious. Wyn wondered suddenly about Torquil, the brother closest to him in age, who he hadn't seen for more than ten years. Rakken had said he'd defected and left the Spires. Perhaps he too was somewhere outside it still, also wondering what was happening in their home court. Or perhaps he'd returned before the borders closed, tempted to try to claim the throne for himself. *But perhaps he doesn't want a future dominated by the Spires either.* Wyn had never had much in common with Torquil, but the thought that he might not be alone in his self-chosen exile from his home court cheered him nonetheless.

An optimistic blackbird flew to one of the stones and then hopped down onto the grass, searching for worms whilst watching them out of one eye.

"How was the lesson, this morning?" Hetta asked softly, and he knew her thoughts had gone from Aroset to the compulsion she'd used on Alexandra. "Are they helping, do you think?" He could see the worry in her, no less than his own, but he could not give the unqualified reassurance he knew she wanted.

He sighed. "I wish I knew a way to make her immune to compulsion entirely, but in truth I do not think such a thing is possible. However, her resistance *is* improving, and even a small advantage may be helpful, if the situation arises, which I intend to do all I can to ensure it does not." The dark shapes of the Indigoes drew his gaze once again.

She squeezed his hand. "*We* will do all we can. You're not solely and wholly responsible for our safety, you know." He turned towards her, and her grey eyes met his, a challenge in them.

"My Star," he said, bowing his head, knowing the non-answer would provoke her.

She poked him in the ribs. "Wyn!"

"Very well; I acknowledge your claim on this land and its people." He could not do otherwise; it was as much a part of her as her pragmatic nature and passion for coffee.

She huffed, but her eyes sparkled before going distant. "Speaking of this land, I invited a flock of piskies to live in the Tower Room."

He gave a startled laugh, and she told him of her day's adventures.

"Well, that will certainly be an interesting thing to explain to the new housekeeper," he mused when she'd finished. The new housekeeper had joined the staff only a month ago. So far, she'd proven a hard-working and pragmatic woman, much less concerned with his fae nature than with him not interfering with her management of the household. Hopefully piskies would be met with a similar attitude.

One couldn't see the house from the Stones, but they both looked in that direction anyway. Hetta's expression tightened. Was she imagining the same scene as him, of one or other of the household coming upon the piskies unprepared? The various obligations they both juggled jostled around them, unspoken but acknowledged.

We should get back. The words sat on the tip of his tongue, unspoken.

But Hetta straightened, a steely determination in her expression. "Well, if we're going to be playing fae politics, we're going to need more practice." She smiled, with a hint of wickedness. "Besides, no one knows we're up here yet."

5

LIGHTNING EXPERIMENTS

"THIS IS *NOT* what I thought you had in mind when you said 'practice'," Wyn groused down at her, the weak spring sunshine glinting in the white-blond of his hair. He stood a few feet from two of the taller Stones, on the opposite side of the hilltop to her. "I thought you wanted to experiment more with your land-sense."

"I do, but you're the one who's most worried about your control, and this is practice for both of us. Maximum efficiency," she pointed out from her seat. She drew her feet up and crossed her legs, glad the skirt she'd worn was loose enough to allow it. If she'd known she was likely to be tramping about the estate, she would've worn her work trousers. With the sun at its peak above them, it was almost warm, despite the bite in the breeze. Deciding to enjoy it while she could, she shucked off her coat and put it neatly beside her.

He sighed. "I won't forgive myself if I electrocute you."

"I don't think that's at all likely. I have complete faith in you." And he had to stop hiding from her—and more importantly, from himself—or this thing between them was never going to work, regardless of the soft, sugary happiness that welled up in her whenever she saw him. It seemed to be one of the irrational side-effects of love.

He eyed the space between them. "Do you realise exactly how unpredictable and powerful my magic has been these past months? How utterly unprepared I was to deal with it? How dangerous I could be if I lost control over it?" His voice had gone tight and angry, not at her but at himself, she knew. In counterpoint to his words, a bumblebee weaved drunkenly around his head before deciding there was no nectar to be had there and continuing on its way.

"We're *all* dealing with new and untried magic. And you're no more dangerous than I am," she continued. "Less, on Stariel's lands, in fact." A fact she preferred not to dwell on, though it was true enough. On the estate, she had more raw magic at her disposal than anyone, though raw magic was not as useful as, say, insulation or linesmen, when it came down to it.

"You've never accidentally called down lightning," Wyn argued.

"You were unprepared then and it was still fine," she disagreed. "It's therefore even more likely to be fine now, with both of us prepared." That was how it had gone the first time his new magic had surfaced unexpectedly: lightning on a clear day, and Stariel snapping it out of the air like a dog catching a stick, leaving both of them wide-eyed with shock, and Hetta's hair standing on end with the static remnants.

Wyn took a deep breath and measured the distance between them again. After a moment, he muttered: "I don't trust my control in this form." He shrugged out of his coat, folding and placing it on top of the nearest stone. His expression was carefully neutral, which meant he was feeling self-conscious.

Between one moment and the next, he shed the proper steward and became fae, complete with wings, horns, and pointed ears. It changed the aspect of his face subtly, his features sharpening, the colour of his eyes deepening. Hetta couldn't help mentally overlaying his two selves, trying to find the man who made her heart sing in the face of the impossibly beautiful prince before her.

She shook her head; she was being ridiculous. It wasn't as if Wyn in this form was unappealing—if anything, there was a trueness to him like this. It was only that he was less familiar, and unfamiliarity, she thought matter-of-factly, was a problem easily solved by exposure. Speaking of which—

"What a pity I had all those shirts specially made for you," she reflected. The shirts she'd given him as a Wintersol gift were made to accommodate wings and meant that he didn't need to go bare-chested anymore when he changed shape. Why had she thought that would be a good idea? Wyn's supply of such shirts had increased over the last few months, so he'd clearly commissioned more, probably feeding the spreading rumours about him, inside the estate and out. But still not any modified coat. Perhaps he didn't think it worth the bother to get one tailored.

"My love, I'm about to undertake a potentially dangerous experiment that depends not only on my focus and self-control but on your quick reflexes if something goes awry, and you are complaining about a missed opportunity to ogle my shirtless self?" His wings shifted restlessly. He was easier to read in his fae form, unable to keep his feathers from betraying his emotions.

She leaned her elbows on her knees and took a moment to consider. "Yes, that's exactly my complaint."

His eyes danced. "*Hetta*. You aren't helping my concentration."

"Isn't that the whole point of this exercise?" she teased. "So you can prove to yourself you won't lose control of your magic under pressure? Who knows, perhaps Stariel's only been so troublesome because it needs reassuring that you're not about to explode into a lightning storm the minute you get excited."

He raised an eyebrow. "The minute *I* get excited? And what about the effect of *your* emotional state on *the land you are magically bonded to?*"

"Well, that's just more reason for me to practice communicating with Stariel, isn't it?" she pointed out. "It has to grasp the concept of privacy eventually, doesn't it?" This last was a skyward plea to her estate, which so far had shown a disheartening lack of comprehension on the subject.

"Both our existences support that conclusion."

She wrinkled her nose. On the one hand, it was reassuring to know it *had* to be possible to have a normal relationship whilst bonded to a faeland. But on the other, she'd much rather not consider either his father or hers from that angle. Instead, she reached for Stariel.

<We're going to try an experiment,> she told the land, supporting her words with images. It was better with images. <I may need your help if it goes awry.>

A feeling of willingness.

"Stariel and I are ready," she told him. "So you can stop delaying."

He rubbed one of his horns, a physical tell that she'd never seen from him in his mortal form. It was oddly endearing, how much easier he was to read like this. "I worry," he admitted.

"You worry too much. Think of the rewards, instead!" She put her hands behind her head and leaned back against the flat rock, knowing it would emphasise the curves of her breasts against her blouse. Wyn tracked the movement, unable to help himself.

"You're doing this on purpose," he accused.

"Well, if your control over your magic is fractured by only very mild flirting, you're of no use to me," she pointed out.

"I intend," he said, voice gone deep, russet irises nearly swallowed by black, "to be of very great use to you, my Star."

She shivered as their gazes locked. "Stop delaying then," she said. "Or with our luck, our 'chaperone' will turn up before you've begun."

He grimaced at the reminder that her cousin Jack was more likely than not to come hunting for them. In Marius's absence, Jack had taken it upon himself to guard Hetta's virtue, whether or not she wanted it guarded. And whether or not it actually needed guarding. Wyn's erratic magic and Stariel's attitude were perfectly adequate chaperones without additional help, she thought sourly.

"You'll do fine." *And Stariel will catch it if you don't*, she added silently, pressing her fingertips into the earth and burrowing a little deeper into Stariel. But she wasn't truly worried. Wyn was rarely reckless and never with magic. She'd never have talked him into this if he thought there was any real danger.

Wyn took a long breath and shifted his stance, fanning out his wings to their full extent in a glory of iridescent azure. A feral wildness rose in him, bringing with it the smell of dust after rain and the thick spice of cardamom. His brown skin grew faintly pearlescent, the strands of his hair shifting into a liquid metal that matched the silver filaments on his blue, blue wings. Pressure beat against her eardrums, and she swallowed to try to release it.

In that moment, he looked both magnificent and inhuman, with no connection to his usual everyday self. Power swelled in the air, and though the sky was clear, in the distance Hetta felt clouds respond to his summons, a storm trying to begin with him at its centre. Leaning in to Stariel, she discouraged the unnatural weather. It felt remarkably like taking handfuls of grain and scattering them, only to have the wind whirl them back into piles as quickly as she could throw.

Wyn corralled the effect with visible effort. The gathering of distant stormclouds ceased, and the power shifted to the here and now, rippling in the air in front of her.

Lightning—or at least its lesser cousin—curled around him in blue-white snakes. He opened his eyes, and she gasped, for in the russet of his irises, tiny bursts of lightning flickered, as if the storm was looking out. Goosebumps broke out on her arms, every fine hair standing on end. Stariel crouched just beneath her surface, waiting to pounce. She held her breath.

He smiled and drew a smooth shape in the air. The lightning

wound down his arm and pooled in his hand, a stuttering ball of blue-white charge. Laughing, he held it up and let the ball spin slowly over his palm.

"Pretty, isn't it?" A rare joy shone in him, and her heart lifted. He didn't often let himself simply *enjoy* magic.

She let her grip on Stariel ease, smiling back at him. "Can I come closer?"

He transferred the blue orb from one hand to the other. "Slowly," he warned. "People carry their own elektrical field. They start to interfere with each other, and I need to adjust for that."

She got up and took one tentative step forward, then another. The air on the grassy hilltop grew dry and thick with ozone, and the storm in Wyn rippled in response to her movement, contained but churning. She took several more steps and felt the moment the magic began to unravel even before he spoke.

"Stop!" he said. "I'm going to have to ground the power." His chest heaved with exertion, primaries spread wide. Little sparks arced from feather to feather, and his silver hair stood on end, rippling in response to currents not caused by wind. The lightning in his eyes almost obscured the russet. He'd never looked less human, an unearthly being of storm and wind.

"I'm ready," she confirmed, gathering up Stariel again. The land bristled under her skin, heather and pine and bluebells in this season.

Wyn nodded.

The power slammed into the ground at his feet in a rush, and Stariel leapt, swallowing it in a single gulp. For a moment, she was blinded by the sudden assault on her magesight, and she stumbled. Strong arms steadied her, and she found herself crushed against a warm male chest.

The lightning was gone from his eyes when she looked up, and she could feel his heart pounding under her hands.

"Do we call that a success or a failure?" he said ruefully.

She was about to answer when the world shuddered. They both

gripped each other for balance before simultaneously realising that the world wasn't literally shaking; something was disturbing Stariel's magic. She reached for Stariel for an answer and received it between one breath and the next. *There*. She turned instinctively towards the source of the disturbance.

Between two of the stones, where Wyn had previously made a portal to the Court of Ten Thousand Spires, a line of dead grass was spreading, reaching towards them. Not *them*, she realised in horror. Reaching for *Wyn*.

The dead grass was just the visible sign of the searching tendril of foreign magic creeping into Stariel, tasting of storms and minerals and blazing heat. In the space between the stones, hints of another landscape glimmered in and out of focus—a city built of towering rock needles.

Anger not all her own blazed up, and for a heartbeat her and Stariel's goals were perfectly synchronised.

<Get out! He's mine.> She wasn't sure if the words came from her or the estate, but both of them meant them. She shoved power at the incursion, her own magic entwined with Stariel's. <Get out!>

ThousandSpire was bigger, older, and probably stronger than Stariel, but they stood in the heart of Stariel's territory. She and Stariel forced the incursion out, inch by inch, until the space between the stones settled to show only the forested foothills of the distant Indigo Mountains once more.

Wyn stood a few feet nearer to the old portal, as if he'd taken the steps without realising. He looked down at himself and back up to where ThousandSpire had tried to reach through, slow horror creeping over his face. Every one of his feathers was raised, making his wings appear larger.

"It wants you," she said. "The Court of Ten Thousand Spires." And that meant—what? That it hadn't bonded a new ruler yet? Or had it been acting under its new ruler's instruction?

"Yes." His voice was hoarse, and the same panicked speculation she felt skittered across his face before he folded his horror under a mask of composure, though his feathers didn't flatten.

Running footsteps sounded on the path, and Jack came crashing into the stone circle like a red-headed dervish.

"What in blazes was that?" he said, spinning around and searching frantically for danger. All the Valstars had a magical connection to Stariel, but Jack's was stronger than most. He spotted the line of dead grass making an arrow from the two stones towards Wyn's feet and whirled on Wyn. "What did you do?" he demanded. A quick glance at Hetta and he added, for good measure: "And what do you two think you're doing, wandering off alone together?"

"In order: I don't know; Wyn was experimenting with his magic; and none of your business," she said.

Jack bristled. He was a broad-shouldered man with brilliant red hair, but when he bristled, he looked like nothing so much as a bulldog with a bone. "What do you mean, experimenting?"

Hetta ignored him for the time being and put a hand on Wyn's shoulder, making him start. "I thought the wards we set were supposed to stop portals from forming inside the borders?" she asked him quietly.

"The resonance here must be stronger than I realised." He stared down at the line of dead grass only a few feet from the tips of his boots, tracking it back across the hilltop to the base of the two stones. "Or ThousandSpire more desperate. My magic just now must have strengthened the link."

"Could it happen again? Was it acting under someone's instructions or of its own accord, do you think?"

"I do not know," he admitted, still staring at the stones. "I never expected ThousandSpire to make another grab for me. I cannot think of a precedent for two faelands warring in such a way."

Jack glowered at where Hetta's hand rested on Wyn's shoulder.

"It's not appropriate, Hetta!" her cousin burst out, unable to help himself. "The two of you lollygagging off together without a care for what people think. You know the rumours are spreading."

She frowned at him. "If anyone knows the two of us are up here alone, it'll be because you told them."

"That's not the point and you know it! I don't like it, and the gods know the family doesn't like it, but you better bloody well be planning to marry him, the sooner the better! Either that or send him away!"

She glared at Jack. He glared back. *Marriage.* Neither she nor Wyn had said it aloud, but Hetta had felt it circling them, becoming ever more conspicuous in its omission from their conversations.

"That's a conversation for Hetta and me, not you," Wyn said with deceptive mildness, his feathers still fluffed up—this time in irritation, she thought. "But was that the only reason you came up here, Jack?"

Jack narrowed hard grey eyes at Wyn. "No, it wasn't." He turned back to Hetta and spoke a sentence Hetta had never thought to hear again: "Lord Penharrow wants to speak to you." He scowled at the thought of their traitorous neighbour. "He's down at the house."

6

AN OLD FLAME

"**F**OR THE LOVE of little green apples, why didn't you send Angus packing?" she asked Jack as she accompanied him back. The Standing Stones were only a short walk from Stariel House, though they were shielded from view by the surrounding forest. Wyn took the sky road so that his return wouldn't coincide with theirs. It was irritating to have to take such measures, but still better than suffering through another round of censure from Aunt Sybil.

"My mother invited him to take tea before I could intervene," Jack said stiffly. He knew as well as she did that Aunt Sybil had her own agenda, which probably involved Hetta marrying Angus and Jack managing the estate while Hetta settled into domestic bliss with the neighbouring lord. Hetta had made it clear she was no longer on speaking terms with Angus, but Aunt Sybil wouldn't let a little thing like that stand in her way.

"Oh, well, that explains everything! We mustn't be uncivil if there are teacakes involved, after all!" Her anxiety about what had happened at the Stones had transformed into anger, aimed at this much easier target. She might not know what to do about ThousandSpire, but she knew exactly how to feel about Lord Angus Penharrow. How could Jack have sided with his mother in this instance? He knew exactly what Angus had done to Stariel.

Jack drew up short and swivelled to face her. Behind him rose the great bulk of Stariel House, the standard of the Valstars fluttering from the tallest of its three towers. "What in the hells else was I supposed to do?" His grey eyes glittered dangerously. "We never made it public knowledge, what he did. Did you want me to open that particular can of worms in front of my mother?"

Hetta glared at him, because he was right. Aunt Sybil had always hoped Jack would be chosen as lord, and she'd make a terrific fuss over the fact that Hetta's lordship had been illegitimate for those first few months thanks to Angus's efforts.

"Oh, very well, you're right," she said ungraciously, wrestling her temper under control. "But what does Angus even want? He must know he isn't welcome here."

"Your guess is as good as mine," Jack said, scowling at the house.

She shared his sentiment. If Angus Penharrow thought he could just waltz in and take tea with her aunt as if nothing had changed… well, she was going to make certain he regretted his choices regarding Stariel. With this goal firmly in mind, she made a detour to change after they reached the house and allowed herself some judicious use of illusion. The magic boiled out of her and knotted itself into tangles on her first efforts, creating the opposite of the smoothly coiffed appearance she'd intended. It didn't help her feel any more in control of today's series of events, and the Hetta who'd earned her mastery in illusion was appalled at the slip.

She sat down in front of the mirror and took several deep breaths before trying again, pushing Stariel away. Her connection to the land might boost her power while she was on the estate, but it didn't change the fact that illusion required fine control and rigid mental focus. *I didn't fight to earn my mastery just to forget it all upon my lordship*, she told herself firmly, visualising the loops and whirls of the spell.

She was glad she'd taken the time both to calm down and to do things properly when she entered the room where her aunt was entertaining their neighbour. Angus caught himself quickly, but not before she saw the pang of mingled admiration and regret cross his expression when he saw her.

I might be petty, she thought, *but that was still very satisfying.*

Angus rose when she entered and bowed a greeting. "Hetta," he said, irritating her with the way he said her name as if he still had some kind of right to do so. But irritating her even more was the fact that he was still just as handsome as ever, continuing to be curly-haired, broad-shouldered, strong-jawed, and smiling the same easy smile that had set her heart fluttering as effectively at sixteen as at twenty-four. Shouldn't villainy make a difference to people's appearances?

"Lord Penharrow," she said frostily. Aunt Sybil's lips pursed, and she pointedly put down her teacup. "You wished to see me?" Her aunt could disapprovingly rearrange china all she liked; Hetta wasn't going to pretend to be happy Angus had come here.

"Yes," he said, and again regret flickered over his face. "Though I know you've not much love for me. I'm deeply sorry for that."

Aunt Sybil looked between the two of them, burning with curiosity but too well-bred to ask for an explanation. Everyone knew that the courtship between Angus and Hetta had cooled very suddenly, but only Jack, Marius, and Wyn knew why.

"Well, if you've something to say to me, come up to my study and say it," she said finally. "Otherwise, I have work to do."

He took his leave of her aunt, and it irritated Hetta all over again that Aunt Sybil didn't protest. She knew exactly how her aunt would react if she'd suggested speaking with Wyn alone.

He silently followed her up, and she shut her study door with a snap. "Well, are you going to explain why you wish to talk to me?"

she said, folding her arms. "Or is this simply an excuse to steal another family heirloom?"

Angus winced. "I suppose I deserve that. For what it's worth, I regret my actions deeply. Are you going to invite me to sit, or are we going to stand here glaring at each other until day's end?"

She'd always liked Angus's frankness, but it irked her now. How dare he try to be likeable?

"You may sit. Don't think it means I forgive you." She took her seat behind her great oak desk, the solid weight of it reminding her of her position. She wasn't the teen girl who'd been infatuated with Angus Penharrow anymore; she wasn't even the woman who'd considered marrying him when he'd proposed several months ago, before his deception had come to light. She bolstered herself against his disarmingly non-villainous appearance. *I'm the lord of a great estate and in love with another man. I don't care what Angus Penharrow thinks of me, and I'm not going to forgive him just because he says sorry nicely.*

Angus seated himself opposite, at ease despite having to fit his large frame into what she knew to be quite an uncomfortable chair. It felt strange to be seated so formally, as if she were interviewing him. They'd never been in this room together before; all their previous encounters had taken place in other, less business-like settings.

Despite vowing not to care what he thought, she wondered how it looked to him. Was he making comparisons to her father's day? She saw him take in the framed picture of the Sun Theatre on the far wall, one of the few changes she'd made to the otherwise old-fashioned room.

"I know the decor is traditional rather than fashionable, but I like it," she said, knowing she was being shrewish but unable to help it. "A happy coincidence, since we can ill afford to redecorate, thanks to our previous steward's dishonesty."

He gripped the armrests tightly, pressing his lips together. "I never knew about Mr Fisk's skimming from the accounts, and I certainly wouldn't have condoned it."

"Perhaps you should've given him a bonus for going beyond the line of duty?" she suggested, her light tone at odds with the white-hot anger flaring up as she remembered that piece of Angus's work all over again. "After all, you were paying him to make sure my father, and then me, got into such financial trouble that we'd be forced to sell you the land you wanted, weren't you? Ha! How dare you try to draw lines between 'acceptable' and 'unacceptable' treachery and tell me you could've done worse!"

He sighed. "I've said I regret my past choices, lass. If you rake up at me about it every other sentence, this conversation's going to take a while."

"Don't you 'lass' me; it's Lord Valstar to you."

Amusement glinted briefly in his hazel eyes. "Well, I will if you insist, though it seems a mite silly to pretend to be strangers. Also, 'Lord Valstar' rather puts me in mind of your father."

"He was Lord of Stariel, as am I. The comparison is appropriate," she said, though she was already regretting her hasty words. She'd known Angus since they were both children; no title in the world would erase the history between them. It *was* silly.

"Yes, but I've never kissed your father," Angus said frankly, startling a laugh out of her.

"You're not going to humour me out of my displeasure," she warned him, even though this was already occurring in spite of herself.

"No harm in trying though, is there?" he said with a quick, disarming grin. His gaze grew thoughtful. "And since you're here permanently now, I've plenty of time to try to make things right, don't I?"

She stiffened. Did Angus still think she was a fake lord? He'd never really believed in Stariel's magic, and they hadn't spoken since

she'd confronted him and forced him to hand back the Star Stone
that was an integral part of Stariel's Choosing Ceremony.

He read her easily enough and shook his head. "Nay, I know
you're no impostor, Hetta. You were right to take me to task for not
believing in the Valstars' land-sense. I don't pretend to understand
exactly how things resolved, but I know Jack wouldn't be looking
at me like I'd killed his dog if he didn't know full well what I'd
done. And if he knows, and you're still lord..." He spread his hands
in a gesture of surrender. "Congratulations on your ascension. I'm
glad of it."

"Forgive me if I doubt your sincerity."

"Credit me with enough personal vanity to be flattered that
Stariel chose the same person as me for lord." He twinkled at her.
"It confirms my great taste."

He's not charming, she reminded herself. *Remember what he did,
for his own gain.* But part of Angus's attraction was his self-assurance.
And though she could lay many faults at his door, he'd never been
driven by malice, and there had been a sliver of sincerity in his
courtship of her. It made it difficult to properly hate him.

"Why are you here, Angus?" she asked him tiredly.

"To offer recompense for my sins." He took a crisp envelope from
his coat pocket and slid it across the desk to her.

She unfolded its contents, skimmed them, and made an exasperated sound. "Really?"

"It's a traditional peace offering, in the North."

He was right, but it still sat badly, accepting anything at all
from him.

"Let my man know when it's convenient to shift them over here,"
he said, taking her silence for assent. He paused, and then leaned
forward, resting his forearms on the desk. "If there's anything
else I can assist you with, I will. I mean to make it up to you, the
harm I did."

She frowned down at his hands, which had stopped just short

of reaching for hers. This was fortunate, because she wasn't sure she could've stopped herself from singeing his eyebrows off if he'd touched her. Irritation and amusement see-sawed in her chest. Did Angus truly think he could simply pick up where they'd left off if he mouthed enough pretty compliments mixed with apologies? Didn't he see that everything was different now?

"I'm not a damsel in distress, Angus," she said quietly. "And we're navigating our way out of our problems without your aid. We've recently come to terms with the bank over an initial loan; there'll be elektricity out to much of the estate soon." And if the repairs to the Dower House stayed on track, further funds for other upgrades would follow. "We may not be updating the decor any time soon, but I mean to make Stariel prosperous once again."

"I hope your new steward knows his job," Angus said, choosing his words carefully, and her internal see-saw settled firmly in amusement. So *that* was why he'd come.

"Really, Angus? All this talk about making reparations when you've actually come here just to satisfy your own morbid curiosity! Or am I supposed to pretend I've no idea of the rumours flying thick and fast around the countryside about my steward and me? Have you come to insult me, or to tell me you're cutting me out of polite society? That won't work, since *I've* been avoiding *you*!"

"That wasn't very subtle, was it?" he acknowledged with a grimace. "I didn't come to insult you, but I have heard some pretty...odd things, Hetta."

"Probably all true, but still none of your business." But her concentration fractured as something tugged, deep inside. The tug came again, inquisitive, bringing with it a hint of spice. She smiled. Stariel's interest in Wyn did have one benefit that they'd taken full advantage of. The land was inclined to pass messages on to her from Wyn if he asked it nicely, and Hetta could touch anyone within her borders once her attention was drawn. It was difficult to convey much more than emotion through the connection, but she knew that Wyn was asking if she wanted him to join them. She sent back a wordless *yes* and came back to her office to find Angus staring at her.

"And that's what you find attractive, is it? A man who's your social inferior, who depends on you for his very employment?" He closed his mouth with a snap and a cut-off curse. Clearly he hadn't meant to say that. He braced himself for her anger. "Ach—that was poorly said of me. I'm sorry."

"You're jealous," she said, her world tilting on its axis. Angus was *jealous* of Wyn? She'd known there was a dash of sincerity in his proposal to her, but she'd assumed it to be a very small dash, since his primary purpose had been to win control over the land that Stariel owned and he coveted. She'd rather thought any attachment he felt would fade quickly once his scheme failed—helped along by the fact that she'd set fire to his office upon that occasion. But if he was irritated enough to say something so deeply untactful just now, then maybe he'd cared a great deal more than she'd realised.

"Is there something to be jealous of?" he countered, colour high. He knew he'd overstepped a line but, in typical Angus fashion, was soldiering on now that he'd done it. He was still leaning forward, the distance between them uncomfortably intimate. She could make out the individual stubble of five o'clock shadow dusting his jawline.

"It's none of your business if there is," she said, leaning away from him. "And it's highly improper of you to ask."

"I still care about you, as a good neighbour if nothing else. I don't like hearing your name bandied about so in idle gossip."

"It's not your job to defend my honour, Angus. And I'd no idea you cared so much about idle gossip." She didn't feel she owed Angus much truth, after the lies he'd tried to sell her. But what were they saying about her, outside the estate? Nine heavens, what were they saying about *Wyn*? They'd both known the news of his nature would spread outside the estate, sooner or later. Whether anyone would believe it was another question. *Though eventually they'll have to, if lowfae like the piskies begin taking up residence outside of Stariel as well.*

"You should care more," Angus said, and something about the way he said it made her pause.

"Why?" she asked, after a moment of trying and failing to work it out. "Taking care of Stariel's interests is far more important to me than what the gossips think." Even if her relationship with Wyn technically had nothing to do with *Stariel's* interests.

Angus shifted, clearly uncomfortable in the hard chair. Good. "It's not only gossips." His gaze suddenly became very serious. "The Conclave hasn't met you yet—all they know about you is what's being bandied about your name."

Although the North was part of Prydein, and thus under the rule of Her Majesty and Her Majesty's government, the Northern Lords' Conclave still held great political power in the North. The Conclave met twice a year, but Hetta had missed the last one, held not long after her father's death. The gods knew her father had rarely bothered to attend, casting his vote by proxy if at all—but Angus, she suspected, was rather more involved in politics. She had an insight then that would've done Marius proud.

"That's the real reason you're here, isn't it? They asked you to investigate the truth of the rumours." She wasn't sure how to feel about a mob of strange lords clucking over the rumour-mill version of her life.

He grimaced. "I meant what I said; I came to apologise. But yes, the Conclave have asked my opinion, though 'investigate' is putting too formal a label on it. Only fools put much stock in hearsay, but the tales that have come out of Stariel lately have been outlandish enough to draw interest." He gave a wry laugh. "You'd not credit half the things I've heard are happening here. Why, if I believed the gossip, I'd have come here searching for fairies under every chair.

Half the North is swearing they know someone who saw with their own eyes your steward transform into a winged fairy!" He grinned broadly, inviting her to share the joke.

"Not under every chair," Wyn said calmly from the doorway. "But there are a few of us here, yes, myself included."

Both of them turned towards him. He wore a slight smile, and he unfurled his great silver-and-blue wings as he entered, filling the space wall-to-wall with gleaming feathers.

7

THE PRINCE AND THE LORD

WYN GAVE LORD Penharrow a cool look, taking a certain satisfaction from the way his mouth dropped open, shock robbing him of both speech and manners. But Penharrow continued to stare, and Wyn's satisfaction changed to discomfit at the forcible reminder of how freakish mortals found his fae form. He folded his wings back with a whisper of feathers. *It is Penharrow and not I who should feel uneasy here*, he reminded himself. And his choice of form had been a deliberate one. It wasn't, after all, supposed to be a secret any longer, and even if it were, he wouldn't have Penharrow doubting Hetta's judgement.

"You're a…fairy," Penharrow mumbled, transfixed, his eyes so wide the whites were visible all around his irises. The fascination wasn't entirely Lord Penharrow's fault. Usually Wyn made an effort to keep his native allure damped down. If he wasn't consciously suppressing it, he naturally exuded a low-level magnetism that made people want to be near him, to please him, even in his mortal form. It was part and parcel of being greater fae, along with his ability to shift forms. It had been harder, of late, to keep his newfound power contained, and it was something of a relief to stop trying.

He met Penharrow's eyes, and the man bowed his head in sub-mission, unable to hold against such a force. Triumph filled him, only to mutate into horror a heartbeat later. Bile rose in his throat. What was he *doing*?

He gritted his teeth and wound the power back under his skin. *I am not the kind of fae who flattens mortals into submission.* King Aeros's expression flashed in his mind's eye, guinea-gold eyes shining as he piled magical compulsion onto his son. *He is dead. He is dead, and I am free of the Spires.* But he could still taste dust and metal, still see that line of dead grass arrowing towards him, and he knew he was lying to himself. Had it been one of his siblings behind the attack, or ThousandSpire itself, still unbonded and reaching for him in desperation? Neither option was comforting.

Hetta gave him an odd look. She was immune to his allure, now. Had she realised what he'd almost tried to do to Penharrow? He took a deep breath, settling his instincts. What was wrong with him, lately? Why had his control threatened to slip for a moment? He could not blame the season; springtime was a mild time for stormdancers.

"You're a fairy," Penharrow repeated, his expression still glazed.

"Yes," he agreed. Making a snap decision, he changed back to his mortal shape, wings compacting with a sensation akin to itching. The lightning charge of his magic subsided a little, the currents harder to influence in this form.

Penharrow straightened as Wyn's power retreated, as if a great weight had been removed from his shoulders, and he managed to tear his attention away from Wyn for the first time since he'd entered the room.

"Your steward is a fairy," he said to Hetta.

She smiled, meeting Wyn's eyes past Penharrow's shoulder.

"Yes," she said. "I know."

"Do I satisfy your purpose in coming here today?" Wyn asked, recalling Penharrow's attention. "You did, after all, come to investigate the wild tales you have heard. Not so wild, as it transpires."

Penharrow glowered at him. "What enchantments have you cast over Hetta?"

Hetta stood and Penharrow rose with her, mortal manners dictating he couldn't remain seated while a woman stood.

"He hasn't enchanted me, Angus." Her lips quirked. "Or at least, not magically. As a person, I find him perfectly enchanting. But I think we're done here."

"I shall escort you out, Lord Penharrow," Wyn said, earning a raised eyebrow from Hetta that said she expected an explanation later, but she didn't question this pronouncement aloud. He nodded slightly.

Penharrow rolled his shoulders, glancing between them. He was a good actor, but Wyn had faced down much better ones, and he could read the man's displeasure despite the neutral expression he was attempting. The world had shifted beneath his feet, but unfortunately he wasn't a stupid man, and he was rapidly recalculating.

Wyn held open the door and said in a low tone: "You are wearing out your welcome. Hetta has dismissed you."

Penharrow's eyes narrowed, noting the deliberate use of Hetta's name. But if he'd truly cared about her affection, he should have valued her over land or power. Thank the High King's horns he hadn't, and that Hetta wanted Wyn, despite all the reasons she might be better off with a mortal man. That still seemed like a wonder beyond all the magic in Faerie.

"And you do her bidding?" Penharrow asked, a sneer colouring his voice. Wyn knew this was meant to insult him, even though that made no sense from a fae perspective—why, after all, would there be dishonour in such a thing?

Still, he chose not to respond and instead continued to pointedly hold the door. Penharrow scowled and stalked out. Throwing Hetta an apologetic glance, Wyn followed.

"Whatever you've done to Hetta, you won't get away with it,"

Penharrow growled as they walked down the long corridor towards the main stairs.

Wyn stopped. Penharrow frowned, drawing to a halt a stride later and turning to face him. Behind him, fading damask wallpaper met the wood panelling at waist height. It needed replacing, but there would be no funds to spare for such trivial matters for some time. Of all the harm Penharrow had done, Wyn found that long-term strategy of deteriorating Stariel's financial position year after year the most unsettling. It was a very fae tactic, both ruthless and patient. *Perhaps there's a reason Hetta was attracted to this man as well as to me*, he thought unwillingly.

"If I had both the power and inclination to bend mortal minds to my will, it would be very stupid to provoke me, wouldn't it?" he said mildly. "So either you are stupider than I estimated"—he ticked off the options on his fingers—"or you are so arrogant you believe you would be immune to such powers, *or*," he paused for emphasis, "you do not believe I have used any such influence on Hetta, but it is more palatable to pretend that magic is the reason she prefers me to you. I suspect the last option to be the truth."

Penharrow bristled. "Are you warning me off?" He gave a bark of harsh laughter. "You might have some kind of…novelty value for now, but do you really think she wants someone like you in the long term? You're her steward, if nothing else, someone she can order about, and she's not the kind of woman who finds weakness attractive. You *should* feel threatened."

The darker parts of his nature flexed, urging him to rise to the man's bait. He took them firmly in hand. This was too important. "I did not accompany you so we could engage in posturing, Lord Penharrow."

"Then why *have* you accompanied me, Mr Tempest?" Penharrow said, folding his arms. A muscle in his cheek twitched with the effort of keeping his temper in check.

Wyn strained, listening to the sounds of the house. There was no one nearby, so he leaned back against the wall and considered Stariel's neighbouring lord. He could feel how close he was to making a permanent enemy here. It wouldn't take much. The man had a deep streak of pride that practically lent itself to such distortion. Resisting the temptation, he picked his words carefully.

"Firstly, I'd like to know the precise nature of what is being said about Hetta and me outside of the estate." And that was something Penharrow wouldn't share with Hetta. Mortals drew strange lines around appropriate topics of conversation, particularly for those between men and women.

Penharrow snorted. "And what makes you think I'd tell you?"

Wyn continued as if he hadn't spoken. "And secondly, I'd like to know whether you stand as Stariel's ally or enemy, and if you are the latter, to attempt to convert you into the former."

"You're a very odd creature," Penharrow said, frowning. Wyn didn't flinch. *Creature.* "Have you no pride?"

Distantly came the sound of chatter and a door slamming. Wyn said, very quietly, "I do, but I have tasted the results of blood feud, and I can sacrifice a hundredweight of pride to stop one before it starts."

"Blood feuds? Is that what you think is happening here?" Penharrow rolled his eyes. "A mite melodramatic, don't you think?"

"You are the ruler of an estate, well-respected amongst the other Northern lords, I would wager. The Lords' Conclave holds great sway in the North. Even in the South, your mortal queen must balance her desires against yours unless she wishes the North to revolt. Hetta is new to her lordship, and unusual in her gender among you. And her membership on the Conclave has not yet been ratified.

"Even if there were nothing else occurring, how you and the rest of the Conclave treat her would affect her rule. But something else very much *is* occurring. I am not the only fae in Prydein, and now that the Iron Law is revoked, that will only become truer with time.

Stariel is a point of overlap between Mortal and Faerie; it stands between the two worlds. If you push for your circles to oppose Hetta, that will bleed into how my people are treated as their presence becomes more widely known. And if the fae encounter only hostility; if your mortal queen is unprepared to negotiate..." He trailed off. "You are a pebble that may begin an avalanche." He gestured. "This is larger than vengeance or jealousy or the love of a single mortal woman, Lord Penharrow, but on such small things wars might turn."

Penharrow's mouth took on a grim line, as if he'd swallowed bitter yarrow tea. "Who are you? You're not just any fairy, are you? Not with a speech like that."

"No," Wyn said, inclining his head. "I am not. My name is Prince Hallowyn Tempestren. My father was king of a fae court, the Court of Ten Thousand Spires."

Penharrow's expression grew even grimmer. "Was?"

"He died very recently. The succession is as yet unconfirmed." A line of spreading dead grass, reaching from ThousandSpire... What in the high wind's eddies was going on in his home faeland?

"My condolences," Penharrow said automatically.

Do not console me; I helped Stariel kill him, Wyn nearly said, but he managed to swallow down the words. It had been an instinctive decision made in the heat of the moment, not a calculated murder attempt, and he couldn't regret it, since it was probably the only reason he and Hetta had gotten out of the Spires alive. But what did that *make* him? *I am not my father.* Even if ThousandSpire had tried to choose him to take his father's place.

"I don't like being made to feel foolish," Penharrow said, and Wyn knew he was referring to the fact that he'd let him believe Wyn a simple servant. Such a trivial thing to focus on, under the circumstances.

"Come into the sitting room," he told the man instead. "You can tell me what I wish to know, and in return I shall answer some of your questions. *Some*," he cautioned. "I might speak of alliances and political expedience, but your actions caused harm to Stariel, and I cannot forget that."

Penharrow weighed the offer. He didn't like Wyn, but he liked ignorance even less. "Very well," he said eventually. He bared his teeth and said mockingly: "Lead the way, *Your Highness.*"

LAND MANAGEMENT

A FTER A BRISK luncheon, Hetta headed off to the Home Farm for the appointment she was now late for, although both the words 'appointment' and 'late' didn't really apply to farmers, she'd learnt. They kept time very accurately in a *yearly* sense, and very inaccurately in any units smaller than an hour. Wyn and Angus still hadn't emerged from whatever they were discussing, but she was determined not to eavesdrop.

All winter, she, Wyn, and Jack had between them been canvassing Stariel's tenant farmers, which had resulted in an extremely long and emphatic list of needs and wants that they had to somehow decide how to prioritise. The bank's initial loan instalment to them had been conservative and so far entirely earmarked for lineswork, but—assuming they *did* actually manage to fix the roof this week— there would be more instalments in future. Which meant Hetta needed to understand a great deal more about farming.

But it was rather hard to keep her mind on the task at hand when her thoughts kept bouncing between Angus's unwelcome news and this morning's arrow of foreign magic from the Spires. *Focus*, she told herself firmly, greeting Mr Brown across the freshly churned field. Jack was already with him, muddied and with rolled-up shirtsleeves, an unsurprising result of the fact that he'd clearly been helping the farmer plough. Hetta couldn't help feeling very surplus to requirements as she walked over to them, the mud sticking to her sturdy boots.

"Good afternoon!" she called. The plough horse gave a huff in her direction as they drew to a halt at the end of a row.

Mr Brown, a weathered man with thinning hair, nodded politely at her. "My lord."

"Hetta," Jack said stiffly, clearly still displeased from this morning.

They talked about soil, and crops, and Mr Brown's opinion on some of the ideas of modern farming practises she'd read about in the latest periodicals. Mr Brown's view on these last items was that new-fangled ideas were all very well in theory, but did they work in practice or was it just ignorant toffs with fancy words and no idea how things really worked? Not that he put it in so many words, but she was unhappily conscious of both her class and inexperience—and of the fact that she was using up the man's valuable time before the rain came tonight.

She left him with Jack, her head swimming with talk of clover and drainage. *No one expects you to know everything immediately*, she told herself sternly, as a guilty kind of melancholy threatened. *And it's not like we have the money to fix everything immediately anyway, even if you did know exactly what needed to be done!* But she couldn't help remembering how much more natural than her Jack had looked in the muddy field.

Angus's kineticar rumbled its way back down the driveway as she emerged from the Home Wood. *Good riddance*, she thought half-heartedly, watching the dust trail rising from the gravel. Why did Angus have to be so complicated? Couldn't he have just continued to stay unapologetically away so she could continue to loathe him without a second thought?

She wanted to go and pin Wyn down on why, exactly, he'd wanted to talk to Angus alone, but Wyn was still occupied, now ensconced with the Head Ranger in his office. She knew this without really trying to know it, and Stariel metaphorically perked up its ears. She sighed and redirected its attention. <We're not going to eavesdrop,> she told it firmly.

She stared at the increasingly overcast sky. The rain tonight would wash away any signs of magic. Coming to a decision, she began to pick her way up to the Standing Stones. The rising wind blew her hair into disarray beneath her hat, and she hugged her arms tightly around her coat.

She passed one of the shepherds as she crossed the fields behind the house. He doffed his cap in grudging respect, dog shivering with nervous energy beside him.

"Storm's coming, milord," he muttered, surprising her, as the shepherds tended to be monosyllabic at best.

"I know," she said. "But it won't break till after dark."

He accepted this without question, nodded, and carried on his way, evidently having exhausted his supply of words. But maybe this was progress—the shepherds at least trusted her land-sense, though the gods knew what they thought of this new world of fae and female lords. She had a sudden urge to yell after him that they were getting new sheep breeding stock, to see if that got a reaction.

The grey skies drained the colours from the landscape, the spring tones taking on a more wintry edge. There was still snow on the foothills, where the highest shepherds' huts were found. Come summer, it would melt from all but the highest caps of the Indigoes, but summer felt years away as Hetta topped the small rise on which the Standing Stones stood.

The grass was yellowed in a direct line between where Wyn had been standing and the two stones where he'd made the portal. She examined the grass, walking slowly closer along its path to the stones. They too were discoloured at the base, a reddish tint on the grey weatherworn material, and there was a bite of ozone in the air. That could be just the aftereffect of Wyn's own lightning magic though. Or it could mean one of his family had created this morning's portal—all his family had an underlayer of storms to their magic. Or had the faeland taken matters into its own hands? Was a faeland capable of taking that sort of action by itself? *Goodness knows Stariel seems to decide quite a lot of things without my telling it to do so.*

Stariel brushed against her as she stopped in front of the stones that had formed the portal. Its communications were complicated things, big and not limited by words, but she knew it didn't like this at all.

<I'm not going to try to open a portal to the Spires,> she told it. <That's decidedly not what I want to achieve here. Don't fret. If it makes you feel better, you can stand guard against another incursion and do whatever seems best to stop it.>

It grew more alarmed as she crouched down in front of one of the stones to examine the discolouration more clearly. The smell of ozone was stronger here, underlaid with something metallic. Copper? Aroset had a copper signature to her magic. *If only I had a fae nose.* She reached out to press a fingertip against the stone, and Stariel roared up at her in warning.

The world spun into black. She was so tightly connected to Stariel that she knew *exactly* what the faeland was attempting even as it happened. *I desperately need to find a manual on faelands,* she thought.

UNCONVENTIONAL METHODS OF
TRANSPORTATION

W YN WAS SITTING at his desk when he sensed the translocation. *Father*, he thought instinctively, fear splintering through him. He leapt to his feet, his magic rising in a wave until the room hummed with potential. Then he remembered it couldn't be his father. King Aeros was dead. Was it DuskRose, somehow? Had the wards failed? Had something happened to Hetta?

It was rather anticlimactic when Hetta emerged, alone and unhurt, with no scent of fae magic following her, and stumbled into his arms.

"That was rather a dramatic entrance, wasn't it?" She shook her head, amused rather than alarmed. "I think Stariel interpreted my instructions a bit too liberally."

His heart pounded as he stared down at her. She was safe. No one was invading. He let out a long, slow breath and carefully unwound his magic, letting it seep back into his bones.

She grinned impishly up at him and wriggled. "Thank you for welcoming me with open arms."

Ah. Right. He probably didn't need to hold her quite so tightly. He forced his muscles to relax. "Are you all right?" he asked.

"Surprised, but fine. And a little annoyed at Stariel's over-protectiveness." She frowned at him. "Are *you* all right? You seem jumpy." She gave a wry laugh. "Which I suppose is fair, since I just magically appeared in your office out of thin air."

"I was…worried. Translocation has rarely heralded anything good, in my experience. I thought—" *that you had been taken again. That Faerie had come to hurt Stariel.* He didn't want to voice his fears aloud, to give them oxygen, but he thought from the way her eyes softened that she'd guessed them anyway. "I'm glad you're well," he said instead. "What happened?" He'd known she'd want to try his father's trick of translocating within her own faeland sooner or later, but she'd have mentioned it if she'd suddenly decided to experiment with that.

She fanned her fingers out on his coat. "I told Stariel to do whatever it thought best if things went sour again at the Stones. Apparently that meant magically whisking me away and dumping me in your office at the first hint of trouble." She wrinkled her nose. "I'm not sure whether there actually *was* trouble or if Stariel was just worried the Spires might reach through and eat me."

He froze. "You went up to the Stones?"

Her brows rose. "Shouldn't I have?"

"I don't know," he said. "I don't know how the portal re-opened earlier either. My list of ignorances is growing quite irksome."

Hetta made a thoughtful noise, and her eyes took on a shine of sudden speculation. "Can I learn to control the translocation, do you think? It would save me a lot of walking."

Laughter rose up in his throat, fond and marvelling all at once. Of course Hetta would take a magic that she'd personally suffered from at the hands of her enemies and not only find joy in the discovery but also put it to practical use.

"I love you," he told her, helplessly, and kissed her. The magic in him thrummed, petrichor and cardamom, curling in the spaces where their bodies touched. Stariel, of course, interrupted before they could get very far, and Hetta slid out of his grasp with a sigh and perched herself on the edge of his desk, a more battered version of the one in her own study. He dropped back into the chair behind it with his own matching sigh.

"All right, tell me about Angus," she said.

Wyn reluctantly recalled his conversation with the neighbouring lord. It was difficult to focus over the roar of sheer want rioting through him, but at least Penharrow's name was extremely cooling. "I wanted to know what was being said about me—about us—outside the estate."

She began to unpin her hat. "And you thought he wouldn't tell me the worst of what they said." It wasn't a question, and she grumbled, half to herself: "Of course he wouldn't. *Men.* Did he tell you?"

"Some. He wanted to prick my conscience, I think. There were some very uncouth words used," he said lightly.

Hetta's eyebrows rose. "And was your conscience pricked?"

"Somewhat," he admitted reluctantly. After a decade in the Mortal Realm, he was familiar enough with the bits of Prydinian culture that governed conduct between men and women. He didn't agree with mortal ideas of respectability, but he couldn't ignore how they affected Hetta. Penharrow had reminded him forcefully of the wider implications.

He told her what they'd discussed, and his attempts to influence Penharrow for the better. From the hallway came the sound of footsteps approaching and then receding as people—the staff, mostly—walked down the passageway. His office was in a busier part of the house than Hetta's study.

Hetta glared down at the open accounts book when he'd finished. "I know it's wiser not to have him as an enemy, but I'll own I can't bear the thought of cultivating Angus's good opinion after what he did!" She sighed. "So thank you for mustering up some efforts at diplomacy on my behalf."

He shrugged. "It's traditional for…inner members of a court to 'muster' on their lord's behalf." *A consort*, he'd almost said, the word cutting too close to the bone. Marriage wasn't necessary for such a position, in Faerie, but Wyn knew things worked differently in Mortal. So far neither of them had broached the subject, and the longer it lurked, silently unacknowledged in the background, the more he fretted. He understood his *own* reasons for not raising it, curse the ties that bound him, but it was unlike Hetta not to state bluntly what she wanted once she'd made up her mind. Which suggested that perhaps she hadn't truly made up her mind.

A smile tugged at her lips. "Angus is giving me sheep." She took a letter from her coat pocket and brandished it at him. "Can you believe it? The effrontery of the man!"

He gave a huff of laughter, though he agreed with her general sentiment. "Well, I understand that they *are* a time-honoured peace offering in the North when one has caused offence. They're not the slateshire sheep?"

"They are indeed. You didn't think I'd accept *inferior* sheep, did you? At least this will help rejuvenate our breeding stock. All that reading of periodicals has done me some good."

"It will also please Jack," he added. Jack had spent a considerable amount of time waxing lyrical about Lord Penharrow's sheep breeding programme and scheming as to how to convince him to part with some.

"Well, that'll be a nice change, since he only ever seems to scowl at me lately." She put the letter down on his desk beside her hat. "Tell Jack *he* can sort out the details of transferring them, if they're so close to his heart. I refuse to have any part in the matter."

He considered the square of stiff paper against the dark wood. "He still thinks he has a chance with you, you know. Lord Penharrow."

"Are you jealous?" He looked up. The grey of her eyes was very clear and penetrating. The hat had cast its shape on her auburn hair, and he had a sudden urge to reach out and tousle it into disarray.

"I have no reason to be," he said, picking his words carefully. He would not have a lack of trust between them. "And you are not an object for us to compete over in any case. Your choices are what matters in this, not whatever Penharrow might or might not think." Her cheeks had gone very pink, and he stood and put his hands flat on the desk to either side of her, boxing her in. "Do you *want* me to be jealous, Hetta?"

"Well, no," she admitted, "But…" She made a helpless gesture, averting her eyes. "I don't know, there's something strangely *thrilling* about the idea of attractive men fighting over you, even if the reality would actually be very irritating. But Angus—no. Definitely not," she said with a firmness that he liked. She shook her head. "Even if he hadn't betrayed me and Stariel, you know how I feel about you." She reached out, oddly shy, and smoothed his hair away from his face, and his heart melted into something soft as dawnlight.

He wanted their relationship to be so firmly set in the world's eyes that no one would think they could wedge them apart. And yet—was that fair, given the potential consequences? Part of him still wondered if maybe the right thing to do was leave and take those consequences with him. It fought with the *other* part of his nature, which growled a savage and not entirely rational song. He remembered Penharrow's unease with his fae shape, the relief when he'd slid his wings away.

He wasn't jealous of Penharrow in any way except one: Penharrow was mortal.

Veering sharply away from that thought, he confessed, "Noble sentiments aside, I would, however, very much like the persistent Lord Penharrow to see no point in persisting." With slow deliberation, he undid the buttons at the wrist of her long-sleeved blouse and drew a small circle with his thumb over the exposed skin there.

Her pulse fluttered bird-fast, and she swallowed, her pupils dilating.

Stariel, of course, chose that moment to make itself known again. It bumped against him in fond affection, knocking him off balance with the force of its enthusiasm, and he cursed as he collapsed back into his seat. "High King's *horns!*"

Hetta giggled, but her expression was pained as she re-buttoned her cuff. "What if Stariel never stops interfering?" She frowned out the window, where the light was becoming greyer as the storm clouds moved in. "I'm not prepared to live a celibate existence forever."

"I think that sooner or later you'll either learn to control it or Stariel will settle down by itself." He added, voice husky: "And there exists accommodation *outside* of Stariel, if nothing else changes."

That made her laugh. "We could go to Alverness, stay overnight," she said. "Surely there's something we could talk about with the bank manager that could justify the visit? Or does that offend your fae morals?"

He shook his head. "The fae have very few compunctions on the subject. From a Prydinian perspective, too few." He still didn't quite understand the mortal obsession with chastity, particularly in its women, and particularly as it related to marriage. Marriage in Faerie was rare and had nothing to do with either sex or inheritance.

"Never mind what Faerie thinks—what about you?" she asked. She fluttered her eyelashes at him. "The act holds significance for you."

"For both of us, I would hope," he said, raising his eyebrows.

"You're embarrassed."

She was getting too good at reading him. Or perhaps he was getting poorer at hiding his emotions. He didn't mind, except— "It's just that—" He broke off and groused, "I'm only a virgin in a very technical sense, Hetta. I'm not ignorant." He was being ridiculous, given their much greater concerns as of this morning, but he did have his pride, stormwinds take it.

"And getting ever more technical by the day." She grinned. "So shall we go to Alverness and rectify that, then? I for one am keener on the sooner rather than later."

"How do you propose to explain the trip to your family?" he said lightly, mainly to give himself time to think.

"I wasn't proposing to explain anything at all to them," she said airily, waving a hand. "The kineticar can suffer a convenient break-down after the last train has left, or something."

Anticipation sparked through his veins, but he looked down at his hands, remembering how the lightning had twined around his wrists earlier. He wasn't as subtle as he'd thought, because she murmured:

"You won't lose control. You're the *most* controlled person I know."

"But if we aren't at Stariel, there won't be any failsafe if I do," he pointed out.

"You controlled it today."

"Only with Stariel's help." He ran a hand through his hair. "And… we cannot keep ignoring the scandal we're creating." The storms knew he didn't want to think about it either, but Penharrow had reminded him that Hetta's reputation could impact on her ability to successfully rule Stariel.

Hetta didn't say anything despite watching him intensely, and he was again afflicted with doubt about the subject.

"I—" he began awkwardly, not knowing quite how to start but knowing that he couldn't bear *not* to talk about it any longer.

A perfunctory knock startled them both.

The door opened barely a second later, and Lady Sybil stalked in. Hetta didn't have time to get off the desk. Wyn was faster and managed to stand and put a few inches of space between them by the time Lady Sybil made it into his office.

"Henrietta Valstar!"

Hetta slid calmly off the desk. "Yes, Aunt?" she said sweetly. "Have you come to remind me to take my tea? How thoughtful of you."

"It's not appropriate for you to be behind closed doors with a man!" Aunt Sybil pronounced in dramatic accents. She shot Wyn a dark look.

"Oh, I know," Hetta said cheerfully, but there was a martial gleam in her eyes.

Wyn thought he'd better intervene, but before he could, Lady Sybil narrowed her eyes at Hetta and said shortly: "A royal courier is here for you."

A SUMMONS

EVEN AUNT SYBIL couldn't conjure royal couriers out of thin air, but Hetta couldn't help feeling like she'd done it on purpose nonetheless. It wasn't as if she could've known Hetta was in here, given how she'd translocated into Wyn's office, so her aunt must've come here *hoping* to catch them engaged in 'inappropriate' behaviour.

"Thank you for alerting us, my lady," Wyn said to Aunt Sybil with a polite smile.

Aunt Sybil merely gave a stiff 'hmmf' and turned to Hetta. Hetta didn't roll her eyes, but it was a near thing—Aunt Sybil didn't know how to treat Wyn now that she knew his true rank, so she generally ignored him if she could. When she absolutely couldn't avoid it, she grudgingly called him 'my lord'. She couldn't stomach 'your highness', but no amount of insisting that Wyn was fine with remaining simply 'Wyn' or 'Mr Tempest' could persuade her to abandon her strict notions of proper manners.

"I'll take you to the man," she informed Hetta. She pivoted without waiting to see if they would follow, head held high.

Wyn wasn't at all dissuaded by her aunt's cold shoulder. He kept gently chipping away with small talk as they walked, playing oblivious to her aunt's rigid disapproval. He'd been doing this dance of reassuring normality for the last two months, to everyone, with mixed results. The staff, he'd won over completely. The villagers remained standoffish. Her family were split on the subject. *And at this rate, it should only take approximately three thousand years to thaw my aunt out.*

Hetta trailed along after her aunt. Honestly, you'd think they lived in the dark ages. It was all so *stupidly* old-fashioned. *And unfair, besides, given that I did far more with people in Meridon than I've done with Wyn.* But she'd been far beneath anyone's notice then, just another illusionist among the theatre crowd. The thought gave her a pang. If Stariel hadn't chosen her, she'd still be back there with her old company, and not having to deal with her ridiculous relations and equally ridiculous societal expectations on top of fae and finances. *And now royal couriers.* Though surely Her Majesty wouldn't trouble herself with idle gossip?

"Why are we going to the west wing?" she asked as Aunt Sybil diverted abruptly in that direction. She'd expected the courier would be waiting somewhere near the entry hall, or possibly in her study, but the west wing lay near neither of these locations.

"The courier is in the Sesquipedalian Lounge," her aunt said shortly. The Sesquipedalian Lounge was so named owing to the peculiarities of Hetta's great-great aunt, a traveller of some renown. That lady had mistakenly believed 'sesquipedalian' to mean 'relating to sea creatures', and since she'd had the word carved above the door into the room, no one had had the heart to enlighten her. It wasn't a room where they normally received guests.

Suspicion prickled and hardened into resignation when they entered the Sesquipedalian Lounge to find an ambush. The ambush consisted of not just the royal courier but a knot of bemused Valstars. *I should've seen this coming.* Aunt Sybil's frustration with her errant niece had been growing, and she'd clearly decided to use the courier as an excuse to stage a confrontation. The poor courier; he had no idea what he'd walked into.

Jack grimaced from behind the royal courier, who turned smartly at the sound of their entry. The courier was blond and pale-skinned—as so many Southerners were—and wore red livery, putting Hetta strongly in mind of a beagle. His gaze flicked first to Wyn, with more than just casual interest, and unease threaded through her before he turned his attention back to her.

"Lord Valstar?"

"Yes," she said, trying to convey some degree of dignity despite the crowd of murmuring relatives. "What's this about?"

The courier bowed and extracted a very official document from his bag. "I am to see this delivered to your hands today, my lord."

Hetta held out her hands obediently. The envelope bore the queen's crest and was sealed and stamped in glittering gold wax.

"I will take my leave then, Lord Valstar," the courier said.

"Don't you want to wait for my response?"

He shook his head, polite but firm. "I was told it wouldn't be necessary, and I must be getting on. Good day, Lord Valstar." He made a beeline for the exit past the glass cases of sea shells.

Hetta frowned down at the thick envelope. Had the queen ever written to her father? *Perhaps she's going to chide me for being tardy in swearing my allegiance.* It was customary to swear fealty in person, but a trip to the South had had to wait on a hundred and one more urgent matters. She and Wyn had talked about trying to arrange it for later in the spring, after planting had finished.

She looked up to see Aunt Sybil, Aunt Maude, her cousin Jack, her stepmother, and her two younger sisters all clustered about in anticipation. Aunt Sybil had done well for such a hasty gathering, though Grandmamma was missing.

"I'm not sure this is any of your business at all," she said to them dryly. "But since you're all here anyway, we may as well find out together." When no one spoke, she unsealed the envelope and pulled out the paper within. "It's a summons," she said after taking in its contents. "Queen Matilda wants me to present myself at an audience with her in a week's time." She met Wyn's eyes. "And she wants me to bring you with me."

Wyn stilled, which meant he was as unsettled as she was.

"Why does she want Wyn to go with you?" Jack wondered aloud. "How would she know anything about him?"

Aunt Sybil sank down onto the nearest seat and clutched at her pearls. "The scandal has spread as far as Meridon, Henrietta!"

"I'm sure Her Majesty has heard far worse scandals," Hetta objected. "I know for a fact that there are lords in the North carrying on far worse activities than me. Why, Lord Orweslyn was found—"

Aunt Sybil purpled and made a noise like a chicken being slaughtered. "Henrietta Isadore Valstar!"

Wyn coughed and said mildly: "I fear I do not perfectly understand the laws that govern your relationship with the Crown. Does Queen Matilda truly pay such close attention to her subjects' personal affairs? Does the North not retain some degree of independence?"

"The South has no right to intervene in our affairs," Jack said fiercely. Hetta's lips curved. You could always count on Northern patriotism, in a pinch.

"It must be because you need royal permission to marry, Hetta," Lady Phoebe said softly. She shrank as all eyes turned towards her. "I mean—that is…" She coloured. "When Henry and I married, we had to get royal consent because he was a lord." Her eyes darted to Wyn. "That is…I mean… You *do* mean to marry him, don't you?" She went bright pink. There was a rumble of general agreement from Hetta's assorted relatives.

Hetta glared at them. Royal permission. It hadn't even occurred to her that she'd need it, and a sharp spear of indignation went through her. Why should other people get a say in her affairs?

"Yes, you must stop shilly-shallying and send him away if you don't plan to," Aunt Sybil said, without looking at Wyn. "And if you're both going to Meridon, I will have to accompany you as a chaperone," she continued without pause.

Hetta slid a look sideways at Wyn. He'd gone very fae, expression unreadable. *Marriage.* She loved him, but—and the 'but' was exactly the problem. *But* he wasn't human, though he was trying so hard to be for her sake. *But* they'd only just freed him from the consequences of his *last* promise to marry someone. *But* how could she marry someone she hadn't even been intimate with? A burble of laughter tried to force its way out. Aunt Sybil would *not* approve of that last thought.

Her stifled laugh made Wyn raise an eyebrow at her, but she shook her head. *But also, he hasn't asked me to marry him, and it's rather a blow to my ego*, she silently admitted.

She blew out a long breath. "Enough. I can't think with you all staring at me. I'm going for a walk. Jack, Angus has given us some sheep. Go and organise to collect them," she instructed, pulling the relevant letter from her pocket and handing it to her cousin.

"Not the slateshire sheep?" His face lit up, followed swiftly by a scowl as he remembered who the sheep had come from.

"The very same," she said, stifling another laugh at how easily her cousin had been distracted from the subject at hand. "I think we should give them in to Hawking's care, since his flocks were hit hardest last year, but use your own judgement."

She threw Wyn a very speaking look as she turned and marched out of the room.

11

FIRE AND AIR

I T TOOK SOME time to extract himself from the Valstars, and when he'd managed it, he found Hetta standing on the lake-shore of Starwater. Ducks quacked indignantly on its rough surface as the shadows deepened and the wind rose. In the distance, small boats from the village dotted the waters, heading for the shore. The location wasn't surprising; since her lordship, she often sought refuge outside when her emotions were stirred.

But she was angrier than he'd realised, because as he drew closer, she flung out her arms and let fire pour forth over the dark waters. Her pyromancy had likely come from the Valstars' distant fae ancestor and—like most elemental magic—it could be fuelled by emotion. Heat shimmered in the air, creating a brief haze of steam that was swallowed up by the wind a moment later. There hadn't been permanent ice on the lake for a week or so now, but the water temperature was still not much above freezing.

"Sometimes I can't *believe* my family!" Hetta threw a hand sky-wards. "Or the foolish rules that apply to the nobility." Another spurt of fire for emphasis. He took the invitation without hesitation.

His control of lightning might be haphazard, but air magic was a more familiar companion. He thought of the Spires clutching towards him and fed his fear into the magic, twining air around her fire and fluting it out to form little sheep. Hetta didn't have fine control of her pyromancy—once it left her hands, if it caught, it became real fire uncontrolled by her magic—and Wyn couldn't call fire from nothing, but they'd found that they could combine their magic this way. *A matched pair*, he thought, chest tight, as the fiery flock frolicked across the sky. Stormwinds, he wanted that.

Hetta began to laugh at the display, and the fire abruptly abated. She kicked at a bit of gravel and watched it sink beneath the surface. "Gods knows what the locals will say about my pyrotechnics," she said wryly. "Though I've quite given up on not causing talk. Maybe that can be my name in the history books: Lord Henrietta the Scandalous." She turned back to him. "Dash it. I *do* have to get royal permission to marry. Sometimes I forget that the same rules don't apply to me now I'm lord."

And here it was—the chance to ask the question he desperately wanted to ask, the one he hadn't the right to. "I'm aware we've both been determinedly ignoring a certain question for some time now," he said. "Your relatives are not very subtle." He grimaced. "Nor are some of the staff."

"Really? Do they drop hints at you?" She shook her head. "No, I'm not getting distracted. Why haven't you said anything before now?"

He held up his hands defensively. "You cannot blame this on my evasiveness alone—you've been equally avoiding the subject."

"You're *still* avoiding the subject." She folded her arms. "Marriage," she said, dropping the word like a stone. "Specifically, of us." A shag emerged from the waters and flapped its way, dripping, onto a tree branch overhanging the lake. The sound was unnaturally loud in the stillness between them.

"I agree with your family that we cannot keep on as we are," he said. Penharrow and the Conclave's censure would only be the start, as the rumours about them spread more and more widely, damaging Hetta's reputation. Nonsensical as it was, it mattered, here in the Mortal Realm, and he'd been unforgivably careless to let himself forget that, risking hurt to Hetta and the Valstars. "And I think you do as well."

No wonder she'd been so angry; she disliked being forced into things, and she'd been forced into so many of them, of late. Was it only that dislike that had stopped her from broaching the subject before now, or was it something more serious? "And I can see why they disapprove of us, as a pairing. After all—what would I bring to such a match except trouble?" Had she been thinking that— weighing up his murderous relations and fae nature and deciding it wasn't worth the cost? He could not blame her, especially in light of today's events.

"Trouble," she repeated flatly. "Is that why you haven't declared yourself?" Colour bloomed in her cheeks. She was embarrassed, and it threw him. Why in the high wind's eddies would she be embarrassed about this?

Oh. *Oh.* He was an idiot, and the sudden relief of knowing it made him laugh.

"*Wyn*, this is *serious!*" Her eyes flashed.

"Oh, I *am* sorry, my love. I'm a fool. I never considered the Prydinian custom, that it is the male's job to do the asking. I didn't mean to make you doubt me." He wrapped his arms around her, leaning his cheek against the top of her head. It didn't satisfy his craving for closeness. "Of course I *want* to marry you, Hetta," he reassured her. If only want was all that mattered here.

She wasn't reassured. She stepped back, forcing him to loosen his arms, and looked up at him, her eyes dark. "Don't try that fae trick on me. I hear what you're not saying."

He sighed. Of course he wouldn't get that past her. "It's not only a matter of my own heart. If Aroset has inherited the Spires, it's very probable that she'll try her best to harm me and anything I hold dear. This morning—that may have been her, trying to do exactly that. It is unfair to bind my fate to yours with that looming over us." His conscience wouldn't let him soar over all the reasons she shouldn't want to marry him, even though he would have liked very much to skirt them in favour of emphasising all the advantages of doing so. The only issue was that there was so very much less in the latter column than the former. "Sunnika, also, will try to manipulate you through me if she can."

"Yes, but she wants Stariel to think favourably of DuskRose," Hetta pointed out. "Which means she's unlikely to ask you for anything too terrible—like this morning, for instance. I don't like her summoning you without warning, but she could've asked for something much more sinister than information about ThousandSpire."

"The next thing she asks of me may not be so. And what of Aroset?"

She shrugged. "I don't see how us marrying would put me in any more or less danger than I'm in now. Aroset already knows you care about me, and we're not even pretending we're not together anymore. Or at least, not very well," she amended. In theory, the relationship between them was only known to her family. In reality, the Valstars were gossips, and Wyn doubted even the most isolated of the hill shepherds had not heard some part of the news.

Her gaze was iron. "Are you going to threaten to leave again for my own good?" There was a warning in the grey of her eyes. *I won't forgive you if you leave*, she'd said once, but it had morphed into a different truth over the last few months, unspoken but acknowledged: *We're past that now. I won't forgive you if you take it back.*

He took a deep breath, met her eyes. "No," he said. "I will not do that." But, oh, how the achingly vulnerable truth of that commitment terrified him.

Her fierce expression softened. "Well, good. Because I won't accept half-measures. Not anymore." She tilted her head. "There's something else you're not telling me."

"Ah…there is another complication. Royal fae need the High King's permission to marry. It may be…difficult to acquire." Difficult was an understatement. The High King of Faerie had decreed that peace between two warring fae courts would be cemented by Wyn marrying Sunnika. Petitioning him for permission to marry a mortal instead seemed unlikely to go down well—if Wyn even knew where to *find* the High King. The High King appeared and disappeared according to no one's schedule. Sometimes no one saw him for years at a time.

Hetta gave him an exasperated look. "If I wanted to live a life free of complications, I wouldn't have run off to join a theatre troupe at seventeen. Or seduced my butler upon my return," she added with a half-smile. "You said difficult—that's not the same thing as impossible, is it?"

"No," he said slowly, thinking. "It is not. So…does this mean you *want* to marry me, then? Hypothetically?"

Her pause probably only lasted a few seconds, but it felt like hours. He repressed the urge to shift restlessly while he waited for an answer.

She began to giggle. "Wyn, you cannot ask people to marry you *hypothetically!*"

"I am fairly certain that I just did. And I am still waiting for a hypothetical answer."

But she shook her head. "Last time you planned to marry someone, it left you with your power stunted for more than a decade and fae from two courts trying to kill you."

"That was because I broke my promise. Which I would not do in this case."

"The case of this hypothetical marriage?"

"Yes. That one."

Her giggles increased until she shook so much she had to put a hand against his shoulder to steady herself.

"It's not very nice to laugh at people who are hypothetically asking you to marry them," he groused down at her. This only made her laugh harder, and he could not help his own mouth curving up reluctantly in response, his heart twisting with painfully intense fondness.

When she sobered, she reached up to tug at his hair. Her eyes were fond. "You impossible man. Of course I'd *hypothetically* like to marry you, everything else aside." Her smile faded, and she pulled the queen's summons from her pocket. "But I don't like that this is all hypothetical, and that anyone other than the two of us gets a say in this decision."

"I know," he said, although a warm, giddy happiness rose in him despite everything. "I don't like it either, and I'm sorry for bringing you so many complications."

Her gaze went faraway, as if she were reaching for her land-sense. "Well, at least half these complications are my fault anyway, since they come from me being lord." She returned to him. "Will we be in danger from whatever's going on in ThousandSpire, if we go to Meridon?"

He shook his head. "Not if the borders remain closed. Whatever was behind that…attack this morning, it was driven by the specific resonance between the Standing Stones and the Spires." *Had* it been an attack? He had not recognised any of his siblings' signatures, but that could be because the strength of ThousandSpire's magic had overshadowed them.

She nodded absently, then straightened, a spark of mischief in her. "Well, shall we try this week to persuade Her Majesty that a complicated fae prince who makes ridiculous not-proposals is a sensible match for her newest lord, then? Next week we can sort out your monarch." Her gaze grew thoughtful. "And while we're petitioning him, I also have a number of questions I'd like to ask him about faelands."

He could not help the soft huff of laughter escaping. If he had not long since fallen for Hetta Valstar, he thought he would have done so at that moment. He pulled her into his arms again, heart swelling. "Let us also try to persuade Lady Sybil that she need not accompany us to Meridon."

12

LADY PEREGRINE'S SOCIETY NEWS

MARIUS VALSTAR WAS deeply absorbed in a book about water lilies when the voices of the nearby students finally penetrated.

"—and speaking of scandals, you know the botany tutor, Mr Valstar?"

"The tall, skinny bloke with the glasses?"

Marius grimaced. The description was accurate, if not exactly flattering. *You could be called worse things.* Unprompted, his brain began to list some: *your father's least favourite son; failed academic; family scandal waiting to happen.* Wait, he'd missed the next words from the students. *Add terrible listener to the list.*

"You know he's from one of the big estates up north? One of those horribly old-fashioned ones," the first student said. He had a thin, nasal voice. There was a murmur of tepid interest. The speakers were obscured by shelves, but they sounded as if they were seated at one of the large tables that lined the outer edges of the library's atrium. If they were referring to Marius as the 'botany tutor', they were probably first or second years. He didn't recognise the voices, but it was only the beginning of term, and he hadn't done much tutoring yet.

He ought to scuttle away. No good ever came from eavesdropping, but curiosity held him in place—curiosity, and a prickle of fear. What scandal were they talking about? *It can't be mine. I've been so careful since I returned.* But what if he hadn't been careful enough? His heart thudded against his ribcage like a jackrabbit.

Calm down. They can't possibly know. Even if they suspect, they can't have proof. There was only one person who could testify against him, and John couldn't do that without implicating himself. *And John's not here anymore.* Marius had heard John's father had gotten him into the Meridon Law School after he'd dropped out of Knoxbridge University. *Dammit, I'm not going to think about John.* Sometimes now he could go days without thinking of him.

Wait, he'd missed the next bit of the conversation as well, but he came back to it with a sharp shock, because it wasn't *his* scandal the students were speaking of at all.

"—anyway, rumour has it that she's fucking her butler. And—it gets better—said butler isn't even human!" Nasal's voice grew ripe with amusement. "The talk of the North is that he's a fairy!"

The latter half of this pronouncement was met with general scepticism.

"I know the Northerners are a superstitious lot, but that's coming on rather too brown, Andy!"

Nasal—Andy, presumably—spoke. "No, it's true, I promise you! My uncle—you know, the Duke of Callasham," he added with a practised emphasis that suggested he dropped mentions of this relative at every opportunity. "He holds a Northern title as well, and he's on the Conclave, and he says the entire North is speaking of it! Fairies!" He chortled.

"She must've been gagging for it to fall for that," another voice added.

"Don't get your hopes up, Fogherty!"

The group snickered, descending into ribald remarks.

Marius stood frozen, his fingers digging into the leather binding of the book. How dare some young idiot speak about his family, about his sister, like that? It wasn't true, the way he'd framed it, and the injustice burned.

You'll only make it worse if you confront them, his inner logician said.

Would he? Gods, he wanted to see their faces if he strolled out from between the shelves right now. An ache started behind his temples.

Yes—currently they just think it's a stupid bit of gossip about someone they don't really know. If you confront them, you'll only make it more likely they'll pass on the story to others.

Dammit. His inner logician was right. Dammit! He glared through the shelves as if the force of his ill will could reach through and strangle the students regardless of all the books in the way. Hetta was worth a thousand of them, and so was Wyn! *If I'm marking any of their classes, they're all failing their next assignments,* he thought viciously.

Seething, he hugged the book to his chest and crept further into the stacks, but he couldn't relax, even when he'd found his way to the darkest corner on the floor, rarely visited by library-goers. He read the spines and nearly choked at the irony: he was in the mythology and folklore section. He'd been meaning to see what resources the library had on the subject of fae, but he was in no mood to browse.

He leaned against the wall and tried to calm his breathing. The ache in his temples increased. He needed to get out of the library, away from the students he could still hear nattering distantly. His legs itched to pace properly. Walking wouldn't solve anything, but it couldn't hurt, and sometimes it helped dislodge loose thoughts. *Walk until you are struck by sudden genius: what a brilliant plan, Marius. Not smacking of cowardice or indecision at all.*

He took a circuitous route out of the library, but his heart didn't stop racing until he was four blocks and an alley away. It was a mild afternoon, and he stuck his hands in his coat pockets and set off at a blistering pace. He knew the central streets of Knoxbridge well from his frequent rambles, so he paid minimal attention to navigation, sticking to the smaller alleys and less crowded paths. It was just gone the hour, and gods knew he couldn't be bothered fighting through the crowds of students swarming from the lecture theatres on Old Street to their colleges at this time of day.

By the time he'd found his way down to the river, he'd mentally composed a long, articulate lecture that explained why gossiping constituted a moral failing and why this was particularly so for anyone publicly discussing his sister. The silent lecture gave form to the worst of his anger as he followed the waterway. By the time he arrived at the east gate of the botanical gardens, he'd progressed from fuming to despondent. There was nothing he could do, really.

I'm a terrible big brother. He'd always felt fiercely protective of all his siblings, but with the youngest three—born after his father had remarried—it had been simpler. He was so much older than them that even his awkward, flailing efforts had impressed. *Although Gregory is rather less impressed with me of late*, he thought morosely. His younger brother had started at Knoxbridge this year, and the dolt was determined not to rely on Marius for anything. But with Hetta, it had always been different. He'd never managed to shield her from Father before she'd left home—if anything, she'd borne the brunt of his moods—and often he'd felt like her younger rather than older brother. *Maybe that's why Stariel chose her for its lord.*

And he still couldn't figure out how to protect her, even now. Gravel crunched under his feet as he strode between flowerbeds and stared moodily at the giant water lilies on display in the pond. The immense white flowers had just risen above the water, petals still tightly furled, and the rich, seductive scent permeated the air. How could he explain the truth to people? He couldn't bear the thought of letting the rumours fly unchecked, but nor could he think of a way to quieten them. He had no authority here; his word would hold no weight. Graduate students were only one step removed from the very bottom of the university's hierarchy. Should he appeal to a higher authority? But who would that be? Maybe his cousin Caro would know—she was better at navigating the social currents of the university than he was. Both her parents were established academics.

He brooded on the matter as he found his way into his greenhouse. At least here there were small tasks he *could* do something about, and he threw himself into potting up seedlings and carting compost. The afternoon darkened, but he didn't notice other than to switch on the elektric lights—a reminder of how backwards Stariel was in comparison to the South.

He was carefully removing stamens from the latest pea hybrids when his cousin Caro spoke behind him.

"Marius Valstar, why are you buried in a glasshouse on a Friday night?"

He started and knocked the container he'd been transferring stamens to onto the floor. Fortunately, it landed right-side-up, and only a few stray threads scattered across the tiled floor. The yellow elektric lights threw hypnotic shadows, making it hard to distinguish the threads from the stone.

Caro had folded her arms, but at the accident she was immediately contrite. "Oh, sorry, Em. Are those important?"

He crouched and picked up the scattered stamens, shaking his head. "No, they're not, actually. These were destined for the compost heap." He frowned as he rose. "But you gave me a fright. Why are you creeping up on me at this time of night?"

"I did not creep! You were just lost in your own little world, like always. In any case, my earlier point stands. Why are you shut away in here? You missed the Spring Fling!" From her dress, that was where she'd been. Her red hair was arranged into perfect ringlets, beneath a hat with curling feathers on it. She dropped down on a stool next to the bench, and a faint scent of liquor hit him. "You haven't come to any of the dances, lately."

"I haven't felt like it," he said defensively. He didn't much like crowds, but normally the lure of dancing was strong enough to overcome that. Lately, however, the crowds had affected him more than usual—that or maybe the new lighting down at the dance floor. Whatever the cause, the eye-watering migraines that resulted made the exercise entirely unappealing.

"Well, you need to come and cheer up Mazie next time we go out," Caro said firmly. "She's suffered a disappointment."

"I told you not to go matchmaking me with your friends, Caro."

She waved airily. She wasn't drunk, but she'd clearly had enough to make her merrily unconcerned. "I'm not! But there's nothing like dancing with a handsome man to make one feel better about oneself. *Please* come next Saturday. As a favour, if nothing else." She huffed. "One might think you hated dancing, the way you've been hiding lately, and I know that's not true."

"Did you break into my glasshouse just to ask me to escort you and your friends next weekend?" he said, secretly flattered by the 'handsome' label. "Where are your friends now? You shouldn't be walking home half-cut and alone at this time of night!"

"Well, obviously *you're* going to walk me home now," she said cheerfully. "My friends walked me here and I saw your light on, and you live on the way to me anyway, so I know it'll be no trouble. Which reminds me." She fished about for her handbag. "This is why I came to find you. One of the girls at the dance showed it to me. Have you seen this?" She pulled out a magazine, laid it on the workbench, and flipped it open.

Marius recognised the magazine as *Lady Peregrine's Society News*, which was a sedate title for a gossip rag. It was his stepmother's guilty pleasure. Aunt Sybil's passion for it was almost as great, though her enjoyment largely derived from loudly rubbishing its contents. This in no way stopped her from reading it.

The article was a tiny one on page 3:

> *A tale has reached our ears, Gentle Readers, almost too scandalous to believe. All I can say is that a certain downstairs personage that we shall call Mr T not only appears to have taken unnatural advantage of a recently titled Northern lord but may not be all he appears to be. A Dramatic Alteration in Alverness is the least of his misdemeanours! Does that whet your appetites? But you shall have to wait until Lady P's next issue for the Full Story!*

When he glanced up, Caro's expression had sobered. "It's about Hetta and Wyn, isn't it? The bank incident in Alverness?"

"I don't see how it could be about anyone else." He stared at the words, furious and futile anger churning in his stomach.

"This is slander, then!" she said, slapping the page. "Or libel. I never can remember which is which."

"It's only libel if it isn't true. And Wyn *isn't* what he's led people to believe."

"Yes, but he hasn't taken 'unnatural advantage' of Hetta," Caro argued. "Can't you ask your lawyer friend if we can, I don't know, get an injunction or something?"

"I don't have a lawyer friend." *John.* She was talking about John. Gods, it hurt, the way Caro said it so casually: *your friend.* Ha.

"Yes, you do. I met you walking one day, and you said '*this is John, my friend. He's reading law*' when I asked to be introduced."

"I meant he's not my friend anymore." Not that he'd ever really been that; friends didn't merrily try to blackmail you and your family. Only Wyn's compulsion had prevented him from succeeding, though Wyn had said he'd lifted it before John had left Stariel.

The compulsion horrified Marius. So did the removal of it, knowing John was no longer bound not to harm him. *Which makes me a hypocrite.*

"Well, that's very inconvenient," Caro groused. Marius nearly laughed, bitterness spiky in his throat. *Inconvenient.* The single most excruciatingly shameful experience of his life was *inconvenient.*

He glared down at the article. What was the Full Story even supposed to be? An account from someone who'd seen something of the attack at the bank last year? Someone from Stariel who'd been there for Wyn's reveal of his fae nature? No doubt whatever it was, a magazine like this would slant it as sensationally as possible. Its publication felt both unreal and strangely inevitable, and the same helpless frustration as this morning rose up again and choked him. His temples began to twinge in a way that meant a migraine was threatening to make a joyful appearance.

"Well, I'm going to write to the editor and demand they not print whatever else it is they're planning. I shall use the word libel liberally," Caro said decisively, sliding off her stool.

"Good plan," he said vaguely, rubbing at his head. And why hadn't he thought of that course of action, obvious as it was? He folded the magazine back in half and gave it back to her. "I'll tell Hetta."

13

LONG DISTANCE COMMUNICATIONS

WHEN MARIUS WAS put through to the gatehouse, the deep, faintly accented voice that answered didn't belong to his sister.

"Marius?"

There was a pause. Did Wyn feel the tension between them, stifling all normal attempts at conversation? Before Hetta had come home and been chosen, he and Wyn had been close. Or, well, Marius had thought so. Maybe Wyn hadn't. Maybe that's why he hadn't told Marius he was fae—Jack and Hetta had both found out before him. *Or maybe he didn't tell me because he knew he couldn't compel me not to tell anyone else*, the traitorous thought snuck in.

Guilt had him arguing with himself. *He probably didn't tell me because he was hiding from his psychopathic family at the time! And I bet Jack only knew because Father told him. Wyn didn't even tell Hetta until he had to!* Was Marius going to hold it against him forever? If only Wyn wasn't courting Hetta—it made it hard to forgive him for everything else.

"Marius?" Wyn repeated, amusement in his tone. "I didn't realise a phone call with me would shock you into silence."

Gods damn it. *Stop getting distracted!* He railed at himself. "Why are you answering the phone anyway?" It was Hetta he'd said he needed to talk to when he'd left the initial message with the gatekeeper to set up a time. The phoneline directly to the house had yet to be installed.

"Hetta is occupied, talking to the linesmen. A minor issue, but she has to sort it before we leave." A pause. "And I wanted to speak to you."

"Leave? Where are you leaving to?"

Wyn told him about the queen's summons. "We're taking the sleeper train down to Meridon. We're staying at the Crane Hotel." He gave Marius the address.

"Not Malvern Place, then?" Stariel Estate owned a townhouse, though only because it was entailed. His father would've sold it otherwise, not having much use for Southern property.

"I understand it needs major repairs to be habitable, even more so than the Dower House, and there are only so many projects the bank will fund, initially." Wyn sighed.

"Father let it fall to rack and ruin too, did he?" Marius guessed. He wasn't surprised. "And you and Hetta are staying in town alone?" he asked sharply.

"No." There was another heartfelt sigh on the other end of the phone. "Alexandra and your Aunt Sybil are accompanying us. Apparently we cannot be trusted alone."

Marius gave a bark of laughter. "Good!" he said. "So why does the queen want you there? Does she know you're fae?" If the rumour had reached as far as Knoxbridge undergrads, it wasn't so far-fetched to think it had reached Her Majesty as well. But would she believe it?

"Perhaps." Wyn's voice was carefully neutral. "We'll be in Meridon for a few days in any case—if you come up, you can have dinner with us and find out what the result of the interview was." Knoxbridge was only an hour's train journey from the Southern capital. "But what were you calling for? If it isn't for Hetta's ears only."

"No, I'd rather burn your damn ears with it." Marius told him about *Lady Peregrine's Society News*. Wyn laughed at the phrase 'downstairs personage'.

"Technically accurate, I suppose."

It was sometimes difficult to remember that Wyn was a prince. He did dignified very well, but there was a strong streak of irreverence in him. *Plus you've seen him wash dishes.* There was something very un-princelike about washing dishes. How did domestic life work in the fae courts? Was it the same as here? Were there fae butlers and housemaids?

"Do you mind it?" he asked. "That we treated you as a servant?" They still did, to a large extent, though it had become an uncomfortable thing. "It's bloody fortunate you were head of staff and not still houseboy when this all came out—at least you haven't had to deal with the servants not knowing what to do with you," he thought aloud.

Wyn laughed. "Marius, I have been treated as per the position I chose to occupy these last ten years. And better than most in such positions."

"But do you resent it?" he pressed. It bothered him when Wyn didn't answer things outright. He was too conscious of the fact that although Wyn couldn't lie, secrets could hide underneath every roundabout response.

"No," Wyn said. "I do not resent you or your family. Quite the opposite: I am deeply grateful that I found you all, and that you accepted me into your world."

Marius snorted. "Yes, we're all so very accepting. That's why you don't take your true form in the house, isn't it, even though we've all seen it now?"

There was a short, pregnant silence on the other end.

"I have not missed your tendency to locate those places where I am most vulnerable."

He wasn't sure what to say to that. "Well, on the other hand, you've made it easier to keep the entirety of Prydein from knowing the truth about you. I mean, no one has more than speculation outside of Stariel, and they're used to believing things no one else does. Half of Knoxbridge would think I was mad if I tried to explain my land-sense to them, for instance, despite the fact that it's neither new nor a secret in the North. Just carry on looking human while you're down in Meridon and everyone will write it off as nothing more than superstitious Northerners," he advised. "Maybe the queen simply wants to meet Hetta and figured she might as well address the gossip at the same time."

He paused, twining the cord of the receiver around his thumb. "Wyn, she *is* my sister. You can't carry on like this forever. I don't want the whole country to be talking about her like she's some kind of…scarlet woman. Caro's going to write to the magazine offices, but the gods know if that'll stop them printing whatever they were intending to."

"I have, as mortals say, 'honest intentions' towards your sister," Wyn said. "But there are…certain complications." A pause. "We'll see you next week."

After the conversation had ended, Marius stared down at the phone and wondered how in the world he was supposed to protect his younger sister from the Queen of Prydein.

14

MERIDON

A STRANGE MIX OF emotions welled up in Hetta's chest as the train came into sight of Meridon.

"It goes for *miles!*" Alexandra exclaimed. The overnight experience in the narrow sleeper compartments hadn't put a dent in her enthusiasm for the trip. She'd never been further south than Greymark.

Aunt Sybil muttered something about how the city had grown since she'd last visited, but Hetta wasn't really listening as she retrieved her overnight bag. Last time she'd been here, she'd been about to make this journey in the opposite direction, setting off to Stariel for the first time in six years. Bradfield's new show had just opened, and she'd lamented the need to be gone for a few weeks to attend her father's funeral and the Choosing Ceremony. It had never occurred to her that she wouldn't be coming back. *I'm sorry I never got to say goodbye to you*, she told the city silently as the train pulled into Celerebank Station.

The three of them bustled to join the crowd spilling out onto the platform. Wyn had lodged in a separate part of the train, as it was divided into 'men', 'women', and 'married couples only'. Wyn had probably had an uncomfortable time of it, as the train billets were not built for those of more than average height.

Overhead, the vast metal-and-glass roof created an effect like a vast birdcage. Sound echoed within its steel ribs, the whistle and grind of engines mingling with footsteps on hard floors and hundreds of voices chattering. Had there always been this many people in Meridon? she wondered as she directed their group towards the back of the train to collect their luggage and tried to locate Wyn.

This would be his first visit to Meridon, she mused as she scanned the crowds. Somehow she'd overlooked that, between one thing and another. A sudden desire to show him the best of her city filled her, and despite the disorienting busyness of the station and the gnawing worry about Queen Matilda, a giddy anticipation began to creep over her. Maybe this trip didn't have to be purely official business, after this audience with the queen was done. She could play tour guide—take Wyn to all her old haunts. Bradfield had invited her to the opening of his newest play, which began later this week. She and Wyn could go together. Who cared what Aunt Sybil thought? This was Meridon, the city that had given Hetta her freedom when she'd most needed it, and she'd be dashed if she let her aunt ruin that with Northern conservatism.

Ignoring her aunt's low grumbling about "too many people; vastly impolite; that girl's hemline is *quite shocking!*", Hetta spun around, trying to spot a glimpse of platinum blond hair in the crowds. Finally, she found him. He was waiting beside the baggage compartment, their luggage already stowed in the trolley beside him. His face lit up when he caught sight of her.

"And I was worried you'd be lost without my guidance," she said wryly when she reached him, gesturing at their luggage. But close up, she could see the odd tightness in his expression. She frowned. "What's wrong?"

"It's the iron," he murmured. His gaze lifted to the glass-and-metal roof. "I didn't realise there would be quite so much of it."

Iron between him and the sky. "Well, it *is* a train station. There'll be less of it outside. I'll go and locate a cab."

She left Aunt Sybil and Alexandra with Wyn and went and found a horse-drawn hackney rather than a kineticar, trying to minimise the amount of iron they'd encounter. Iron didn't hurt fae, he'd told her, just interfered with their magic. He'd never shown unease around iron before—so why was it affecting him so badly now? Perhaps it was an issue of scale, since she supposed there was significantly less of it at Stariel. Or was he more sensitive to it now with his increased powers? Would he be all right, in the hotel they were staying in?

She was fretting, and only realised she was doing so when Wyn climbed in beside her—to Aunt Sybil's displeasure—and said in an undertone: "I'm not about to expire, Hetta. I was only…unprepared for the station."

"Do people truly choose to live so very squashed together?" Alexandra peered out the hackney window, humming with excitement. "What's that building with all the stone gargoyles on the top?"

"The Natural History Museum," Hetta told her absently, trying to read Wyn's expression. He was always so very good at pretending to be all right when he wasn't.

He raised a sardonic eyebrow at her. *Stop worrying; I'm fine,* he might as well have said. She wasn't sure she believed him, but he did at least look a little less tense than he had on the platform.

The hotel they'd chosen was in a good but not fashionable part of Meridon, more comfortable than the hostels she'd stayed in between flats in her years away, but far from the grandest accommodations on offer. She was Lord Valstar now, not an anonymous illusionist, but Stariel was still financially struggling. The hotel was a compromise between those two facts. Aunt Sybil had grumbled about staying in a hotel at all—apparently it wasn't "quite the thing!"— but this sadly hadn't been enough to dissuade her from coming.

The hotel staff treated them all with utmost politeness as they ferried them all to their rooms, but their expressions held a spark of interest that suggested at least some rumours about her had reached as far as Meridon. So this was what infamy felt like. *I suppose my anonymous days truly are behind me then, even here.* The thought cost her an odd pang.

Nostalgia is giving you a rose-tinted view of the past, she admonished herself. *Remember how ghastly some of those boarding houses you lodged in were!* This hotel was worlds nicer. She couldn't go back to her illusionist days, so she might as well enjoy some of the privileges that came with rank—such as the fact that she'd gotten bigger and better rooms than the rest of the party. Rooms *plural*—she had a separate sitting room as well as a bedroom dominated by an enormous metal-framed bed.

She considered the bed, and butterflies swirled lazily in her stomach. There was no Stariel here to interfere. The bond pinged very faintly as she stretched absently towards the estate. At this distance, it was barely there at all. Excellent. What were the chances of getting Wyn alone, in that bed, without risk of interruption from her relatives?

Could she set Aunt Sybil and Alexandra loose on Malvern Place, the dilapidated townhouse? Perhaps the lure of planning renovations could keep them out of her hair. Her aunt loved to have opinions about things. *Though do I really trust her opinions on décor?* She'd better first make sure it wasn't her aunt who'd approved the aged pink-and-green wallpaper in the hallway outside her bedroom at Stariel.

She shook herself out of her thoughts as she began to change into formal clothing. *Get through the audience with the queen first before you start making plans for house refurbishments you definitely can't afford yet.* She set about making up her face, falling into the familiar routine.

Now, the question was, should she augment her cosmetics with illusion? With Hetta's luck, Queen Matilda would be like Aunt Sybil and think illusion low-class. Her aunt had taken to wearing a quizzing glass in the last few months, just so she could criticise Hetta if she used magic to alter her appearance—the specially made lense allowed people to see the distortions caused by illusion. It hadn't stopped Hetta from using illusion as she pleased. But perhaps discretion might be the better part of valour today. *Although if Queen Matilda is the sort of person who examines people through quizzing glasses, then she's going to disapprove of me regardless.*

She stared thoughtfully into the mirror when she'd finished. Her face didn't look anywhere near serious or old enough to be a lord, despite her efforts. *On the other hand, I do look extremely pretty.* Prettiness was just another sort of illusion, a construct of skill, paint, and fashion rather than magic, but it was nice to have the armour in place, regardless. Her dress was blue, with long sleeves and a high collar, suitable for the formality of the occasion, and she'd paired it with long dangling earrings containing sapphires. They'd been her mother's. She tapped at the silver, sending the jewels spinning. What would her mother have thought of all this? Hetta had never known her, as she'd died in childbirth. She frowned at her reflection, wondering suddenly about Wyn's mother. She'd been conspicuously absent from both the Court of Ten Thousand Spires last year and from all of Wyn's stories of growing up in Faerie. Was his mother dead too? The subject had somehow never come up between them.

How can I marry someone who I still know so little about? But she knew the important things, she argued with herself. She knew Wyn was kind and loyal and wryly humorous and so determined to do the right thing she worried it would be the death of him. A fierce possessiveness curled through her veins. He was *hers.*

The thought gave her pause. She wasn't on Stariel lands now; that possessiveness hadn't been due to the faeland's influence. In a way it was reassuring—not that she'd doubted her attachment to Wyn, but Stariel's newfound enthusiasm for its steward had muddied the line between her and Lord Valstar's wants. Of course, Lord Valstar was welcome to want to marry Wyn as well—and it was, in fact, rather convenient that she did, since the separation between the two of them was entirely fictitious—but the point still stood.

There was a soft knock at the internal door, and Hetta had a moment of disorientation where she reached for Stariel for information and received nothing in return. How inconvenient not to be able to just magically *know* who was knocking at her door. But it wasn't hard to guess, judging from the timepiece that said they'd better leave for the palace soon.

"Come in," she said, turning away from her reflection.

He'd changed into more formal attire as well, his pale hair slicked back, black bowtie crisp below the strong column of his neck. He looked very human, but the sight woke dissonance in her. He *wasn't* human. She saw him once again at the Standing Stones, with glittering blue wings unfurled, hair disordered from the wind, lightning curling around his forearms. Which one was the truer him? Both? Neither? Was it right that she was making this impossible man try to be human, just for her?

"You look beautiful." His russet eyes warmed as he took in her appearance.

"You're wearing one of your shirts," she noticed suddenly—the ones with button-up slits at the back to allow for wings. With his coat and waistcoat in place, there was no outward difference between his ordinary shirts and the modified ones, except that she recognised his wardrobe now.

"I suspect it would scandalise your queen if I did not wear a shirt."

She rolled her eyes at him, unimpressed. "Are you planning to go all fae on her?" Was that sensible?

He spread his arms wide. "I am not planning to flaunt my…less than human attributes, but I thought it best to be prepared. It's not, after all, supposed to be a secret anymore."

"True," she said, uneasy for reasons she couldn't explain. She looked at the timepiece. "We'd better leave."

He hesitated. "Hetta, I have a…gift for you."

"That's not usually a reason to look anxious." Because he *was* anxious; she could tell.

He went to speak but stopped himself before reaching into his trouser pocket to retrieve something. He brought his closed hand up into the space between them and uncurled long fingers to reveal a ring.

The ring rang with familiarity, and she stared at it, her pulse loud as an oncoming train as she reached out to take it from him. The stone set into the silver was almost but not quite star indigo, a rare substance found within Stariel's borders. Her bond with Stariel, muted at this long distance, sparked as the stone touched her bare skin.

"It's like it has a piece of Stariel inside," she said wonderingly when the land's response came. "How did you…?"

"I cannot take credit for it," Wyn admitted. "The stone came to me through Lamorkin, as the vessel for a powerful translocation spell, but Stariel did something to it when we found out you were imprisoned in the Spires. The translocation spell is no more, but Stariel's imprint on that stone remains. I'm curious as to whether it might allow you to draw on the estate's magic even outside its boundaries."

"I thought we were trying to encourage Stariel to be *less* involved in our affairs?" she said archly as she turned the ring over in her hands. "But this does seem to magnify the link." She sent a question towards Stariel and felt the land reach towards her curiously, muted but definitely more *there* than when she'd tried before. Just how much would it allow her to draw on Stariel's magic outside its bounds?

"I thought it best to increase our advantages. Just in case," he said.

She considered him evenly. "Wyn, you *cannot* be unaware of the connotations attached to this particular gift. Particularly in light of recent conversations we've had on the subject. This isn't a hypothetical object."

"I'm aware of the Prydinian customs you refer to." He looked sheepish. "But since neither of us is free to make the promises that should come with it, think of it rather as a statement of intent."

She turned the ring over in her hands. How long had he spent on this? The silver band was deceptively simple, but the closer she looked, the more detail was revealed. The setting invoked feathers that morphed into abstract lines twisting around the band—wind currents? Tree branches? The high peaks of the Indigoes dark against the setting sun? Her mind spun into increasingly sentimental imagery, and she pulled it firmly back.

"It's lovely," she said. "But I'm growing rather tired of your hypothetical proposals. Let's hope the queen will give me permission to make it only half-hypothetical." The other half of the problem, the High King, loomed on the horizon, a knot Hetta wasn't sure yet how to unravel. Wyn had tried again to contact his godparent for advice on the subject before they'd left Stariel, but without success. *Well, we can deal with that after we deal with Queen Matilda.*

Wyn grimaced, clearly thinking along the same lines. "Yes. But regardless of custom, it seemed too useful an object to keep from you, since we're outside of Stariel."

"Surely whatever is happening in the Spires won't endanger us here?"

"I hope not. But I've misjudged dangers before."

"Alexandra wasn't your fault, and nor was Marius," she said sharply.

He made a loose motion with one hand, disagreeing.

"You know, it's arrogant to assume everything is your fault."

He smiled, fleetingly, the flecks of brandy gold gleaming in the russet of his irises. "I *am* arrogant, Hetta."

She reached to pull him down into a kiss, but he shifted away.

"I'll ruin your lipstick."

She sighed. He was right, dash it. Why had she decided caution was a good idea today when it came to cosmetic illusion? "Well," she said brightly. "How fortunate that this matches my mother's earrings." She rummaged in her jewellery box and pulled out a long silver chain, threading the ring through, and slipped it on and under her dress. At Wyn's inquisitive look, she shrugged.

"I think it would be impolitic to appear before the queen wearing an obvious betrothal ring *before* I've asked for her permission to marry."

He chuckled as she smoothed down the collar of her dress and stood.

Fortunately, they were already in the hallway when Aunt Sybil barrelled along it, intent on preventing any clandestine goings-on.

"My lady," Wyn greeted her cordially. "We were just on our way out. I hope you and Miss Alex enjoy your morning without us."

She narrowed her eyes at both of them and looked Hetta over from top to toe, making liberal use of her quizzing glass.

"Do *try* to uphold the family name, Henrietta," she admonished, when she couldn't find anything to criticise in Hetta's appearance.

15

QUEEN MATILDA

ERIDON PALACE WAS surrounded by a vast park, and the long vehicle approach gave visitors plenty of time to be intimidated by its imposing rectangular form. Hetta had been here before, on a public day, as one anonymous tourist among many, shown around its public galleries by a very superior tour guide. But that only made it more surreal now, approaching the gates without the protection of a crowd. In front of the great gates, the driveway encircled an enormous statue of a winged woman holding a trident. The woman was Pyrania, the sea goddess responsible for lifting Prydein above the waves. Hetta stared up at the golden face and tried to borrow some of Pyrania's serenity for herself.

I'm a lord now, she reminded herself as she smoothed her dress. Here, she represented more than just herself. Renewing Stariel's agreements with the Crown might only be a formality, but she was still determined not to show any sign of shabbiness while doing so.

Wyn had a very curious look on his face as he surveyed the many fluted columns running along the palace's frontage, an emotion more complicated than mere sadness, and one that Hetta recognised because it was what she felt whenever she caught sight of her father's portrait in the long gallery—not grief, exactly, but a sober awareness of the past. She put a hand on his arm, and he gave himself a tiny shake.

A rigid manservant took their names and coats with cold formality and ushered them through the palace to a waiting room. Everything about it was designed to keep visitors unbalanced, from the uncomfortably upholstered chairs, to the large portraits of past monarchs staring disapprovingly down from every wall, to the temperature, which was slightly too cool. They couldn't even talk openly, for they were left in the care of a footman, who remained standing so still next to the doorway that he might as well have been part of the furnishings too.

They waited. Time ticked by in tiny increments marked by the ornate grandfather clock. Hetta got up after a while and began to pace. The footman watched her impassively, and she was gripped by a temptation to pull faces at him, just to see if that got a reaction.

Wyn stared unseeingly at the wallpaper, that strange tightness back in his expression, and she suspected he was thinking of the Spires again. If only the footman would leave them alone so she could ask him about it! She'd seen only glimpses of the Court of Ten Thousand Spires, but they'd left her with an overwhelming impression of lavish wealth, gold leaf everywhere that could be leafed, and jewels sparkling in any surface that could be jewelled. Just when she was about to break the silence, unable to stand it any longer, the far door opened, and another liveried footman appeared.

"Lord Valstar, Mr Tempest," he said with a nod to each of them. "Her Majesty will see you now."

They were shown in to a drawing room. It was as old-fashioned as one of Stariel's public rooms, every item no doubt a family heirloom, but its atmosphere differed markedly. Where Stariel House gave off a faintly dilapidated air of neglect, this room reeked of wealth and attentive care.

A row of palace guards in stiff uniforms lined each wall. *Well, it's certainly not a very private private audience*, Hetta thought, blinking at them in surprise. Was such an excessive number of guards usual?

Queen Matilda sat in a high-backed chair that brought to mind the word 'throne'. Two advisors stood to either side of her, both men, one dark-skinned and one fair, but Hetta didn't know enough about the queen's court to recognise either. She did, however, know enough to kneel, spreading her skirts in a smooth movement that would've made her old school mistress proud. What a lowering thought, that her old school mistress had been right to see that the correct protocols were drummed into her. At the time she'd thought it pointless to learn how to interact with royalty. *And it's not like I needed it to interact with Wyn*, she thought with a wisp of inappropriately timed humour.

She bowed her head and waited for permission to rise and speak. To her surprise, Wyn didn't kneel, and instead cut a very deep bow. One of the queen's advisors made a small noise of shocked displeasure and would've objected aloud except that the queen cut him off with a single commanding hand movement. Hetta shot Wyn a meaningful glance. What was he *doing*? Weren't they supposed to be showing the queen what good, non-scandalous citizens they were?

"You may rise, Lord Valstar," the queen said. "Though I see such permission will be wasted on your companion." Her tone was very dry.

"Forgive me, Your Majesty," Wyn said quietly. "I honour your position greatly, and I mean no offence, but you are not my queen, and it would be impolitic of me to rank you above my own liege."

The queen ignored him. Up close, Hetta could see that there were tiny strands of illusion wound into her blonde hair, hiding the grey. Interesting. *I wonder if Aunt Sybil knows the queen uses cosmetic illusion?* Hetta would probably do the same for her own auburn locks when the time came, but who was employed as the queen's personal illusionist? She wished she'd known that was a career option back when she'd been seeking financial reward in exchange for her magic, though the theatre crowd appealed to her for more than monetary reasons.

"You have been tardy in paying your respects, Lord Valstar," Queen Matilda said. "You have not yet sworn your oath to the Crown. You inherited in October, and it is now March, is it not?"

"Yes, Your Majesty." She fought the urge to fidget under the queen's piercing blue-eyed gaze, feeling as if she truly had regressed back to her schoolgirl self.

"You make no excuses, Lord Valstar." It was a statement rather than a question, but Hetta answered it anyway.

"Well, I certainly *have* excuses. I didn't intend to delay quite so much, but it's been a very busy six months since my father passed away." Had it truly only been six months?

"So I understand," Queen Matilda said, her attention shifting to Wyn. He met her gaze without trouble, expression neutral. "This is your steward?"

Hetta opened her mouth to confirm, but before she could, Wyn spoke, a hint of steel in his tone.

"I think you suspect precisely what I am, Your Majesty." He gestured at the many guards. "Unless you always employ such a large number of people wearing yarrow charms to guard you."

Hetta took a sharp breath. Yarrow! The herb had anti-fae properties. It had disoriented Wyn, last time they'd encountered it, but he didn't appear disoriented now. He held himself tightly, his posture very erect.

This room had a grandfather clock too, the twin of the one in the waiting room, and its ponderous tick grated as the queen considered Wyn in silence for a long, long moment.

"And what are you, Mr Tempest?" she said finally.

"Fae. Greater fae, to be precise." He enunciated each syllable with cold, clipped precision.

The queen's expression didn't change, but her grip on the arm-rests of her chair tightened. "Then you are on dangerous ground. Interaction between Faerie and the Mortal Realm has been forbidden for the last three centuries."

The conversation had spun so rapidly beyond what Hetta had expected that she felt a strong urge to ask everyone to pause for a few moments so she could catch up. From the faces of the queen's advisors, they felt similarly wrongfooted. Both men were staring from Wyn to their monarch like spectators at a tennis match, each looking like they wanted to interject but didn't quite dare.

"The High King has revoked the Iron Law," Wyn said evenly. "The ways are open once more, for those that care to find them."

"Excuse me, Your Majesty, but if you already knew about the fae, why didn't you say so in your summons?" Hetta said, deciding that it was time she re-inserted herself back into this conversation.

"The fae are dangerous. They can enchant the mind, Lord Valstar," the queen said without taking her attention from Wyn. Hetta didn't like her expression—as if Wyn were a specimen in a glass case. A dangerous specimen. "I had heard you were…entangled with this one."

"'This one' is Prince Hallowyn Tempestren," Hetta retorted, needled. The shape of it felt strange—she could count on one hand the number of times she'd used Wyn's real name, and she'd never prefaced it with the word 'prince' before. "And my friend. He hasn't enchanted me."

"I would like to hear that from his lips, thank you." Queen Matilda didn't take her attention off Wyn.

"I have used no compulsive magic on Lord Valstar, Your Majesty," he said. His expression was dangerously neutral, and there was a faint edge about him that Hetta knew meant his fae side was close to the surface. The faintest hint of spice touched the back of Hetta's tongue.

"And have you enchanted any other of my citizens?"

Of course Wyn hadn't enchanted anyone! Hetta opened her mouth to say so but shut it as she abruptly remembered Mr John Tidwell, her brother's ex-paramour. And Alexandra—Wyn had been practising compulsion resistance with her. A panicky sensation spiked in her chest. How could they explain that to Her Majesty in a way that didn't sound nefarious?

Wyn, of course, had no trouble doling out truth untruthfully. "There are no compulsions of mine on any of your citizens. I mean no harm to any mortals. I am here in my capacity as Lord Valstar's steward, and my loyalties lie with her."

Relief and unease twined around her heart. There were a *lot* of guards, and they were half a country away from Stariel.

The queen made a sound, not quite disbelief but not approval either. "Nonetheless, this is an unusual state of affairs. We had not expected to encounter fae in Prydein, in our reign, and we wish to understand the ramifications of this. You will stay here under our supervision, Prince Hallowyn." She said the words so matter-of-factly that it took Hetta a second to understand their meaning.

"You aren't proposing to imprison him?" She clenched her fists, a spark of fire threatening to light in her palms.

The row of guards shifted very slightly, as if they had all tensed as one.

"What precisely are you proposing, Your Majesty?" Wyn said quickly.

"If the fae have truly returned to this world, then we must be sure of their intentions. We cannot grant you freedom of movement before we have satisfied ourself as to this point. If you are truly as loyal to Lord Valstar as you profess, then you will do as her queen commands." Queen Matilda gave Hetta a dry, fleeting glance.

Hetta bristled and thought about reminding Queen Matilda that she hadn't sworn her oath of fealty yet, but she settled on: "I don't think keeping Prince Hallowyn here would tell you much about the fae's intentions. He doesn't represent them, and he isn't a danger to anyone." She used Wyn's title again deliberately, hoping that would make the queen take them both more seriously.

"That is a judgement we need to make for ourself, Lord Valstar." The queen's tone was cold.

Wyn shot Hetta a warning look that said, very plainly, that arguing with your monarch in front of a roomful of people was generally not a good way to make them warm to you. Hetta glared black, trying to convey that this was no time for him to play martyr.

"I am willing to prove my loyalty, to a point," he said. "I mean your people no harm, Your Majesty."

"Then you will stay here," Queen Matilda said calmly. "As my guest."

"For how long?"

"Until we are satisfied," she said. She gave Hetta a very cool look. "We do not think you have been a good influence on Lord Valstar."

"On the contrary, Prince Hallowyn is an excellent influence, as he's by far the more level-headed of the two of us," Hetta couldn't help saying. The queen's eyes narrowed, and the fair-skinned advisor looked down his nose at Hetta, as if she were a dog that had made a mess on the carpet. She was speaking too frankly, too informally. *Remember you're talking to the Queen of Prydein!* She took a deep, calming breath. "And how long until you are satisfied? Your Majesty," she added belatedly. She reached for Stariel, but the stone from the ring wasn't touching her skin, and all she got was a distant murmur.

"You shall be informed when we know the answer to that." The words rang with frosty hauteur.

"I will be your guest, you say?" Wyn said. "Not, and forgive me, but I would like to be very sure on this point, a prisoner? Lord Valstar may visit me?"

"Let us say an entirely house-bound guest," the queen countered.

"You will be provided with rooms here, the same accommodations as any ambassador. You may receive visitors, but they must declare themselves upon entry." She paused. "We have only one additional requirement."

"Which is?"

The queen turned to her dark-skinned advisor. Hetta wished she'd introduce them. It was more intimidating, being faced with nameless nobles. Or were they so high up in the hierarchy that she was supposed to know who they were on sight? Southern titles were more convoluted than Northern ones, where you were either a lord or you weren't. "The box, Your Grace."

The man—a duke, apparently, which meant Hetta really ought to know who he was because there were only about seven of those, she was fairly sure—obediently retrieved a small chest from a nearby table, presenting it to the queen with steady hands. She opened the lid and lifted free two metal arm cuffs. They glimmered strangely, as if there was water beneath the surface of them, and intricate sigils were etched into the metal. Still resting in velvet inside the box was a large, ornate key made of the same strange metal.

Wyn went absolutely still, and the taste of spice in the air strengthened.

"What are they?" Hetta asked. "Your Majesty."

The queen raised one slender eyebrow, a silent commentary that said she'd noticed Hetta's poor manners. "They are called *dismae*, Lord Valstar."

"They bind greater fae," Wyn murmured. "I did not know there were any left." He raised his voice. "And if I refuse?"

The queen's blue eyes were unwavering. "Then you declare yourself an enemy of the state. As do those who harbour you."

"No," Hetta said, low and fierce. "This is completely unnecessary."

"Very well," Wyn said. He smiled at Hetta, soft and sad. "I am trying to prevent a war, my Star, not start one." He turned back to the queen and took a deep breath. She watched, helpless and furious, as he held out his arms. "Give them to me."

16

THE GRIFFIN THEATRE

HETTA STALKED OUT of the palace after being dismissed, a seething, acid anger churning in her stomach. How dare the queen treat Wyn like an enemy? How dare he agree to this so easily? But beneath that was a worse emotion, a spiralling panic at how quickly everything had changed, at the flat calm of Wyn's expression after donning the iron cuffs—never a good sign.

She paused in the public avenue outside the palace and balled her hands into fists. The statue of Pyrania gazed impassively down at her. What was she supposed to do now? How could she convince the queen to let Wyn go? It had all gotten so much bigger than Stariel and gossipy magazine articles. *Politics*, she thought, remembering how the queen's advisors had looked at her with disdain. This wasn't her world, and they'd known it.

She couldn't face the hotel, not yet. Aunt Sybil might have gone out—but knowing her, she'd be crouched waiting for Hetta and Wyn to return. Would her aunt hold her to blame for this? Would she take the queen's side? *At least she no longer needs to worry about protecting my imaginary virtue!* But she couldn't laugh at that because she wasn't sure she'd be able to stop.

Agitation impelled her back into motion, and she found herself walking the familiar streets towards the part of Meridon still filed under 'home' in her heart. The theatre district was quieter than usual at this hour, and she drew to a stop outside the Sun Theatre with something cold and thorny settling in her chest. Was it home-sickness? *Last time I was here we'd just opened our first show at the Sun,* she thought. A replacement illusionist had seen out the rest of the show's run when she'd been summoned north.

And now the show was finished, an unqualified success without her, and Bradfield and the company had moved on. Upgraded, even. Bradfield's newest show opening this week would be at the Griffin, several steps up in the theatre hierarchy from the Sun, which in turn had been several steps up from the tiny ramshackle places Bradfield had run shows out of in his early years as director.

Hetta picked at a spot on the pasteboard, revealing a sliver of familiar poster in amongst the new. Had it truly only been six months since she'd been here? It seemed much longer. It was unreasonable, but part of her hadn't quite accepted that the company both would and could move on without her. *This will never be home again, not really.* Her heart gave a queer thump.

She shook her head and briskly set off for the Griffin. The stage door was located down a side entry, and a twist of the handle found it unlocked. She took a deep breath, not entirely sure what reception she'd get. The distance between her past and present selves yawned. Would Bradfield still treat her the same way? There'd been a handful of phone calls and letters that suggested nothing had changed between them, but in person, things might be different. Brad wouldn't be expecting to see her so soon, though she'd promised they'd make it to opening night.

Anger swarmed up again as she thought of the queen's high-handedness. She *would* prise Wyn out of the palace's clutches before

Brad's show opened. She wouldn't let herself consider the alternative, that this might drag on, that the queen's uncertainty would
change to enmity. *She promised he'd be treated as an honoured guest,*
Hetta reminded herself. It didn't ease the knot of fear in her belly.
There'd been so many guards. And Wyn pretending very hard that
the dismae didn't affect him, attempting to project only warm and
harmless humanity. And why should he have to pretend to be something he wasn't?

She ignored the small voice that pointed out that he was doing
all this for her. But why was he always so willing to martyr himself,
anyway? She needed to free him as soon as possible just so she could
shake him for his stupidly self-sacrificing tendencies.

Backstage was a hive of activity, and she wove her way through it
unchallenged for about thirty seconds before she was noticed.

The company's long-time lead actress, Sally-Ann, did a double-take. "Hetta!" she shrieked in her carrying stage-voice. Heads
emerged from out of alcoves and behind bits of stored scenery.
"You're back!"

Hetta quickly found herself surrounded by a throng of actors,
seamstresses, and stagehands. She didn't recognise all the faces, but
most of the old crowd was still here. They all knew of her rise in
station, of course, and there was a hesitancy to them she hadn't
seen before.

"It's Lady Valstar now, isn't it? Do you want us to curtsey?" the
backstage manager asked warily, folding her arms as she looked
down at Hetta from her considerable height—Marjorie was six foot
two, and broadly built.

Hetta grinned up at her. "Only if you consider it a necessary
formality when greeting all your old friends."

Marjorie's face relaxed into a smile. "Omar does do a lovely
curtsey," she said thoughtfully, with a nod in the direction of one of
the young actors. "He's been practising!"

Omar dutifully spread his non-existent skirts in a grandiose curtsey, to a general rumble of laughter, and the tension broke. Now assured that Hetta hadn't transformed into an autocratic ogre, they began to pepper her with varying degrees of inappropriate questions.

"Did you get sick of the Northerners and come back to join the company again?"

"Is that dress illusion or did you get up all fancy just to see us?"

"Do you have scads of money now? We could name a box after you for a very reasonable fee…"

Hetta laughed and tried to answer them all, strangely dislocated in time and space. They hadn't changed at all, this irreverent crowd, most of whom had never been further than an hour north of Meridon.

"The dress is real, and I'm just back for a visit. Oh, I've missed you all terribly." And she had. Her throat closed, thick with sudden emotion. She'd never had the chance to say goodbye to her old life, and here it was, hammering her with poignancy and laughter and the smell of cheap fabric and fresh paint. They talked excitedly over each other without waiting for her answers, trying to cram six months of news into single sentences.

"You won't believe what happened to Angela while you were gone!"

"We heard the wildest stories about you, Hetta!"

"Yeah, we even heard you was shagging a fairy prince!" This came from one of the seamstresses, who grinned nervously when her words created a small hush as everyone waited to see if she'd crossed a line or not.

"Alas, you are misinformed," Hetta told her primly. She heaved a great sigh. "There has, I regret, been no shagging. My prince has stronger principles than I and has so far held out against me."

They burst into laughter, and she smiled. It felt good despite the anxiety tearing her apart. *I'm picking up bad habits from Wyn, misleading with truth.* What would he make of her theatre friends?

"All right, all right," she said after the initial round of greetings had simmered down a fraction, "I'd no intention of causing such a riot. Where's Bradfield? Don't you all have jobs to be getting on with?"

They groaned, but eventually dispersed and even provided directions, and she found herself with a free path to Brad's office, a tiny room half-below street level.

"My gods, they're making a racket out there, Arthur!" Brad said without looking up as she came into his office. The narrow windows near the ceiling looked out at foot-height into the alley behind the theatre, letting in only dim light. Her ex-director was hunched over what looked like stage plans, paper covering the entire surface of his battered desk. His black, wildly curly hair stuck up in a way that meant he'd been grabbing handfuls of it in frustration.

"It's not Arthur, Brad," she said softly. "It's Hetta, descending upon you in all her lordly glory."

That sent him spinning about like a top, his elbow catching on a ruler and sending it clattering to the floor. "By the marsh goddess, Hetta! I thought I wouldn't see you till tomorrow earliest!"

"A change of plans," she said wryly as he rose and embraced her.

He was still reed-thin, and he wore his favourite plum velvet smoking jacket paired with a soft white cravat, though the fashion was decades out of date. Bradfield's style had always been both finicky and entirely individual. He was much the same height as her, and they stood face to face, drinking each other in for several long seconds.

"You look well," she said. It wasn't surprising. He always looked well, if slightly manic, in the lead up to opening night, deep brown skin and eyes glowing with the fires of obsession. It was only afterwards that the weight of exhaustion would hit him.

He grimaced. "A painfully inane observation, my girl. But if we must exchange such everyday pleasantries, you look terrible." He flourished a hand at her outfit. "Though very smartly turned out, I will say."

"I've been visiting the queen."

He laughed and then choked when he realised she was quite serious. "Egads, you really *are* a lord!"

"Did you think I made it up?"

"It's just"—he smoothed a hand over his jacket—"a bit of a mental adjustment. Is it too early for a drink?"

"It's definitely not too early," she said fervently.

"Well, in that case, let us celebrate both your rise in the world and your return," he said with a grin, returning to his desk. He fished a bottle of brandy out of his bottom drawer and eyed it. "Gods only know where to find a clean glass though. I think we left the last lot up on the roof."

Hetta sat down on the only other chair in his office and held out a hand imperiously.

He raised his eyebrows but gave her the bottle. "Very lordly."

"You've no idea, Brad. None." She wiped the lip of the bottle, took a swig, coughed, and handed it back with a shake of her head. "This is vile!"

"It is," he agreed. He put the bottle aside without drinking any himself. "Not that I mind, but what brings you here needing my brandy at such an ungodly hour?"

"Hardly ungodly. It's nearly midday." She sighed and began to pull off her gloves, more for something to do than because she particularly wanted them off. "And I came because I need a favour."

"That doesn't sound ominous at all," he said, crossing one leg over the other.

She smirked. "I need to know who has the queen's ear—who has influence at court—and I've no idea where to even start. I thought you might know some names, at least."

Bradfield's eyebrows went up. "And you're asking me?" He smoothed his velvet jacket grandly. "Obviously, I just came from tea with the queen myself!"

"Don't tell me you don't read the society pages, because I know you do. And even if you don't, you've been dropping hints like rocks about your latest conquest being blue-blooded, so you can't be completely ignorant of court politics." She'd been half-amused, half-worried that Brad was tangling with someone titled and—from the sounds of it—in the public eye. Meridon was much more liberal than the North, but still, it seemed dicey, pursuing someone whose rank would protect him, but not Bradfield, if things went sour.

A short, annoyed silence fell.

"His name was Simon," he said at last. He reached for the brandy, unscrewed the cap, and took a deep draught. "And he was a bloody dickhead. Threw me over for a fresh-faced lawyer, if you can believe it."

"Oh, I'm so sorry," she said, reaching out to pat his arm. She *was* sorry, though not exactly surprised. Brad's love affairs were usually short-lived things.

He waved her away. "No, no, it's for the best. Better not to get caught up with the aristocracy. See also previous remarks regarding general dickishness." A glimmer of humour caught at his mouth. "And I don't mean that in the enjoyable sense." He gave a long, theatrical sigh. "Besides, he was awfully strait-laced everywhere except where he wasn't...laced. It was growing tiresome."

"Well, if you *will* have a weakness for uptight men, what can you expect?" she teased.

He raised the brandy bottle in a half-salute of agreement. "You wound me." But his eyes sparkled, his humour restored. "Ah, well. Enough of that maudlinry. You're right, I could probably give you a list of names cobbled together from gossip and hearsay. But what have you gotten yourself mixed up with, old girl, that you need the queen's ear for?"

Hetta wrapped her fingers around her folded gloves, tried to think of the right words, and then gave up with a trill of laughter. "Oh, there's no way to explain it that won't sound completely ludicrous to you! So here it is, the shortest and most ludicrous of explanations: I've a beau." Her hand went to the lump of the ring under her neckline.

"Well, congratulations, but that's not exactly ludicrous. Or news." The twinkle in his eye said he'd seen the dashed magazine article.

"Oh, hush. I've a beau who it so happens is both Stariel's steward and a winged fae prince. The queen has taken exception to this, mainly for the latter reason, and he's foolishly agreed to let her imprison him in the palace, which I know is at least half because he wants her permission to marry me and probably half because he thinks he's solely responsible for cementing peace between humans and fae or some such thing. And despite his occasionally extremely trying tendencies towards martyrdom, I'm not going to simply leave him there and hope it all works out and Her Majesty doesn't suddenly decide executing him would be the best course of action." She fought an uncharacteristic urge to burst into tears and pasted a smile on her face instead. "Sorry, Brad. That was rather more than I ought to have burdened you with." She felt very small and alone suddenly, conscious of the distance between her and Stariel.

Bradfield was a difficult man to truly surprise, though he often adopted the emotion if he thought it would help him deal with the dramatic personalities of the actors. But he stared at her for a moment, the bottle frozen halfway to his lips. His eyes went wide.

"Egads, you're serious!"

"Afraid so."

He offered her the bottle again. "You need this more than me."

She laughed but refused. "Would you recognise any of the nobles on sight? There were two advisors with the queen, but she didn't introduce them." It seemed as good a place as any to start. She grimaced. "One of them was a duke, but I admit to not paying much attention to the list of Southern peerage at school."

"Astound me, then," he said, gesturing broadly.

She'd forgotten that Brad was used to her illusion, comfortable with it in a way that no one at Stariel yet was. Still, she remembered how to play to an audience. Concentrating, she pulled up the images in her mind's eye, using Brad's chair as a stand-in for the queen's throne-like one. He laughed as the queen's image overlaid him and the worn wood became stiff brocade beneath him.

"Gods, you're a loss to the company, Hetta," he lamented. "Not to say anything against Ida," he added hastily of Hetta's friend and the illusionist who'd replaced her. "But she's not yet a master." He drummed his fingers on the arm of his chair, chuckling as they rose in and out of the ghost shapes of the queen's slender hands. Hetta had kept the illusion of the queen simple, focusing her energies on the two advisors.

"Do you know either of them?" she asked, glad to be sitting down. The draw of magic left her tired. She'd gotten too used to having Stariel to draw on, made the illusions too detailed too quickly. She wrapped her hands around Wyn's ring and pulled. A trickle of energy came from the stone, the taste of Stariel suddenly strong on the back of her tongue, the effect not unlike swallowing a strong shot of coffee.

Bradfield's amusement snapped off as he stood to examine the men. He narrowed his eyes at the fair-skinned advisor and said shortly: "That's Simon. The Earl of Wolver." He glared at the illusion for several long seconds before forcing himself to look at the other. "And that is the Duke of Callasham," he identified the dark-skinned man, then went straight back to glaring at the Earl of Wolver. "He looks tired, don't you think? Bloody prettyboy running him ragged," he grumbled.

She snapped her fingers, winking the illusion out of existence. "Sorry, Brad, I didn't mean to confront you with your ex-paramour in your own office."

Bradfield took a swig of the brandy and collapsed back into his seat, his expression dark.

Hells—not only an earl, Brad, but one active at court? Really? That was skating awfully close to potential disaster if it came out, but Brad had never had much sense when it came to his love life.

"But thank you," she said, keeping her worries to herself. Brad had said the relationship was over now, after all, and even if he hadn't, he wouldn't thank her for sticking her oar in. She'd never had the smallest ability to persuade him to take the path of less risk. "Do you know anything about the Duke of Callasham?" she asked, to distract him from the earl.

Brad was still scowling at the patch of carpet that had recently contained the Earl of Wolver, and he visibly shook himself out of his sullenness before answering. "His grace's wife likes experimental theatre. She's booked a box for opening night with a bunch of other nobs. Come along and you can hoity-toity with the rest of them beforehand, if you think it will help get your prince out of his golden cage."

"I'm willing to try anything," she admitted. On impulse, she reached out and gripped his hand. "Thank you, Brad." She felt a little less alone than before, though still woefully out of her depth.

He waved her off. "It's nothing. Lordship's making you sentimental." But he looked pleased.

POLITICKING

THE DISMAE ITCHED, and Wyn resisted scratching at them for the thousandth time as he examined his reflection critically. He hadn't slept well under the suffocating weight of them, but he was determined not to let it show. Queen Matilda and her court mustn't know how much they affected him. He'd demanded the palace send for his belongings from the hotel yesterday, so he was at least clean and well-presented this morning. *Though not quite princely*, he thought with narrowed eyes. Appearances mattered, in Mortal just as much as Faerie, though the specifics of appropriate attire differed greatly between the two. He wondered if he could demand an appropriate wardrobe from the queen by arguing that she was forcing him into an ambassadorial role that he, obviously, hadn't packed for. At least mortal males' formal costuming was reasonably similar regardless of rank. The problem would've been much worse in Faerie.

He buttoned his shirt-sleeves and slipped on his coat, continuing to ignore the cold itch of the dismae. It wasn't a physical sensation anyway. He could itch his wrists raw without effect, but even knowing this didn't quieten the urge. The spellworked iron tangled his innate magic into knots that, well, *itched* to be unravelled. It also dampened his leysight to the point of non-existence, as if he wore a thick veil all over, his sense of the world extending no further than his skin. He ran his hands through his hair just to feel something. How did mortals live like this? The fact that his magic had been growing stronger since the Maelstorm only made the sudden absence of it worse.

The desire to change forms was nearly as strong as the urge to scratch, his instincts seeking an escape from the muffling effect of the dismae. *No point*, he told his instincts. The dismae would block his magic just as well in his fae form, and he suspected it would be even more disorienting. At least in his mortal form he was somewhat accustomed to having his magic flattened out.

And at least this is a comfortable prison, he reflected as he began to absent-mindedly straighten his things. They'd given him a suite with a grand sitting room, which boded well. After all, why have a sitting room unless they meant to let him entertain people here? The rooms they'd put him in were lavish, undoubtedly meant for visiting ambassadors or heads of state. Although he supposed he *was* a visiting ambassador, of sorts—the first fae to officially interact with a mortal court in centuries. Hetta and Stariel could not truly be considered official, since he had adopted a human guise for most of his service there. He looked down at his wrists again, his coat sleeves hiding the metal. Not a promising start.

He closed his eyes, drawing up calm enough to strategise. If he must be imprisoned here, he meant to make the most of his location, erase the difference between 'enforced guest' and 'honoured guest'. *And so I must become a prince again.* Mention of his title had already shifted the queen and her advisors' attitudes slightly in his favour, he judged. Or at least made them more wary of what influence he held in Faerie. He'd have to dance a fine line with that.

Do you think if you play at being human for long enough, it will become truth? His brother Rakken's words came to him, mocking, and he pushed them aside just as a soft knock sounded at the interior door. He opened it to find they'd sent him a servant to bring him breakfast and tidy his room, which astonished him more than it should have. He'd played a servant too long to fall comfortably back into the appropriate manner, which was to pretend that such people were invisible. *And why ignore a potential source of information, anyway?*

"Good morning," he said, waving her inside. "Mrs…?"

She bobbed a curtsey. "Mrs Lovelock, Your Highness." So the news of his rank had already been passed on to the staff. Good.

Mrs Lovelock was a middle-aged woman with wary eyes that said she'd heard the rumours and that she didn't trust him as far as she could throw him. Had she drawn the short straw, or had she volunteered in place of someone considered more impressionable? After a few moments of trying to draw her out, he was almost certain it was the latter. *She wanted to protect innocent young maids from my bad influence and possibly unwanted attentions, if I had any.* He did his best to be as human and non-threatening as possible. Usually he'd twist his natural allure sideways in an attempt to reassure, but perhaps the dismae would achieve the same effect? It was difficult to say—but in any case, Mrs Lovelock did not seem unnaturally distracted by him, so that was something.

She bustled around, seeming determined to do her job and be gone, but drew up short at his already-made bed and spotless rooms.

"I'd like to thank you—and the rest of the palace staff—for accommodating me so swiftly, since you did not know I was coming." He smiled apologetically.

"It's no problem, Your Highness," she said automatically, and not for the first time he envied the mortal ability to lie so casually and so trivially.

"Would you take tea with me as thanks?" he asked her, indicating the tray she'd brought. "And if I selfishly confess to finding it somewhat lonely, breakfasting by myself?"

She wavered, wrongfooted by this confusion of the normal hierarchy. He pretended he hadn't noticed and poured her a cup of tea, gesturing firmly at the seat opposite. "Do you take milk, Mrs Lovelock?"

She sat down uncertainly, apparently deciding it would be a greater sin to refuse than accept. "Ah, thank you, Your Highness, I do."

He handed her the cup. "Are there many other guests staying in the palace, at the moment?"

He learnt that there were two small delegations in the palace at present, that the royal family took breakfast in their private quarters, that the Ekaran ambassador was to play an informal croquet round with some of the members of parliament on the Green Lawn in the palace gardens this morning, and that the new house manager really needed his head looking at if he thought untrained girls could be turned into acceptable maids overnight.

He thanked Mrs Lovelock and let her go. She went with a slightly guilty expression. She hadn't meant to chat with him for so long. *Time to test how far my leash stretches, I think.* He took a deep breath, fortifying himself and trying to ignore the disorientation of the dismae. *I am a prince of royal blood. I can channel lightning. The Queen of Prydein is not my queen.*

Opening his door, he greeted the guard posted there with a polite but distant smile. "Good morning. Would you be so good as to accompany me to the Green Lawn? I have a great wish to take the air." He stepped out as if he could not imagine a world in which the guard would not comply.

"Ah—I'm not sure…" the guard stuttered, instinctively turning slightly leftwards. That must be the direction of the Green Lawn, then. "Your Highness, I think you'd better…"

"Take you with me?" Wyn finished. "Yes, I quite agree. I perfectly understand Her Majesty's desire to take precautions, but the Green Lawn *is* within the palace, is it not?" He smiled brightly at the man and began to walk down the left corridor. The guard followed, helplessly. "Tell me, what is your name?"

18

NEWSPAPERS AND COFFEE

"A CERTAIN FEMALE NORTHERN *lord*," Hetta read aloud in disgust over breakfast. "Is that supposed to obscure my identity somehow?" She sat in her sitting room at the hotel, with Alexandra beside her on the chesterfield. Both of them were surrounded by newspapers, spread over every nearby available surface. An empty coffee carafe stood on the sideboard—and thank Simulsen that coffee was considered one of the standards of civilisation here, because it was the only thing keeping Hetta's temper in check right now. Aunt Sybil brooded into a teacup from her armchair, uncharacteristically—but thankfully—silent.

Alexandra gave an uncertain giggle. "It's very silly, isn't it, since you're the *only* female Northern lord?" She put her own paper down. It was the most respectable of the papers, since Aunt Sybil had objected to Alexandra reading any of the scandal sheets. "They name you in the *Meridon Times*, but it's buried in the back pages and very dull—they just say you had an audience with the queen to swear fealty. They don't mention Wyn at all."

Hetta had asked the hotel to send up all the Meridon newssheets with breakfast. It had seemed a slightly outrageous demand, but she'd made it in her loftiest tone, and the hotelier had merely nodded and said: "Of course, my lord." The perks of rank, indeed. *If only I still didn't have to channel my father in order to acquire them.* She could try to emulate Wyn's manner, but which one? The mild, respectful camouflage he adopted with Hetta's stepmother? The kind but firm way he spoke to the staff? The gentle reproof he reserved for children? The frosty hauteur he used on the bank manager? His dry way of needling Jack when he was being stuffy? The wild passion she'd so far only glimpsed?

Probably not that last one. She sighed.

"It'll be all right, Hetta," Alexandra said, smoothing her paper nervously. "Won't it?"

"It will if I have anything to do with it," Hetta vowed.

Aunt Sybil sniffed. "Alexandra is right. These newspaper bleatings are for fools, and so I shall tell Seraphina when I call on her today. I cannot agree with Her Majesty's position on this. Prince... Wyn is about as dangerous as a robin." She grimaced at the choice between Wyn's title and his name. Still, Hetta was oddly touched by her aunt's willingness to wage war on her—or at least Wyn's—behalf. "I do not approve of his—or your—conduct these past weeks, but I cannot deny his long years of loyal service to the estate."

"Thank you, Aunt," Hetta said softly. Did any of Aunt Sybil's friends have the queen's ear? She doubted it, somehow, but it was still worth asking. "Do you know the Duke or Duchess of Callasham? Or the Earl of Wolver?"

"The Duke of Callasham is also Lord Greymark," Aunt Sybil said disapprovingly and with a heavy subtext of: *which you ought to already know.*

"Oh." Her aunt was right; she really ought to have known that the duke also held one of the most prominent Northern titles, because that meant he was on the Northern Lords Conclave. Which meant Angus had been right too—she ought to have cared more about politics. Guilt and irritation both prickled at her. "Have you met him and his wife?"

Aunt Sybil grew thin-lipped. "The duchess is very young and lively, or so I have heard." Hetta took that for a 'no'.

She frowned at the sheet under her hands and snorted again at the headline: *A Brewing Northern Scandal?* The paper hadn't quite been able to bring itself to print the word 'fae', instead making do with 'wild rumours about Mr. T's past' and 'eye-witnesses report a concerning altercation in Alverness'—which was just repeating what *Lady Peregrine's Society News* had already said.

I need to find out what they're going to print in their next issue, she thought grimly. The magazine was printed in Meridon. How had they gotten hold of a story so far to the north in the first place, and why had it surfaced now, just when she and Wyn most needed to make a good impression on the queen? She mulled over who 'eye-witnesses' might be, turning her memory back to last year, when she and Wyn had made rather a mess at the bank in Alverness after a swarm of fae creatures had attacked. None of the staff had seen Wyn in his fae form. Well, none except the bank manager's wife. Who admittedly did dislike Wyn. Could Mrs Thompson have written to the editor? But why wait until now to do it?

She put the newspaper to the side. "I'm going to the palace," she announced.

"May I come?" Alexandra asked. It was plain she didn't wish to be left to visit Seraphina with Aunt Sybil. "I mean, if it won't cause trouble," she added quickly.

"I don't think we can be in any more trouble than we are already," Hetta said with a sigh, contemplating the papers.

PROBABLY IT WOULD'VE BEEN more proper to take a hackney from the hotel to the palace, but she needed to work off some of her restless energy, and the centre of Meridon was dense but surprisingly compact. Everything enchanted her sister as the two of them walked: the elektric street lights, the black liveried kineticars, the shop windows, even the street hawkers. The air had a gritty tang to it—not strong in this quarter, where the wealthy had long since converted to heat stones rather than the old coal fires, but still present.

"Do you ever miss living here?" Alexandra asked, eyes wide as she took in a man walking four large poodles past a telephone box.

"Sometimes," Hetta said absently. Memories swam up: arguing illusionary theory in coffee shops, exploring street markets, late-night revelries, glorying in being young and free and wild. The images thronged around her, close enough to touch and yet as distant as if they belonged to someone else. What did you do with the knowledge that you could never truly return to a place you'd once called home? More than mere miles separated her from her old life, now. She put a palm against her dress and pressed the ring beneath it against her skin, and Stariel gave a low beat of acknowledgement.

She realised Alexandra had been quiet for several blocks. *Do try to be a better tour guide*, Hetta's conscience prodded her. It wasn't her sister's fault that Hetta was having an internal crisis. She began to point out landmarks with snippets of information—for a given value of 'landmarks'.

"The Dresborough market is held down that way, under the glass roof, on Saturdays. There's a stall there that sells the most incredible baked goods—we should go if we're still here next weekend."

"Hetta," Alexandra said suddenly, pulling on her elbow to bring the pair of them to a stop. Hetta followed her gaze through the crowd but couldn't see what had worried her sister. "I think..." She bit her lip.

"What do you think?" Hetta coaxed.

"I thought I saw Gwendelfear," she blurted. "But she can't be here, can she?"

"Where?" Had Princess Sunnika sent her handmaiden to spy on them? What in the nine heavens for?

Alexandra pointed between a flower stall and a paper stand. "It was just a moment, and then she turned the corner." A crease formed between her brows. "I could see under her glamour without even trying. I couldn't do that, last time." Gwendelfear was lesser fae, which meant she couldn't change shape and used glamour to make her appearance more human-like. But Alexandra could see through illusion and glamour both, and her Sight had been growing in strength these past few months.

They crossed the street to inspect the location, but there was no sign of the fae girl. Was Alexandra disappointed or glad about that, Hetta wondered? Aroset had used Gwendelfear's enchanted locket to lure Alexandra beyond the bounds of the estate last year. Did her sister blame Gwendelfear for that?

"Well, if she is here and following us, I wish her much joy of it," she said eventually. But what did it mean that DuskRose was watching them?

19

HOLDING COURT

WHEN HETTA ARRIVED at the palace, two guards escorted her and Alexandra to the green, where she found Wyn ingratiating himself with two members of Parliament and a foreign ambassador over croquet. For a good few seconds, she simply stared at the tableau. He was all right, then. A laugh tickled in her throat. Here she was, fretting herself to pieces over fae and mortal politics both, while Wyn was playing sports in the spring sunshine! Of course, she knew that wasn't what was truly going on here—but still!

However, her amusement turned to a strange unease as she drew closer. Wyn looked particularly human and buttoned-up, the cuffs hidden under his coat. He'd clearly been ruthlessly channelling his most charming self, because the group looked utterly relaxed, with the kind of casual masculine camaraderie that came with knowing yourself to be both among and one of the social elite—and Hetta felt abruptly like an outsider, peering in.

Wyn looked round and met her gaze, and for a moment, relief shone in his eyes; he was just as uneasy with the situation as she was.

"My Star," he said, inclining his head. The two men with him gave Hetta and Alexandra once-overs, and the atmosphere changed subtly as Wyn performed introductions, becoming more guarded in that way that men so often were in the presence of women. Hetta wasn't sure if it was only that or if they'd heard something more about the infamous Lord Valstar to make them look at her with a kind of interested wariness. *Though you'd think a female lord wouldn't be so astonishing, in the court of a female monarch*, she couldn't help thinking irritably.

There followed an extremely tedious interchange of small talk, and she heaved a sigh of relief when the politicians finally excused themselves, leaving the three of them alone. Or, well, not alone at all, since three guards still watched from a polite distance. Was it really necessary to be so personally guarded within the grounds of the palace itself?

Deciding she didn't care what the guards thought, she tucked her arm into Wyn's. Alexandra tilted her head like a bird, as if she wondered whether she ought to object in Aunt Sybil's stead. Hetta gave her her best older-sister look, and Alexandra blushed and looked away.

"I admit I didn't expect you to begin politicking right off the bat, though clearly I should've," she said to Wyn. "I'm amazed you haven't managed to stage a coup yet." Wyn was right that getting anyone and everyone at court on their side was a sensible idea, but it still sat oddly with her.

Wyn smiled down at her. "Give me time."

As they strolled the edge of the green, she asked Alexandra to repeat what she'd said about spotting Gwendelfear. There were bluebells starting to bloom beneath the trees, and the air was almost warm. Winter lingered longer in Stariel.

"It wouldn't surprise me if Princess Sunnika sent one—or more—of her court to keep track of us," Wyn said after listening to Alexandra's account.

A faint crease had formed between his brows, but his tone was gentle as he directed his words at her sister. "But only greater fae can compel, so you need not fear that from Gwendelfear."

"Of course I'm not afraid of Gwen!" Alexandra said, in an exasperated way that made Hetta believe her. Did that mean her sister still considered herself friends with the lesser fae?

Alexandra looked between the two of them, lingering on their joined hands, and wrinkled her nose. Her shoulders drew up, and she abruptly announced: "*I'm* not going to hover like Aunt Sybil." She glared at the guards. "Or *them*," she muttered. "I'll go sit over there and sketch the building." She waved her ever-present sketchbook in the direction of a bench under the stately line of trees.

"Thank you, Miss Alex," Wyn said, half-smiling.

"Well, if you're going to be my brother-in-law, you might as well just call me Alex, you know." She ducked her head and trotted off to the bench, her cheeks red. The guards watched her impassively.

Wyn had frozen in place. Hetta had never seen him so completely taken aback before, his expression curiously vulnerable.

"It hadn't occurred to you that I came with family attached?" she couldn't resist teasing him.

"Not that particular aspect of it," he admitted, still staring after Alexandra.

She laughed, tugging him back into motion again. "Just remember you also get Aunt Sybil as *your* aunt too." But her amusement faded as she told him about Bradfield's information, and the stirrings of interest from the newspapers.

Wyn grimaced. "I confess, it would surprise me if Mrs Thompson gave an interview. I had thought she'd forgiven me for the bank incident. Besides, spreading rumours doesn't seem like her—she was considerably more, ah, direct in her approach in the past."

Hetta gave him a look, because while he might be able to joke about it, she still remembered the sharp spike of fear at the sound of the gunshot, the bright red of blood staining his feathers.

"Well, I'm going to visit the magazine's offices, here in Meridon," Hetta decided. "Caro never got a response to her letter, but it'll be much harder for them to ignore me in person."

He looked down at her with such a depth of emotion that for a moment she couldn't breathe. "I never intended to make you infamous," he said softly. "I am sorry for that."

She poked his shoulder. "You forget I've been the cause of my own infamy for years." Though that infamy had been on a much smaller scale than this.

A weight of anxiety began to creep back. Information was all very well, but how were they going to convince the queen to let Wyn go? She put this to Wyn, who tried not to look troubled.

"I did not handle things yesterday as well as I might," he admitted.

"Yes, you shouldn't have agreed to these." She slid her hand down his arm and squeezed the hard outlines of the dismae beneath his coat.

He blinked. "No, I meant that I should perhaps have been more conciliatory. Queen Matilda is right to be worried about what my— or rather, my kind's—presence in the Mortal Realm means. But my temper got the better of me, I'm afraid."

Hetta huffed, not liking the way he'd phrased that, as if he were an invasive species of bird. "Well, I'm not signing my oath of fealty until she frees you," she said in a low, fierce tone so as not to be overheard.

"Hetta—"

"No. It's the only bit of leverage I have here, and I'm not going to pretend it's reasonable to treat you as a danger to the realm. We can conjure up ten years' worth of testament to your non-dangerousness, if needed. If Queen Matilda doesn't believe that, then that's as good as saying she doesn't trust Stariel to deal with its own internal affairs, and—and I'll go to the Conclave with that if I have to."

Wyn didn't point out that her membership in the Northern Lords Conclave hadn't yet been ratified. He drew to a soft halt, looking down on her with dark eyes, and there was a tiny hint of cardamom-and-storms for a heartbeat. It snapped out, and he winced.

She put a hand on his wrist again. "It's a small torture, isn't it?"

"I'm not worth Stariel, my love."

Hetta wanted to argue that he most certainly *was*, except that she made it a rule not to lie to him. It wouldn't be fair, since she was the only one of the two of them that could. A prickle of guilt set up camp in her conscience. Ought she to be so reckless with Stariel's fate over one man?

"I don't see why it has to be one or the other. And I *am* thinking of Stariel. The Iron Law coming down has already affected the estate—and it's going to affect all of Prydein, sooner or later. Treating you like a criminal isn't going to help make a bright united future between humans and fae, and neither is you martyring yourself." She met his eyes steadily, her heartbeat suddenly loud in her ears. "Or you pretending to be human."

Wyn sucked in a sharp breath, but before he could respond, a *fourth* guard—really, was this necessary?—appeared, accompanying a pageboy with a summons from the queen.

CHOICES

WYN TRIED TO settle his very unsettled emotions as they were escorted to the same room as yesterday, and not least because he kept accidentally activating the dismae. They left Alexandra unhappily waiting in the uncomfortable antechamber.

At least today there were only two guards standing unobtrusively by the door, one of whom announced them as they came in. Progress? It wasn't a formal audience, and Queen Matilda was standing rather than seated this time. Only one of her advisors was with her—the blond-haired Earl of Wolver. He frowned at the sight of Hetta's arm linked with Wyn's.

Queen Matilda weighed the two of them before she met Wyn's eyes. "I have heard you found sufficient activity to entertain yourself this morning."

She wasn't using the royal plural today—was that a good or bad sign? Or merely a shift in tactics?

"Yes, Your Majesty, I did," he said mildly, playing oblivious to the subtext. "Thank you for the quality of the rooms you assigned me."

She narrowed her eyes and sat, allowing them to follow suit with a wave of her hand.

"I'm sure all the palace is very fine," Hetta said tiredly. "But can you tell us what you want, Your Majesty, and how we can change your mind about keeping Prince Hallowyn here?" Hearing his name and title on her lips sent a strange, quivering emotion through him. *Prince Hallowyn.* He both wanted and did not want to hear her say it again.

Queen Matilda smiled very slightly. "It is customary to open the conversation with pleasantries, Lord Valstar, before launching into blunt demands. Such are the hallmarks of civilisation." She turned to Wyn. "I find we are sadly lacking in information on the fae courts, Your Highness. If you mean to be an ambassador for your people, I would know more of them, and yourself. Which court do you hail from?"

He was going to have to be very, very careful here. "I am a prince of the Court of Ten Thousand Spires, Your Majesty. There are many courts in Faerie, some large, some small, but thinking of them as equivalent to different human countries is not an unreasonable comparison. ThousandSpire is one of the upper courts, which means it is one of the most influential in all of Faerie." It pained him to place so much weight on his bloodline, but he needed her to see more than just a single, easily disposable individual when she considered him, needed to give the impression that he represented vast numbers. In a way, he did.

"And how is it that you come to be in Prydein?"

He danced around that one. "A disagreement with my father, now resolved." He looked at Hetta, let his feelings for her rise to the surface. "But now I have more reason to stay than to return."

Queen Matilda hmmed, apparently not swayed by this

sentimentality. Ah, well. It had been worth a try. She moved on, her interrogation far more thorough than Penharrow's. How great an area did the Spires comprise? What were its armies and resources? How many other fae courts were there? Oh, it was all phrased very delicately, but Wyn could read the subtext as well as anyone.

The grandfather clock ticked. Hetta kept quiet during the conversation, though he could tell she was thinking furiously. He couldn't read the queen's hawk-blue expression as she folded her hands neatly in her lap.

She let the silence build for a time. Eventually she said to Hetta: "I cannot have my lords' loyalties divided. I will grant you permission to marry him, Lord Valstar, if Prince Hallowyn will agree to renounce his ties to Faerie and pledge allegiance to the throne of Prydein."

There was a weightless moment just before a dive, when you folded your wings back and before gravity took hold. Between one second and the next the earth would tighten its grip and suddenly you would be dropping as swift and deadly as a stone. Wyn had never experienced that moment whilst earthbound, but he felt it now, breathless as if he were miles above the Indigoes.

He should accept the offer, if Hetta would. The stormwinds knew he didn't want the Spires. Why then, this hesitation? But Faerie was more than just his tie to ThousandSpire, and he wasn't sure what breaking his ties to it would do to him. *But I spent nearly a decade living with a broken oath, as a shadow of myself. It wasn't unbearable.* How often had he wished to be human, for Hetta, without the complications of his fae heritage? This was merely the logical extension of that. It was simple. He could do it. He *should* do it.

He opened his mouth to express willingness, but Hetta spoke, cold and hard: "No." She put her hand on Wyn's arm and met his eyes, something steely in their grey depths. "No. Those terms are not acceptable."

He closed his mouth, unable to speak even if he knew what to say. Gratitude and guilt tangled together in a jagged ball of razors in his throat.

The queen's eyebrows went up. "Well, then, I hope you find your accommodation comfortable, Your Highness, for it seems your stay may be an extended one."

21

BALCONY ENCOUNTERS

L ATER THAT DAY, Wyn stared through the glass of his balcony doors at the ivy-covered walls of the internal courtyard, feeling oddly raw. There'd been no chance to discuss anything with Hetta, since the queen had all but thrown her out of the palace after she'd flared up in his defence, and his door-guard—William, he'd learnt his name was—had regretfully informed him he was under orders not to let him wander.

At least Queen Matilda had *offered* her permission for them to marry, despite the strings attached. He stared unseeing at leaf, brick, and mortar and turned his mind to his own liege. The High King wasn't the sort of person you summoned; rather the reverse. But it *must* be possible to find him. If only his godparent wasn't still trapped by whatever was going on in the Spires—Lamorkin would know where to begin seeking the High King, he felt sure. Stormwinds, he hoped they were all right.

Claustrophobia clawed at his chest, and he rested a hand against the panes of the glass doors, spreading his fingers over their cool fragility. Was this a test? Even setting the glass aside, this entire setup was ludicrously insecure. Did the mortal queen want him to escape and thus draw cleaner lines between enemy and friend?

He reached for the ornate brass latch, not truly expecting the doors to be unlocked, but the latch turned easily, opening onto the private balcony. Floral-scented night air wafted in as he stood there, blinking in surprise. Was this unguarded balcony door a trap or simply a mortal oversight? In Faerie it would certainly be the former, but mortals weren't as casually duplicitous, in his experience. Then again, he didn't know these Southern mortals so well as their Northern counterparts. Maybe baited traps were as commonplace here as in Faerie.

Cautiously, he stepped onto the balcony. Below was a carefully cultivated courtyard of flowerbeds and shrubs, cut through by paved walkways. It lay deep in the shadows cast by the tall buildings on all four sides, untouched by light from the setting sun.

A small figure burst into the courtyard. It was a girl-child, her braid swinging out behind her as she charged along the path, head down like a tiny blonde bullet. She drew to a panting halt below his balcony, out of sight but not earshot, and he heard her begin to climb up the trellis towards him. He strained, and sure enough, through the door across the courtyard came the sound of someone calling, with irritation rather than alarm.

The girl was making excellent progress up her makeshift ladder, but the gap between the balcony and the trellis was tricky, and she faltered as she reached the top. The trellis shook violently, threatening to peel itself from the wall and take its cargo with it. Quick as a cat, Wyn reached down, took hold of one thin arm, and hauled the girl over the ledge.

The girl's wide eyes were a familiar piercing blue, so he wasn't especially surprised when a woman emerged into the courtyard calling: "Your Highness! Your Highness!" The woman harrumphed, as if she was accustomed to losing her ward and out of patience with it.

The girl—the princess—shot him an urgent plea, imploring

him not to reveal her. Wyn wasn't proof against mischievous children, so he merely quirked an eyebrow and stepped back through the balcony doors. She scrambled after him and they both stilled, waiting. The woman below made a circuit of the courtyard, her exasperation increasing, but eventually she decided that her quarry was elsewhere. Her receding footsteps echoed on the stone paths and then faded into nothing as she entered the building on the other side of the courtyard.

Meanwhile, Wyn and his new friend inspected each other. Now, was it sensible, helping the queen's offspring evade her caregivers? Possibly not—although it did give him the chance to practice his ambassadorial diplomacy. It was cheering to think at least one royal mortal might not dislike him on sight, even if the royal in question was under the age of ten.

"Who are you?" the girl demanded when the woman had left. She looked around the room accusingly. "And why are you in here? There's never anyone in here."

"I could ask you much the same questions," he said, folding himself down onto the nearest chair so as not to tower over the child.

The girl frowned, her chin jutting forward. "Everyone knows who I am," she declared. "And this is *my* palace. And you should not sit."

"Why not?" he asked mildly.

"Because I outrank you! And I'm a girl," she added as an afterthought. "You have to wait for me to sit."

"What if you were a boy?" he couldn't resist asking. "And I were a girl?"

"I would still outrank you," she said primly.

"But we have not been introduced, so how can you be sure?" A smile tugged at his lips. The princess saw it and flared up.

"Because I am Crown Princess Evangeline!" she announced, stamping one small foot.

Wyn bowed his head "I am honoured to make your acquaintance, Crown Princess Evangeline."

The princess narrowed her eyes. "You're laughing at me."

"I am, a little," he agreed. "It is only that our meeting was something of a surprise to me. I did not expect to encounter princesses climbing in my balcony, nor for them to upbraid me on my manners, having done so. Now I wonder: Should I rise, having already sat, or will that only make the situation worse?"

She giggled, imperiousness melting into childish delight in an eyeblink. "Well, I suppose it's all right for you to sit, since you didn't tell Lady Hawkins where I was."

"Thank you," he said solemnly. "Will it make you very angry if I tell you that I'm not sure you *do* outrank me, Your Highness?"

"I outrank *everyone*," she informed him. "Except Mama and Papa." Her face fell. "And maybe the baby, if it's a boy."

Interest quickened, but he didn't let it show in his expression. The queen was with child? "That seems unfair." Mortal inheritance laws still puzzled him.

She shrugged. "It's the law." Her attention wandered towards the door, and he knew she was contemplating her exit route. "Who are you, anyway?"

"I am Prince Hallowyn Tempestren of the Court of Ten Thousand Spires." An iron truth on his lips, despite his ambivalence in invoking it.

She blinked at him. "That sounds like a made-up name."

That startled a genuine laugh out of him. "It is my true name; it is impolite to make fun of it."

Her mouth grew mulish. "Princesses do not apologise."

"Never? I do not recall either of my sisters being given such a far-reaching exemption."

"You have sisters? Are they older than you?" There was a yearning in her expression.

"I have two sisters," he told her. "And three brothers as well." It was peculiar to be speaking so freely of his family when even at Stariel so few people knew such details. "All of them are older than me. And all of them have names you would likely think made-up."

"You're not the Crown Prince, then," she said smugly. "You *don't* outrank me."

He spread his hands. "Ah, but we don't have such a thing, where I come from. Any one of us might inherit the throne." Cold crept into him and curled up around his heart.

"How do you decide then?"

"We don't. The land decides for us." It was very nearly a lie, and the words were thick and difficult in his mouth as a result. The land did decide, but hadn't he made his own decision on that front? Would he rule the Spires now if he'd embraced rather than fled its touch, after King Aeros's death?

The thought chilled him. He hadn't let himself put it in those terms before: *the Spires wanted me for its king.* He made himself think the words: *I could have been king. I could still be king, if the faeland hasn't bonded yet.* But he would *not* be the King of Ten Thousand Spires. He would not. Thwarted storm energy crawled through his veins, seeking an outlet and not finding it, painful in its constraint. Stormcrows, what if his choice didn't matter in the end? Dust and metal, arrowing towards him across Stariel lands...

"There's a Northern estate like that," Princess Evangeline said, and he grasped at the new subject with relief.

"Yes," he agreed with a smile. "I know."

Growing restless, she began to investigate the depths of his room with quick, birdlike movements. Confidently, she trotted towards the interior door.

"I wouldn't leave that way if I were you. There's a guard."

She skidded to a halt, and he suddenly wondered what the guard would think if a small, grubby princess emerged. There was a leaf caught in her braid, and her dress was smudged in places from her climb. Why in the high wind's eddies did her carers choose to dress her in such pale, delicately embroidered fabric? It seemed a waste, or at least an unfair burden upon the laundrymaids if this was a regular occurrence. Ten years ago, the thought wouldn't have occurred to him; such trivialities were not of concern to princes. But a decade of domestic service had left its mark.

"Why is there a guard?" Her eyes grew round and interested.

"Because I'm a prisoner," he said. "Because I'm fae."

This information did not disturb her in the least. Instead, she inspected him from top to toe, clearly unimpressed. "You don't look like a fairy."

He smiled. He couldn't help it; there was nothing more endearing than the frankness of mortal children, before the world taught them to censor themselves. "And how do you know what fairies look like?"

To his surprise, her expression grew serious, and she chewed her lip as some complex internal decision-making process occurred. "Well," she said, her tone defensive, her little shoulders stiffening as if she expected to be ridiculed. "There's a fairy that lives in the kitchens. And you don't look anything like her."

He stilled. "What does she look like?"

"Well," she said warily. "She's a lot shorter." She held out a hand below her own child's waist height. "She comes up to about here, and she has big gold eyes. And funny ears."

A brownie. There was a brownie in the palace kitchens. He supposed it had only been a matter of time. The Iron Law had never strictly applied to the lowfae, but they had nonetheless largely retreated with their more powerful brethren, needing the magic that greater and lesser fae tended to propagate just by existing. Brownies liked human households and they tolerated iron well. They didn't have much magic, but even brownies could use the small don't-see-me glamour. Which meant—

"No one else can see her," she admitted, confirming his suspicions.

High King's *horns*. The Crown Princess of Prydein had the Sight. And no one had told her.

"Some people can see things others can't," he said. "It doesn't mean they aren't real. It's called 'the Sight', the ability to see through fae glamour. It is a gift."

Princess Evangeline's whole body sagged with relief. Had she thought she was going mad, seeing things that weren't there?

"Oh. Her name is Bessie, she told me," she added shyly. "I spoke to her once."

"Well, I am not the same kind of fae as Bessie." It was a good thing he and not any other greater fae was the one having this conversation. Any other greater fae would have been greatly offended at being compared to a mere brownie.

Footsteps sounded in the hallway outside. "You'd better go by way of the window," he said. "We'll both be in trouble if you're found here, I imagine."

"Can I come back and visit you? How long are you here for?"

He ought not to encourage her, but her expression was so hopeful that he could not bear to crush it. "I'm not sure. But I'm glad to have met you." He got to his feet and swept her a grand bow. "Crown Princess Evangeline."

She giggled. "I'm glad to meet you too, Prince Hallow—"

"Hallowyn Tempestren," he supplied.

"Prince Hallowyn Tempestren. I'll ask Mother if you can join us in the Octagon Garden. We always walk there before breakfast."

It had been a long time since anyone had said his true name so many times in one day. He'd adopted 'Wyn' years ago as a precaution against his father locating him. Obviously that was no longer a risk. Still, the sound of his name made him curiously uneasy.

"Wait," he said, as she began to scamper for the balcony. "You have a leaf in your hair." He reached out to remove it and made sure he pulled a few hair strands with it, churning with self-loathing. She was a child, and far too trusting, and to use that naïveté for his own ends was repugnant, even though it wouldn't harm her. He curled his fingers around the leaf and hair, careful not to lose the prize.

Evangeline didn't notice and beamed at him as he lifted her carefully over the edge and made sure she had a firm grip.

Once she was out of sight, he closed the balcony doors and grimly contemplated the strands of long blonde hair he'd captured. It might not be enough, but it was worth a try. The spellwork on the dismae was keyed to the Prydinian throne, after all.

22

THE DEFINITIVE COMPENDIUM OF FAIRIES IN COMMON FOLK LORE

MARIUS WAS BEGINNING to suspect the *Definitive Compendium of Fairies in Common Folk Lore* wasn't as comprehensive as its name suggested. There was absolutely no mention of stormdancers in the index, for one thing. He sighed and added it to his pile anyway. It couldn't be less helpful than *Nymphs Through The Ages*, which contained nothing useful—the author had merely illustrated a number of suggestively posed women wearing little more than a few fig leaves between them. He'd left that one on the shelf.

He was cynically surveying the rest of the spines filed in the 'Mythology and Folklore' section of the library when the shelf opposite *exploded*. He dropped his pile, automatically bringing his arms up to shield against the light. The world smelled suddenly of thunderstorms, tinged oddly with tangerine, but he hadn't processed what that meant before he was flung to the ground as someone crashed through the bright wall of light and landed on top of him.

Books and sharp corners dug into his back as the weight of

someone large, male, feathery, and oddly familiar knocked the wind out of him. Familiarity snapped into sudden recognition: Prince Rakken, Wyn's brother. Marius had never seen him in his fae form before. The light—it was a portal. As he stared past Rakken's shoulder, a winged woman holding an enormous sword stumbled through the portal before it winked out of existence, leaving untouched shelves behind it. *How does that work?* The library went dim again, and he blinked rapidly, struggling to adjust to the change.

The winged woman's green eyes fixed on Marius. "Go to sleep, mortal," she said, low and menacing. "Believe this a dream."

He felt the familiar ache in his head that indicated someone was trying to compel him. Shaking his head, he made an inarticulate sound of protest and wriggled, trying to shove Rakken off him.

"Prince Rakk—" But Rakken's hand covered his mouth before he got the name out. Vivid green eyes glared into his as Rakken's weight pressed him uncomfortably into the toppled shelves. Rage burned in the fae's expression, though the hand covering Marius's mouth was ice-cold. Last time Marius had seen Rakken, he'd radiated glossy composure, but now he was jarringly dishevelled. Blood smeared his temples, and his dark hair was damp and half-escaped from its queue. Bronze horns rose from his head, and Marius stared at them in shocked fascination.

"Compulsion doesn't work on this one, Cat," Rakken said to the woman without taking his attention away from Marius. His voice wasn't the polished tones Marius was familiar with, instead coarse and strained as dry gravel.

"Kill him then."

Marius jerked. What? Had she really just said *kill?* Was that a *normal* activity for Wyn's brother? They were in a *library!* You couldn't murder people in *libraries!* He struggled, which had absolutely no effect.

Rakken's eyes bored into his, so close Marius could make out the few gold threads among his otherwise dark eyelashes. "Do not try to speak my name again," he bit out, each word clipped, as if it cost him an effort to speak. "Do you understand me, Marius Rufus Valstar?"

Marius swallowed and nodded. He'd never seen Rakken like this. In his mortal form he'd been all mocking, languid charm and amusement at everyone else's expense. There was no amusement in him now.

Rakken nodded and removed the hand covering Marius's mouth. He rose to his feet with a hiss of pain and a rustle of feathers, using the shelf for leverage. His wings were bronze, shading to green at the tips, and the feathers were as disarrayed as his hair, bent at odd angles and torn away in places.

"You know him?" the woman asked Rakken. What had he called her? Cat—that must make her Princess Catsmere, Rakken's twin sister, then. Aroset was the oldest sibling, wasn't she? No, wait, there was another brother whose name he couldn't remember. Curse Wyn and his confusing family. Was it a bad sign that both of Wyn's sisters had tried to compel Marius within thirty seconds of meeting him? What in the hells was going on?

Princess Catsmere had the same bronze-and-green wings as Rakken, though her feathers were straight and undamaged. Her pointed, pixie-like face was at odds with both her cold expression and the intimidating sword she held, made of some glittering substance. Not iron, presumably. Fae couldn't magic iron.

"He's the brother of the Lord of FallingStar," Rakken ground out, narrowing his eyes at Marius.

Both fae wore black leathers embellished with strange patterns on their wrist-guards and boots. Rakken had some kind of throwing stars attached to his belt, along with a long, glittering knife. *And don't forget Catsmere's sword.* Not that it was the sort of thing you *could* forget. The weapon wasn't angled at Marius, but it wasn't *not* angled at him either. It radiated an aura of hostile sharpness such that Marius couldn't help leaning subtly away from it even though that probably wouldn't make any difference if Catsmere decided to go back to being murderously threatening again.

"You look like a pair of assassins," Marius said without thinking. His gaze snagged on a long gash in the fabric across Rakken's chest. Touching his own shirt where the fae had fallen against him, Marius brought away fingers red with blood. "Are you all right? You seem to be bleeding." It was hard to tell, in the dim confines between the shelves.

Both fae ignored him. "Why is he here? Where did we come out, Mouse?" Catsmere asked her twin.

Rakken's gaze flicked over Marius and the shelves. "A mortal library, perhaps Knoxbridge. It's in the south of this land. The resonance makes sense."

"Hey, are you all right down there? What's going on?" Voices came from the far end of the shelf stack. Students. Marius struggled his way to standing. What should he do?

"See nothing out of the ordinary," Catsmere commanded in the direction of the voices, and a cold wave passed over Marius's skin. "Leave this building now." The students subsided and left without another word.

"You can't just—just compel people because you want to!" Marius said, skin crawling.

"Yes," Catsmere told him with a flash of teeth. "I can."

"A man's mind is sacrosanct!"

"To you, perhaps," Catsmere said, bored. "If you are of FallingStar, do you know where our youngest brother is?"

"What do you want with Wyn?" Marius sure as hells wasn't going to give Wyn up just for the asking of it, especially not knowing whether these two were allies or enemies. "And why are you bleeding?" he asked Rakken again.

The pair exchanged glances, and Rakken's expression smoothed, a civilised mask sliding into place over the burning rage.

Sudden realisation thrilled through Marius. "You're angry

because you've failed. You lost the battle for your court. Your sister is ruling the Court of Ten Thousand Spires. Princess Aro—" He cut off as Rakken's knife was suddenly at his throat.

He hadn't even seen the fae *move*. He should be afraid, but it was all too unreal. Instead, he blinked uncertainly up at Rakken, frozen in place. It was rare that he had to look up at other men. This close, the impossible green of his eyes was even more impossible. No one had eyes that colour. *Like sphagnum moss*, he thought inanely. *Or new spring growth. Why the fuck am I thinking about plants? He has a knife!*

"I am loath to kill you, Marius Valstar," Rakken said silkily, "but I will, if you give away our location through your careless use of true names."

"Sorry," he croaked. "I didn't know. How does that work, exactly?"

Rakken considered him for a moment and then lowered the knife and stepped back. "Magic." He definitely *was* injured. Despite his sudden movement, or perhaps because of it, his breathing was laboured, and he rested one hand on a shelf for balance.

"Yes, but how? And what exactly constitutes a true name?" Another realisation hit him. "You're going by Cat and Mouse? Really? *You're* Mouse?" *Shut up shut up shut up*, he censored himself, too late.

"You do not have permission to call me thus, Marius Valstar." But something that might have been humour glinted in Rakken's eyes, so Marius took that as permission to start breathing again. *Almighty Pyrania and all the little gods.*

"Well, what do you want me to call you then?" Marius asked.

"Your Highness seems perfectly sufficient."

"You do realise that's going to cause a stir if anyone overhears us?"

"Rake, then, in extremis."

"We are *wasting time*, Mouse," Catsmere broke in.

"If Set knew where we'd gone, she'd already be here," Rakken replied calmly. He pressed a hand to his chest, against the wound, and narrowed his eyes at his bloodied fingers.

Catsmere looked unconvinced. "Yes, but she won't have to search hard to find little Hollow, if he's still at FallingStar." They were talking about Aroset, Marius realised. Catsmere shot him a sharp look. "Is our brother on your faeland? Mouse claims you mortals care for our youngest sibling's welfare. If this is true, you should tell us where he is."

Fae couldn't lie, but... "Why? Because your sister's the new Queen of Ten Thousand Spires?"

"No," said Rakken. "Because she *isn't*." His voice snapped on the last word, citrus and rain swirling in response to his sudden anger.

Marius rubbed at his forehead. "I forgot how exhausting fae are. So someone else is ruling ThousandSpire then?"

"Oh no, our sister is definitely *ruling* ThousandSpire," Catsmere said with a worried glance at Rakken. She took Marius's measure. "Where are your healing supplies? I need to bind my brother's wounds."

Rakken looked like he was about to argue with her, but she stared him down, and after a fraught silence he bowed his head in acquiescence.

Interesting, Marius couldn't help thinking. He hadn't expected to see anyone tell Rakken to shut up and have it actually work.

"Well?" Catsmere prompted.

Marius tried to think. It felt like corralling a flock of pigeons, some part of him still having trouble accepting that two greater fae were here in Knoxbridge, bleeding on the carpet. "I have some supplies in my greenhouse," he said eventually. "But you can't come traipsing through the library dressed as fae assassins with wings and horns and bleeding everywhere. Can you...change or something?"

Catsmere frowned. "You wish us to take mortal forms to draw less attention?"

"Er...yes. *Can* you?" he asked, looking at Rakken. He knew from Wyn that fae healed better in their native forms.

"I appreciate your concern for my welfare," Rakken said, "but it is unnecessary." Between one moment and the next, he shifted forms. The great bronze wings folded away, and his features became softer, less angular, his ears losing their upswept tips. Despite his words, he staggered, throwing out a hand to catch himself on the shelf, the other automatically going to the wound on his abdomen.

Catsmere followed suit, though humanity didn't fit her as easily. There was still something a little too alien in the way she held herself, in the restless way her eyes swept their surroundings. The leather outfit and sword only exacerbated things. After puzzling at it, Marius realised it was because everything about her still screamed *warrior*, jarringly unfeminine.

He looked to Rakken uncertainly. Should he offer him a supportive shoulder or would the fae take offence? Catsmere took the decision from him by matter-of-factly arranging her twin's arm about her left shoulder, still holding the sword in her right hand. There was something terrifyingly focused about her, like a hunting falcon.

He pulled out his handkerchief and offered it to Rakken. "Press that to the wound so you stop dripping everywhere."

Rakken took the offered scrap of material without comment.

He wasn't sure how to explain the twins' appearances, even minus the wings and horns. *Some kind of student shenanigans, maybe? A costume party? Oh, don't mind the blood, it's just tomato sauce...* But such explanations weren't required, as the gazes of the few people they passed slid away from them as if there was nothing surprising about them at all.

"You're using glamour," Marius said disapprovingly to Princess Catsmere, though he wasn't actually sure which one of the twins was responsible. "Why isn't it affecting me?"

"Do you always say whatever comes into your head out loud?" she said acerbically.

"In my experience, yes," Rakken said. He'd put on a mask of insouciance with his human form, but his coolly amused tone didn't quite hide the strain in his voice. Just how badly was he wounded? The black leather hid bloodstains, but Marius could see flashes of red in the handkerchief scrunched under Rakken's fingers.

He nodded at Rakken's injury. "Was that from your sister? Your *other* sister, I mean, unless you have a charming nickname for her as well?" Rakken's expression grew smooth and remote, and Marius had a strange flash of familiarity: it was exactly how Wyn reacted under stress. "And what did you mean, back there with the portal, that the resonance made sense? Why would ThousandSpire share a connection to the university library?" *For Simulsen's sake. Stop! Talking!* he instructed himself.

Catsmere frowned at him. Supporting her brother's weight didn't appear to affect her, though they'd now descended two flights of stairs and Rakken looked frayed about the edges. He sighed at Marius's question.

"It makes sense that my library would resonate with another in the Mortal Realm," he said. "Though I didn't anticipate *your* presence."

"*You* have a library?" Marius couldn't help the surprise in his voice, for Rakken couldn't look less like an academic. He was so powerfully muscular, and now they were out on the street, the sunshine brought out the gold strands in his dark hair and warmed the deep bronze of his skin. Oh dear. *You shouldn't be noticing things like that! Do not admire the dangerous and possibly evil and definitely male fae!* If he'd needed any more confirmation of just how terrible his judgement was when it came to base matters, here it was. He boxed up and squashed the attraction into the deepest corner of his mind and imagined slamming the door shut on it.

"I can even *read*, Marius Valstar," Rakken said dryly.

Catsmere huffed at them both. "How much further, mortal?"

They'd left the library behind a block ago, walking through the cobbled streets and aged stone buildings that characterised Knoxbridge.

"Not far," he said, as they came to the walkway he'd been aiming for. "Down here." He diverted them down the path beside the Maudlin Bridge, which led to a side entrance to the Knoxbridge Botanical Gardens. Unlatching the gate, he gestured them through.

"In there," he said, pointing at the shed a stone's throw from the fence. Although the Botanical Gardens were open to the public during the day, few people came in this particular entrance, since it consisted of sheds, piles of compost, and glass houses rather than flowerbeds. He unlocked the shed he'd taken over for his own experiments and waved the two inside.

Princess Catsmere deposited Rakken onto one of the benches next to the door while Marius hurried to find the first-aid kit. Rakken changed back to his fae form as he sank down, which said he was more badly wounded than he'd admitted to.

"The taps run only cold water, I'm afraid, but I'll put the kettle on for hot," Marius said as he handed Catsmere the kit.

She didn't say anything, so he went and put the kettle on and filled a bowl with water. When he returned, the twins were engaged in a dance of coordinated efficiency. Catsmere undid straps as Rakken peeled off his leather harness and undershirt, suddenly bare to the waist.

Marius swallowed, taken aback by the deep wound in Rakken's side, as if someone had tried to disembowel him with something the size of a sword; if Marius had been injured like that, he wouldn't have been upright, let alone able to walk. Let alone *conscious*.

Catsmere gestured impatiently for the water bowl. Marius put it down beside her with a thump, feeling entirely superfluous to the proceedings as she began to clean the wound. Rakken held still and impassive as stone. He looked up and met Marius's eyes.

"Admiring my musculature, Marius Valstar?"

"This is horror, not admiration!" Marius snapped. "Since someone seems to have tried to slice you right through!"

"How foolish of me to confuse the two." Rakken grinned, slow and wicked, clearly enjoying discomfiting him. A spike of panic threatened to pierce through the fog of surreality. Had Rakken figured out his secret or was he just being flippant? Marius wanted to ask for clarification, but it wasn't the sort of thing you *could* ask about.

Catsmere didn't look up but whacked her brother with the damp cloth, making him wince. "Leave the mortal alone, Mouse. This needs stitches." She didn't seem nearly concerned enough, given the severity of the injury, but then fae did heal faster than humans.

"Probably," Rakken agreed dispassionately. "But I'm unwilling to be stuck with iron needles." He tapped the first-aid kit.

Marius stared at him for a moment, heart still beating twice its normal speed. "You're not allergic to blackthorn, are you?"

Rakken didn't know the species, but when Marius went out and returned with a branch of the shrub from the nearby hedge—and several scratches for his trouble—he sniffed it cautiously and said, "It has no hostile properties that I can tell." His gaze went meaningfully to a tub near the door, where a yarrow plant was flourishing, and he gave Marius an edged smile.

Marius ignored the subtext, and the guilt that came with it. It was just plain good *sense*, investigating plants with anti-fae properties, wasn't it? Not everyone was resistant to compulsion, after all, and it wasn't as if the two fae even seemed particularly worried by the yarrow plant's presence. Maybe it was the preparation of it that mattered. Did it need to be dried or some such thing?

Marius looked at the wound in Rakken's side and decided now wasn't the time to ask, although the fae wasn't likely to tell him in any case. He focused back on the blackthorn, worrying. "It's not sterile, though." Two blank looks. "It means you're more likely to get infected."

Their expressions cleared. "I am not a mere mortal, Marius Valstar, to sicken from every stray disease," Rakken said with a shrug, then winced at the motion.

"Yes, well, at your own risk be it then," he said, exasperated. "I'm just trying to help, though the gods know why, since I'm sure you're both up to something nefarious."

Catsmere ignored them both and used the long thorns and thread from the first-aid kit to begin stitching Rakken's wounds. It must have hurt, but Rakken showed no sign of discomfort other than to lean back against the wall and shut his eyes. Fatigue emanated from him.

"Keep still," she instructed.

"Are the two of you ever going to explain what you're doing here?" Marius asked. "Or what you want with Wyn?"

Rakken spoke without opening his eyes. "Because, dear mortal, our sister might have claimed the Court of Ten Thousand Spires, but it has not claimed *her*. She has not bonded to the faeland; it does not recognise her as queen." His tone got even colder, until each word carried frostbite, and when he opened his eyes, they burned with arctic fury. "Neither does it want me, nor Cat, nor any of our other siblings."

Marius's eyes widened. "You think the Court of Ten Thousand Spires wants Wyn as its new king?"

"Yes," said Catsmere.

"And our sister will have come to the conclusion that if the faeland's favourite is dead, then it will have to choose from those remaining of the bloodline," Rakken finished.

NIGHT FLIGHTS

A
S DUSK DEEPENED into true night, Wyn frowned down at
the three remaining golden hairs he'd taken from Princess
Evangeline where they glinted against the dark wood of
the coffee table, shining pieces of guilt and failure. *One more try,* he
steeled himself.

Half of him wondered why he was bothering; he'd voluntarily donned the dismae for good reason, after all, and that hadn't
changed even after twenty-four hours of wearing the miserable
constructions. But if he could work out the release mechanism, he
could at least gain a temporary respite from them, enough to sleep…
and the part of him that had grown up in a fae court disliked relying
on Queen Matilda's goodwill for his freedom.

In theory, it should be possible to coax the spell into believing
Princess Evangeline's hair was the same as receiving permission from
Queen Matilda's bloodline, even in the absence of the key. Theory
was all very well, but in practice, every time he thought he'd nearly
unravelled the thing, it collapsed in on itself, bit down on his magic,
and sent a punishing shock of storm-magic through him.

But this time... he held his breath and carefully touched the tip of one golden hair to a fine weft of the spell. If he'd judged correctly, this ought to—

He hissed as distorted elektricity punched through him and broke off the attempt, the single hair sizzling up in a puff of smoke. Usually he was immune to his own charge, but whoever had constructed the dismae had a nasty streak, turning the prisoner's magic against them. They'd also known their business when it came to spellwork, unfortunately.

This is the problem with trying to understand magical constraints from the inside, he thought, collapsing back into his seat with a sigh. *Or perhaps it is merely my mediocre magery.* The repair of his broken oath and the Maelstrom might have flooded him with new power, but power wasn't the same thing as knowledge.

He considered the remaining two hairs, shook his head, and tucked them away in a little fold of paper placed carefully in his pocket. The acrid smell of burnt hair lingered, and he got up and pushed open the balcony doors, stepping out into the cooler night air.

The little courtyard lay deep in shadow as he stood, listening to the quiet of the sleeping palace. Cut off from his leysight, the world seemed emptier than usual. He looked up. No starlight penetrated the thick cloud layer above, and the reflected glow of the city's lights washed the sky a deep yellowish grey. It drew him, nonetheless.

No, he told himself sternly. *That would be foolishness.*

But what if he was letting paranoia rule him? His unlocked balcony doors could be mere mortal oversight—Queen Matilda did not seem the type to set such a trap, and he had not told her that stormdancers came winged. In any case, he could be out and back again before anyone noticed.

Without glamour, though? What if someone looked up at the wrong moment? But mortals rarely looked up. *And I can fly high, if I can get out of the courtyard unnoticed.* Hmmm. He eyed the distance required to clear the top of the courtyard. Not much room for error and even less without magic. Stormdancers had air magic that helped them fly, particularly crucial when taking off, but with his magic crippled, he'd be relying on pure muscle power.

Still half-undecided, he changed forms, and it was almost but not quite like stretching a sore muscle, relief mingled with frustration at not being able to complete the motion. Disorientation riddled him, just as he'd suspected might happen when the magic that should have flowed smoothly in this form didn't. The itch of the dismae magnified a thousandfold, and he furled and unfurled his wings several times, trying and failing to dispel the sensation.

He climbed up on the ledge, spreading his wings for balance. If he misjudged this and ended up on the ground, he'd have to climb up to the balcony again—a vertical takeoff from ground level within the tight constraints of the tiny courtyard would be impossible without magic.

He looked down again and grimaced. *Perhaps this is not the time for complete recklessness.* Skirting along the balcony until he faced the wall of the building, he began to climb. The stonework provided a reasonable number of footholds, and he was tall enough to reach windowsills, pulling himself up to higher levels. Eventually he hauled himself onto the roof of the palace and flared out his wings, feeling much more confident. His stomach lurched as he leapt and gravity took hold, but he beat powerful downstrokes, bearing him upwards and out of its grip.

The air over Meridon had a comfortable degree of heat in it, and gaining height wasn't as hard as he'd feared. Without the dismae, the sheer quantity of the city's iron would have tangled his leysight into knots. With them, there was only a vast, eerie vacuum below.

Even so, his tension eased as the air rushed past his feathers, giving the illusion of freedom. The world spread small beneath him, the palace shrunken to a series of pale rectangles surrounded by dark parkland on three sides. The walkways were easy to make out, lit up like lines of tinsel, and beyond them the bright stretches of streetlights marked the roads. The houses and shops were darker squares, their occupants mostly asleep at this time of night.

He could not help drifting towards the hotel. Hetta. He could fly to her. And then…? They could run back to Stariel, but Stariel was part of Prydein. Hetta couldn't just ignore her queen's commands, not without consequence. And Stariel and Hetta aside, the fae were coming back to the Mortal Realm. The world was changing. He could not leave such important negotiations to fae who did not look so kindly on mortals as he.

Reluctantly, he banked, turning back towards the palace. As he drew closer, soaring over the grand buildings, something glinted in the moonlight. Something white, amidst strange-shaped shadows, at the entrance to one of the inner palace buildings. He banked again, frowning at the shapes, and the shadows resolved into recognisable forms.

Bodies.

His magic rose in a wave, crashing against the iron constraints like the tide hitting a seawall with a spray of pain. He pushed the magic down with a wince, folded his wings, and plummeted, landing in a clumsy rush.

In the shadow of great locked doors lay two bodies of guards, and specifically two of *his* guards, from earlier today. Lightning buzzed under his skin, shorting out and snapping down his nerve endings, but he couldn't rein it in until he saw the small movements of their chests. They were alive. Thank the stormwinds. But what was going on?

He crouched to inspect the men, but there was no obvious wound on either. He shook William's shoulder, but the man remained locked in slumber. Both men had the slow breathing of the deeply unconscious. Stormcrows, but he wished for his leysight; without it, he couldn't tell if it was magic holding them under, nor use his own to bring them out of it. How long had they been like this? He thought of Gwendelfear, here in this mortal city. If she was here, her princess could be also—or some other DuskRose greater fae with the power to compel. But how would enchanting guards benefit the Court of Dusken Roses?

A glint of whiteness again, in the corner of his eye. Wyn turned and stared numbly at the white feather on the stone steps. Oh dear. The unlocked balcony *had* been a trap. He scanned the scene for other tell-tale signs. Yes, there was a second feather peeking from beneath the second guard's body. They were both wispy down feathers, making it hard to identify species at a glance, but he knew what whoever found this scene was supposed to assume. Someone had wanted to make very sure the right person—or rather, the *wrong* person—got the blame for this, whatever this, exactly, was. Which meant—what? His eyes fell on the great ornate doors to the building. He didn't know what lay behind them, but no doubt it was something intended to incriminate him.

He let out a small, bitter laugh, quickly stifled. *Whoever did this didn't know my wings have changed.* His mind raced, counting up possibilities and motivations. Did whoever had done this want him to flee, thus proving his guilt? Or was this scene to provide an excuse to drop the privileges of 'honoured guest', to justify the extraction of information from him in harsher ways than mere questioning? He hadn't thought the queen the type to take that route, but her patience with his vague answers had been wearing thin today.

If it was the first, he needed to get back to his room immediately and hope Queen Matilda wasn't persuaded by this amateur attempt to frame him.

If it was the second…he swallowed. *I am here to prevent a war,* he reminded himself. He had to hope his judgement was sound, that Queen Matilda hadn't set this up herself.

He climbed up the side of the building, a dark emotion he hadn't felt in a long time hard in his chest—betrayal. He'd been unforgivably careless, too trusting, not expecting treachery from mortals in the ways he would've from the fae courts. His own magic, petrichor and cardamom, lay thick and heavy on the back of his tongue, frustrated by the dismae, but the height made it easier to get airborne again, and he swept up into the night sky.

The palace was still silent when he made it back to his rooms. When would the outcry come? Abruptly not prepared to wait, he stalked through to the interior door without bothering to change to his human form and yanked it open.

The captain of the guard had his fist raised to knock, and stared at him in shock. Behind him were several other guards, all of them braced for hostile action, and Wyn knew, in that moment, that they had not come to treat him gently. *The second route, then,* he thought with a sinking heart. He'd misjudged.

The captain recovered himself with a shake and straightened. "Prince Hallowyn Tempestren, by order of Her Majesty—" He broke off as the ground shuddered.

Danger screamed against his senses, every feather standing on end. Again, storm magic instinctively flared out only to be reflected back, and he winced at the shock. *The storm winds curse iron and those who spellwork it.* He strained, listening, gritting his teeth with the effort of not stretching out with his leysight to identify whatever was causing the ground to shake.

The guard captain's eyes went wide with fear. "Prince Hallowyn, I must ask you to desist your magic—"

Wyn stared at him in incomprehension and then raised a cuff, about to protest that there was no possible way *he* could be responsible for any magic, but then the scent hit him and he froze, froze in mingled disbelief and fear, the fear of feathered things trapped deep underground. *No.* But that darkness-and-rock scent, of caves and things unseen by daylight, was unmistakable.

A wyrm. Someone had sent an actual wyrm into an actual human city for him. *Ah well,* he thought faintly, *at least that simplifies matters.*

24

WYRM

DISTANTLY, WYN SUPPOSED that the wyrm meant Aroset was now the Queen of Ten Thousand Spires, and beneath his panic, he felt a stab of worry for his other siblings. But there had been three of them, united. How had Aroset overcome that?

Think about that later: survive the wyrm first.

The guard captain was still staring at him in guilty confusion, and Wyn whipped the man's ornamental dagger out of his belt before he had a chance to protest. It was as laughable as a toothpick, but better that than nothing.

"Hey, you can't—"

"Run," he snarled at the man, pushing him back into his men, making no attempt to soften his strength to mortal levels. The captain staggered.

"Now, Your Highness—" His eyes went wide as something roared in the courtyard behind Wyn.

"Run!" Wyn repeated. "It's me it wants!"

The men took one look at his expression and fled.

The palace would become his tomb, if he was trapped here. He didn't have his magic; he desperately needed his wings if he was to have any chance at all against the wyrm. He whirled, determined to make it back to the balcony, but a shadow blocked out the sky, and he caught a glimpse of thick, maggot-pale flesh: a nightwyrm, then. *Too late.*

He darted back through the door into the hallway, wrenching it closed behind him just as the wyrm crashed through the balcony glass and into his rooms. The wyrm slammed against the interior door. Splinters ricocheted, and he ran down the hallway in the opposite direction to the guards. Behind him, the wyrm hit the door again and went through it with a crunch.

It was huge, but it wasn't very manoeuvrable, and therein might lie his only advantage. He couldn't let it build up momentum. He didn't dare slow down to look, but he heard it gaining speed and dashed through a doorway to his right, slamming that door shut as well, just in time. The hair on his neck rose as it rushed past, bringing with it the smell of mould and dank earth.

He was in a music room, dominated by an enormous golden harp and grand piano. He twisted, searching desperately for another door, but there was none. Trapped. His thoughts flew hard and sharp as crystal shards, and he tore a handkerchief from his pocket, spat in it, and flung it at the chesterfield farthest from the door before leaping atop the piano. From there a beat of his wings took him up to the chandelier, where he hauled himself on top of the fitting, crouched beneath the ceiling. The chandelier swayed and shifted as he found his balance, but he steadied it before the wyrm crashed its way into the room.

The dagger felt ludicrous against a monster of such size, but he gripped it tightly and forced his heartbeat to quiet, curling his magic in as tightly as he could. The dismae actually made that easier. Thank the high winds for small blessings.

The wyrm snarled as its head thrust through the door, baring diamond teeth as long as Wyn's forearm. It scented the room, eyeless head swaying side to side as it did so. Wyn didn't dare breathe, keeping absolutely still as his heart hammered in his ears. Nightwyrms might be blind, but their other senses were acute.

With a sound of tortured wood, it forced its way through the doorframe and undulated its way into the room, pure muscle under its armour, curling its way around the perimeter with its head raised. Its long, pale body was thick as a centuries-old oak and covered in chitinous armour plates. A lesser nightwyrm. Thank the Maelstrom. A greater wyrm would have had aggressive magic to draw on as well; at least this one only had its physical attributes. *Only.*

His gaze fixed on one of its claws. Nightwyrms had only the two forelimbs, tipped with diamond claws that they used to tunnel through anything and everything in their native environment, far beneath the surface. They used nightwyrms in the mines of ThousandSpire, and if it caught him, this one's claws would tear his flesh far more easily than stone.

The nightwyrm made a wet snuffling noise, nostrils flaring. With a snarl of triumph, it threw itself towards the chesterfield where Wyn had thrown the handkerchief, scattering and smashing straight through the furniture in its path. The grand piano hit the wall with a discordant clash, and stray ornaments shattered as they ricocheted off the walls. Wyn swallowed, tightened his grip on the dagger, took aim, and threw.

His aim was off. He knew it as soon as the dagger left his hand. Unsurprising, with his unsteady footing on the chandelier making accuracy impossible. He'd meant to hit the nightwyrm's eardrum, one of the few vulnerable spots in its armour, but instead the dagger clattered against its forehead. The wyrm's neck-spines flushed out, and it bellowed in anger, unhurt. *Damn.*

Wyn hurled himself from the chandelier a split second before the wyrm lunged, tucking his wings in and hurtling through the shredded doorway, splinters biting into his skin. He slammed his shoulder into the hallway wall opposite in his haste and pushed off again without giving himself time to think.

He ran. He ran, and the nightwyrm chased.

The chase blurred into primal terror, the desperate need to get out, out, *out* of this claustrophobic rabbit warren and away from this creature of earth. His wings were dead weight in here, but there was no time to change, no time to think. *Out.* He had to get out. He was a flightless bird, and the wyrm was in its element, a snake in a burrow.

The nightwyrm was so focused on Wyn that it ignored anyone else in its path of destruction. *Small mercies.* The noise it made was incredible. Stone shrieked under its claws as it smashed its way down hallways, shattering wood and brick, furniture, gold leaf, ornaments, *anything*. Wyn ran, leaving a sovereign's ransom of ruined wealth in his wake. Fear became a constant shock of elektrical charge as his magic hit the dismae again and again, trying to find its own way out.

He ran, slamming doors where he could, darting down hallways. The wyrm would tear him to ribbons in seconds if it caught him, parting flesh and bone like butter under its diamond teeth. Distantly, he registered that the palace was waking up—impossible that it should not—but mainly his focus was on the next doorway, the next room. *Out. There must be a way out of this damned palace.* But each twist and turn seemed only to bury him ever deeper in the warren.

He hit the kitchens and flung shut the great doors, amused despair thrilling through him when he realised his location. Had his serving years given him some kind of automatic kitchen-centric homing instinct? But at least kitchens were full of sharp iron implements. *Something I never thought to be thankful for.*

He seized a pair of carving knives, and as he did so, he met the wide eyes of Princess Evangeline, who was frozen in shock beside the kitchen counter, a stolen pasty in one hand. Stormwinds. Her wide eyes took in his wings and horns.

"You really *are* a fairy prince," she said.

"Run!" he told her, dropping a knife so he could haul her up and thrust her towards the back door. She gave a squeak of protest. "Run!" His urgency finally communicated itself to her, and she began to scramble just as the nightwyrm pounded against the kitchen door.

High King's horns. He couldn't lead the wyrm in the same direction as a child, and there were only the two exits. He spun frantically as it crashed against the doors again, searching for something, *anything*. His gaze fell on the rack of herbs and spices, and he began to tear them from their shelf, throwing the glass jars in all directions so they smashed, releasing pungent clouds of different scents: rosemary, chilli, cinnamon, dried lemon peel, cloves, sage, *cardamom*. The cacophony of smells was unbearable to his heightened fae senses, but he grit his teeth and kept throwing, fanning his wings out and flapping for all he was worth, throwing the scents into further disarray, until it was impossible to pinpoint where any individual one was coming from.

The wyrm broke through the kitchen door, and Wyn had the satisfaction of seeing tonnes of fae monster recoil. But it had too much momentum to stop, and it slid into the room on an ear-splitting shriek of protest. He didn't hesitate. He slammed the first knife into one of its nostrils and the second into one of its eardrums before it had time to recover.

It went mad, whether from the iron lodged in its skull or the spices overwhelming its senses, he didn't know and didn't care as it knocked over cabinets, sending plates shattering. Claws caught him a glancing blow as it writhed, slicing through his side so sharply he barely noticed it. He picked up another set of knives and backed away, his aim steadier now he was on firm ground. He missed as much as he hit, his grip oddly slippery, but it was a confined space, and there were a lot of knives, and they were all made of iron.

He didn't know how many knives it took to kill the nightwyrm except that its agonised screams split his skull by the end. It crashed its head and claws about, trying to find its tormentor, but it couldn't manoeuvre quickly enough in the cluttered room, not when the riot of scents meant it didn't know where to aim. Its death was a long and bloody thing, but it never stopped trying to find him or made an attempt to escape, not even in its death throes. A *geas*, then. Only magical compulsion could make a creature continue through such pain.

Aroset had sent creatures to kill him before, but this was different, somehow. Before had been at Father's direction, and which of them hadn't done terrible things to avoid Father's wrath or court his favour? This, though, this was Aroset alone, with no King Aeros to either punish or reward her.

Was this her opening sally as ThousandSpire's new queen? The thought brought a swell of terrible horror-tinged relief, and he had never loathed himself more than at that moment. How could he find any relief in *this*?

He stood panting down at the nightwyrm's still-twitching corpse, sickened. *It's done. It's done.* He had to repeat it several times before he could believe it, the nightwyrm's screams still seeming to echo from the walls. He put his hand to his side with a wince. It came away red and dripping, and he stared at his palm, the next thought taking an oddly long time to form: *I am bleeding.*

A sound behind him. He looked up to find the horrified faces of the palace guard peering around the doorframe. As if operating on pure reflex, one lifted his ornamental rifle to his shoulder and aimed dreamily at Wyn. Stormcrows. Wyn tore open the door that Princess Evangeline had used and flung himself through. The bullet hit the doorframe with a sound that seemed both obscenely loud and oddly muted, compared to the nightwyrm's ear-splitting screams.

He stared up at the dark sky. He was outside. The other door to the kitchen was a bloody outside door, which seemed a completely obvious location for it to go. He began to laugh, an edge of hysteria in it. There was no sign of the princess.

The sound of another shot shook him back to himself. He looked down at the dismae. Aroset had sent a nightwyrm into the heart of a mortal city, and the humans here were liable to kill him out of sheer fright before he managed to explain himself. There was really only one choice left. Pressing a hand to his side, he flung himself painfully into the air.

25

RUDE AWAKENINGS

LOUD HAMMERING JERKED Hetta from uneasy dreams. She flailed at the bedclothes, disoriented in the darkness. Who was making such a godsawful racket at this hour? *If the pigs have got into the Home Wood again, I'm not dealing with it until after breakfast.* The knocking came again, sharply demanding. She reached for Stariel for answers, found none, and abruptly realised she was in a hotel bed, half a country away from home.

Too bleary to remember where the light switch was, she stretched out her fingers, summoned a ball of silvery light into being, and flung it ceiling-wards. The pounding continued.

"Lord Valstar!" a man's voice, unfamiliar and unfriendly.

She scrambled out of bed and retrieved her dressing-gown, wrapping it around her pyjamas as she padded through into the sitting room and towards the door of the suite. The muzzy dregs of sleep were quickly giving way to alarm. Angry people didn't knock on doors before dawn to deliver good news.

She opened the door a crack, throwing the person on the other side off-balance, as he'd been just about to knock again. It was a member of the queensguard, resplendent in his red-and-purple uniform, and he wasn't alone. Three other guards stood in the hallway behind him, all of them with grim expressions. The hotelier lurked a little further back, eyeing Hetta nervously, clearly torn between royal authority and the impulse to protect his guests' privacy.

"Lord Valstar," the first guard said again. "I am Captain Marleigh. I have a warrant to search your rooms."

Hetta frowned at him but couldn't make sense of the situation. "What for?"

"We have reason to suspect you may be hiding a fugitive." Captain Marleigh nodded to his men and put a hand meaningfully on the door. "Please remove yourself from the doorway, my lord."

"Or?" She felt like she ought to object to ill-explained early-morning invasions on principle, no matter how polite. Her mind whirled. "And what do you mean, hiding a fugitive?"

He ignored her question. "If you will not open this door, I regret I will be forced to open it myself."

Not so polite an invasion, then. She'd worn Wyn's ring to bed, and it lay warm against her skin, heightening her land-sense. Through it, Stariel flared in anger, a distant thunderstorm, and she repressed the urge to demonstrate to the captain that she wasn't going to be bullied before she'd even gotten dressed. <Primal responses are generally unhelpful,> she told Stariel, though she wasn't sure it could understand her at this distance.

"I must insist you allow us in, Lord Valstar." Captain Marleigh drew himself up, and Hetta sighed in exasperation and threw open the door.

"Come in, then," she said. "And see for yourself there's no one but me here."

The four guards ignored her as they entered. Three of them reached into pockets and retrieved sets of quizzing glasses before spreading out in a search pattern. The fourth man didn't don glasses before moving towards her bedroom. Hetta noticed that on his lapel he had an insignia that none of his comrades bore: a stylised eye. The conclusion wasn't hard to draw: he must have the Sight.

"For the nine heavens' sake, you don't truly think a person could fit under the sofa?" she said, when one of the men crouched to peer under it. A hard knot of suspicion was forming, a twisted almost-nausea in her stomach. "And you'd better not be looking for Prince Hallowyn, because that means you've lost him, and the queen herself assured me he would be treated as an honoured guest. He *is* still at the palace, isn't he?"

The man checking under the sofa glanced up at the captain for guidance on how to answer this apparently difficult question, which told her that Wyn *wasn't* at the palace anymore. What had happened? He'd been so very resolved not to embark on any daring escape attempts; what had made him change his mind? Had they hurt him?

"Well, you have a terrible poker face," she said. "So I can see that *something* has happened. Where is the prince?"

The captain frowned, as if he wasn't sure her reaction was genuine. "There was an…incident. The prince is no longer at the palace." He pressed his lips shut and glanced at the guard with the eye insignia who'd just emerged from her bedroom. "Anything, Severn?"

The guard shook his head. "No. Wait and I'll check this room as well."

"Your compatriots have already checked it most diligently for secret sofa-hiders," Hetta said acerbically but was again ignored. What was the point in being a lord if people still ignored you? She tightened the belt of her dressing gown and straightened. How had her father behaved when he was displeased with underlings? "Captain Marleigh, I'm not accustomed to being woken at strange hours and having my quarters searched as if I were a criminal, without any real explanation."

"I'm checking for fairy glamour," Severn said, to his captain's displeasure.

"You're checking for fae glamour because you don't know where Prince Hallowyn is and you believe he's hiding in my hotel room?"

"We're merely following our orders, Lord Valstar," Captain Marleigh said when Severn shook his head.

Aunt Sybil, Alexandra, and three more guards tumbled into the room at this point. Aunt Sybil was doing a very good impression of a large, indignant crow. Her dressing gown was an ancient black monstrosity, and she drew herself up to her not inconsiderable height and hissed at the captain:

"What is the meaning of this, young man?"

The captain, to give him credit, didn't quail at the sight. He looked to his men, who shook their heads. "Nothing, sir."

The captain bowed to Aunt Sybil. "Thank you for your cooperation, ladies, Lord Valstar. We apologise for the intrusion. If you have questions, I suggest you take them up with my employer."

And they marched out the door as if that were a completely satisfactory answer, leaving only the apologetic hotelier in their wake. Aunt Sybil began to give him a dressing down at this appallingly unacceptable treatment of guests, commenting liberally on his intelligence, class, and manners, and threatening to blacken his name to every person she knew.

"Something's happened to Wyn, hasn't it?" asked Alexandra while their aunt was preoccupied. Her blue eyes were wide and worried. "What are you going to do, Hetta?"

Hetta frowned at the sofa where the guard with the Sight had searched. "I'm going to get some answers."

IT WAS STILL VERY early when she reached the palace, the overcast dawn so grey as not to be worth the name. Despite the hour, the palace reminded her strongly of a kicked anthill. Official-looking people were piling out of dark kineticars whilst servants hurried out of the way. Already several newspaper reporters had gathered at the front gates, attempting to interview stony-faced guards.

Hetta considered the grand main entrance and decided she didn't have much taste for sitting in ornate waiting rooms for who knew how long. She wanted answers now. Slipping towards the back entrance, she drew up the uniform of a palace kitchen maid, overlaying it on her dress. It took longer than it should've to get it right, with her emotions tangling the magic. She took long, steadying breaths, taking the time to iron out the details. If she was found out, it dashed well wouldn't be because of shabby magic, not in Meridon, where she'd earned her mastery fair and square.

After that, well, she became invisible in the way that servants are invisible. This was much easier than true invisibility, which only worked with any degree of success while one stood still. Still, limited invisibility was better than none, and she took advantage of her skills to work her way into the palace. She headed in the direction that appeared to be the focal point of the foot traffic, stepping into doorways and throwing up a veil whenever it looked like someone might question her presence.

Something had wrecked the palace to an incredible degree. Whole walls were missing in places, splinters and plaster shards everywhere, furniture flung about as if a dog had worried at it. Already workmen were beginning to clear away the mess. Hetta didn't dare imagine the cost of the repairs.

I hope they can't charge Stariel for damages, she thought, mostly because she was trying not to think about what lay at the end of this path of destruction or what had caused it. But if the queensguard were searching for Wyn, that meant he had to be alive, at least, didn't he? They wouldn't search for a dead man. *But he didn't have access to his magic.* What if whatever had caused this mess had caught him? What if he was bleeding out somewhere, alone and in hiding? A cold, needly feeling dug into her chest. Oh, gods, why hadn't she told him she loved him yesterday? It always seemed too sugary sentimental to say aloud, but what if he wasn't all right… She paused and took a deep, sharp breath. This wasn't the time or place to panic. *Find out what happened first.*

She followed the increasing guard presence towards the epicentre, relying more and more on illusion as she got close. Two maids passed her as she hid in a doorway. One of them said to the other with a kind of unholy relish: "They said he was bleeding like a stuck pig. He can't have got far."

Her heart squeezed so tight she thought it would burst. The door to the kitchens was shredded, and she clambered through to find a stomach-turning mess of blood and spices and an enormous fae creature dead and glittering between ruined shelves. There was no sign of Wyn.

Wyn had given her one of his old white feathers, months ago, as a Wintersol gift, and Hetta often carried it with her, not liking the idea of it falling into someone else's possession. She pulled it out now and gripped the nib so tightly it dug into skin as she stared down at the fae monster. It looked something like a giant, armour-plated snake with two forelegs. Its eyeless head bristled with kitchen knives, and rivulets of blood dripped sluggishly onto the floor from each wound. *Well, Meridon will have to believe in fae now.*

But where was Wyn?

26

THE QUEEN IS NOT AMUSED

ETTA FACED A rigidly displeased monarch shortly after finishing her covert explorations and re-entering the palace officially, to a different receiving room this time. This one was, if possible, even less friendly than the first, or perhaps it was just the way the queen's blue eyes flashed when they saw her, cold and hard. The Duke of Callasham—Lord Greymark—accompanied her this time, and he looked at Hetta like she was something the cat had dragged in.

"And where is Prince Hallowyn, Lord Valstar?" the queen demanded.

"I was hoping you could tell me, Your Majesty, since last time I saw him was in this palace," Hetta said. "I assume he fled in fear of his life." That had to be why he'd run, and she couldn't blame him, not after seeing the size of the dead fae monster in the kitchens. There was no Stariel to keep out monsters here, and whoever had sent that creature might send another—and Wyn had no magic to defend himself, thanks to those cuffs.

"Fear of a dead monster? We warned you both that if Prince

Hallowyn chose not to remain in our custody, we would consider him a hostile agent."

"You cannot blame him for not wanting to be a sitting duck if the Spires send another monster! For that's what your cuffs have made him!"

"And why, exactly, is his home court sending monsters after him?"

Because his psychopathic sister Aroset has inherited the Spires? Wyn's other siblings probably wouldn't send murderous fae creatures to assassinate him if they'd inherited. And if Aroset hadn't inherited, why would she bother sending creatures after a sibling who'd opted out of the Spires' succession war?

But the queen wasn't a fool. "We assume it has something to do with this 'as-yet unsettled succession' that he mentioned?"

"It could do, Your Majesty," Hetta temporised. What would Wyn say in this situation? "Not all fae are equally keen to broker peace between the fae realms and mortal," she said carefully. "And I think it's likely that the fae who sent that monster is one of those who holds decidedly anti-human views. You should—"

The queen's eyes sparked a warning. *Right. Don't tell the queen what to do.* Hetta shut her mouth hastily.

"The destruction of large sections of this palace has not endeared the fae to us, Lord Valstar. We do not like the idea that there may be further attacks."

"Well, you should be thankful that Wyn has left the palace in order to spare you then!" Hetta snapped before she could stop herself.

The queen's eyes narrowed. "And how do my two enchanted palace guards fit into your narrative of noble self-sacrifice, Lord Valstar?" She told Hetta, in clipped tones, that two guards on the nightshift outside the Treasury had been found unconscious. "The Treasury is where the keys to the dismae are kept," she added.

The only reason Hetta could think of for Wyn to go seeking the keys to the dismae was if he'd had some warning of the fae monster's attack and knew he'd need his magic. He could've made guards sleep—Hetta had seen him do it once before, with Gwendelfear. It made her feel slightly better, thinking that he might've freed himself from the cuffs before he'd escaped.

The queen continued: "My guards tell me the men were found some time before the appearance of the monster, in an enchanted sleep from which they could not be woken. They were on their way to question him when it arrived. Which suggests Prince Hallowyn may have either summoned the creature as vengeance after having secured his freedom from the dismae, or that he knew of its pending arrival and intended to flee and leave us to its mercy."

"Both of those are ridiculous suggestions," Hetta said flatly. "Wyn would never—"

The duke puffed up. "Remember who you speak to, Lord Valstar. Besides, you're defending a criminal; they found his feathers at the scene." He wrinkled his nose in faint revulsion. "We know the man's not human in his other shape."

Hetta swallowed down a hot response. It wouldn't do Wyn any good. "What did the guards say when they woke up?"

The queen's eyes narrowed. "They do not remember what happened."

"Then this is all speculation!" Hetta tried to keep her tone even, reasonable. "Doesn't he deserve some benefit of the doubt? He put on those dismae just to reassure you he meant no harm—that's the sort of person he is! And when we find him, he'll have a very good explanation for all of this that will probably be because he was trying to protect you all from that creature!"

Queen Matilda didn't look convinced. "We have only your word for this, Lord Valstar. And against that, two enchanted guards, a missing fae prince, and an alarming sum in property damages."

"The property damages weren't his fault. He's not responsible for the actions of other fae." *Please don't let her hold Stariel responsible for damages either.*

"Hmmm." Queen Matilda pursed her lips. "Do not leave town,

Lord Valstar," she said after a moment. "And if Prince Hallowyn's whereabouts should be made known to you, I expect you to waste no time in informing us."

Hetta curtseyed, despite her simmering anger. "As you wish, Your Majesty."

"And perhaps while we wait for Prince Hallowyn to reappear, you can sign the necessary paperwork ratifying Stariel's agreements with the Crown."

Hetta smiled through gritted teeth and said sweetly: "Oh, I cannot sign anything without my steward to advise me. I'm sure you'll forgive me for the delay."

Queen Matilda's eyes flashed. "Four days, Lord Valstar," she said after a pause. "We shall set the appointment for Monday morning. If, as you say, your 'steward' is merely temporarily absent, that should be plenty of time for him to clear his name, shouldn't it?"

✦✦✦

HETTA HAD YET TO leave the palace in a good mood, and today was no different. Obviously she'd no intention of leaving Meridon without Wyn, but it was quite another thing to be commanded not to. The maid's words about Wyn bleeding everywhere went round and round like a stuck phonograph. *He heals very quickly*, she tried to reassure herself. The fact that she knew this was in and of itself depressing. How many times now had she seen him clawed up by some new and horrible fae monster?

At the palace entrance, the newspaper reporters had multiplied like flies buzzing around a corpse. Hetta took the precaution of adopting a demure manner and illusing herself to appear as a middle-aged blonde Southerner, and they didn't tag her as anyone worth notice. *Long may that last.* Sooner or later, someone would make the connection between Stariel, Wyn, and the damaged palace. Or perhaps the news that the fae were real might overshadow that?

She traipsed back to the hotel, both hoping and fearing to find a bloodied Wyn there, but all she got was an anxious sister and irate aunt.

"Wyn wouldn't just run away!" Alexandra flared up when Hetta had explained the situation. "Not without reason!"

"Yes, I know," Hetta said. She felt utterly unable to reassure her sister; her own emotions were too tumultuous.

She focused on taking care of small necessities, such as ringing Stariel's gatehouse and telling the gatekeeper to pass on a message to Jack. *It will be so much more convenient when there's a direct line to the house.* Worry kept intruding. Why hadn't Wyn contacted her, somehow, if he insisted on staying in hiding? He must know she'd want reassurance after seeing that fae creature. He wouldn't simply run, would he, in a misguided attempt to try to protect her from the political fallout?

She slammed the phone back into its rest, not comforted by the thought. It would be far too like Wyn to think that was a sensible course of action. *I'll set his feathers on fire if that's the case.* But better that than the alternative; that he was lying bleeding in a ditch somewhere. *Though probably not a literal ditch, since we're in the capital. An alley, rather.* Her heart squeezed tight, and her hand went automatically to the ring.

"He's not at Stariel, is he?" Alexandra asked. Hetta stared at her, feeling unusually dim-witted. "Wyn." Alexandra bit her lip. "I mean, he could fly there, couldn't he?"

Hetta blinked. "He could, I suppose." *Though not if he's injured.* "I'm sure someone will tell us if he drops from the sky up there."

She had to believe Wyn was all right and that he would

communicate his whereabouts in a timely fashion. *In the meantime, think*, she told herself sternly. When—not if—she found Wyn, they would need to deal with the queen.

Feathers and enchanted guards... The more Hetta thought about it, the less sense it made. If Wyn had known the monster was coming, he would've wanted to protect people from it. Which, in fairness, might've included him attempting to get the keys to the dismae. She knew how uneasy he'd been about using compulsion, of late, but the monster might've outweighed that consideration. But even so, he wouldn't have left guards still unconscious and thus vulnerable behind him, especially in such a deep sleep that other people hadn't been able to wake them. And why hadn't he tried to get people to evacuate or attempted to lead the monster away rather than into the interior of the palace?

The fact that he'd done neither of those suggested he *hadn't* known the monster was coming—in which case, why had he wanted to rid himself of the dismae badly enough to enchant guards? She brooded at the coffee table, trying to pull the threads together. The bloodied wreckage in the kitchen rose in her mind's eye. Broken cabinets. The knives sticking out of the monster's dead head. Glass shards. A fine dust of spices lying over everything.

Wait. *Literal* spice—that's what the smell had been. Not Wyn's magic, as she'd assumed. Had *anywhere* in the destruction actually smelled like storms? Horror welled up as she realised it hadn't and what that might mean if Wyn was still wearing the dismae, still cut off from his magic.

But if he'd still been wearing the dismae, that would mean he couldn't have compelled the guards... *Which takes me right back to square one.*

A knock startled her from the tangled chain of thoughts. It was the bellboy, with both a telegram and an envelope. The envelope had Brad's name scrawled across it: tickets to opening night, no doubt.

Hetta thanked the bellboy and frowned at the telegram. It was from Marius, its contents short and to the point. Prince Rakken and Princess Catsmere had popped out of a portal in Knoxbridge, Wyn was in danger, and the three of them were arriving by train this afternoon. *Oh good*, she thought faintly. *They can answer some questions.*

27

THE TRAIN STATION

ETTA WAITED AT Pickering Station alone. As she'd told Alexandra when she'd objected to staying behind— what if Wyn turned up at the hotel in her absence? She shut her eyes briefly. *Please let him be at the hotel when I return.* Then he could be responsible for figuring out how to re-introduce Prince Rakken to Aunt Sybil with a minimum of fuss. He'd previously masqueraded as Lord Featherstone, the son of Aunt Sybil's old friend, and that deception was bound to create awkwardness. *And when Wyn returns, I'm sure we can sort out this business with the queen. Somehow.* Even if they couldn't untangle the knots, he would still be *here* and *alive.* She was having difficulty caring much about scandal and politics in comparison.

She shook her head to clear it. Fretting wasn't going to help. She glanced up at the large station clock: two minutes till the train was due. How often had she waited on this platform during her six years in Meridon, counting down the minutes until her brother's arrival? Admittedly, never with quite this degree of anxiety, but the sharp pang of familiarity was there all the same. Knoxbridge was only an hour's journey from Meridon, and Marius had studied at the university there until Father had decreed his academic career must come to an end.

One minute. She hopped impatiently from foot to foot. Hopefully Marius was all right after dealing with the two fae alone. She didn't know Princess Catsmere at all, but Prince Rakken had been sharp-tongued enough to easily bruise a much less sensitive soul than Marius.

The train finally came into sight and pulled into Pickering Station with a slow grind of brakes, and the station attendant began to briskly walk the length of the train, opening doors to release a modest stream of passengers. Hetta craned her neck, though it probably wasn't necessary. Both her brother and Prince Rakken were tall and would be visible above the crowd.

Marius emerged first, looking irritable rather than anxious. The two royal fae followed him, both in human form and wearing well-cut suits. Their features held echoes of Wyn's, and her heart gave a tight, painful pulse at the sight.

Hetta's wasn't the only head turning towards the tall, sleek pair. It was something more than beauty that drew the eye, something that put her in mind of the brightly scaled snakes she'd seen once in the Meridon Zoological Gardens. The way the deadly animals had moved had held the same sinuous, mesmerising fascination.

Neither of the twins appeared aware of the attention, but Marius definitely was, because by the time the group reached Hetta, his face was flushed, his shoulders hunched defensively as he carted his battered valise. The royal twins apparently did not come with their own luggage.

"Don't call them by their names," he blurted out before she could utter a greeting. "It's some magic thing, apparently, that allows their sister to find them. You can call them Cat and…Rake." He grinned at the last, to Hetta's amazement. Apparently she'd significantly underestimated her brother's ability to cope with intimidating fae if he was actively *provoking* them.

"Your Highness is also appropriate, as I have previously explained," Prince Rakken said dryly. "Good afternoon, Lord Valstar. We meet again."

If she hadn't known Wyn so well, known the signs of him under strain, she would've thought Prince Rakken coolly composed. As it was, she could tell he was ill at ease. *The iron*, she realised abruptly. All the iron in the station was affecting him as it had Wyn. Princess Catsmere also seemed to be strung tight, greeting Hetta with a clipped nod. She was a very tall, willowy woman with short dark hair and the same vivid green eyes as her twin.

"Lord Valstar," she said. "This mortal tells us you know our brother's location?"

"I don't, unfortunately. You, me, and half of Meridon are currently searching for him," Hetta said. "Also, good afternoon, ah, Cat. It's nice to meet you properly."

Catsmere blinked. "I have seen you before, Lord Valstar, though I accept you were preoccupied at the time," she said with significant understatement, as this referred to the scene in the throne room at ThousandSpire, when King Aeros had been taunting Wyn. "Why is half of Meridon currently searching for our brother?"

"Why are you two suddenly in Meridon, looking for him?" Hetta returned.

"We were fleeing our sister's wrath. And armies. She controls the Spires." The bluntness of the answer threw Hetta off balance. How refreshing, to meet a fae who didn't talk in circles.

"At present," Rakken added sharply. Anger flashed across his face, there and gone in a second.

"The Spires wants Wyn as its new king so their sister whose name starts with A is trying to kill him to stop that happening," Marius summarised, watching her carefully.

She sucked in a deep breath, not surprise but despair threatening to overwhelm her. Of course. It made sense that Aroset would try to kill Wyn if she thought he stood in her way. She'd been deliberately not thinking about how the Spires had reached out for Wyn a week ago, about what that might mean. She'd even hoped, deep down, that Aroset *had* bonded with the faeland, because it would make it safely not Wyn's destiny once and for all.

"She sent that creature after him at the palace." She wrapped her arms around herself. Maybe the maid had been wrong about how injured Wyn had been. But the creature had been so very enormous.

Catsmere's head snapped to her. "What creature?"

Hetta described the armoured creature from the palace, and the ruin it had left in its wake. "That's why half the city is looking for Wyn—he hasn't been seen since the attack." She swallowed. "You'd—you'd know if he were…" *dead*, she tried to say, but it stuck on her tongue, as if saying it would somehow make it so.

Rakken gave a dismissive shrug. "He's not dead. We would know."

She could suddenly breathe again. Marius looked similarly relieved. "Gods, Hetta," he said.

"What you describe is called a nightwyrm." Catsmere's expression was grim. "It is indeed a creature from the Spires."

"If Set is already sending creatures to this city, then why are we standing idly on this platform?" Rakken asked, waving irritably at the thinning stream of people on the narrow strip as the rest of the passengers found their way into the station proper.

Hetta was tempted to tell him that his attitude wasn't fooling her; she knew he just wanted to get away from the iron, but instead she said flatly: "We're going to stand here until I know whether you two want to kill Wyn too." After all, if the Court of Ten Thousand Spires truly wanted Wyn as its ruler—and she'd be dashed if she let that happen—then he also stood between the twins and the throne.

She'd thought saying so might anger them, but Catsmere seemed to think it a perfectly natural concern. She momentarily ceased her restless scanning of the crowd to say: "We vowed, my brother and I, that we would not let our sister damage little Hollow as she did Koi." Aroset had blinded their brother Irokoi in one eye.

"Well, that's good to know, but I'd like a more precise answer." She knew very well how fae could slide around truth unless you pinned them down.

Rakken said, a trace of impatience in his tone: "We don't plan to kill him." He didn't sound particularly happy about it.

"I wouldn't have brought them here if I thought they wanted Wyn dead. Do give me *some* credit," Marius said, folding his arms and looking down at her crossly. "Wyn and I might've had our differences lately, but, he's still, well, *ours*. But I think *Their Most Royal Highnesses*"—he emphasised the words with a pointed glare at Rakken—"actually are worried about his safety. Family means more to these two than they let on."

Rakken shot Marius a look with daggers in it. "You are being impolite, Marius Valstar." Marius frowned, confused, and that seemed to satisfy Rakken in some way that made no sense to Hetta. His expression smoothed into amusement. "Very impolite."

Marius threw his hands up. "Well, I'm not sure why me vouching for your good intentions offends you, but you can't expect me to just magically know and abide by all your daft fae rules."

Hetta's eyebrows went up, but Rakken just said mildly: "They are only daft from your perspective, which is, naturally, a limited one."

"Because you know *so much* about mortal customs and are clearly a *completely unbiased judge!*"

Hetta met Catsmere's eyes, seeking confirmation that their respective brothers truly were having a petty argument in the middle of a crowded train station while Wyn was still who knew where. The princess was difficult to read, even for a fae, but Hetta thought she detected amusement in the gleam of her emerald eyes. Or perhaps merely exasperation. Had Marius and Rakken been sniping at each other like this the entire train ride?

And then Catsmere went still as a hunting hound scenting prey. Her stillness spread to Rakken half a second later, and the pair of them scanned the crowded station as if they'd already discussed how to efficiently divvy up the space between them.

"Yarrow," Rakken murmured.

Catsmere nodded. "Yes…"

Neither twin lost their human form, but they were both sharpened, their beauty strange and overpowering.

"There!" The two of them zeroed their attention in on one particular section of the crowd, and Rakken's eyes blazed a brighter green. In a heartbeat, the steam and grit were masked with the smell of storms and citrus. *Wyn*, Hetta thought, but it wasn't his scent, not quite.

The huge, soundless force of Rakken's magic radiated outwards, and the crowds became still in its wake, the entire station falling silent but for the engines. It spooled out and out until it…caught, was the only word Hetta could think of to describe the sensation, like a hook on a fishing line. The force abruptly released the eerily quiet mass. Chatter broke out again, and hundreds of people jerked back into motion, as if they hadn't all been trapped for a moment in frozen soundlessness.

Rakken made a grasping motion, and a man with straw-coloured hair began to stagger towards him. No one reacted to this. Instead, the crowds parted around the man without appearing to notice that they were doing so. *Compulsion*, Hetta thought. *Rakken's using compulsion.* A chill went down her spine.

"What are you *doing*? Who is he?" she demanded.

Rakken frowned down at her, and the man shuddered to a halt at the end of their platform, his face unnervingly blank.

"He has been watching us this entire time, and he carries anti-fae charms." A grim satisfaction glinted in his expression. "For lesser fae, at least."

Rakken and Catsmere stalked towards their prey, leaving Hetta and Marius to trail behind them. Hetta shared a look with her brother. His grey eyes were wide and horrified, a mirror of her own emotions. Rakken had held the whole station in thrall for that gut-wrenching heartbeat, and he'd plucked a single man from the crowd as easily as a fish from a barrel. She'd had no idea compulsion could do something like that.

The thought snuck into her, unwillingly: *Could Wyn do that, if he wanted to?* But that wasn't the point—he wouldn't. The twins held no such moral compunctions. *I mustn't let myself forget that.* Their resemblance to Wyn made it too easy to assume they'd act as he would.

Before the twins reached the blond man, a pair of men pushed out of the milling crowd and took hold of his arms. Hetta recognised one—the guard with the Sight—though he wasn't in uniform now. The other man waved a posy of something under his nose and he jerked, breaking out of the compulsion with a gasp. Again, that terrifying hammer of Rakken's will spread out, and the newcomers reeled under the blow.

"Stop!" Hetta cried, hurrying after them. "They're palace guards!"

The guards staggered away, pulling the other man with them. The twins teetered on the brink of giving chase, but by the time Marius and Hetta reached them, they'd decided against it, both tense as un-hooded falcons.

"Why were guards from the palace watching you, Lord Valstar?" Rakken asked with narrowed eyes.

"Still watching you," Catsmere added. "Don't look!" she hissed as Hetta instinctively began to do just that. "Or they will know that you know they are there."

"How many are there watching us?" Marius asked.

"Five, not counting the three before," Rakken said.

Hetta swallowed, a cold lump settling in her stomach. "Her Majesty must have sent her guards to follow me in case I contacted Wyn." Anger balled in her fists, threatening to manifest as fire. She almost regretted stopping Rakken from interrogating that guard.

How dare the queensguard follow her around? But no; she'd done the right thing. She was, after all, trying to convince Her Majesty that Hetta and Wyn were trustworthy, upstanding citizens.

Besides, it's also ethically questionable, she thought, somewhat belatedly.

She looked around the train station, where there was now no sign of the vast compulsion of before. Gods, that wasn't going to help her case with the queen at all.

"Will they remember it? The compulsion?" Marius asked before she could.

Rakken eyed him oddly. "No. They will not. I am no amateur."

Hetta didn't know whether to find that a relief or even more unsettling.

Catsmere spoke as if impatient with the subject. "And do you have a way to contact our brother? Or something of his?"

Hetta was about to shake her head when she remembered. "I don't have a way to contact him. What do you mean by 'something of his'?" She thought of the ring, lying warm against her skin. Stariel gave a distant hum of acknowledgement.

"Something that carries his essence may allow us to trace him," Rakken explained patiently.

"Ah—I have one of his feathers," Hetta said, feeling hope for the first time today. "Will that work?"

Both twins stared at her as if she'd grown a third head, and Catsmere smiled for the very first time. It wasn't Rakken's sharp, sarcastic expression, but something warmer and almost familiar, and it made Hetta's heart ache suddenly with missing Wyn.

"Yes," she said. "That should work."

28

SILVERSINE PARK

HETTA HAD IMAGINED quite a different tone to her first visit to Silversine Park—her favourite park—since her return to Meridon. Her mental version had, firstly and most importantly, involved only her and Wyn. His siblings and her brother were very poor substitutes. She'd also envisaged far more romantic strolling arm-in-arm and chaperone evasion and far less furtive spell-casting in secluded copses. Not that either Rakken or Catsmere was particularly furtive, having shaken off their guard escort with a combination of compulsion and glamour. It was certainly useful, but Hetta kept remembering that silent force swelling out at the train station and shuddered. *Thank the gods my bond with Stariel makes me immune.*

Marius liked it even less than she did. Every time a passer-by came close and then abruptly diverted their route, he glared at Rakken, which was unfair, because Hetta suspected Catsmere was responsible for that bit of traffic management. Rakken was constructing some kind of ritual preparations, which he did with a casual display of magic, scooping a circle in the earth with invisible hands, muttering something too quietly for Hetta to hear.

"I don't think they really think of humans as people," Marius reflected beside her. Hetta was fairly sure both fae could hear him, but they ignored the remark. Rakken finished his preparations and stalked over to Hetta.

"Give me my brother's feather," he said, extending his palm.

Hetta made no move to do so. "What are you going to do with it?"

He frowned. "As previously stated: attempt to find him."

"And what then?" she asked. "You'll welcome him as your prospective king with open arms?"

They might've convinced Marius they meant no harm to Wyn—and heavens only knew how they'd achieved that—but Hetta was still suspicious of their motives. "You said you weren't here to kill him, so what *do* you want?" Probably she should've asked this sooner, but the queensguard had been an effective distraction.

He narrowed his eyes. "Sometimes, Lord Valstar, our choices are not what we would like."

"You mean you'd rather Wyn than—" She remembered not to say Aroset's name at the last moment and finished, "—your other sister."

Rakken gave a tight smile. "We do not know for certain what ThousandSpire wants. But yes, if it comes to it."

Marius and Hetta exchanged a look. Rakken's slim hope that he might still be chosen seemed like a simple case of denial.

"I know about not being chosen," Marius said suddenly. "It's not always the end of the world." He smiled at Hetta. "I've come to respect the choices of faelands."

Warm affection for her brother bloomed, despite the fact that she had no intention of respecting ThousandSpire's choices in this. *Oh, Marius.*

Rakken ignored this sentimental moment. Hetta was beginning to suspect this was his way of dealing with things he didn't know what to do with. "Regardless, I assume you'd like to know my brother's location also, Lord Valstar?" He held out a hand.

She did, but it was still hard to relinquish the feather. "I'd like it back when you're done."

"Very well." He continued to hold out his hand, expression impassive.

Taking a deep breath, she handed it over. He prowled back to his circle, whereupon he folded himself to the ground. He looked extremely odd sitting cross-legged in a tailored suit beneath a birch tree in Silversine Park, but he was supremely unselfconscious. A blackbird chirped in the tree above his head and then took flight, and she wasn't sure if it was magic or not that had disturbed it.

"How does this work, exactly?" Marius asked, but Catsmere hushed him absently. Her attention was still on the perimeter of the area, diverting foot traffic.

Rakken's eyes were closed, a faint crease between his brows. Dappled light glinted in the ebony and gold of his hair. His magic had the same storm underlayer as Wyn's, but overlaying it were woodier citrus notes instead of spice.

Stariel bristled, and Hetta sent a soothing reassurance down the bond, through the ring. <He's trying to help. I think.> Stariel wasn't reassured, and Hetta felt a swell of longing down the gossamer-thin thread. Stariel longed for her to be home. The land included Wyn in its longing too, to her surprise. What did that mean? *Probably that I'm still not doing this lord business right, letting my emotions bleed too much into my faeland.* But that was a concern for another day.

Rakken opened his hand, and Wyn's feather lay there, silvery white and somehow clearly *other*. Hetta swallowed to release the sudden pressure against her eardrums, and then realised it wasn't a physical sensation but a magical one. The pressure increased, and with it the citrus scent of Rakken's magic, until the feather began to vibrate. Power built for long moments, the feather now humming so intensely it was nothing more than a pale blur floating a fraction above Rakken's palm—and then with a crack, it burst into flame.

Rakken hissed and closed his hand around the flame, snuffing it out. His eyes burned a brilliant, poisonous green, and he opened his fist to reveal a palm smudged with grey ash. As Hetta watched, the breeze caught a few of the insubstantial grey flakes and carried them up through the budding branches and out of sight, leaving her feeling more bereft than the loss of one feather really ought to warrant. Wyn would be perfectly happy to give her another, when they found him.

Rakken rose, brushing the smudges of ash from his hands. "There is something stopping the connection from forming."

Catsmere spared a glance away from her glamour. "Why would Hollow be blocking such magic?"

"Could dismae block your spell?" Hetta asked. Both fae's attention snapped to her, green eyes glowing faintly.

"Dismae?" Catsmere snapped out the word.

"Yes, Wyn said they block the magic of greater fae. The queen made him put a pair on." She stopped. Despite their sharp edges and their casual use of compulsion and glamour, Hetta hadn't truly felt in danger from the pair before. Now they'd both gone still. It wasn't Wyn's stillness of thinking furiously for the correct reaction—it was the stillness of predators before an attack, and there was abruptly nothing human about them, despite the lack of wings.

"Your mortal queen placed *dismae* on our brother?" Rakken asked, voice low and menacing. Hetta had to stop herself from taking a step back. Around their private bubble, people strolled in oblivious twos and threes, their unconcerned chatter a jarring counterpoint.

"Well, strictly speaking, he agreed to it," she said, holding her ground. "And you can stop going all prickly at me. I didn't like it either, but he was determined that it was the best course of action."

The twins exchanged meaningful glances. Hetta was already very tired of this secret communication method.

"No, Wyn's not insane," Marius said, answering as if the twins had spoken. "He just places more value on Stariel and Hetta than on himself, which I know may be a foreign concept to the two of you. Maybe that's why ThousandSpire likes him better."

She appreciated the defence of Wyn, but was it a good idea to bait his siblings? There was a deep and vicious anger in Rakken that he was masking, but flashes of it came through now and then, and she didn't want to find out what would happen if the mask slipped completely.

"If our brother made himself so vulnerable at your mortal queen's request and she failed to protect him, she owes him a debt," Catsmere said flatly.

"I happen to agree," Hetta said, to Marius' disapproval. "Well, I do. That creature—the nightwyrm. You didn't see it, but it was huge. I have no idea how he killed it without any magic to call on, but he wouldn't have been half so vulnerable if the queen hadn't insisted he wear those cuffs."

"Because fae are all sweetness and light and should be trusted on general principle?" Marius said sarcastically. He had a point, but she didn't want to hear it right now. What did it *matter* what other fae were like, when they both knew Wyn was different?

"Well, I'm glad to hear you say so," Rakken drawled with a smirk.

Hetta rubbed her temples. "This isn't getting us anywhere. I take it if Wyn's still wearing the dismae, your tracking spell won't work?"

Catsmere frowned. "No. But there are other methods, Lord Valstar." She looked at her twin, who sighed.

"There are few lowfae in this city, and the nightwyrm will have frightened them badly," Rakken said. "I fear it may take some time for them to speak to me."

"Then we go hunting," Catsmere told her brother. "Beginning at the palace."

Rakken nodded, and the two of them began to walk off without regard for whether Hetta and Marius were following.

"Are they always like this?" Hetta grumbled to Marius as she trotted to catch up. They all had longer legs than her.

He wrinkled his nose. "Yes."

On the one hand, it was a relief to be taking action—any action—but on the other, Hetta had become accustomed to taking charge. She didn't appreciate the usurpation, particularly not after having to bow to Queen Matilda's wishes.

"I think even they think they're grasping at straws though," Marius added. "If they can't trace him because of the dismae, how are they going to pick up his magical signature? And Rake is still recovering from an injury and probably can't keep gallivanting around the city all day. So we'd better think of a back-up plan. What else did the queen say?" Rakken shot him a narrow-eyed look over his shoulder and Marius shrugged. "Yes, I know you can hear us."

The twins didn't look like they were grasping at straws; on the contrary, they moved with a supreme confidence that Hetta privately envied. But she trusted her brother's intuition. He'd always had an uncanny knack for understanding people, when he wasn't buried in his own thoughts, oblivious to the outside world. She told him about the queen demanding Wyn renounce his ties to Faerie, the newspaper articles, and the unconscious palace guards. Rakken and Catsmere were listening too, judging from the tense line of their shoulders that relaxed when they heard Wyn had refused to swear fealty to Queen Matilda.

Hetta didn't object to the twins using glamour to gain entrance to the palace; she didn't really have any high ground, since she'd used illusion in the same manner. She'd seen Wyn do this once before too, creating a kind of cocoon of invisibility about himself, wholly different from the ways illusion could fool the eye. At the thought, a cold lump formed in her throat.

The corpse of the nightwyrm had been removed from the kitchen, though the whole room still reeked of blood and spices, not yet disguised by the industrious cleaning that was currently underway. Rakken evicted the cleaning crew without compunction, informing them that they should take a break outside for a few minutes. Hetta watched uneasily as the maids cheerfully filed out the kitchen door, leaving a wake of buckets and mops.

"Was that really necessary? Wouldn't glamour have hidden us as effectively?" Marius objected.

Hetta made a vague sound of agreement. Obviously, she cared about the principle of the thing, but just now it was difficult not to care quite a lot more about finding Wyn as quickly as possible. Besides, had this specific use of compulsion done any harm? But she knew that was a dangerous way to start thinking; it felt like the same type of danger that came with having a land-sense that allowed one to know too much about people too easily, if one didn't resist the temptation.

Rakken ignored them both, feeling absolutely no sense of ethical quandary, and he and Catsmere prowled around the room like a pair of territorial tomcats.

Hugging her arms close, she stepped her way carefully into the centre of the room and managed to avoid accidentally brushing up against anything. It didn't stop the heavy feeling of contamination from the thick atmosphere, and her gaze fell on a dark, reddish stain on the wooden floor. *Bleeding like a stuck pig.* Her heart gave a painful lurch. "Could you tell if Wyn used magic here? In case he did manage to free himself from the dismae and there's some other reason your tracking spell didn't work?"

Rakken looked down his nose at her, as if she'd asked a child's question, and she glared back until he said icily: "Imagine the imprint of a feather falling on soft earth. And then imagine blood-letting and violent death as hammering that same earth with hailstones the size of fists."

"You could've just said 'no'." She hugged herself more tightly. "What about compulsion? Could you tell if it was used on the guards? *Without* compelling them?" She directed the question at Catsmere, who so far had seemed the slightly more sympathetic of the twins.

Catsmere weighed the question. "No. Not for something as simple as sleep, not with so many hours passed since it was done." She looked to her twin. "Mouse?"

He gave Hetta a very sardonic smile. "I was under the impression Lord Valstar wished for me to leave the palace guards alone."

Marius made an impatient sound. "Obviously this isn't the same thing. Do you want to play games, or do you want to find Wyn?"

Hetta stared at her brother, both surprised by and in firm agreement with his fierceness.

Rakken's eyes narrowed, the green of them flaring bright. But after a moment, he subtly inclined his head to Hetta. "Very well, Lord Valstar."

❦

OUTSIDE THE GUARDHOUSE, HETTA held a small internal battle between ethics and pragmatism. Before she could come down on one side or the other, a man emerged from the low, rectangular building who she recognised as one of the guards who'd been present at the green yesterday.

"Excuse me, sir," she said, stepping forward.

Rakken gave her an irritated glance, but the man heard her, so he must've released the glamour.

The man started. "Lord Valstar." He frowned, but his frown was all reserved for her; his gaze slid off the others like water. "What are you—"

Hetta interrupted quickly. "I'm here to interview the guards who were enchanted last night." She said it with as much confidence as she could muster and soldiered on before he could think to ask if her visit was authorised. "Please summon the relevant men." Maybe sheer bluffing would work.

He blinked uncertainly at her. The space between the buildings where they stood was quiet, but the muted rumble of men's voices could be heard through the windows. "Well, that would be me. And James—but it's his day off today. Does the captain know you're—"

"Relax," Rakken said, his tone smooth and irresistible as sunlight. "Trust us. What is your name?"

"William Chudleigh, sir." His expression went slack, his eyes oddly glassy. A chill went through her.

"And what do you remember of last night, outside the doors of the Treasury?"

William answered without hesitation. "Got assigned Treasury duty last-minute; it's a bugger, getting roped into an extra night shift without notice. Least it wasn't raining; nothing worse than a night shift in the rain," he added, his conversational tone unsettlingly at odds with his vacant expression. "I told James we must've pissed off the powers-that-be, to both pull double-shift."

"What is the last thing you remember before you fell asleep?"

He frowned in thought, his eyes still eerily unfocused. "It's a bit fuzzy," he said slowly. "I remember feeling pretty woolly all evening, and it getting harder and harder to keep my eyes open by the time it came midnight—and that must've been the prince's spell, because I've never fallen asleep on the job, extra shifts or not, I swear—and then I'm waking up in the barracks with a crick in my neck and it's bloody morning. They told me I'd kept sleeping like a babe even when they picked me up to cart me over from Treasury. James, too."

That didn't sound like the compulsion Hetta had seen Wyn use before—he'd told Gwendelfear to sleep and she'd just, well, *slept*. Instantly.

Rakken made an inquisitive sound in the back of his throat, like a cat coaxing a kitten. "Did you see the prince?"

William frowned. "No. Was surprised to hear he'd done it, actually. Seemed a decent chap. Guess you can never tell."

Rakken and Catsmere exchanged one of their secret communicatory looks.

"Thank you; you may go," Rakken told him.

Frowning, but still somewhat glassy-eyed, William stuttered back into motion. After taking half a dozen steps, he turned back, his frown deepening as he scanned the space outside the guardhouse without appearing to see them. He gave himself a shake, straightened his shoulders, and marched off.

Hetta couldn't exactly be angry with Rakken for compelling the man, since that was what she'd brought him here for—but it didn't stop guilt pricking at her. "Well?" she prompted him.

He shook his head, his expression grim. "That man wasn't compelled last night. Perhaps you should look closer to your own nest, Lord Valstar, for the cause of this. I assume there are mortal means of inducing sleep?"

Oh. *Oh.* "There are." Drugs and tonics and sedatives. Aunt Maude was fond of a 'soother' that led to her dozing on the sofa if no one chivvied her into her bed in time. But Hetta didn't need to know exactly what had been used to drug the guards to understand what it meant: this was a human act, not a fae one.

Her hands curled into fists. She'd march up to the queen and tell her that not only were her accusations against Wyn baseless but that *humans* had tried to set him up so how dare she treat him being fae so—vengefulness came to a screeching halt as several cold realisations hit her in quick succession.

Even if the queen accepted Rakken's word as proof—unlikely in and of itself—the way they'd obtained the information wouldn't please her, and she might very well try to imprison the twins once she knew what and who they were. Hetta went cold, imagining how Rakken and Catsmere would react to that.

And what if this whole mess was the queen's doing in the first place? Hetta had thought the queen's reaction genuine at the time, but then what else was politics but acting, really? They were her palace guards, after all. *Maybe I've been even more naïve than I thought.*

"Mortal politics," Catsmere said in disgust. "We have wasted enough time on this." She began to stalk away, and Rakken followed without comment.

Hetta stood frozen for a long moment, until Marius came up beside her and squeezed her arm. "Why did someone want us to think Wyn had enchanted the guards?"

"I don't know," she said. She thought furiously. Whoever had done this had also planted feathers. Someone was trying to blacken Wyn's name, and whoever it was knew something of his nature. The duke had sneered that they knew Wyn wasn't human in his other shape, and the words from *Lady Peregrine's Society News* came back to her: *Mr T…may not be all he appears to be.* Was there any connection there? It seemed a stretch, but at the same time it would be awfully unfair for there to be *two* persons out there with an anti-Wyn agenda.

She brooded over that as they trailed the twins around the palace in a bubble of glamour. Neither of them could pick up any trace of Wyn's trail, and they were all stiff with frustration by the time the pair finally gave up, spilling out onto the pavement into the darkness of the now-evening.

"Well, although I'm just as keen as anyone else to locate Wyn, I'm also now extremely hungry," she said prosaically. "So I vote in favour of dinner in the absence of any other good ideas."

DESPITE HER ANXIETY, THERE was something inherently amusing about watching the two royals' first encounter with a corner chippy. Neither of them said: *this is not what we are accustomed to*, but Hetta could almost hear them thinking it. She swapped looks with Marius, who grinned and kept placidly eating chips out of his twist of newspaper.

She probably could've taken them back to the hotel and fed them there, but she'd smelled the fried fish and been swamped by a wave of hungry nostalgia. The salt-and-vinegar taste was everything she remembered. *Besides, this saves us an awkward mealtime conversation with Aunt Sybil.*

"So what next?" Marius said, his mouth twitching as Catsmere inspected a piece of battered fish with all the suspicion of a child encountering a broccoli floret. "You can't find Wyn with your magic, and the queensguard clearly haven't found him either if they're still trying to follow us."

"Well, tomorrow I'm going to go and plague *Lady Peregrine's Society News* until they tell me who tipped them off about Wyn," Hetta said firmly.

"Playing politics, Lord Valstar?" Rakken asked, one eyebrow rising.

"If I have to."

"And you think this will help you find our brother?" Catsmere said doubtfully. She ate the piece of fish in small, delicate bites.

Hetta sighed. "I think it will help me figure out who has it in for him besides your sister, which may or may not help me find him. You're welcome to suggest any better ideas."

They were silent.

Marius crumpled up his grease-stained newspaper and frowned into the middle distance. "I'm going to the Law Library tomorrow, when it opens." He shrugged in answer to Hetta's questioning glance. "I haven't looked at the treaty between Stariel and the Crown in an age. If you're dealing with Queen Matilda, you ought to know exactly what's in it."

He was right, and a more conscientious lord would probably have thought to check Stariel's copy before she'd left her estate—but she hadn't realised it might be relevant. Swearing fealty to the Crown was supposed to be ceremonial only, after all, not an actual political decision. But nothing had gone according to plan since leaving Meridon. No—since before then, since the day at the Standing Stones when the Spires had reached for Wyn. She stared up at the sky, no stars visible against the murky darkness with all the light pollution. *Where are you, Wyn?*

29

BREAKFAST FLIRTATIONS

"T HEY'RE *HERE*?" ALEXANDRA'S voice went up in pitch, her eyes wide. "In our *hotel*?" She and Aunt Sybil had been waiting up in Hetta's suite when they returned. Hetta had arranged extra rooms for Rakken, Catsmere, and Marius with the hotelier, who hadn't blinked at the explanation of "My brother and his university friends."

"Well, not at this exact moment. They went out looking for Wyn again," Hetta said. Was it poor-spirited of her not to offer to accompany them? But it seemed pointless to wander the streets vaguely with no set direction—especially since Hetta was already tired from their earlier wanderings. "Though presumably they will return to sleep at some point, so you'll probably see them at breakfast."

Aunt Sybil glared. "You cannot mean for us to sit at table with them! Lor-Princ"—she stumbled over Rakken's title—"*he* hasn't even apologised for his deception last year!"

"We won't let them compel you, Alex," Marius said softly, ignoring his aunt to focus on his sister. "Though I don't think they'll try."

Oh. Obviously Alexandra would be nervous the next time she encountered greater fae—especially since it had been one of Wyn's siblings who'd compelled her last time. Rakken and Catsmere weren't like Aroset—but they weren't like Wyn either. And Hetta could hardly tell Alexandra she had nothing to fear from the twins when she'd spent the day witnessing their liberal use of compulsion on Meridon's unsuspecting citizenry. *I should have thought of Alexandra sooner.*

"Yes, I shall set fire to both of them if necessary, though I also don't think you've anything to fear from them." Rakken probably wouldn't bother to compel anyone at the breakfast table, but Hetta understood why Alexandra might not find that particularly reassuring. "But you don't have to see them if you'd rather not. You can eat breakfast in your room, or in here, if you like." She gestured around the sitting room.

Alexandra had wrapped her arms around herself very tightly, but she shook her head. "No. It's all right. You're right." She bit her lip and then blurted: "It's stupid, being so afraid."

"It's *not* stupid," Marius said firmly. He hugged Alexandra. "And you're not stupid either."

Hetta awkwardly patted Alexandra's shoulder as her sister took deep, shuddering breaths. Aunt Sybil hovered in the background like a disgruntled hen. Hetta felt the six long years of her absence sharply—despite these last few months, she still didn't have Marius's ease with their younger siblings. *And maybe I never will, if I keep putting fae before my own family's interests.* The thought sat uneasily on her conscience, coming as it did with the guilty addition: *if only Wyn wasn't fae.*

IN ANY EVENT, BREAKFAST turned out to be awkward in an entirely unanticipated direction. Hetta had forgotten that Rakken could be charming when he tried, and that he had fewer compunctions than Wyn. *Stop flirting with my aunt!* she nearly snapped from her end of the table. It was distressing to see Aunt Sybil's stone-faced demeanour melt into girlish fluster. *Honestly, the single one of my relatives I thought I could rely on to maintain a proper degree of caution!*

Catsmere ignored both her brother and Aunt Sybil and seemed to feel no particular need for small talk. As Alexandra was entirely occupied in counting the stitches along the edge of the table-cloth, and Marius was busy trying to vaporise Rakken by glaring at him over his teacup, there wasn't much conversation.

The hotel's dining room wasn't private, and they drew a fair degree of attention despite their relative silence. *Everyone's seen the papers*, Hetta thought glumly. The press hadn't quite figured out all the connections yet, but even the *Meridon Times*—by far the most respectable of Meridon's broadsheets—had run the headline: '*Fairy' Beast Attacks Palace!* They'd gone with '*eye-witness accounts describe a species of large, exotic snake*', but they'd also interviewed one of the members of Parliament who'd met Wyn, and he'd named '*Lord Henrietta Valstar of Stariel Estate*' as having '*some connection to a visiting ambassador*'.

Or maybe no one had recognised her and it was just Rakken and Catsmere drawing interest. Even in mortal form, they were both so very *other*. It gave her an idea.

"If we haven't found Wyn by tomorrow, will you two come with me to the Duchess of Callasham's soirée before Bradfield's play?" Surely they'd find him before then? But she was unhappily aware that if they didn't, she was running out of time. It was Friday today, which meant there was only the weekend between her and the queen's set date for her signing the oath of fealty on Monday, and she knew she wouldn't be able to put that off any longer than she already had. She wasn't about to march up to Queen Matilda and announce "I have allies! Ha!" to her face in case she decided to imprison them too, but that didn't mean she couldn't get the news to her in other ways. *So this is what playing politics means.* She felt horribly out of her depth. *This isn't just about me and Wyn, not anymore.* She knew she had to think rationally about Stariel's role in this new world where it wasn't a secret that the fae were real. But it would be significantly easier to be rational if Wyn hadn't been missing for two days now. Again, she pushed down the panic clawing up in her chest.

Marius lifted his head. "The Duchess of Callasham?" He frowned. "The duke's on the Northern Lords Conclave, isn't he?"

"Yes. Why?"

He coloured faintly. "I, er, overheard some of the students talking. His nephew, apparently, is at the university. They treated the news of fae as a joke, but the nephew did say his uncle had said the whole North was talking about it."

Hetta absorbed this. The duke had certainly seemed very set against Wyn. "Maybe he's the one who warned Her Majesty about Wyn in the first place. Well, that just gives me more reason to want to speak to him." She turned to the twins. "Will you come?"

Both fae approved of her plan, once she'd explained her reasoning, which made her fear it might actually be a *terrible* idea. But if it made Wyn safer, once they found him...her heart hardened.

Marius reached out and gripped her hand, as if he'd heard her thought. "We'll find him, Hetta." He gave her the ghost of a grin. "Even if we have to question all of Meridon and outrage Queen Matilda herself to do it."

The sound of a teaspoon being worried against a china plate came from Alexandra's end of the table. She was biting her lip. "Um," she said without raising her gaze from the tablecloth.

"Alex?" Hetta prompted gently.

"I will not eat you, Alexandra Valstar," Catsmere said,

straight-faced. "I do not eat children."

"Um, what about Gwendelfear?" Alexandra said. She lifted her head, eyes very blue and determined. "If she *is* here to watch you, maybe she saw where Wyn went?"

This comment required no small amount of explaining to the two fae.

"You are treating with DuskRose, Lord Valstar?" Catsmere asked with narrowed eyes.

"Well, I'm not at war with them, if that's what you mean," Hetta said. Honestly, 'treating'—was it *compulsory* for all fae to speak in the most old-fashioned manner possible? "But we're not exactly negotiating a treaty." Could Stariel even do that, by itself, or was that something *else* they would need Queen Matilda's permission for? Princess Sunnika had mentioned negotiations when she'd first come to Stariel. What would a treaty between a single estate and an entire fae kingdom even look like? *Maybe we agree to swap sheep for teleportation services on demand,* Hetta mused.

Catsmere and Rakken exchanged one of their silent communications.

"I do not trust the Court of Dusken Roses," Catsmere said grimly.

Rakken's mouth curled as he watched Hetta. "I believe Lord Valstar wishes to say that she doesn't trust *us*."

"I don't trust *either* of the courts, Your Highness. I'm treating you all with equal-opportunity suspicion."

Rakken canted his head, the gesture eerily similar to Wyn's. "Tell me, do you include my brother in this broad-brush distrust of fae? He isn't human, and he won't be, no matter how the two of you try to pretend."

"You can't be offended that Hetta doesn't trust the Spires. They did, after all, kidnap her last year," Marius said into the tense silence.

Aunt Sybil made a highly offended sound, and everyone ignored her.

"*I* was not involved in that," Rakken said.

"Yes, but you did think it was funny to poison Wyn," Hetta pointed out.

"A poison I made sure he had an antidote to." Rakken's eyes gleamed. "Tell me, Lord Valstar, does he still?" She scowled at him, refusing to answer, and he laughed, low and chocolate-rich. Even Aunt Sybil's outraged expression softened at the sound. "Oh, you make me suspect he *does*. What a poor-spirited beau, to leave you so unsatisfied."

The antidote to that poison had been the blood of a virgin. Which Hetta was *definitely* not discussing with Wyn's brother, ever, and particularly not at the breakfast table surrounded by the rest of her family.

Catsmere had grown impatient with their exchange. She stood, tall and imperial and oddly fashionable with her short, sleek haircut. "If this lesser fae is in the city and involved in our brother's disappearance, we will find her and she will pay," she promised. She raised a brow at Rakken, who shook his head.

"No—you hunt. I intend to see Stariel's treaty with their mortal queen."

Marius choked on a mouthful of tea.

Rakken smiled sardonically. "Yes, Marius Valstar. That *does* mean you get the pleasure of my company."

Hetta looked at her brother. "In that case, shall I—"

But Marius flushed and interrupted her before she could offer to accompany them. "I don't need a babysitter, Hetta, and he can't compel me. He's welcome to come and be as heartily bored as he likes." He coughed, still recovering from the tea, and hastily took a sip of water instead. The liquid seemed to steel him, and his grey eyes were determined when they met hers. "Go and talk to the newspaper."

"All right," she said. There wasn't really any other answer to give, now that Marius had stuck his stubborn feet in. She'd only hurt him if she implied he couldn't handle Rakken. At least he was immune to compulsion. And really, what was the worst that could happen, in a library? Still, she pinned both twins with her gaze. "But both of you remember this is a *human* city."

THE MERIDON TIMES

*L*ADY PEREGRINE'S SOCIETY *News'* street address turned out to be located at the offices of a much larger and more respectable newspaper, and Hetta narrowed her eyes as she took in the familiar logo, which she'd seen staring at her from every street corner for six years: the *Meridon Times*. Presumably *Lady Peregrine's* was a lucrative sideline for the larger press. Did Lady Peregrine even exist, or was the alias merely a convenient fiction? Hetta had always assumed the latter, though it tickled her to imagine the namesake as a real-life woman looming in corners (she bore a more-than-passing resemblance to Aunt Maude) and pursing her lips in delight as she caught morsels of scandal.

The entrance was bustling with paper boys and reporters going in and out through a revolving glass door. No one paid any attention to her, though she was fairly sure she had at least one queensguard watcher following her. There hadn't seemed much point trying to lose the tail; it wasn't as if the reason for her visit here would be any great mystery to anyone who'd read that magazine article.

She felt brittle, like an ice sheet shot through with spiderweb-thin cracks, and she'd reached for the ring so often in the last two days that it had become an unconscious tic, the warm metal pressing against her breastbone beneath her dress. Stariel reflected back an echo of her worry. *Wyn's alive. There's no reason to think otherwise,* she told herself sternly. *Rakken and Catsmere would know somehow if he wasn't.*

She took a deep breath and marched up the steps. She *would* wring the name of Lady Peregrine's source from them, and hopefully it would tell her where to go next. *Where to find Wyn.* Gods, she missed him. For a moment, the ice creaked, but she couldn't—wouldn't—fall apart now.

She suffered a check at the reception desk in the form of a steely-eyed receptionist who informed Hetta in clipped tones that the editor of *Lady Peregrine's* was not available.

"Well, when *will* they be available?"

The receptionist looked down her nose at Hetta, a tactic she was used to, since the Valstar nose was also very good for looking down, and many of her relatives frequently used it for this purpose. "For what purpose do you want an appointment, Miss...?"

"It's Lord, actually. Lord Valstar. *Lady Peregrine's Society News* made some petty aspersions about my staff recently and threatened to make more in their next issue, which I rather object to." The receptionist's eyes widened slightly at Hetta's name. "Yes, I see you remember the article. I'd like to speak to whoever is responsible for that."

The receptionist told Hetta to wait. After that, there were a lot of conversations in hushed whispers and people hurrying off, hopefully to tell someone higher up in the organisation that there was an unhappy lord sitting in their reception and they'd dashed well better *become* available. Maybe she shouldn't have charged into things quite so bluntly, but she was sick of all this shadow boxing. And why shouldn't the magazine know what she thought of them? *She* was the wronged party here!

Eventually, Hetta was shown into the office of a gaunt middle-aged man wreathed in smiles, who introduced himself as Mr Walter.

"Please sit, Lord Valstar." He waved at a chair across from his desk. "My apologies for the quality of the accommodations. We're not used to entertaining."

He had no idea what kind of life she'd led before her lordship, she realised. *And no idea that old and venerable though Stariel House might be, it's hardly luxurious.* "Are you Lady Peregrine?" she asked.

The man twinkled at her. "Ah, her ladyship doesn't take interviews, but you can trust that she hears all from us mere underlings. What can I do for you, my lord?" He had bright eyes, like a magpie, ready to swoop down on any gleam of information. A frisson of unease went through her. She must be careful not to tell this man anything he didn't already know, or no doubt it would make an appearance in tomorrow's *Times*.

"I want to know what information you based your article on."

Mr Walter chuckled. "Now, now, Lord Valstar, a newspaperman never reveals his sources."

"So you claim to have a source, then, rather than fabricating a story from hearsay?"

Mr Walter bristled. "*Lady Peregrine's* may not be the *Times*, my lady, but we do not print hearsay."

"The correct address is 'my lord'," Hetta said coolly. It was a common error for Southerners. "But if you were so sure of your sources, why was that article so anxious to avoid naming me or my steward? To me, that implies you were worried about a defamation case."

"Now, that's a—"

"And correct me if I'm wrong, but an article could only be considered defamatory if the claims it makes aren't true."

Irritation crossed Mr Walter's face, quickly papered over with insincere concern. "I can understand your feelings, Lord Valstar. Would you like to make a statement, correct the public misconception, as it were?" He picked up a pen and folded open a notebook. "Your steward, for instance. Is it true that he's related to Lord Featherstone?"

Hetta burst out laughing. "No, he's not," she said, deciding there was no harm in that snippet and probably quite a lot of good. Goodness knows what the real Lord Featherstone would make of that rumour if it reached his ears, but it probably wouldn't move him to support her on the Northern Lords Conclave. "But I'm not going to give you an interview. I just want to know who your source is." She watched him carefully for a reaction. "Did they write to you?"

"Alas, I am obliged to keep their identity anonymous."

"Can you tell me if it's a man or a woman, at least?" That might narrow it down a little.

"Perhaps we could trade information." His eyes narrowed in sudden calculation. "What do you know of the incident at the palace yesterday?"

Hetta eyed the man with dislike, though she supposed he was only doing his job. "Will you give me the name of your source if I tell you?" It was probably only a matter of time before the story of the nightwyrm came out. Maybe it would be better for a factually correct account to be published instead of the mishmash of nonsense she'd so far seen.

Mr Walter looked torn, but eventually shook his head. "The anonymity of our sources is sacrosanct."

Hetta could see he meant it. She tried another tack. "What if I tell you in exchange for you promising not to run another article?" She felt very fae, all of a sudden, bartering favours. She gestured vaguely in the direction of the palace. "Since I don't believe you can top *that* for newsworthiness." The bank attack in Alverness by a swarm of lowfae had nothing on the nightwyrm.

He smiled, a narrow smile full of sudden delight. "Oh, you don't think so, Lord Valstar? You don't think Meridon or the queen will care about you endorsing fae attacks on Prydein's citizenry?"

"*What?*"

Mr Walter shrugged. "Our source suggests that you are under an enchantment and that you're not responsible for your actions." He paused. "But you don't *seem* to be enchanted, do you?"

The word triggered a memory of Lord Angus glaring at Wyn: "*What enchantments have you cast over Hetta?*"

She dug her nails into her palms. Oh, if Angus was responsible for this, she'd burn Penharrow Estate to the ground.

HETTA LEFT THE INTERVIEW in a fury that faltered at the sight of Catsmere waiting by the receptionist's desk. The fae woman had to be doing something with glamour to make people's gazes slide around her, because she was making absolutely no attempt to blend in. She didn't have her wings out, but that was the only concession she'd made to being in a mortal city. Otherwise, she was dressed in—well, Hetta would've called it 'men's clothing' except it was clearly designed for Catsmere, and she didn't look at all male in it. She looked dangerous, comfortable, and expensive—*not a combination I would've thought possible, before now.* It made Hetta eye the outfit speculatively and reflect that the introduction of fae fashions into the Mortal Realm might be one of the few unambiguous benefits to come out of the Iron Law's revocation.

"Lord Valstar," Catsmere greeted. The receptionist didn't appear to hear or notice her. She watched Hetta walk over to Catsmere but abruptly lost interest as soon as soon as she got within three feet of the fae. *Glamour.*

Exhausted of politeness, she simply asked: "Why are you here? Did you find Gwendelfear?"

Catsmere shook her head. "I did not."

"Do you know if she's still in the city? Is there some way you can tell?" It seemed unfair for everyone's quests this morning to fail to bear fruit.

"I do not know. Faerie is thin and weak here." Something of Hetta's frustration clearly showed, for Catsmere added, "Mouse has made contact with the local wyldfae; if the lesser fae is here, we will get word of it, sooner or later."

"Oh," she said vaguely. 'Sooner or later' didn't feel very reassuring, and the receptionist's continued inattention prickled against her neck. Abruptly, she couldn't bear to just keep standing here and ignoring her presence. "Well, I'm going back to the hotel to call my cousin," she said, moving away from Catsmere. She mightn't be able to put her own hands round Angus's throat, but Jack would make a fair proxy in the meantime.

Catsmere canted her head. "May I accompany you?"

Hetta paused mid-step, curious despite herself. "Is this why you followed me here after you failed to find Gwendelfear? To talk to me alone?"

"Yes," Catsmere agreed easily. Her frankness was oddly refreshing.

"Well, I was planning to cut across Crown Park to the main road to catch a hackney, but you're welcome to talk to me as I do." She gestured for the fae to go before her through the revolving door. Catsmere's expression narrowed, and she drew herself up to her not-inconsiderable height, much like a cat bristling, as if about to forcefully refuse the direction, but then she smoothed out again and led the way out into the morning without comment.

Was there some kind of royal protocol for exiting buildings?

Hetta wondered, bemused by the whole interaction. *Or perhaps she just doesn't like having people at her back.* The Spires seemed like the kind of violent place that would encourage that degree of mistrust. Her bemusement changed to something heavier.

Catsmere was silent as they made their way out of the newspaper's stableyard and onto the public street. The morning was bright and hopeful, though there was a wet hint in the air that promised rain later. Hetta almost reached for Stariel for more information on the weather before remembering there was no point.

Catsmere reminded her strongly of a guard dog, constantly scanning her surroundings, alert but not alarmed as they crossed the street towards the park. "Will you try to make my brother choose you over the Spires?" she asked, as if this was the kind of question you could just *ask* a person with no warning.

Hetta bristled. "I'm not going to *make* Wyn do anything. But you have to know he doesn't *want* to go back to the Spires." She clung to that certainty. Wyn wanted to stay with her, and Stariel, and why shouldn't both of them get what they wanted in this instance? The oaths she'd made when she became lord were to think of Stariel's interests, not ThousandSpire's. The other faeland could just find someone else to bond to.

"And is he happy here, playing human?" Catsmere sounded genuinely curious.

"If this is some attempt to persuade me to give him up—" she began suspiciously, but Catsmere waved a dismissive hand.

"We have agreed it is Mouse's job to do the persuading—or the sweet-talking, should such be required," she said with absolute seriousness.

Hetta raised an eyebrow. "Is that what you call his flirting with my aunt this morning?"

Catsmere shrugged. "Flirtation is a form of persuasion, Lord Valstar. I would not attempt it with either you or your aunt, but then I have no taste for mortals. You are all so very...fragile. Mouse is less discerning, and he has little compunctions about employing whatever methods he deems appropriate."

Hetta stumbled on the gravel path, not quite sure she'd understood that correctly. She gave the fae woman a sidelong glance, trying to judge.

A slight smile curled on Catsmere's lips. "Don't encourage Mouse, unless you wish to pursue that kind of intimacy from him." She wrinkled her nose. "Which I would rather not hear about, if that *is* the case."

So she *had* understood correctly. Her cheeks felt hot. Could this truly be an acceptable topic of conversation in Faerie? "Thank you, but I don't wish to encourage anything from anyone except Wyn," she said firmly, trying to get her expression under control. She'd be dashed if she'd let Catsmere discompose her here in *her* city. "Is this Rake's cunning plan then? Attempt to seduce me so I forget Wyn and don't try to stop him going to the Spires?" It didn't sound any less laughable said out loud.

"Oh, no, Lord Valstar," Catsmere said blandly. "You've misunderstood me. I think Mouse is, on the contrary, interested in the potential advantages to be had for the Spires from a relationship between you and little Hollow, and I don't think he wishes to sever that tie. I was merely giving you warning that he will take his lead from you in this."

Hetta stopped in the middle of the footpath, not sure whether she wanted to laugh or set fire to the fae princess. "You're trying to test how loyal I am to Wyn?!" she accused. "Using Rake as bait!"

Catsmere blinked down at her. "Obviously."

"No, that *wasn't* obvious, thank you very much! *Obviously* I'm not going to swap Wyn for the nearest pretty face! *Obviously* if he meant so little to me, I wouldn't be here! And *even more obviously*, if I did choose to stray—which I have no intention of doing, just to be excruciatingly clear—it certainly wouldn't be with Rake!"

"You do look at him a lot." Catsmere's eyes were wide and guileless, an eerie match for Wyn's expression when he was being deliberately provoking, and Hetta knew in that moment that she was being teased. It didn't make her any less irritated.

"That doesn't mean I like him! It just means I have eyes! And I *love* Wyn!" The word came out as half a shout, but it clanged even louder in her chest. She hadn't said it nearly enough to Wyn to be saying it to everyone else in his absence. She glared at Catsmere and began to walk again, anger in every step. *Honestly.* The woman fell in beside her without comment, and they strode past several sets of less-energetic pedestrians. The branches of the park's trees were still largely bare, but little bursts of vividly green new growth were scattered here and there, almost a match for the colour of Catsmere's eyes.

"Why are you telling me your—or Rake's—nefarious plan, anyway? Isn't the whole point of a nefarious plan that it's also secret?" Hetta asked, when the heat of her anger had ebbed a bit.

"Have I told you anything you didn't already suspect, Lord Valstar?" Still with that same bland expression, she added: "I thought I would save us all some time."

Hetta glared at her. "And if you're not trying to persuade me to give Wyn up, then why are you insinuating that he'd be happier in the Spires? That seems unlikely. He's never described his time there using anything even approaching the word 'happy'." And he still carried the scars of his upbringing, the tendency to flatten down any emotions he thought he ought not to have, the habit of freezing and assessing rather than simply reacting.

Catsmere sighed. "Yes. Our father was unpleasant, even more so after our mother left."

She desperately wanted to ask about Wyn's mother, but equally she didn't want Catsmere to know her ignorance. It was the sort of thing you ought to already have talked about with the man you were trying to marry, wasn't it? But what did she care what Catsmere thought of her? She took a deep breath. "What happened to your mother?"

"He never told you?" There was no judgement in Catsmere's tone, but Hetta felt it nonetheless. "We don't know." Catsmere examined the branches of a cherry tree overhanging the footpath. It was more optimistic than its brethren, buds of pale pink already forming despite the earliness of the season. "Mouse thinks she's probably dead, that perhaps Father killed her and hid it from us," she added conversationally. "He may be right. Little Hollow has always believed in a more optimistic outcome. Her departure affected him badly. He is, after all, the youngest."

Hetta stumbled again. "I'm sorry," she whispered.

Catsmere looked down at her. "I believe you are." She sounded surprised. "Thank you."

Hetta shook her head. "And yet you're trying to convince me Wyn would be better off there than here?" She'd known there was probably some tragic story attached to Wyn's mother, but she hadn't imagined anything like this. The calm way Catsmere had announced that it was perfectly possible their father had murdered their mother sent chills through her.

"I am not trying to convince you of that, Lord Valstar."

"What do you want then? Do you want Wyn to be King of Ten Thousand Spires?"

Catsmere laughed. The sound was silvery, but with none of her brother's sensuality.

"This isn't about what I want, Lord Valstar. This is about blood and duty. We are royal stormdancers, bound to the Court of Ten Thousand Spires as your family is bound to FallingStar. We owe a duty to our land and its people." Her expression grew bleak, and she surveyed the park as if seeing a different landscape, one made of soaring rock towers. "There are many there who will suffer under my older sister's rule. She is powerful enough, perhaps, to hold it, and she has modelled herself on our father, but she lacks his self-control."

Something about the phrasing puzzled Hetta. "Wait—you think your father was a good ruler?"

"He held the Spires against the might of DuskRose for generations," Catsmere pointed out. "We were one of the largest and most influential courts under his rule. He built what is now our greatest city, Aerest, from nothing."

"And the fact that he was a sadistic tyrant who imprisoned me and tried to kill Wyn?" Perhaps she ought to feel bad about King Aeros's death, since he *was* Wyn's father, but she didn't. The world was well rid of him, in her opinion.

"I do not agree with all of his choices. This does not make him a bad ruler. There are realms in Faerie that have seen worse. If Set succeeds in her goals, I fear she may be one such."

"Why does it have to be Wyn though? Wouldn't one of you rather rule the Spires? Don't you have other siblings?" All right, none of Wyn's siblings had so far struck her as being particularly virtuous, even if they weren't as actively murderous as Aroset, but on the other hand, virtue wasn't exactly a requirement for rulership in the human world either. Guilt wound its way around her insides, and she ignored it. Why should who ruled ThousandSpire be her or Wyn's responsibility? She had *enough* responsibilities as it was.

Something in Catsmere hardened. "There is no one else, now." Her anger was a colder thing that Rakken's, the merest hint of ice in the depths of that blindingly green gaze. "It is not for me to argue with the choices of faelands. If the Spires favours little Hollow, then that is who I will pledge my allegiance to."

"Then why are you asking about Wyn's happiness, if it doesn't weigh into your calculations at all?"

Catsmere stared into the middle distance as they cut their way across Crown Park. "Why indeed?"

31

BLOOD AND IRON

THE FIRST FEW times Wyn woke, his magic instinctively flared out in panic at full strength, hit the dismae, and shocked him back into unconsciousness. The defensive response to pain was designed to keep him safe, so he could protect himself even in sleep. Now, it caught him in an endless loop each time he grew awake enough to feel but not quite awake enough to suppress his instincts before activating the cuff's recoil. He became a leaf in a gale, letting the pain and magic flow and ebb, dragging him where it would. This reaction, too, was one bred in the bone rather than a conscious choice, a way to survive when the world had narrowed to nothing but terrible sensation.

Awareness came and went, sound and smell and touch. The air tasted gritty. He was cold and that was strange; stormdancers were resistant to cold. It meant... But he faded out again before he could finish the thought.

At one point he opened his eyes and met the glowing green gaze of a catshee, the colour reminding him of his sister Catsmere's eyes. The wyldfae gave him a very unimpressed look, as if he were a kitten that had gotten itself stuck in a too-tall tree. <Birds shouldn't fly underground, storm prince.>

He should say something, he knew, but the catshee slunk away before he could find his voice. He swam back to consciousness inch by inch. It was cold and dark, he was lying on something hard, and he felt like he'd been split in two. Was he in his father's dungeons? He'd been sent there only once, briefly—but that had been enough for him to vow he'd never, ever make the mistake of angering King Aeros again. How had he slipped up?

But my father is dead. I helped kill him.

The thought startled him enough that he only just managed to avoid shocking himself again. *I will be very adept at controlling my magic the longer these dismae stay on.* He should point this benefit out to Hetta; it would make her laugh, though it wouldn't entirely defuse her anger at him for letting himself be cuffed in the first place.

Hetta. Another layer of memory peeled back. *Hetta.* How could he have forgotten her? He could see her so clearly in his mind's eye, the way a faint crease formed between her brows when she was thinking, the line of her nose, the storm's grey of her eyes. Where was Hetta? Was she safe? Why was he lying here when he didn't know that very important fact?

I am lying on my wings, he realised with a jolt. It was an unnatural position for a stormdancer. They protested when he tried to move, cramped and heavy, and for a single, terrified moment he feared they were broken. *I can't be earthbound again. Not if another wyrm comes.* For a moment, his magic threatened to surge again, but he grit his teeth and held it back, mainly because he *wasn't* broken. The discomfort was merely chains, weighing his wings down and preventing him from unfurling them.

They're not broken; I'm not broken. The flash of terror dispelled the last of his dizziness, and he finally managed to haul himself awake. For long moments he lay panting. Little aftershocks crawled over his skin and eventually faded. He sat up, the movement taking an embarrassing amount of effort. Every muscle protested but—thank the high wind's eddies—none of them actually refused to work. His chest burned in a long line from his hip across to the opposite shoulder, and his shirt was crusted with dried blood. Was he still bleeding? He touched it, gingerly, and brought away fingers spotted with fresh blood. At least it appeared to be oozing now rather than gushing. He wrinkled his nose, deciding it might be better not to try to unstick his shirt in case that made it worse. *Damn these dismae.* They were slowing his healing. How long had he been here?

He stared down at the dismae on each forearm. *How ironic, that they should be more effective on greater fae than on the lower ranks of Faerie, since they turn our power against us.* The markings on them were blackened around the edges, almost singed, as if his unintended battering at them had taken a toll on the spellwork. *Well, if Princess Evangeline's hair doesn't free me, I suppose there's always the option of sheer magical persistence.* That would have to be a last resort, since there was a high chance his own strength would give out before the ancient spellwork. He reached for the little packet of hair in his pocket and realised in that moment that he'd acquired extra restraints: someone had placed iron manacles above the dismae, binding his hands together with about a foot of free movement between them.

His temper snapped. It had been a very trying day.

"Oh, Maelstrom take it!" He shook his manacled arms in frustration. It didn't achieve anything except a loud, metallic rattle that filled the space. Leaning back against the wall, wings cramping, he tried to sort through the muddle. Instinctively, he went to look at the world with his leysight and hissed in discomfort as the dismae reminded him of his constraints. He closed his eyes, breathing in and out in time to his heartbeat before opening them again.

Where was he and how had he gotten here? The room was dark, with no windows or furniture, and a layer of grime covered every surface. The hard metal floor hummed under him, bringing with it a faint rattling noise that swelled and then subsided, along with the vibration.

He remembered the nightwyrm with a shudder, and his decision to flee before the guards shot him out of sheer fright. He hadn't wanted to go to Hetta, not until he knew what else Aroset might have sent, but his wing-beats had grown sluggish, his vision darkening at the edges. *I landed on a rooftop to think, and—ah.* That was when the world had gone dark. He examined his blood-stained fingers. *Well, I suppose that explains why. Blood loss.* That was a new one. He didn't think he'd ever fainted from blood loss before. *The nightwyrm hurt me worse than I realised.* That was the problem with their diamond claws—the blow had cut too sharp and too deep. Had anyone at the palace been hurt? There had been those unconscious guards outside, safe at least from the wyrm if not from whoever had been responsible for their state. What of the palace staff? Thank the high winds the attack had been after midnight, when most were asleep—it was all a blur, but he could not recall that he'd led the wyrm into sleeping quarters, at least. *Please let no one else have been hurt.*

Before he could sift through any more of his jumbled thoughts, light flooded the room, and his brother Irokoi was standing before him without so much as a ripple in the fabric of reality. Nor the use of any doors. Wyn reached for his magic, but the dismae clamped down on him, hard. He winced, and tried and failed to get to his feet. His limbs felt weak as jelly.

"Brother!" Irokoi said, his face splitting into a smile. His silver hair was unbound, parting softly around his dark horns, and his black wings flared out a fraction in excitement.

"Koi," Wyn said. "How are you here? Where are we? *What is going on?*" Had *Irokoi* brought him here?

"No, this is definitely not the time for family arguments," Irokoi scolded himself with a frown. He looked momentarily blank and then beamed at Wyn again, the sudden change jarring. "That was the right name! Well done."

Of course—that must be how Aroset's nightwyrm had found Wyn, through the trace of his true name.

Irokoi canted his head as he examined Wyn's wings. His pale hair fell away from his face to reveal his mismatched eyes: one gold, one a fractured arctic blue where Aroset had blinded him.

"They'll say we resemble each other now that Father is no longer there to compare us to," Irokoi remarked. All King Aeros's children had inherited something of his looks, but in Wyn and Irokoi the resemblance was strongest, though neither now had his wing colouration—King Aeros's bloodfeathers had been silver and crimson. "They are very pretty, you know. I am nearly jealous." He fanned out ink-dark feathers. "But mine are good for sneaking, don't you think? You sparkle a little too much for such things."

Wyn bit back impatience and tried again. Prising information out of Irokoi had something in common with herding catshee. "Koi, where are we? Is Set looking for us? Is she Queen of the Spires?"

Irokoi frowned at him for a few seconds. "She's very childish, isn't she?" He sighed. "She never liked me much." Sadness edged into his expression. "I'm not here. That's why I'm here. Am I making any sense?"

"Not a lot, no." Wyn held up his manacles. "Will you help me remove these?"

Irokoi shook his head. "They're not important. *I'm* important. I need *your* help. And you need mine, if you truly wish to take those vows." He pursed his lips thoughtfully. "Bring the other one, if you can."

"Koi—" Wyn said, even more lost than usual in the conversation. "What do you mean you need my help?"

"I'm stuck," he said, expression falling comically. "So stupid, I know, at my age, but there it is." Whimsy danced across his face, and his eyes brightened. "But I do have *some* advice to offer, for the time being." His tone grew sly. "If you want to ensure you can't be torn from FallingStar, you need to put down deeper roots—and I don't mean that entirely metaphorically." He paused, feathers rustling thoughtfully. "Tell Cat I looked, but there isn't another way. Sleep is not death."

And then he was gone.

Wyn gaped at the space he'd left behind. There hadn't been a portal, and when Wyn shuffled closer to inspect the ground, pulling to end of his chain, there was no sign of footprints, even if Irokoi was capable of teleporting, which he wasn't—at least to Wyn's knowledge. He sagged back down against the wall with a groan of disbelief, the chains clanking in grating counterpoint. His brother had spoken truly: he *hadn't* been here, not really.

But astral projection wasn't a stormdancer talent. Was it? How else had Irokoi done such a thing? And why had he thought it necessary to deliver such irritatingly cryptic advice instead of, say, helping Wyn escape?

The effort of moving had cost him, pain pounding him with every heartbeat, his cramped wings a dull background ache. His thoughts moved sluggishly. If Koi had come to him, that meant he wasn't with Wyn's other siblings. Didn't it? Which meant the others were... somewhere. Not here, certainly, which was... darkness, cool and quiet and so tempting to slip under and... *Focus!* He couldn't be unconscious when whoever had dragged him here and put these manacles on him returned. But his thoughts unravelled like streamers of fog, giving way beneath the pain and exhaustion battering at him. Consciousness was clearly a losing battle.

He gritted his teeth and Changed. His mortal form juddered into place, and the world grew darker but a little less disorienting, since at least in this form he was accustomed to dampened senses. Normally this form would slow his healing, but since the dismae were already doing such an excellent job of that, at least this might prevent him being stuck in the psychic pain loop again.

And at least this way I cannot cramp my wings, was his last thought before he surrendered and darkness towed him under once again.

32

THE LAW LIBRARY

LIBRARIES USUALLY SOOTHED Marius, but the imposing dome of the Law Library didn't have the usual effect. Instead, the sight made his stomach tie itself in knots. It wasn't just Rakken's unsettling presence next to him. *Though let's be honest, that's definitely not helping.* It was the knowledge that this was the *Law* Library, i.e. plausibly contained law *students*, and it would be just his luck to encounter the one law student in all of Meridon he most wanted to avoid. Except a part of him hoped desperately he *would* see John, just so he could finally say all the things that had been burning in him over the intervening months, like *I should've been the one who ended it, not you* and *I don't love you anymore.* Which was a completely stupid hope, because it wasn't like he could say any of those things in a public forum, even if John gave him the chance and the words didn't dry up in his mouth.

"I appreciate that the building has an impressive facade, but do you intend to admire it for much longer?" Rakken said dryly. "Or were you attempting to imitate the architecture?"

Marius jerked out of his thoughts. "This way," he mumbled,

marching into the building.

The Law Library was built around a soaring stone foyer that spanned the full height of its three floors, circled by an open staircase. High, narrow clerestory windows let in sharp shafts of light, and intricate stone owls nested amidst the elaborate architecture; the animal most closely associated with Eracene, the Goddess of Justice.

There was a reasonable amount of traffic in and out of the library, and the high foyer echoed with the sharp clicking of various footwear crossing its polished floors. No one gave Marius a second glance; he looked like he belonged here. It was almost certainly his spectacles.

People's disinterest didn't extend to his companion; their gazes caught on Rakken, and they'd blink as if they weren't quite sure they were seeing correctly. *Maybe the effect is magnified after you've spent hours buried under legal records.* And there was undeniably an effect. One older woman nearly dropped a stack of files when she came hurrying out of a nearby doorway and encountered them, and only Rakken's quick reflexes saved them. She stammered her thanks, but Rakken merely smiled and walked on without giving her the opportunity to start a conversation. She looked after him forlornly. Rakken was either oblivious to or uncaring of people's reactions as they walked up the winding stairs to the special requests desk on the second floor. Probably uncaring. What would it be like to be so inured to admiration that it didn't even register?

It was something of a relief to know that Rakken's magnetism wasn't Marius-specific—though it would be even better if Rakken didn't exude *any* magnetism at all. Was it glamour? Marius wasn't immune to that, though sometimes he could tell it was being used, like a procession of spiders scrambling over his scalp, but there was no such feeling now. Of course there wasn't. That would be much too convenient, being able to blame this unwanted attraction on magic rather than his abysmal taste in men.

Gods above, how could he be worrying about such petty anxieties when Wyn was still missing? He remembered Hetta's expression when she'd held that feather, distress and longing all rolled up together. Wyn *had* to be all right. The alternative was unthinkable. His heart squeezed tight.

Wait, Rakken had said something and he'd missed it, too wrapped up in his own thoughts.

"Sorry?" he said when Rakken stared down his nose at him, intent as a panther. "I didn't hear what you said."

Rakken considered him for a moment. "And what is it, little scholar, that so preoccupies you?"

Little scholar, he huffed internally. He was skinny, certainly, but it still wasn't a reasonable label. "Ah—your brother. Wyn," he added stupidly, as if Rakken somehow didn't know his own brother's name. "Sorry. I was wondering if he was all right." Rakken made a noncommittal noise, and Marius rolled his eyes and made his way past him. "The special requests desk is up here." He'd visited the Law Library before, on one of his trips to see Hetta in Meridon, but that had only been to the public areas. They'd have to request access to the undercroft to view the old legal documents.

Hetta had been different, then, and not just because she'd been younger. Marius tried to pinpoint exactly what he meant by that, and was so caught up in doing so that he failed to pay adequate attention to where he was going.

Smack! He collided with a blond man descending the stairs. The scent of familiar cologne punched straight to his gut, and recognition rose up in a wave of longing and despair even before he looked up and met the blue eyes that had haunted his dreams for so many months. *John.* It seemed so completely unfair of the universe to arrange this meeting that for a moment he couldn't do anything more than stare in disbelief as another, less-frozen part of him drank in every detail of John's appearance, looking for—he didn't know. Guilt? Absolution? But John looked exactly the same as always, still achingly handsome, lithe and smooth-cheeked, and a flurry of images assaulted Marius—that same face, relaxed in sleep, the heavy-lidded way John would look at him, teasing, when—

John's eyes widened as he recovered from his own shock, and then such a look of open contempt came over him that Marius couldn't move or speak, stunned into paralysis by the force of it. The words John had hurled during that horrible final argument rang in his ears, his head starting to pound as if they were hammer blows against it. Heat flooded his cheeks, and he wanted to sink into the staircase and melt straight down through it into the centre of the earth.

He felt the sudden weight of an arm across his shoulders, and Rakken spoke, coolly arrogant, before Marius could process the strange intimacy of his nearness. "You are blocking the stairwell," he said to John with casual arrogance. "Move, or I shall move you."

John's expression shifted to disbelief, and Marius read his thoughts as easily as if he'd spoken them aloud: *He's not—he can't be with Marius.* If Marius hadn't been glued in place, he might've laughed at the sheer, mind-numbing pettiness of that.

"I do not like to repeat myself." Menace in his tone, a hint of storms in the air. Horrified recognition flashed across John's face, and he went white.

Marius jerked back into motion, shrugging out from under Rakken's arm. "John—"

But John was already gone, fleeing down the stairs in real terror, boots sharp against the stone.

Marius whirled on Rakken. "What did you do?"

Rakken looked surprised. "Nothing magical."

Marius stared down the empty stairwell, unwilling guilt curling around him. He didn't want to feel sorry for John, but the way he'd reacted... He must've realised what Rakken was, from his resemblance to Wyn, and thought he was about to be compelled again. *I shouldn't have to feel guilty about that!* John was the one who'd blackmailed *him*, after all, and a bitter, angry part of him was *glad*

Rakken had terrified him. But oh gods, the way John had looked at Marius at first, with such contempt...

Rakken made a thoughtful sound, and Marius braced himself for an interrogation, adding panic to his already turbulent emotions. But Rakken's expression was uncharacteristically gentle.

"Shall we go retrieve your charter?" Without waiting for an answer, he turned and continued up the stairs. After a moment, Marius swallowed and went after him. What else could he do, really? He felt peculiarly off-balance and faintly nauseous, as if someone had given him several shots of strong whiskey on an empty stomach.

The librarian was a middle-aged man with iron-shot hair and a forbidding expression. The forbidding expression turned out to be an omen, for the man wasn't at all amenable to Marius's request for access to the old charters, and specifically, to the treaty signed between Marius's ancestor and the then-monarch of the rest of Prydein.

"I'm not going to hurt it!" Marius said, exasperated. "I know how to handle old artefacts. And as for needing permission to view it, we've our own copy in the Stariel library. You're not protecting state secrets."

The librarian puffed up, and Marius knew he was going to tell them to leave, but Rakken's smooth voice interrupted.

"Take us to see this charter. You should not be worried we will damage it; see how trustworthy we appear."

All the hairs on Marius' neck rose. Compulsion. Horror twisted in his stomach, a live thing made of jagged edges. This was what John had feared.

The librarian's face went blank, and he nodded and reached behind the desk to retrieve a set of keys. Should Marius do something to snap him out of it? *Could* you snap people out of compulsion without specific anti-fae materials? Why hadn't he brought some of his experimental mixtures with him from Knoxbridge so he could at least try? What would happen if he shouted at the man or slapped him? But he did none of these things as the librarian made his way out from behind his desk and led them down a locked staircase into the library's understoreys, and he hated himself a little bit for it.

The temperature dropped a little as they descended in the steady glow of the lightspells. The room the librarian showed them into was below ground level, with a reading area in the centre of the room and walls lined floor-to-ceiling with shelves and shallow drawers, each labelled with a series of numbers.

"The Northern treaties?" Rakken suggested to the man, though he looked at Marius for further guidance. *Oh no,* Marius thought grimly. He might not have done anything to stop it, but he wasn't going to *help* Rakken carry out this crime.

The librarian went muttering along the rows and began opening drawers.

"Are these originals?" Marius couldn't help asking. There was a faint vanilla-y smell to the room, the comforting whiff of old paper.

"Some of them," the librarian answered, absently, pulling on a thin pair of gloves from a box next to the door. "Some are copies of older documents too fragile for handling. Those are stored elsewhere. We periodically audit the files and copy them when necessary. Ah, yes." He returned and laid a brown leather-bound book on the reading table. "This is the charter that was signed between the Crown and the Conclave of Northern Lords," he said reverently. The charter marked the official beginning of one united Prydein between North and South. "And this is the additional treaty between Stariel and the Crown."

"What do you mean, additional?" Marius asked. Stariel had its own copy of the charter, but he didn't remember any additional documentation.

The librarian shrugged. "Northern legalities are not my area of speciality. I am merely showing you what you asked for." He frowned, and for a moment it looked like the compulsion was fading, but that cold sensation came again, and the librarian's expression softened with it.

"You may leave us here," Rakken told him.

"Remember to use the gloves," the librarian said sternly. "The oil from fingertips can be very damaging to old documents."

"We'll remember," Marius promised him. "Won't we, Mouse?"

Rakken's eyes narrowed in irritation, but to Marius's surprise he agreed. "Yes. We will remember the gloves."

The librarian nodded unconcernedly and left.

"You can't just use compulsion on people because it's easy!" Marius burst out as soon as he'd left.

"That is scarcely an argument against it," Rakken said, with the kind of cool amusement he so often used on Marius, as if this was some trivial and faintly amusing notion on Marius's part.

"It's wrong!" Marius said. "A mind is the ultimate sanctum. To invade it is…a horror beyond anything."

He'd amused Rakken again, the hard lines of the fae's mouth curving. "I do not hurt the mortals, little scholar, so I don't see why it troubles you so."

"Don't call me that!" he objected before he could help it.

"Scholar?" Rakken's gaze flicked up and down the length of him, and Marius flushed. "Or little?"

"I'm not—the adjective isn't even *correct!*" Marius spluttered, not sure how they'd gotten to this tangent but seizing on that as at least one thing he *was* sure of. He was taller than the average man; it was rare that he found himself looking up as he was now. And, yes, he might not have the breadth of Rakken's shoulders, but he sure as hells wasn't going to let Rakken insult him for it. *Brilliant. Just brilliant. I sound like a bratty teenager.* He took a breath. "You're trying to wind me up."

"Well *done*, little mortal," Rakken said, eyes gleaming. He took a step forward and loomed over Marius. On purpose. "You are, you must admit, smaller than me."

"You are not the objective standard of size against which everyone else is measured!" Marius said. *Do not think about sizes. Do NOT go down that mental path. Think about something else. Anything else!* What had he been talking about before? Compulsion!

"Stop trying to change the subject!" he told Rakken, taking a step back. His back hit a shelving unit. *And stop being so damned attractive*, he added mentally. He was excruciatingly aware of the fae's closeness in the small room, of the faint citrus notes in his scent.

"How is it that you care so much for the trifling redirections of dull mortal minds?"

Honestly, what was he supposed to do with Rakken's complete inability to take this seriously? It was pointless. He rubbed at his head, which was starting to pound again.

"Never mind," he said, suddenly tired. He tried to push past Rakken towards the reading table, but Rakken caught his wrists.

"Do not try to strike me, Marius Valstar. I am not my brother; I will not tolerate the insult. And do not call me by my sister's pet name. I have not granted you the right."

For a moment Marius just stared at him, uncomprehending, and then he laughed. "I was trying to get past you, Prince Melodramatic, so I could look at the damn charter, not trying to attack you. Maybe I'm not a terrifying fae warrior-assassin, but I'm not so inept that my punches look like flailing!"

"Forgive me if I find that difficult to believe," Rakken said. But he released Marius's wrists and stepped away. He was *definitely* amused.

Had he truly thought Marius meant to hit him or could the entire bizarre interaction be filed under 'strange fae humour'? But maybe people did frequently try to strangle Rakken. *And I for one wouldn't blame them*, Marius thought darkly. He took a deep breath, struggling to focus, and went to retrieve a pair of thin reading gloves. Rakken followed suit.

Still unsettled, Marius sat down at the central table and pulled the document the librarian had named the 'additional treaty' towards him. The cover was made of wooden boards joined by leather thongs with metal clasps. Iron? But iron would rust, and it was the wrong colour besides—a shade between copper and silver. An alloy of some sort?

Rakken sat opposite Marius, examining the Northern Charter with appropriately gloved hands. He leaned over it with a slight frown, apparently fascinated, even though from Marius's vague memories of Stariel's copy it was a very dry and archaic document.

Just ignore him. You're here to help Hetta, remember? Marius rearranged the square book and undid the metal clasps. They clicked open easily enough, despite their age, and Rakken looked up at the sound.

"That," he said, "has a magical residue on it." He held out a hand imperiously, and Marius sighed and slid the book over to him. Despite its age, it wasn't at all fragile.

Rakken hummed to himself as he turned the pages in what Marius considered a highly irritating manner.

"Well?" Marius said. "Are you going to explain or are you going to sit there making entirely non-illuminating noises to yourself?"

Rakken chuckled, the sound chocolate-rich and sinful. "Settle your feathers, Marius Valstar. Not everything I do is designed purely to provoke you." His lips curved in a close-lipped smile. "Though you are very easy to provoke." Before Marius could respond, Rakken had returned his attention to the thick vellum pages. "This tastes of the High King. And it pre-dates the Iron Law. Three hundred mortal years, give or take," he expanded at Marius's blank look.

"Your fae High King came to Stariel when the Northern Charter was signed?" Marius asked.

Rakken turned the book to a page of signatures, tapping on one written in runes that shifted oddly as Marius stared at them. Printed underneath, in reassuringly non-headache-inducing letters, were the words: *Her Royal Majesty Oberyn, High Queen of Faerie.*

"He was the High Queen then. He has been the High King for only a few decades past."

Wyn had told Marius this before, the gender-changing nature of their fae ruler. It was so strange, and Marius couldn't quite get his head around it, but Rakken didn't seem to find it at all odd.

"So the, er, High Queen was there because Stariel is a faeland and so sort of part of her kingdom too?" Marius guessed, trying to imagine the world before the Iron Law had cut off interaction between Faerie and Mortal. *And now we're to live in that world again.* Had Hetta truly thought about the ramifications of her relationship with Wyn from that perspective? It would be like her to think she could bull her way through them with sheer stubbornness.

"*His* kingdom. One uses current pronouns when speaking of him, regardless of his various titles," Rakken corrected gently. "But yes, the Court of Falling Stars is a faeland, and that is likely the reason for the High Queen's presence at the time this was signed." He smoothed the vellum, and his gaze grew faraway, his fingers stilling on the pages.

He's sad, Marius realised, recognising the yearning emotion with a start. "You're thinking of home," he said aloud. "The Court of Ten Thousand Spires."

He didn't expect the fae to acknowledge his words, but Rakken sighed and rubbed at the nape of his neck.

"Yes," he agreed. "I was." He turned vivid emerald eyes to Marius, as if he could see through flesh right into Marius's thoughts. What a terrifying idea. "You are a very dangerous man, Marius Valstar, and yet as ignorant as an unfledged chick. I am beginning to wonder how it is that you've survived so long thus."

Marius stiffened. *Unfledged chick?* he thought indignantly, followed by, *Wait, Rakken thinks I'm dangerous?* Which was such an improbable sentiment that he laughed.

"What do you mean *dangerous*? Dangerous to your plans, whatever they are?"

The corner of Rakken's mouth twitched, but he didn't look up from the charter as he said, "No, I'm not going to explain myself, Marius Valstar. I suspect it may be for the best that you do not know." He turned a page and pushed the separate treaty towards Marius. "Besides, are you not here to aid Lord Valstar? Should you not cease admiring me and begin your research?"

Marius glared at Rakken. He was right, damn him. They *were* here to help Hetta. Or at least, Marius was. Gods only knew what Rakken's motivations were in all this. Marius firmly cordoned off the growing field of questions Rakken's words has sprouted. *Later, think about that later. This document in front of you is the only thing that is important right now.* He hunched over the treaty and began to read, desperate to be taken away from his whirling thoughts. Fortunately, the mundane magic of words still worked, catching him in its spell, and the world dropped away as he sank into the convoluted lega-lese. He stopped to make notes occasionally in the notebook he'd brought with him. A library hush fell, the background noise of pen scratching and page turning.

He was concentrating so hard that he wasn't sure how much time had passed when something snapped him out of it. He glanced up to find Rakken wearing a very sardonic expression.

"You are not good for my ego, Marius Valstar," the fae reflected. "I am not accustomed to repeating myself so frequently."

"Sorry," Marius apologised. "I tend not to hear things when I'm concentrating."

"So I have discovered," Rakken said. He was leaned back from the table, hands loosely steepled in front of him. "My amazement at your continued survival only increases."

"You might take this slightly more seriously, since it's *your* brother who's currently most at risk from Queen Matilda's wrath."

"I *am* taking this seriously, Marius Valstar," Rakken said. He unlaced his hands and leaned forward. "As I understand it, this charter of yours is a written mortal oath that binds your queen and all the Northern estates, Stariel included." At Marius's nod, he continued. "And the estates agreed to give up certain powers in exchange for various promises from your mortal monarchy. The power to make laws or negotiate treaties is one of the powers they gave up. But this specifically does *not*"—he tapped the charter meaningfully—"apply to FallingStar."

"We can make our own laws?" Marius repeated, sure this couldn't be true. Yes, long ago, before Prydein became Prydein, justice had been whatever the relevant lord decreed, but that was definitely not the case anymore. The Crown's laws applied everywhere.

Rakken waved this away. "Oh, not entirely. There are merely a small number of exemptions that refer to the separate Addendum for specifics. More to the point, Marius Valstar, you can make your own *treaties* as an independent entity. And your monarch must take those relationships into account in their dealings with your court."

Well, that certainly *sounded* promising, though Marius was suspicious of it. Rakken looked very pleased with himself, so Marius said: "If you're thinking that this means Stariel can make some kind of treaty with ThousandSpire, no one's currently ruling it, are they? So it can't make any treaties with *anyone*. Unless you're thinking that that's what Wyn could do, if he becomes king there." Which might be the best outcome, if it wouldn't also leave Hetta broken-hearted. She'd get over it though, wouldn't she? Marius felt guilty for even thinking that, but it didn't stop it from being true, did it?

Rakken's eyes narrowed, and that anger he'd been doing such a fine job of hiding burned briefly in them, an inferno cast in emerald.

"Nothing is certain, Marius Valstar," he bit out. "Perhaps my brother is dead." Marius was pretty sure Rakken had meant to say that provokingly, to show he didn't care at all if that was the case, but it came out hollow.

"Wouldn't you know, if he was?" He'd been drawing comfort from the assumption that Wyn's siblings would know if something had happened to him. If they *didn't* know, if Wyn could be dead and *no one* know it... Marius swallowed, a cold sense of dread settling in his belly.

Rakken sighed. "Usually, yes, but I don't know how the dismae would affect that. Maybe we would not sense it." His gaze went unfocused, and he looked so uncharacteristically vulnerable that Marius risked a very brief pat on his shoulder. He had very muscular biceps. Rakken's mask slid back into place at the touch, once more all sardonic amusement, and he raised an eyebrow at Marius until he withdrew his hand.

Marius pulled the charter back towards him like a shield. "Don't worry, I won't shatter your stoic image by blabbing to everyone how worried you are about him."

Rakken's lips curved. "Thank you."

33

OPENING NIGHT

ETTA SMOOTHED THE sleeves of her coat over her dress, a long flowing chiffon confection in pale apricot with a draping neckline. She and Marius were standing in the lobby of the hotel, dressed to the nines, waiting for Catsmere and Rakken so they could make their way to Bradfield's opening night.

"Do you really think this is going to help us find Wyn?" Marius grumbled, fidgeting with his cuff links. He looked considerably smarter than usual in his evening suit, with his hair unnaturally tidy.

"Probably not," Hetta admitted glumly. "But even if I can't get anything out of the duke, it can't hurt to try to turn the tide of public opinion in our favour so we don't have a riot on our hands when we find Wyn, and we're not going to do that by hiding." *When* they found him; not *if*. The queen had refused Hetta's request for an audience today. That could mean nothing, or it could mean they'd found Wyn and didn't want to tell her. If that was the case, maybe the duke would know. At this point, Hetta was starting to not care *who* found him so long as *someone* did.

She sighed. "Besides, I can't think of anything *more* helpful to do right now, so we may as well as not support Bradfield's artistic endeavours." She'd relayed her concerns about Angus to Jack in their brief phone call, but her inability to chase that lead right now chafed. How life had changed. Six months ago, the play would have been her first priority. She reached for Wyn's ring where it hung on its silver chain, on public display along with a generous amount of cleavage, and Stariel gave a beat of acknowledgement through the stone.

Marius chose this moment to notice the object. "Why are you wearing a ring as a necklace?"

"Because Wyn gave it to me. And because I'd much rather people viewed Wyn and me as star-crossed lovers than as a dangerous liaison," she said matter-of-factly, but her heart beat fast as a hummingbird's wings. Her brother wasn't stupid.

Marius's frowned. "What do you mean— Oh," he said, eyes widening. "Oh. I thought… But does it mean—are you——has Wyn asked… But why…?" He trailed off, took a deep breath and tried again. "Congratulations."

Hetta laid a gloved hand on his arm. "Congratulations are a little premature; we need royal permission to marry. Two lots of royal permission actually: both Queen Matilda and the fae High King, but I appreciate the sentiment nonetheless. I haven't told anyone else," she said in a rush as Marius looked down at her.

His frown deepened, and he said exactly the thing she didn't want to hear. "Are you hoping a public declaration that you're engaged will keep Wyn from leaving for the Spires?"

She folded her arms. "I'm not making a *public declaration*."

"You're wearing what is very obviously a betrothal ring in a very attention-drawing location." He flushed.

"Are you criticising my *dress*?"

He looked determinedly at the ceiling, cheeks pink. "That's not what I meant, Hetta, and you know it," he said in a pained voice. "You can pretend all you like that there aren't any unresolved issues between you, but you haven't seen Wyn for three days, and now you're suddenly telling the world you're engaged? Clearly this isn't a decision he was part of."

"Are you saying you think I would *make this up*?" She shook the chain at him.

"No! But I think you're terrified that once we find him and he finds out what's happening in ThousandSpire, he'll decide he has to go back there and be their king." Marius met her gaze. "And I think you think that might actually be for the best, even though you don't want it to be. So you're trying to ensure he'll stay and ignoring the consequences."

Was she? "Do you hate the idea of us marrying so much?"

He blinked. "No, of course not." He wrinkled his nose. "In fact, I told him he needed to stop vacillating and make an honest woman of you when I spoke to him last."

"That's a very outdated way of thinking, brother mine. And I didn't think you'd side with the gossips," she said tartly, unexpectedly hurt.

His eyes flashed. "I don't give a fig for the scandal." When Hetta raised an eyebrow, he conceded: "Oh, very well, I don't like it when people talk about us in the papers. But that's not what I meant, Hetta." He grew oddly serious, glancing up the ornate entry stairs. "You can't keep pretending it doesn't matter that he's fae."

"It *doesn't* matter that he's fae! Not to me."

"It's not just about you though, is it, anymore? What about Stariel and the rest of Prydein? What about his home court?" He sighed. "I know he's a good man. But he's got some very…questionable family connections, and you just told me yourself that you're going to have to fight two different sets of royalty just to marry him. But if that's what you want, then, well, I'll gladly dance at your wedding. You better be damned sure though." He took a deep breath. "You're not doing this just because everyone's opposed to it?"

She huffed and poked him in the shoulder. "I'm not going to

marry a man out of sheer contrariness!" That, at least, she could safely refute. She didn't know what to say to the rest of Marius's other words. They held too much truth for comfort.

Marius laughed, but his expression grew thoughtful. "I wonder if you actually do need the queen's permission to marry, though."

"What?"

"You know that Addendum to the Northern Charter I told you about and the exemption about making treaties? What if your marrying Wyn is part of a treaty between you and his kingdom?"

Hetta blinked. "He's not going to be king of ThousandSpire."

Marius didn't argue with her, which was a jolly good thing, because she wasn't sure what she'd have said if he had.

"Do you think the queen knows about the Addendum?" she wondered aloud. "She never mentioned it." She frowned. "Oh, of *course* she must have known. She didn't want to give up the advantage. Gods, the human court is just as bad as the fae ones, isn't it?" She felt a sharp yearning to be home, away from the politics.

Marius patted her shoulder. "He'll be all right, Hetta. He's a resourceful man. Fae." But she could see he was worried about Wyn as well. How strange, for Marius to be reassuring her rather than the other way around. She watched him wrestle with himself before he added, reluctantly: "Isn't wearing a betrothal ring in public tonight a touch undiplomatic, since the queen *hasn't* given you permission?"

"That's what's going to make us star-crossed lovers in the public's eyes," she said lightly.

Before he could respond, the royal twins appeared at the top of the main hotel staircase.

They were still in their human forms, but they were somehow inhuman, everything about them drawing the eye in the same way a master's painting did. *Or a live tiger.* Wyn did that too, on rare occasions when he lost control of his emotions, fae shining through his mortal skin, but she hadn't realised it was a thing they could turn on consciously. They wore white-and-bronze clothing cut in an unfamiliar style, and Hetta would bet good money that Meridon's tailors would be besieged with requests to imitate it by tomorrow morning.

Adorning them was a king's ransom in gold and emerald jewellery, the colours sharp against their oak-brown skin, bringing out the strands of gold in their dark hair. Though their colours matched, it served only to emphasise the differences between them: Rakken's broad shoulders and cut-glass cheekbones, Catsmere's willowy grace and pixie-like features. They were mesmerising, impossibly beautiful and altogether other.

In fairness, Hetta had *asked* them to emphasise their foreignness. The news of the nightwyrm would paint the fae as monsters; let people see that they could also be entirely civilised—or at least dress up nicely for parties. She couldn't openly announce Rakken and Catsmere's true identities without risking the queen's wrath, but if Lord Valstar—who the entire world had probably heard was involved with fae by now—turned up with a couple of eerily beautiful companions of mysterious identity, well, Hetta couldn't be blamed for the conclusions people might draw.

Stariel stirred, restless, and she realised she'd been staring dumbstruck at the two fae for their entire descent to the lobby, unable to tear her attention away. *Thank you*, she sent through the ring, not liking that she'd nearly been caught in the allure.

Rakken's lips curved in slow, sensuous amusement. "Are we to your liking, Lord Valstar?" he purred. "I should hate to disappoint at my first mortal event." His eyes were impossibly green as he took in her and Marius, like someone had crushed emeralds with sunlight and new spring leaves to create a hue that redefined the colour entirely. "You look ravishing."

Stariel grumbled again, and she realised she'd almost been caught once more. Drat. She took a firmer hold on herself.

"Stop it."

"Stop what, Lord Valstar?" He looked genuinely puzzled.

"Stop whatever it is you're doing to make yourselves…" She made a vague motion at him. "That."

"Inordinately good-looking?" Rakken suggested. "Devilishly handsome? You wanted us to be ourselves, as much as possible in mortal skin. This is a natural side-effect. It's not my fault if you find royal stormdancers particularly alluring." He angled his head, as if he knew that would make the gold threads in his hair glint in the light from the vast elektric candelabra that lit the lobby. He probably did. "Or if you find my brother…unsatisfying in comparison."

Marius sighed. "Stop flirting with Hetta, Rake."

"Are you jealous?" Rakken said archly.

Hetta had a moment's panic on her brother's behalf, but Marius ignored the fae and offered an arm to Hetta.

"Let's get this over with then," he said with a sigh.

***

HETTA WANTED TO QUIZ Marius, but she didn't have the opportunity to speak to him alone before they reached the theatre. It was probably for the best; Marius didn't like crowds much, and a better person than Hetta would avoid upsetting him in such a situation. But Rakken's remark had made her intensely curious. There were very, very few people who Marius had trusted with the truth of his own preferences, and Hetta wasn't strictly one of them: he'd only admitted it when confronted. He *had* told Wyn, during the years when Hetta had been away, and possibly some of his Knoxbridge friends knew, though she wouldn't stake her life on that. He'd never tell someone like Rakken. Which meant either Rakken had guessed and was deliberately taunting him, or…?

Or Rakken just flirts with everyone, she thought. *In which case, it will be an interesting night.*

Marius's arm was tense under hers as he escorted her inside the Griffin Theatre. The front entrance could hardly have contrasted more vividly with the back. Here, at the public-facing end, the Griffin was a wildly ornate creature made of false gold curlicues, pillars, and mosaics showing frolicking mythical beasts.

The duchess' guests were ushered upstairs into the Griffin's private bar that ran behind the boxes. It was a long room, decorated with more mosaic tiles and potted plants with long, spiky leaves. A string quartet gave it a fashionable ambiance—as did the throng of bejewelled and elegant partygoers, who all seemed to know each other.

There was no herald—it wasn't that kind of event—but Hetta could still see the news of her arrival passing from mouth to mouth down the room, amplified when everyone caught sight of Rakken and Catsmere.

Hetta took a deep breath. *I can do this; I am the lord of a great Northern estate, and I've been to plenty of parties before.* But she'd never faced a room full of strangers examining her so intensely, as if they wanted to find flaws. The parties she'd loved were mad things where no one cared who your parents were or where you came from, where you could argue about plays and invent new drinks and dance to wild, fast-paced tunes until you dripped with sweat. No doubt the parties of the aristocracy could get just as crazily out of hand, but she'd never been in an atmosphere so prickling with malice. Or at least, not in the mortal world.

But apparently this was an atmosphere that the two fae royals knew exactly how to thrive in. Rakken gave Hetta a single, sharp-edged smile before he and Catsmere set off to do battle. Hetta watched them go, not sure how to feel about the way people turned towards them, caught by that tug of allure that wasn't exactly compulsion but also wasn't exactly *not* compulsion. Probably she ought to be appalled by it, but honestly all she could think was that if it helped her find Wyn then she would happily watch them enthral the whole of Meridon.

"Well, at least *some* of us are enjoying themselves," Marius said, looking in the same direction. "What now?"

"Now we find the Duke of Callasham or his wife before the play starts. Or Brad, if he's here." She knew Brad would want to be downstairs, preparing, but his business instincts might demand he at least put in an appearance here, for his patron's sake.

They found the duke first, drunk out of his socks in the card room adjoining the bar.

"Lord Valssssstar!" he said exuberantly, throwing his arms wide. The drink he held sloshed dangerously close to the rim. "I don't know you!" he told Marius.

"This is my brother, Mr Marius Valstar," Hetta said impatiently. "Your Grace, I wanted to ask you—"

"You don't have a drink!" He narrowed his eyes at Hetta's empty hands. "You're not one of those damned teetotallers, are you? You should have a brandy. The brandy's excellent here, you know."

"I'm sure it is, but I wanted to ask you about the Northern Lords Conclave," she said quickly before the duke could interrupt. She watched for a reaction, but he merely homed in on her cleavage.

"Want advice, eh?" he said to her breasts. "Well, if you wear that dress, you'll certainly grab them by the balls."

Marius swelled, and Hetta quickly tried another tack. "Your Grace, did you read the article about me in the last issue of *Lady Peregrine's Society News?*"

"Simon's gossip rag?" The duke laughed uproariously. "Not to my taste, m'girl."

"Simon?" Hetta pressed. "Who's he?"

The duke blinked at her. "The Earl of Wolver. He owns the magazine, along with half the papers in town." He patted the seat beside him. "Why don't you sit here and try the brandy?"

"Thank you, Your Grace, but I'm afraid I have to go now." She dragged a purpling Marius away.

"The Earl of Wolver," she mused once they were safely back in the main bar. "I wonder if that's coincidence?" Bradfield had given the strong impression he and the earl hadn't parted friends, but surely that was no reason for the earl to strike out at Hetta? Did the earl even know she and Brad used to work together?

"Knowing our luck, probably not," Marius said. "Though if he owns half the papers in town, he might not keep track of what each publishes in any detail. Owner's not the same as editor-in-chief."

"Yes, but he probably *could* get them to publish whatever he wanted." Her thoughts flew to Angus again. Angus had been a lord for several years, and the political circles he moved in would've likely overlapped with the earl's at some point. What if that was the connection? What if *Angus* had asked the earl to put that article in? She shared her thoughts with Marius.

"Maybe," he said doubtfully.

The duchess was lounging on a chaise amidst a flock of admirers. *Oh, I can see why Aunt Sybil disapproves of her.* Hetta, however, felt a flash of envy for her dress, a daring confection in pink silk. The duchess was a statuesque woman, much younger than the duke, unmistakably fashionable, and unmistakably risqué, from her bold outfit to the sultry smile she wore as she leaned towards the man she was sharing the chaise with. Hetta did a double-take as the crowd parted slightly, revealing the man's hair: Rakken. He laughed at something the duchess said, and the chocolate-rich sound rolled over the duchess and her flock, drawing them in like moths to a flame. *Apparently he does flirt with everyone.* Marius gave a small, disgusted huff.

A harried Bradfield appeared suddenly at her shoulder.

"Ah, old girl, you made it!" he said, stopping to greet her though he was clearly in a hurry. He caught their line of gaze. "Ah, yes, eye-catching, isn't he? No idea who he is, but I'm grateful for the timely distraction of Her Grace." He grinned. "Her favourite *artiste* is going to have bloody hell to pay if I don't get down there and rouse the rabble soon."

"This is Bradfield, Marius." Hetta performed the introductions.

Marius was stiffly correct, which meant he was feeling self-conscious. "Good evening, Mr Bradfield," he said, eyes darting everywhere except to the man in front of him. Hetta heaved an internal sigh. *Honestly, Marius, you are your own worst enemy sometimes.*

Brad was too distracted to notice. "Good to finally meet Hetta's older brother." He made a face at Hetta. "Sorry to leave you to these wolves—got to dash. You know how it is!"

"I do," she said. "Go, Brad! Break a leg!"

After Brad had disappeared in the direction of the door, Hetta wondered whether to interrupt Rakken or leave him to it. *Leave him to it,* she decided after a moment. His flirting would probably do more to endear the fae to the duchess than anything Hetta could muster, and hopefully the duke would be too drunk to notice. She talked to the assorted aristocrats instead—or rather, they talked to her, all desperately wanting to know who Rakken and Catsmere were. Did that mean she could count this as a clever political venture? Word would certainly get back to the queen, if nothing else, but it didn't feel very clever, attending parties while Wyn was still missing. *But what else was I going to do? Sit at home and twiddle my thumbs, hoping for him to fall out of the sky?*

"Well, they're both fae royalty," she told everyone who asked. There didn't seem much point in pretending otherwise, and aristocrats liked titles. "Like the queen's honoured guest who's been missing these past few days." She lowered her voice conspiratorially. "My fiancé, though we've not yet announced it, of course."

This generally made people gape and resulted in one of two responses: an urgent need to excuse themselves so they could go away and whisper to their friends, or increasingly inappropriate questions which she excused herself from with teeth bared in a barely civil smile. No one reacted as if they knew anything about Wyn's disappearance.

"You're good at this," Marius said quietly after they'd extracted themselves from another conversation in which no one knew anything useful.

"Ha!" Hetta said bitterly. She gulped down a flute of iced lemonade. She'd much rather be drinking the strong liquor on offer, but she wanted a clear head.

"Well, better than me, in any case," he clarified with a grimace.

"You don't have to stay with me; I know you hate this kind of thing." She was tremendously grateful for her brother's presence; it would've been so much worse facing this crowd of strangers alone.

He rubbed at his temples in the way that meant he had a headache. "If you think I'd leave you alone in this pit of vipers... No." He contemplated the wider room. "Do you think they're actually finding out anything useful or just enjoying themselves?" he complained, and she saw he was watching Rakken dance his fingers lightly up the sloped back of the chaise, inches away from the duchess's shoulder. Her lips were half-parted, and she coloured as he asked her something. "He doesn't really see humans as quite real, you know. We're just amusing toys to him."

"I think they *do* want to protect Wyn from their sister, though," she said, not disagreeing with his assessment. "I'm hopeful that their attitudes towards humanity will improve with exposure."

Marius gave a short laugh. "With exposure to this lot?"

"Well, they should feel right at home, shouldn't they? Backstabbing and posturing?"

He laughed again, but it faded quickly as he frowned down at his own drink. They were standing next to the bar, a brief respite from the crowd. "But should we really be encouraging people to welcome the fae with open arms? They're not exactly...good."

"What about Wyn?" she asked quietly, a strange, painful tightness in her chest.

"He's different," Marius said. "More, I don't know, human."

That's why he's in this mess now, she couldn't help thinking. Rakken and Catsmere wouldn't have put on the dismae at the queen's command. She surveyed the room, trying to decide where they should go next. There was still another half-hour before the curtain rose.

"Hetta!" a familiar voice said behind her, and she turned to face, of all people, Lord Angus Penharrow.

His presence was so completely out of place that for a moment all she could do was stare blankly at him. What was Angus doing here? The duke and newspaperman's words had been enough to make her suspect his involvement, but this seemed like confirmation. Angus didn't look nearly villainous enough in his evening finery, but Hetta glared at him anyway.

"Penharrow," Marius said curtly, shoulders going up like a cat's. "What are you doing here?"

Angus gestured at the bar. "Getting a drink," he said blandly. He took in Hetta's dress. "You look lovely, Hetta." He frowned as his gaze snagged on the ring.

"What are you doing here *in Meridon*?" Hetta repeated.

"I *do* do business in town, occasionally. You don't hold a monopoly on the city." He shrugged, and the lights glinted in his warm brown curls.

Hetta eyed him incredulously. "Are you trying to tell me it's coincidence you're here at *my old company's play*?"

A hint of chagrin crept into his expression. "Ach, very well. No, it's not a coincidence that I'm here tonight, though I truly do have other business in town I'd already planned. But I did come here tonight to talk to you, though I'd hoped to be somewhat subtler about it." He grimaced around at the party, clearly ill at ease with the nature of it. "Can we talk somewhere quieter?" He glanced at Marius. "Alone?"

"Absolutely not," said Marius flatly. "Do you *want* to tear my sister's reputation to ribbons in front of half of Meridon society?"

Hetta didn't actually think she had any good name left to ruin at this point, but she appreciated her brother's support nonetheless.

"Bradfield gave us a box for the night," she said. "You can come and talk to *both* of us in there." She narrowed her eyes. "As it happens, I would quite like to ask you a few questions myself."

BOX SEATS

THE BOX HAD five seats upholstered in plush red, but Hetta was too agitated to sit. Instead she went and stood by the heavy decorative curtains that framed the view. It felt jarringly strange to be in a Meridon theatre with two people from Stariel. The stalls below were beginning to fill, people's voices echoing as they shuffled into their seats. A fake, empty throne sat on the stage in preparation for the first scene, covered in glittering jewels that were paste beneath the illusion. Hetta grimaced; it reminded her unpleasantly of the bejewelled throne room in ThousandSpire.

Angus came to stand beside her, leaving Marius awkwardly cramped into the space by the door. The boxes weren't really made for milling about in.

Angus looked between them, a crease forming between his brows. "Have I done something more than ambush you to make you angry? You both look like you could spit tacks."

"What did you say to *Lady Peregrine's* about me?" Hetta said, working her fingers restlessly into the tassel of the curtain tie-back.

Angus rocked back on his heels. "*Lady Peregrine's*? The gossip rag?" he repeated, sounding genuinely puzzled before his eyes widened in realisation. "I heard there was an article slighting you. You think *I* went to the papers about…Prince Hallowyn Tempestren?" He said the name with distaste, but it wasn't that that sent a cold shiver over Hetta's neck. Catsmere had said not using true names was merely a precaution, but it still made her uneasy, as if Aroset would spring suddenly from the upholstery.

"It wouldn't be the first time you've acted dishonourably," she said icily, but her certainty was fading in the face of the anger in Angus's eyes.

Angus's mouth thinned, but he held back his instinctive response. "I suppose I've earned your suspicion, but I had nothing to do with that article. You truly think I'd take your affairs to the *press*, Hetta?" He shook his head. "I told you I've no taste for seeing your name raked through the mud."

Hetta met Marius's eyes. He grimaced, his face in deep shadow at the back of the box. "I believe him." He paused and then added, challengingly: "But you're happy enough that Wyn's suddenly out of the picture, aren't you, my lord?"

Angus shrugged but directed his answer to Hetta. "I'm not going to pretend I think he's worthy of you, though actually, no, I'm *not* happy with the way he's disappeared, leaving you alone to hold off scandal."

"I'm hardly alone, Angus," Hetta said, waving a hand at Marius. She smiled. "My sister and aunt are also in town."

"Your family can't protect you from the talk, though," Angus pointed out. He hesitated, glancing fleetingly at Marius.

A horrible suspicion dropped into her stomach, and she held up a hand to interrupt him. "Angus, if your next words are anything resembling an offer, I shall have hysterics."

Marius choked.

"You've never had hysterics in your life, Hetta," Angus said, but there was a deflated angle to his shoulders. He *had* been going to say something along those lines. *Oh, Angus.* She reminded herself of his treachery; she definitely *shouldn't* feel sorry for him.

He took the setback with grace. "Very well, I won't add to the awkwardness then, so you can stop spluttering, Valstar." He shot a wry smile in Marius's direction before turning back to Hetta. "That's not the only subject I wanted to broach, though. I wanted to warn you about the Conclave."

Hetta blew out a breath. "You already warned me about them, Angus."

He shook his head. "The situation has changed. Someone tipped off the Chair—no, not me, Valstar"—he added at Marius's accusatory "Ha!"—"and I'm fairly certain that you won't receive an official summons to the next meeting; he'll try to deliberately exclude you."

"Why? Ratifying my membership on the Conclave should be a simple formality." But she knew why, though she wasn't sure if the Conclave cared more about the fae business or if they were primarily concerned with her being young, female, unmarried, and 'unvirtuous'. The latter made her angry but was easy to brush off. The Conclave had had far more scandalous members than Hetta, and she'd force them to acknowledge that, if she had to. But the fae—the Conclave weren't wrong to be concerned about them as a whole, even if they were wrong about Wyn specifically. Dash it— why did Marius have to be right? *Was* she being a bad lord, not thinking more about what was good for Stariel rather than just her own interests?

Below came the sounds of the orchestra's warm-up, punctuated with conversation and the occasional louder burst of laughter. Footsteps passed the box door as the duchess's partygoers made their way to their seats.

"The Conclave want to discuss you without your being present— decide if you're 'respectable' enough," Marius guessed, anger stirring in his tone. "They have no right to make such judgements.

It shouldn't matter in the slightest how respectable she is; she's still Lord of Stariel."

Hetta laughed bitterly. "And it would be the highest of hypocrisies for them to declare me not respectable enough given that I know at least one of their members is conducting a very torrid and scandalous affair entirely in the public eye, and no doubt half of them are doing so privately." Fire simmered under her skin, itching for release, and she took a deep breath. Her pyromancy had been slowly gaining in potency since she'd bonded to Stariel, but she hadn't lost control of it since she'd been a teenager. She wouldn't do so now.

"Your brother is correct about the Conclave's motives," Angus said quietly. "Though they're concerned about this fairy business as well. But I agree with you both, and no, not just because I wish to be back in your good books, Hetta. I wanted you to have warning of it, so we have time to plan." Something in his expression hardened. "We must not become like these Southern nobles, driven by petty rivalries and desire for the queen's favour. The North shouldn't be divided against itself. Especially not at such a time, with change on the horizon whether we would have it or not." He glanced at her necklace again and shook his head. "Fairies. I never imagined we'd have to deal with such things."

Marius jerked suddenly, alarm in every line, just before the door slammed open and Catsmere stalked in, a sword in one hand and power rolling off her in waves. She brushed Marius aside and bounded over the seats to land next to Hetta, staring keenly out over the balcony.

Angus gaped at her; the movement had been too smooth to be possible, especially in a dress, though Hetta realised now that there were slits all the way up to Catsmere's waist, and that she wore loose-fitting trousers beneath the exotic bronze-coloured over-dress.

Catsmere's attention flickered out over the stalls, searching for something. The room was suddenly filled with the scent of rainstorms, mixed with notes that made dread seep into Hetta's stomach: copper and old-fashioned roses. Aroset's magic.

"You should leave, Lord Valstar," Catsmere said without taking her attention from the auditorium. She looked across to the stage and stiffened. Hetta followed her gaze down to the throne, which rippled in a very alarming and familiar way a split second before a portal opened and something hurtled through it.

THE KUTRASS

"**G**ET DOWN!" CATSMERE snarled, brandishing her sword. Hetta's first, confused impression was of a monstrous stick insect made of blades and wings. It fell out of the portal in a mess of oddly jointed limbs and flitted up straight for their box.

Catsmere met it with her sword, but it was only a glancing blow, and the creature darted back, making an angry rattling sound with one set of wings.

From below came a cheer, and Hetta had a confused second of incomprehension as to why *anyone* would be cheering the attack. Surely she wasn't *that* disliked? But then she realised—illusion. The audience thought it was part of the special effects for the show, starting early.

The creature hovered, trying and failing to get past Catsmere's guard while Hetta and the others scrambled back from the balcony. Fire boiled up beneath her skin, but she fought it down. The tight confines of the box were far too flammable.

The monster abruptly changed tactics, swooping up and out of view. Had it given up? But then the box shuddered as something heavy landed inside the box above them. Oh no. Hopefully it had been empty.

A razor-sharp claw stabbed through the ceiling above her, and she flung herself away from it, landing in a tangle on top of Angus. His eyes were very wide, but he wrapped an arm around her waist and hauled them both up, towards the door.

"Open the door!" she prompted Marius, who was still frozen in shock. He jerked into motion, clumsily reaching for the handle as the creature stabbed more holes through the ceiling. Ceramic fragments ricocheted off the wall, and Marius yelped as one stung his cheek.

They tumbled out into the hallway, just as the ceiling collapsed. The creature tore its way through after them with a shriek of triumph, and Hetta got her first good look at it: six spindly legs tipped with blades and hard, metallic silver wings. Its eyes were obscenely large, multi-faceted like an insect's and covering the entire upper half of its head.

Had Catsmere been caught under the falling masonry? She'd been on the other side of the box, but the creature wasn't heading in that direction now. Instead it clicked two of its bladed claws together with a horrible sound like glass-on-glass and hurtled down the hallway towards them.

The eyes gave her an idea. There was no time to think or weave anything complicated, so she closed her eyes and drew in as much calm as she could—a feat in itself, under the circumstances—and flung simple light at the creature. Lots of it.

The monster stumbled, temporarily blinded, slowing its rush. Hetta and the others sprinted down the hallway into the bar. It was emptier than before but not empty enough, with a few drunken stragglers still scattered about. The monster followed them in, shaking its head in irritation, its spinning wings loud as struck blades.

"Over here, beast!" Angus shouted, throwing a heavy ornament at the creature. It struck just behind its head joint with about as much effect as a cushion.

Flammable theatres be dashed. Hetta abandoned all attempts at calm and let fire run down her arms, pooling in her palms, heightened by fear. But before she could throw it, Catsmere was suddenly there in a blur of grace and violence. There was a whir of blades followed by a heavy, fleshy sound, and before Hetta could quite process what had happened, the monster's severed head rolled to a halt at her feet. She stared down into its dimming many-faceted eyes and struggled with sudden nausea.

"Hetta!" Her name came from two directions at once: her brother and Angus. She looked to Marius. A single drop of blood had rolled down his check where the ceramic shard had hit him before, and he rubbed it with the back of his hand without thinking, then scowled as he realised he'd only smeared it. But, she thought with relief, if he was scowling in distaste, he wasn't seriously hurt.

Angus scanned her from top to toe. "Are you all right, Hetta?"

She looked down at her dress, which was flecked with bits of broken mosaic. It could've been much worse; at least it didn't appear to be torn. "Yes," she said shakily. She didn't let herself think too hard about what had just happened, about how close the monster had gotten, because she thought she might be sick if she did. "I think so."

Catsmere had pieces of plaster in her hair but didn't seem hurt. She glanced up suddenly as the door opened. Rakken stalked in. He checked only slightly on the threshold, absorbing the scene before him in one impressive sweep of the room, and his mouth thinned as he took in the stunned and inebriated partygoers, who were just beginning to break into alarm.

"Hey, I say, what *is* that thing?" A thin, pale man staggered towards them.

"I think you should all leave now and recall this as a drunken fever-dream," Rakken suggested to the remaining patrons. His power expanded through the room effortlessly, as it had at the station, and for a moment fae shone beneath his mortal skin. Thunder and citrus replaced the smoky liquor ambiance.

The partygoers fell silent and began to file towards the door as if sleep-walking, their faces slack. Hetta shuddered, but she didn't try to stop them. Did that make her just as culpable?

"What's going on?" Angus demanded in a low, angry voice.

"It's just you, isn't it?" Marius said to Rakken. "That's not—you can't *all* do that, can you?"

"All greater fae can compel," Catsmere said. "It is part of what makes us such."

"That's not what I—" Marius began, but Rakken interrupted him, the deep anger Hetta had glimpsed in him before suddenly there and blazing in his eyes.

"Yes," Rakken said. "My compulsion is magnified. *That* is one of the gifts the Maelstrom gave me. What do you think that means, Marius Valstar?"

"It means you're sorely in need of a stronger code of ethics," Hetta said matter-of-factly. *Or a ruler who has one.* "But what *is* this thing?" She indicated the severed head with a slippered toe, her voice trembling slightly. The adrenaline from earlier was wearing off. "Another of your sister's creatures?"

"It's called a kutrass. That trick with the light was well done," Catsmere said. She drew a snow-white handkerchief from the folds of her elegant gown and wiped off her blade. The kutrass bled a pale greenish blue.

"How did she find you?" Rakken asked his sister. He'd folded his rage away, neat as a scalpel, but his expression remained uncharacteristically grim.

"Lord Penharrow said Wyn's true name," Marius said. "It wasn't his fault; he didn't know not to. And where were *you*?"

Rakken frowned at Angus, who returned the expression as the two men sized each other up. Hetta had to give Angus credit for taking the situation in stride. He was shaken but clinging on to his composure.

"There must have been a close resonance with the theatre, for Set to build a portal here so quickly. Unlucky," Catsmere commented.

"We haven't been introduced...Your Highnesses?" Angus hazarded. There was a strong familial resemblance between Rakken and Wyn; Hetta herself had noticed it the first time she'd met Rakken.

"This is Lord Angus Penharrow, Stariel's neighbour. Angus, these are two of Wyn's siblings," she said tiredly.

Rakken dismissed Angus and turned his attention back to Marius, lingering on the blood on his cheek. "It's just a scratch," Marius said tiredly. "So stop fussing."

Hetta didn't think Rakken's dispassionate inspection really counted as 'fussing', but Rakken merely shook his head.

"You are being impolite again, Marius Valstar."

"Why is it only me who gets accused of impoliteness?" Marius complained bitterly.

Catsmere gave a soft huff of amusement and looked to her brother, whose expression darkened. He jerked his head in a stiff negative, and Catsmere shrugged as if to say it was none of her business.

"Well, when the two of you are finished being cryptic, can you do anything about this creature? I've probably ruined Brad's opening night, but I can at least not leave a fae corpse behind for him to deal with." Besides, leaving a dead monster here would only encourage people to think of the fae as dangerous. Which wasn't exactly untrue, but that was quite beside the point. She hoped Brad's patron wouldn't blame him for the attack. *And that Brad can forgive me for staining his carpet.* A pool of greenish-blue blood was slowly spreading from the corpse. Maybe, if they were lucky and the audience continued to think it had all been illusion, the show could go on with no one the wiser. *Surely even silly Southerners must realise that wasn't illusion, though?* The thought brought a half-smile to her lips. *Listen to me embracing Northern superiority.* She'd always dismissed the Northern tendency towards superstition as foolishly old-fashioned, but it *had* made it easier for them to believe in the fae.

"Well, Cat, shall we do Lord Valstar's bidding and rain down destruction?" Rakken's eyes glittered, lit with some uncanny inner light. Stariel quivered along her bond, uneasy.

Catsmere considered the scene. Hetta had the feeling she was assessing whether or not they could summon lightning within the confines of the room. "No," she said decisively. Apparently even the twins' control over their lightning powers had its limitations.

"What do you suggest, Lord Valstar? I can compel the mortals to believe whatever I want," Rakken said unconcernedly, "but I do not have much taste for dragging a corpse about. And where did you plan to put it, besides?"

"Can you do air magic?" she asked. It felt oddly like a betrayal to ask someone who wasn't Wyn to work with her, but one had to be pragmatic. She held out a hand and summoned a small flame to the palm of her hand. "I can burn it, but I'd rather not set the building on fire by accident."

Rakken languidly stretched out an arm. "*Alamein*," he commanded, and wind suddenly rushed into the room, lifting up the kutrass's body and twisting its limbs in on themselves, a grotesque compacting of carapace and flesh into a wind-confined ball.

It was a relief to give her anger and distress an outlet. Fire sprang forth, white-hot and terrible. The twins twisted the air currents, and the corpse of the fae blazed bright as the noonday sun for a moment. Hetta snapped off the flames, though she wanted to keep pouring them forth, pour out fire as if it could take every negative emotion with it. There was nothing they could do about the blue bloodstain on the carpet, but it was much less incriminating than a body, and she'd run out of brilliant ideas.

Lord Angus tentatively nudged the pile of ash with a boot, and she started. She'd forgotten he was still here.

Marius spoke suddenly to Rakken, looking accusingly at his

neck where, Hetta realised with a jolt, there was a very incriminating smudge of lipstick. "You didn't answer my question: where were *you* when this kutrass attacked?"

"Talking to lowfae, as it happens." Rakken gave a sharp, quick grin to Hetta. "A brownie saw my brother, the night of the palace attack, atop a building adorned with stone gargoyles."

"Could they be more specific? There happen to be a lot of gargoyles in Meridon's architecture."

Rakken shook his head. "That is not my main point, Lord Valstar. My brother wasn't alone—a lesser fae was with him. A lesser fae from the Court of Dusken Roses."

"Gwendelfear." Her heart raced. It was the first piece of actual *fact* and not speculation they had. "But where are they now?"

Rakken shrugged. "That, Lord Valstar, is what we are going to find out. I've heard there is a catshee in this city who knows more."

Catsmere nodded, and the two of them made to leave, a pair of predators moving out on the hunt.

"Wait!"

Rakken looked at her impatiently. "Go and sit safe in your mortal lodgings." His eyes were very green, like a jungle cat's in the dusk. "We have hunting to be doing."

"Not without me." She was sick of twiddling her thumbs, waiting and hoping that things would become clearer. And she didn't trust the two of them not to drag Wyn straight to the Spires, if they found him.

Catsmere met her eyes, as if she knew exactly what Hetta was thinking. "He is *our* brother, Lord Valstar, our blood." *Perhaps our king*, she didn't say, but Hetta knew that's what she meant anyway. "Your claim on him is weak, in comparison. Besides, you cannot fly. I am sorry." And then they were gone.

36

OF LESSER AND GREATER FAE

WYN SNAPPED AWAKE to the knowledge that he wasn't alone.

"Well, that took you much longer than I thought it would, Your Highness," a cool feminine voice said.

He stumbled from his half-risen position and landed painfully on his knees, so he wasn't able to glare nearly as intensely as he wished to. *I probably look ridiculous.*

"Gwendelfear," he growled. The lesser fae smiled, showing faintly pointed teeth. She leaned against the far wall of the tiny metal room, entirely too relaxed for a lesser fae confronting a greater one. Her skin was dark and greenish in the dim light, her hair the yellows and greens of summer grass. Gwendelfear's bright blue eyes with their flower-lobed pupils lingered on his dismae with something like satisfaction.

"You highlight very vividly the disadvantages of being greater fae." Gwendelfear had more reason than most to feel the sharpness of the difference. Her father was a greater naiad, she'd told Wyn once, when he'd pressed her as to how she came by her healing abilities. That inheritance was unusual. The higher ranks of Faerie were less fecund, as a rule, but when they did bear children, the greater magics usually bred true, even if the bloodlines were mixed. By rights, Gwendelfear *should* have been greater fae.

"I take it you are responsible for my restraints? And does your mistress know of it?"

"Yes." She smiled.

He realised his mistake in asking two questions at once and shook his head, trying to clear it. The dismae hadn't shocked him again, but he still felt weak and watery. At least his limbs obeyed him this time as he struggled to his feet.

"Does Princess Sunnika know I'm here?" he repeated, watching her closely for confirmation. Would Sunnika truly be party to this? It didn't match with their recent interactions, but perhaps he'd misjudged her. *The High King knows it wouldn't be the first time I trusted someone when I shouldn't have.* Had he been unforgivably naïve, believing an enemy princess might be sincere? After all, what fae *wouldn't* have taken advantage of him, in the state he'd been in?

Gwendelfear didn't answer, only hummed a small sound of pleasure. "Let me savour this moment: a mighty stormdancer bound by a DuskRose lesser fae. You cannot, after all, compel me not to." Her smile sharpened, and he knew she was thinking of their last interactions. She had good reason not to like him much.

"No, but I *can* point out that I was already injured, already bound, and already unconscious when you brought me here." He didn't remember anything after that embarrassing fade-to-black on the roof. Gwendelfear must have found him there. "Is there much glory in taking such a prisoner?"

"I could still probably kill you now, crippled as you are," she continued, as he took slow inventory of his various hurts. "Think of the glory that could be mine, ending a prince of the Spires!"

"It probably would've been better to try while I was unconscious," he pointed out. "I shall take your lack of such attempts as a positive sign."

Her sharp smile only widened. "Perhaps I wanted the pleasure of seeing you realise you owed your death to a lesser fae."

He shrugged, faking a calm he was far from feeling. "I didn't think you cared so greatly for my feelings." The dried blood on his abdomen stuck and unstuck to his shirt as he got to his feet. However, no fresh blood dotted the material, suggesting the wound had finally scabbed over. How long had he been out this time? He wouldn't be easy prey if he could help it. He tried to read Gwendelfear's intentions. She might hate Wyn, but she didn't necessarily hate the Valstars. She'd saved Alexandra's life, once—and moreover, Alex seemed to consider her a friend, though he wasn't sure whether Gwendelfear did. He thought about testing how much influence that relationship held and decided against it for the moment. It sat badly, bringing Alexandra into this.

"Oh, I don't," Gwendelfear admitted. "But your death tempts me, nonetheless." Her eyes gleamed, the expression of avarice one he knew well, so common was it in Faerie and Mortal both. "I heard you swallowed your father's powers, when you killed him," she breathed.

The jolt from the dismae nearly had him flat on his back again, and he panted while the surge subsided.

"Is it true?" she asked, enjoying his discomfort. "Everyone is speaking of ThousandSpire's youngest prince, powerful before his time." In Faerie, power often but not always came with age.

"Your princess freed me of my broken oath. I went into the Maelstrom," he said flatly. "That's why my powers increased."

Gwendelfear's blue, whiteless eyes widened. Even a DuskRose lesser fae knew of the Spires' Maelstrom. "But what of your siblings?" she asked, hunger still in her eyes.

"What of them?" he asked, trying not to show his confusion. What did Gwendelfear want from him? And where were they? He tried to hear anything beyond the dark room, but all he got was a kind of growling rumble, growing louder and then receding.

"They are more powerful than they should be, too."

She wasn't going to attack him, he decided. This sudden preoccupation with his family was odd but apparently made him valuable as a source of information. Maybe DuskRose wanted to know more about Aroset, her potential weaknesses, now that she was Queen of ThousandSpire, though if they intended to use him as a bargaining chip against her, they would soon discover his worthlessness in that regard. His lungs froze. ThousandSpire wasn't the only court he could be used against.

"Are they?" he said eventually, deciding that was a safe enough answer.

Gwendelfear laughed. "All the courts know the storm children are unnatural." Her eyes narrowed. "What other court has six royal offspring from the same pairing?"

Wyn laughed. It was true that such fertility was unusual for greater fae, and especially for royal fae, but: "I think it's a stretch to call that unnatural." Quietly, he tested how much the chains of the manacles would stretch.

"How else could two unblooded youths have killed Prince Orren?" she shot back, unwilling to be shifted off the subject. The enmity between the two courts had raged a long, long time in one form or another, but that was the moment that had fanned the fires to breaking point and led to the intervention of the High King himself.

But that had been *years* ago—why was Gwendelfear asking about it now? Her whiteless eyes glittered eagerly, but with a kind of desperation, as if the answer meant something personal to her. He forced his way back through her last few questions, trying to make sense of her train of thought. Understanding lit suddenly. *She wants to be greater fae.* He knew, in that moment, that this was one half of why she'd imprisoned him and that the other was vengeance for the way he'd imprisoned her. What a temptation he must have presented, defenceless and practically gift-wrapped with the dismae.

"Sunnika doesn't know I'm here, does she?" he asked. "Are you hoping I have some secret to share that will transform you into greater fae? I do not know of such a magic."

She jerked towards him with a snarl but pulled back before she came within reach. "I see no reason to answer your questions, stormdancer. *I* am not the prisoner here."

Wyn pulled the chain taut again. The link closest to his left manacle had a worn spot, thinner than the surrounding iron. "Shall we stare menacingly at each other in silence, then? Or do you propose an alternative course of action?"

"There is no small pleasure to be had in watching you shock yourself into unconsciousness," she purred.

"That may be, but I am no longer doing so at present," he said mildly. "So my entertainment value is presumably limited." That vibration came again, like an oncoming train. Trains! Hetta had described the underground trains of Meridon in her letters. They must be in one of the maintenance tunnels. Unease crawled down his spine. Just how far underground were these trains? How much iron was between him and the sky? At least the dismae meant he couldn't tell if it was two feet or two hundred.

She tilted her head to one side. "What would you give me, if I freed you?"

Ah, here was the crux of it. "What do you want, Gwendelfear?"

SUMMONING

THE KUTRASS ATTACK didn't stop the play, as it turned out, but Hetta couldn't have faced it even if their seats hadn't been destroyed. Similarly, she had no time for Angus's attempts to take care of her. She thanked him for the news about the Lords Conclave, bid him a very firm farewell, and dragged Marius into the nearest hackney. Not that Marius required much dragging—he looked frayed nearly to pieces, deep shadows under his eyes. Hetta, in contrast, was jittery. She burned to run out into the night. The only problem was: then what? She couldn't sprout wings to follow Wyn's siblings.

It began to rain as the hackney took them back to the hotel. Hetta stared out into the rippling lamp-light reflections, wondering if Wyn was out there in the same rain. With Gwendelfear? Hetta wrapped her arms around herself. She remembered the way Gwendelfear had looked at Wyn with undisguised malice, the last time Hetta had seen her.

"Do you think Gwendelfear would…" But she couldn't finish the thought.

Marius leaned forward and took her hand. "He'll be all right, Hetta."

She shook her head. "Just saying that won't make it so. What if—" She took a breath. "What if Gwendelfear has hurt him?" *Killed him*, she couldn't say. She began to shake. It was shock, she knew, the aftermath of the kutrass attack mixed with days of worry.

"What could Gwendelfear possibly hope to gain from that? I'm sure DuskRose would much rather Wyn rule ThousandSpire than any of the other candidates on offer, and you said Princess Sunnika wants an alliance with Stariel. She knows what Wyn means to you. They wouldn't harm him."

Marius's calm logic steadied her. She took a deep breath. "You're right. It doesn't make sense." She shook her head. "I don't know why I'm being so featherbrained about it. I just—"

"You love him," he murmured.

"Obviously."

He made a face.

"It's all right, I'm not going to start waxing lyrical about it."

That made him chuckle. He squeezed her knuckles and sat back. "Heavens forfend."

They fell into silence filled with the jingle of harnesses, the thrum of rain, and the clatter of traffic. Hetta brooded. Marius's words had reassured her somewhat, but she couldn't stop worrying at the puzzle pieces, trying to make them fit. She couldn't make sense of Gwendelfear's role in all this. If DuskRose had Wyn, why hadn't they contacted her?

She hadn't reached any satisfying conclusions by the time they reached the hotel, but she'd thought of even more worries. What if Rakken and Catsmere found Wyn? He wouldn't just agree to go to ThousandSpire without talking to her first, would he? What if they *didn't* find him? What if they *did* but managed to re-ignite a fae war in the middle of Meridon in the attempt?

I should never have let them leave without me, she thought furiously, *though how I was supposed to make that happen, I don't know.*

"Do you want me to wait up with you?" Marius asked. His complexion had taken on a greyish edge. The party had taken more out of him than she'd realised.

She waved his concern away. "No. You may as well go to bed. At least one of us ought to be well rested."

After he'd left, she changed into her pyjamas and dressing gown and paced the edges of her hotel room. If she concentrated, she could almost pick out the faint traces of Wyn's magic from that first morning before they'd left for the palace. *I'm being ridiculously sappy,* she reflected, but it didn't stop her pausing by the window and breathing in, wondering if she was just imagining the hint of spice in the air. He had to be all right, didn't he? She hugged herself, pressing her dressing gown against her skin and wishing miserably that it was Wyn holding her instead.

It doesn't make political sense for Gwendelfear to harm him, she reminded herself, trying to argue the anxiety into submission. But what if Gwendelfear wasn't interested in politics? She had a very personal grudge against Wyn, since he was the one responsible for her imprisonment at Stariel.

Fear shot through her like a bucket of ice water down her back. *Oh gods.* Princess Sunnika might see Wyn as more valuable as a live bargaining chip, but what if Gwendelfear wasn't acting on her mistress's instructions? What if the princess had no more idea than Hetta what was going on?

She couldn't bear it, this not knowing, and she cursed the twins again for running off without her. If only she could contact Sunnika somehow… Wait. She slid to a halt on the heels of that thought.

Wyn had summoned his godparent. Gregory had summoned Gwendelfear. As she understood it, all a summons did was create a kind of resonance between two locations, which then allowed the person summoned—the summonee?—to build a portal, if they chose and the location wasn't warded against translocation.

She swallowed. "I summon thee, Princess Sunnika Meragii." She repeated the name three times and waited, heart racing. Would the princess answer?

"It is bad manners to summon royalty in such a fashion, Lord Valstar," a low feminine voice said behind her. She spun to find Princess Sunnika standing next to the coffee table. The fae woman sighed. "But I suspect you did not know that." Despite the fact that she couldn't have had any time to prepare before she'd teleported, she was perfectly coiffed and composed. The sleek black waterfall of her hair was even threaded with tiny pink flowers that matched the colour of its tips. Had she come from some public appearance, or did she just live permanently in the fae equivalent of court dress?

Hetta brushed the idle thought aside for more urgent concerns. "Do you know where Wyn is?" she asked in a rush.

The princess frowned. "Prince—"

"Don't say his name," Hetta hissed, flailing a hand at her. "Or you may invite a surprise fae monster visit from his sister."

Princess Sunnika's eyebrows went up. "Very well." She pursed her lips and considered the hotel room, lip curling in sudden distaste. "But I see he is not the only royal stormdancer you are keeping company with." Her eyes narrowed and her stance shifted, tensing. "Have you taken sides, Lord Valstar? I am a shadowcat; you cannot hope to ambush me." She scanned the room as if expecting just that.

"I haven't taken *any* sides," Hetta said impatiently. "And the others aren't here right now anyway. Never mind them. What have you done with Wyn?"

The princess's confusion seemed genuine. "You are accusing me of...?"

"Gwendelfear. You sent her to follow us. Do you know where she is now? What she's been doing?"

"It is also poor manners to accuse members of other courts of spying," Princess Sunnika said bluntly.

"Worse manners than sending the spies themselves?"

The princess's lips curved very slightly. "Obviously."

Obviously! If one more fae said that to her, she wouldn't be responsible for her actions. "Well, bad manners or not, do you know why Gwendelfear was with Wyn? And where they are now?"

A slight frown marred Princess Sunnika's brow.

"You don't know anything about it, do you?" Hetta guessed, impatient for answers. "But she's *your* spy, isn't she? If she's hurt Wyn, then I am very much holding the Court of Dusken Roses responsible. There will be no agreements between Stariel and DuskRose. You'll owe *me*." Hetta wasn't at all sure that was how fae debts worked, but she didn't care.

Princess Sunnika pursed her lips and looked as if she was about to speak. Anger flashed in her dark eyes, but in the end she shook her head and disappeared, leaving only the faintest trace of beeswax and cherries.

Well, that had gone fantastically, hadn't it? Hetta slumped onto the sofa, fighting the urge to laugh. Or cry. She wasn't sure. *Did I just threaten a foreign nation?* Possibly she ought to worry about that, but she'd reached her quota of worry for the day. Princess Sunnika could jockey with Queen Matilda for Most Offended By Ill-Mannered Northern Lords.

I suppose there's nothing to do but wait now for Rakken and Catsmere to return. If they return. She drew patterns along the armrest, sighed, and got to her feet again. Maybe she could work off this restless anxiety by pacing the hotel's hallways. Maybe then she could sleep. It would be sensible to try to sleep.

There was a very faint popping noise. Hetta whirled, to find an extremely angry Princess Sunnika standing in front of the mantelpiece, gripping Wyn's arm.

Her eyes blazed with anger. "DuskRose owes you no debt, Lord Valstar," she said, and disappeared.

SOAP AND POLITICS

Wyn had seen Hetta in a lot of heightened emotional states over the years, but he'd never before seen her burst into tears out of sheer, helpless relief. Something splintered in his chest, and he shook off the disorientation of the teleport and closed the gap between them.

"Oh, my love," he murmured, gathering her to his chest even though he was still reeling from the sudden change in his circumstances. She was warm and soft and *safe*, and the closeness began to thaw the bone-deep chill of the past few days.

She made an angry gurgle and clutched at his shirt, and he knew she was furious at herself for crying.

"I'm all right," he told her, stroking her hair. "My ego is very bruised, but I'm all right, Hetta." It tore at him, to be the cause of her anxiety. He tightened his arms around her, nuzzling the top of her head. "And I'm here now." Stormwinds, did he owe Sunnika yet *another* favour for that? She hadn't bargained, merely appearing and transporting him away before he'd had time to speak. He put the fleeting thought aside—it could wait.

Hetta's hands found the half-healed wound.

"You're *not* all right." Her voice quavered. "Show me!" she demanded, fingers flying to his shirt buttons. He didn't resist as she undid the buttons one by one, tugging his shirt away, and he obediently lifted his arms to let her peel off his undershirt. To his relief, the wound didn't start bleeding again as the material was removed. Thank the stormwinds it had scabbed over properly at last.

The task steadied Hetta, and she dashed her tears away impatiently. He lifted a hand to cup her cheek, the knot of anxiety in him unwinding as he drank in the sight of her, whole and unharmed.

"Hetta," he said.

"You need washing and bandaging," she said, taking a firmer grip on herself as she frowned at his abdomen. "Why do I have to spend so much time patching you up?"

"Hetta," he repeated, and she looked up. The grey of her irises was pale as willow catkins. "I love you."

She gave a watery smile. "I love you too, but you're trying to distract me."

"Yes." He leaned down and brushed a kiss over her mouth. "Is it working?"

"No," she said. "Come into the bathroom and distract me there while I clean this. And tell me where in the nine heavens you've been."

She took him by the arm and steered him towards her bathroom, a luxury his own hotel room had lacked. His shared the use of the common bathroom with the rooms on the rest of his corridor.

"You're still wearing the dismae," she said quietly once he was seated on the lip of the heavy claw-footed bathtub.

"Yes, and they've caused me no small amount of trouble," he admitted, while she filled the sink with warm water.

She looked tired, he thought, wishing he could smooth the fatigue away. Was that only because of worry for him, or had something worse occurred in his absence? He caught her free hand with his, tangling their fingers. Even the foot of space between them seemed like too much distance, and he had an overwhelming urge

to close it, to fold his arms around her and simply breathe in the
steady reassurance of her nearness.

She squeezed his hand briefly but disentangled herself so that
she could wring out the cloth. When she began to dab away the
old blood, it stung only a little in places. Without his magic, his
sense of smell and touch seemed sharpened. The roughened texture
of the wet cloth against his skin was magnified, more intimate. He
rested his hands loosely on the cool ceramic of the bath, the solidity
reassuring. *I am here; Hetta is safe.* The transition had been too rapid
for easy adjustment.

When she'd washed the blood away, the wound cut an angry red
slash of thinly healed skin from his hip to his shoulder. Hetta glared
down at it, as if convinced it was somehow worse than it looked.

"Was this from three nights ago?"

"You heard of my adventures with the nightwyrm, then?"

Her lips softened. "Wyn, a blind man would've noticed the path
of destruction that creature tore through the palace."

Wyn grimaced. "Yes. Precisely how angry have I made your
monarch?" He could smell the faint daphne of her perfume, and it
made him acutely conscious of his own dishevelled state, an unpleasant reminder of iron and blood and the tunnel beneath the earth.

Hetta sighed and wrung the cloth out, little plink-plinks hitting
the basin. "She's not happy with either of us. I've had her queensguard following me not very subtly around town for the last three
days." She rested the pads of her fingers on his stomach, and little
butterflies stirred in response. "Exactly how bad was this, Wyn, if
it's still like this three nights later?" She traced the length of the
wound without touching it. Her hands did not stop there, skimming up to frame his face. It was an unusual perspective, having
to look *up* rather than down to meet her eyes as she kissed him.
Her mouth was full of worry, and he brought his arms around to
nestle at her waist. *Yes,* said the clawing need inside. *This.* It was
the first time he'd kissed her without being simultaneously aware

of the signature of her magic, but it added a new dimension rather than subtracting one. This was pure Hetta, warm and fervent, and tasting very faintly of lemonade.

Her eyes were the colour of thunderstorms when she released him.

"I take it you missed me too?" he said.

"Quite desperately," she murmured, stroking her thumbs over his cheekbones. "I feel like I have five thousand or so things I need to tell you, but the first one is that you're *not* allowed to get yourself injured by any more fae monsters."

"I shall endeavour to obey that command."

"Good. See that you do," she said shortly. Her eyes were still red-rimmed as her gaze dragged back to the mark of the nightwyrm's attack. "What happened?"

An echo of that night's terror whispered down his spine. "The nightwyrm hurt me worse than I realised." He brought a hand to his shoulder, probing the newly healed skin. It was tender, but that was all. *It still shouldn't have taken three days to close over, not with my new powers.* The dismae had much to answer for. "I forgot what someone once told me: their claws and fangs are so sharp it's possible to take a death-wound but not know it until it's too late." He told her, a little sheepishly, about losing consciousness on top of a building adorned with stone statues of sea creatures.

"The Natural History Museum," she identified. "Honestly, only you would be embarrassed to lose consciousness after nearly taking a *death-wound* from a gargantuan fae monster." Her eyes flashed, and he wasn't sure if she was more annoyed at him or the nightwyrm, but her hands were gentle as she smoothed over the wound again. "Well, you're not bleeding, at least, but I can't help but feel this should still be bandaged." She made as if to move to find such materials then and there, and he silently mourned the loss of her touch.

"You may swaddle me in bandages if you wish, but I would like to wash first." He wrinkled his nose. "My accommodation these last few days has been somewhat sub par."

Hetta paused. "All right," she said after a moment. Her eyes met his, a dare in them, and she leaned past him and turned on the taps to the tub. "You can wash and explain where you've been at the same time."

His pulse quickened, and conflicting thoughts flashed through him between heartbeats. He wasn't an idiot; he knew where this was likely to go. He might not agree with certain mortal rules of proper behaviour, but he knew very well what they were, and the consequences for Hetta of breaking them. Was it really fair to entangle her fate with his, when stormcrows knew what Aroset might send for him next now she was queen? His chest tightened, thinking Aroset wasn't the only queen to consider. It might be best for Stariel if he distanced himself from Hetta to try to cool the mortal queen's wrath.

But there was vulnerability in Hetta's red-rimmed eyes, as if she feared he'd disappear once out of her sight. He recognised the match for his own crushing need for reassurance, for *closeness*. Perhaps he could've denied his own need, but it wasn't in him to deny hers. And he wanted… Stormcrows, he didn't know what he wanted, but he knew it had nothing to do with any mortal notion of propriety. Desire pulsed through him, jagged and raw as lightning. *Though considerably less painful.*

"That seems a very…practical suggestion," he said slowly, quirking an eyebrow at her. She didn't look away. He wasn't body-shy—the fae had little use for modesty—but this was different. Not shyness, but anticipation.

Her chin tilted upwards in unconscious challenge. "Yes, I thought so too."

"Excuse me, then." He stood, and the generously sized bathroom shrank as they contemplated each other. He could feel the weight of Hetta's gaze as he divested himself of the rest of his clothes and climbed into the tub. The sound of water filling the tub was nearly louder than his own heartbeat. A sigh of pleasure escaped him at the feel of the water on his skin, almost but not quite too hot to bear. *I'd begun to think I'd never be warm again.*

The tub had only a few inches of water in it, and he leaned back against the far end, out of the way of the running taps.

"Well?" he said to Hetta. "Are you going to check me over for further injuries?"

She laughed, throaty and delighted. "I should know better than to dare you by now, shouldn't I?" she reflected ruefully. "You always did like to try to shock me."

"This was your idea," he said mildly, hunting for the soap. He paused to grin at her. "Are you regretting it?"

"Not even slightly. Tell me about Gwendelfear."

He began to work up a lather as he told her about the lesser fae and the underground maintenance tunnel. "I suppose I must've presented too much of a temptation, unconscious and bound." He frowned down at the dismae. "I cannot truly blame her for her grudge against me. I *did* compel her and hold her prisoner. Though I'm glad I didn't have to promise her anything in exchange for my release." Hetta didn't say anything, and he tilted his head to find her tracing his soap-strokes with her eyes. "Hetta?"

She started. "What?"

He chuckled. "You are doing my vanity a world of good. Did you promise Princess Sunnika anything for returning me?"

"Oh, um, no. No, I didn't." Red bloomed in her cheeks. What had she been imagining? He himself was suffering from some very vivid imaginings that involved *both* of them in this tub. "In fact, I told her she'd owe me a debt if DuskRose was responsible for your absence, but I'm surprised it worked," she said to the ceiling, her voice breathier than usual.

He frowned. "Perhaps Sunnika is trying out mortal politics? Magically enforced obligations aren't the only ones."

"That's a rather terrifying thought," she agreed. "Though I'm finding I don't really have much thought for politics right this moment." She had laced her fingers together as if to stop herself from reaching out, but her gaze roved where her fingers would not, tracking water droplets as they rolled from his collarbone, down to his chest, to the waterline. Lower.

The tub was nearly full now, and he leaned forward and twisted the taps off. The bathroom echoed with small sloshing sounds, and clouds of steam rose from the water, scented faintly with the honeysuckle of the soap. It was strange again not to taste any magic. He'd thought his energy levels drained down to their dregs, but awareness sparked through him as he felt her gaze on him, until he imagined he could feel every tiny hair on his body, every vein and sinew.

Hetta gave in, perching on the lip of the bath and smoothing a hand over his shoulders. The touch lit up his nerve endings like the many braided paths of a lowland river as she followed the line of muscle around to the nape of his neck. He leaned into it, half-closing his eyes.

"Do you?" she asked, scooping up a handful of water and running it through his hair.

"Hmmm?" It was hard to focus on anything except the sensation. He wanted to lose himself in it, but at the same time it wasn't nearly enough. He wanted skin against skin, to kiss his way in a long line down to—

She laughed and prompted: "Do you have much thought for politics right now?"

He gestured at the evidence of his distraction. "Probably as much as you do." His voice came out deeper than usual.

Hetta's eyes were very dark. "I can't believe I'm about to say this— but shouldn't you, well, rest?"

"I've heard that beds are very good for resting."

"Wyn!" She laughed, splashing water at him. "Behave!"

"Do you want me to?" he asked seriously.

Her lips curved. "Well, no, but I felt that someone ought to make an effort to be reasonable."

"I feel distinctly *un*reasonable." He twisted around to embrace her, but she extricated herself with a squawk of outrage. "You're all wet!" she protested.

"A risk associated with bathing," He widened his eyes. "See how wet and bedraggled I am! Don't I deserve some coddling?"

She backed away, wise to his tricks. "Oh, no, I'm not going to be pulled into the bath with you. These are silk pyjamas!" The vulnerability he'd seen in her earlier was washing away, replaced with something warm and full of sensual mischief.

He sighed. "Hand me a towel then." Her eyes sparkled but she did as he bid as he stood, dripping water. "Perhaps you should check whether I'm hiding any other injuries?" he asked, twisting this way and that. He couldn't resist. The way she looked at him—it was like a flood of magic rising up through his toes, a rush of energy and sensation. Since his identity had been revealed, so many people had looked at him with distrust or unsettling fascination. But Hetta didn't look at him as if he were a monster or curiosity. There was only heat in her expression, and a tenderness that made it hard to draw a full breath.

She smirked but didn't come closer. Instead she opened the bathroom door, letting out billows of steam.

"Perhaps you should come out so I can do so properly," she said over her shoulder as she left.

He clambered out of the tub, wrapped the towel around his waist, and followed her out into her bedroom. This was the moment before a dive, where he could still change the angle of his wings, but he didn't want to alter course. *Selfish*, the word murmured in the back of his mind. He was being selfish, but he didn't care. Hetta wanted this. He wanted this. They were alone and safe, and no one need know what happened here. Why not finally give in to this reckless, lightning-soaked desire?

He felt drunk on anticipation, thick and heavy as treacle. It was too much and not enough all at once, and his magic shifted restlessly within its confines. He stroked the boundaries of his magic, feeling the cool metal at his wrists, reassuring himself. *I am safe.*

Hetta sat on the edge of the bed, a temptress in a dressing gown. The humidity had twisted her hair into interesting shapes, damp against her forehead. He paused, looking down at her, and smoothed the curls back. The pulse at her throat fluttered like a hummingbird's wings, but her eyes were a clear, penetrating grey. She flicked a fingernail at the metal dismae, and it vibrated slightly against his wrist, cold and unbending.

He raised his arms. "Do you know, there is a singular benefit to these? They keep my magic under control, regardless of… provocation."

"I've never been as worried as you are about losing control." She grinned, unexpectedly wicked. "You *do* know some loss of control is required in order to achieve satisfaction?"

There was only one possible answer to that. He leaned down and kissed her. The cold echo of the iron melted, and everything grew hard and desperate with wanting.

"Yes," he whispered against her skin. "I know." He stroked a fingertip over her quivering pulse, soft as thistledown. "I want this."

She let out a throaty laugh. "Good, because I certainly do."

"Ah…" He paused. "I realise that in my haste I did not ask you about precautions—"

"Fortunately, *I* have been taking precautions for months in the hope of tempting you into bed." She put her palms flat against his chest, the warmth thrilling through him. He found the ties to her dressing gown and undid them, pushing the material off Hetta's shoulders. The material swished gently as it fell. It landed on his feet, and he kicked it aside absently.

"They are very nice pyjamas," he said diplomatically.

"Are you suggesting they might look better elsewhere?" She lifted her arms obediently.

"The floor," he agreed, drawing the top garment over her head and tossing it somewhere in the vicinity of the dresser.

She laughed, her eyes full of sultry teasing, and lust blazed up in him like wildfire. It wasn't the first time he'd seen Hetta bare-breasted. Last time had been under a snow moon, when the wintertide magic had risen up and threatened to drag them both under. His memories of that night were slightly fogged at the edges.

This was much better than a magic-drunk memory. It was more than the call of flesh to flesh, more than magic. It was sheer concentrated Hetta-ness, the essence of her vibrantly alive and fiercely attractive.

She raised her eyebrows, utterly unselfconscious, and pointed at his towel. "Fair is fair."

He chuckled and removed the offending item before joining her on the bed. The mattress gave slightly under his weight. For a moment, neither of them moved, the potential humming between them holding them in place. Hetta watched him with darkly sensual eyes.

And then they both shifted at the same time and met in the middle. It sparked an entirely new level of sensation, kissing skin-to-skin, like the difference between humidity and a rainstorm.

"Henrietta Isadore Valstar," he said into the dip of her collarbone, using her full name giving him a little shiver of pleasure.

"So formal," she gasped as he traced his hands over her skin, over the curve of her breasts. Leysight notwithstanding, she felt like pure magic.

"It's a fae thing," he said. "Later." He hadn't the coherence to string enough words together for an explanation just now, not when Hetta's hands were performing their own exploration, each touch setting off a tiny starburst of sensation.

He'd worried that it would matter, his inexperience, but after all, this was Hetta, who understood him even when he didn't always understand himself, and that worry fell away as they learnt each other in teasing caresses and guided hands and small, urgent words like *there* and *yes* and *more*.

He'd known Hetta Valstar for more than ten years now, but this was a different kind of knowing, the shape of something growing between them that was more than their sum—something raw and physical and yet somehow more. The contrasts between their bodies sharpened. He followed the warm curves of her, enthralled, as she did the same to him.

When, panting, she pulled him towards her, he resisted, holding his weight above her as she arched in frustration. "Wyn!"

"Is there something you wanted?" He nuzzled at her neck.

She gave a low, throaty laugh. "Not as innocent as all that, are you?" She wriggled provocatively, and he groaned.

"You're debauching me thoroughly," he agreed roughly.

Exhilaration burned through his blood, as if he was riding the air currents above a hurricane. When he bridged the final space between them, the world fell away, as if he'd emerged suddenly into the perfect eye of the storm.

"Hetta," he said, his voice unrecognisable, sweat a slick line down his spine. Her eyes blazed dark as winter skies and caught him in their hold. He'd never been so wholly aware of the entirety of his being down to the last straining sinew, of her flesh and his, joined.

She rocked her hips, and then there was no more thought. Control surrendered to the instinct of rhythm, spiralling them higher and higher until the world fractured, and he with it.

NORMAL AWARENESS SLOWLY RETURNED. He was trembling, little forks of lightning shivering under his skin. A fog of magic filled the room, drifting in lazy eddies. They stared at each other, each of them still breathing hard. He felt raw and vulnerable and yet still filled with a deep want he had no name for. Hetta's eyes were wide and dark as the night, and he felt as if she could see through him, down to the burning emotion he was struggling to express. The intimacy was unbearable. He wanted to break away from it. He wanted it to go on forever.

Hetta reached up and stroked his hair without breaking the eye contact.

"I love you," he told her. He kissed her forehead, her cheeks, her lips. "I love you." Inadequate words, but all he had.

"I love you too," she said, a little shyly. She smiled in a very satisfied way. "Did the act meet your expectations, then?" she teased.

He struggled to find his levity, something shaken loose in his chest. "Yes. No." Both truth. Something dark and fierce clutched at him, almost like terror. Rakken's mocking repetition of the old saying hit him with sudden crystal clarity: *Love is for fools and mortals.* He'd dismissed the words as irrelevant—obviously fae were capable of love—but now he wondered if Rakken had meant it as a warning. Perhaps fae hearts weren't designed to bear this much feeling. How did mortals live like this? "Perhaps we ought to repeat the experience in order to make sure that wasn't a mere fluke. I'm certainly in favour of as much repetition as possible."

She chuckled. Her focus flickered away from his for a moment, and her eyes widened. "Wyn…" Amusement quivered in her voice. "Your fae is showing."

He frowned. But abruptly he realised what she meant; he was

in his fae form. His wings rose behind him, draping across the bed in great shimmering sheets of indigo. She reached up to curl her fingers around one of his horns, and he held still under the touch, frozen with shock. When had he changed? How could he have failed to notice?

Wait. He could *see* the magic in the room. He rolled to the side, feathers rustling against the bed, and looked down at his wrists. Both the dismae were black and cracked. He pulled at one, and it came free, the metal crumbling under pressure. He tore the other off, not quite daring to believe it until he stretched out with his leysight and met no resistance.

He held the broken dismae up to Hetta.

She blinked, then giggled. "Well, that's a convenient side effect."

I lost myself, he wanted to say. *I lost control again. What would that have meant without the dismae to stop me?* Abruptly he couldn't bear to be here like this, exposed in his fae form, and changed.

PILLOW TALK

ETTA COULD TELL Wyn was trying to reconstruct his careful walls. She would've been more annoyed, but it was hard to feel very annoyed by anything just now, with her limbs gone soft as pudding. Aftershocks of pleasure had her curling like a cat around the object of her affection. The object of her affection absently stroked circles over her stomach, his gaze unfocused, hair tufted into disarray.

"Am I imagining it, or does that look better than it did?" She stroked a line next to the gash across his torso, careful not to touch.

"Quite possibly," he agreed. "Since I should heal faster without the dismae."

"You're welcome, then."

He chuckled, and she wriggled up to rest her head on his shoulder. The moment stretched soft and long as taffy, the sound of his heartbeat a murmur of reassurance. She wanted to wallow in the languor, but the political thoughts she'd pushed aside earlier kept intruding. "Wyn?"

"Hmmm?" he asked sleepily.

How much responsibility did one owe to the wider world, set

against one's own needs and wants? She thought of piskies, and the nightwyrm, and a train station held in thrall to a single greater fae. Even if they stopped Aroset, that wouldn't stop every future problem stemming from Faerie. She thought of Alexandra's pale face, fearing she might be compelled once again.

"You said ThousandSpire was one of the most powerful courts in Faerie. Could its ruler control what fae do in the Mortal Realm?"

He tensed under her cheek, and all signs of sleep had gone from his tone when he spoke, low and careful. "Some fae—yes. But many fae—no. DuskRose and its allies would certainly not heed any directive given by ThousandSpire, at least. And no one really controls the wyldfae, outside the boundaries of faelands." He turned towards her, his eyes dark and worried. "I don't know how to stop Aroset, as Queen of the Spires, except perhaps to petition the High King himself."

"Your oldest sister hasn't been claimed by the faeland," she said quietly, meeting his gaze. "*No one* has bonded to the faeland." She told him about Marius arriving with the twins, about the attack at the theatre.

He absorbed this, going so still that only the rapid beat of his heart gave him away. "They think the Spires wants me." There was a plea in the russet of his eyes. He wanted her to tell him he was wrong. But she thought of dust and metal, arrowing towards him across the grass at the Standing Stones.

"Yes," she said instead. "What would it mean, if you were King of Ten Thousand Spires?"

"I'd have to leave Stariel."

Cold began to weave its way into her heart, and she wrapped her arms around him to ward it off. "You could visit though, couldn't you?"

The room filled with the threat of rainstorm, and he remained stiff under her touch. Eventually he said: "You're probably feeling it already, a pull back to Stariel, a sense that you're not where you ought to be in the world. The longer you're away, the stronger that feeling will become. I don't know how long it would take before you had to return, but eventually you would or else risk dire consequences. For you and Stariel both."

Hetta frowned. That put her yearning for home in a different light. "I wish you'd told me this before we left home! Am I about to keel over unexpectedly with pining, then, or will I get some warning?" The bond was wafer-thin without the ring, but she gave it a suspicious tug anyway. *So I really can't escape my lordship*, she couldn't help thinking.

"I don't know how long you could stretch your bond for. A month? Six months? A year? You are mortal, and every faeland is different. Besides, I suspect Stariel is more accustomed to mortal comings-and-goings than ThousandSpire. But, no, it would not be a sudden thing in any case."

"So you *could* still visit Stariel. If you were king." Why was she trying to argue with him about this? She didn't want him to rule ThousandSpire either.

He flinched slightly at the word king, the movement apparent only because she was draped over him. "Yes, I could visit," he told her. "But it isn't just the faelord that suffers when the bond is stretched. The land suffers as well. How absent could I be from it, how often, before it would be detrimental to the Spires?"

"We could alternate," Hetta pointed out. "That would share the burden, at least."

"Stop being practical!" he growled at her. "Is that what you want? Half a life together?"

"And stop being so unnecessarily dramatic!" She poked him in the ribs. "I'd rather that than nothing at all. Of course I don't want you to have to leave Stariel," she said more calmly. "But I'd rather know what our options are than fear unknowns."

Wyn stared unseeing into space, and Hetta didn't say anything more, even though she could feel the thoughts sliding between them.

"The palace guards," he said, after a long silence. "There were a pair of them unconscious, before the nightwyrm came. Someone had planted feathers on them." He gave a hollow laugh. "*White* feathers. The guards were very keen to interrogate me about it before the nightwyrm's arrival. Someone wanted them to have an excuse to do so."

Hetta sucked in a breath. "Whoever wanted to frame you based it on out-of-date information, then. Oh, I wished I'd asked to see those feathers! Though I don't know if it would've made much difference—the queen didn't believe me when I defended your honour." She told him what she'd learnt, watched him work through the same calculations she had.

"There are not so many people who've seen me in my fae form." He ticked them off. "The Valstars, the staff, the bank manager and his wife." He hesitated. "Lord Penharrow—though he didn't see me with my old plumage."

"Satisfying as it would be to pin this on Angus, I'm pretty sure it wasn't him." She walked her fingers down his chest, thinking. "I found out last night that the Earl of Wolver owns *Lady Peregrine's*, though I don't know what his motives would be in this. But I guess he'd have access to the palace guards as well. He could've drugged them or arranged for someone else to do so. He could've planted those feathers." She told him about her encounter with the reporter. "I don't think I did much good there—they're going to continue to do their best to besmirch your name, from the sounds of it." She rubbed her cheek against his shoulder.

"Besmirching *your* name as well," he said grimly. "Hetta—"

"Don't, Wyn. Don't tell me you're to blame for everything and that you should leave for my own good." She pulled away and rose up on her knees to glare at him. "You're not allowed to hypothetically ask me to marry you and then take it back. Stop trying to protect me!"

He might be an oh-so-tightly-controlled fae prince, but he was still very *male*, and few men could maintain detachment in the face of naked breasts. Heat sparked in his expression, desire and anger both.

"What if I said I'd marry you, *non-hypothetically*, the Spires, Queen Matilda, and the High King's permission be damned? Would you marry *me*?"

She rocked back on her heels. "What happens if you marry without the High King's permission?"

He followed her movement, reaching out to clasp her hips, as if he couldn't stop himself. "Why? Are you trying to protect me from the consequences of reckless decisions?"

Oh, *that* was unfair. "It would fracture your power again, wouldn't it?" she guessed. His narrowed gaze told her she'd guessed right. "Me having to deal with gossip isn't the same, and don't try to pretend it is." She leaned forward and put her palms flat against his chest. "I can handle scandal, but if you're going to give up on us so easily, you can get out of this bed right now."

He skimmed his hands up, slowly, and little pinpricks of sensation shivered through her.

"Hetta," he said, her name a caress. His voice had gone deep and husky, but there was still a hitch of amusement in it. "In that case, I am definitely not giving up."

40

THE MORNING AFTER

WYN WOKE TO a flood of glorious awareness. Where there had been only a numb void, the background magic of the world's leylines now shimmered against his skin as it should. He leisurely extended his senses, like a cat stretching in a pool of sunlight. *And to think I assumed I was doing a fine job of playing human for all those years.* Mortals didn't feel as if they were missing a limb without magic, did they?

The differences between fae and mortals are greater than I realised. A memory bubbled up from a few months before: Marius, sitting in the library's windowseat, a book resting on his knees, his gaze heavy. "How do you expect us to accept you if you can't accept yourself?" he'd asked, in his characteristic fashion of cutting right to the heart of your vulnerabilities without warning.

Hetta was curled against him, still asleep, the coverlet loose around her waist. She didn't wake as he snaked an arm over her side and splayed his hand possessively over her stomach, or as he shaped his body to the curve of her spine and kissed the top of her head, tucked beneath his. Her hair smelled floral from her own soap—and his, he thought with a grin, remembering the clouds of honeysuckle-scented steam from the bath the night before. She made a sleepy "mmmfff" and burrowed further into the pillow.

He'd loved her so deeply and for so long that he hadn't thought it possible to feel any further increase in intensity, but something made of a thousand razored edges grew in his chest as he watched her. He'd touched the outer edges of the Maelstrom, and the power of it had shredded his wings. And yet, the terror he'd felt then was nothing to what he felt now, contemplating the possibility of losing this woman.

He should think of how to resolve things with the mortal queen, of what he should do regarding ThousandSpire, of the identity and motivations of his hidden enemy in this mortal city, and how in the high wind's eddies he was going to find the High King.

Instead, he thought of Stariel.

This was the longest he'd been away from the estate since his arrival there. The new housekeeper was competent but inexperienced. Had she managed to keep Buddle from bullying her over the correct procedures? Had the thatchers sent in their quote for the cottages? He and Jack had discussed trialling some new seed varieties on the Home Farm, with Hetta to adjust the drainage slightly. Would the soil be warm enough yet to try? How had the new sheep from Penharrow been received? How were the repairs to the Dower House proceeding?

The hotel was quiet, and the bright light edging over the top of the curtains told him it was after dawn. He'd slept later than usual, but then he'd had an unusually tiring few days. *And nights*, he thought wryly, watching the rise and fall of Hetta's chest.

What had happened last night to break the dismae? *Did I lose control, or was that something else?* Was such a surge of power at such a time normal, for greater fae? Reluctantly, he considered that there were two greater fae in the city who might know the answer to that question. *Am I brave enough to ask Catsmere whether her own powers changed so dramatically as she aged? Or when she experienced physical intimacy for the first time?* Catsmere had always been fondest of him, of all his siblings. She might even tell him, though she would *definitely* tease him first. He frowned, wondering suddenly where his other siblings were. Why wasn't Irokoi with the twins? At least Wyn knew he was alive, based on that strange astral projection. *That's three out of five accounted for.* Torquil ought to be safest of all of them, under the protection of a foreign court.

He abruptly realised why his thoughts had drifted to family. On cue, Marius knocked sharply on Hetta's door, the sound amplified in the morning quiet. What had brought him here at this hour? Marius wasn't a naturally early riser.

"Hetta? Are you awake? I've news!" Marius knocked again. "Let me in!" Hetta must've given him the key to her suite, since he was knocking on the internal door between her bedroom and the sitting room. Oh dear.

"Hetta, love," Wyn murmured. "Wake up."

Hetta grumbled her way to consciousness as Marius repeated his hammering. He sounded excited rather than alarmed. Wyn sighed and slid out of the bed, to Hetta's general disapproval.

"Can't we just pretend we haven't heard him?" Hetta said in an undertone.

Marius knocked again. "Hetta? Is everything all right?"

Wyn just raised his eyebrows. "How well do you know your brother?" He stalked off to find his trousers. His ruined shirt he'd have to do without, since they'd left it in the sitting room, but Marius would melt into the ground with embarrassment if Wyn appeared without any clothing at all. He found his trousers still on the floor of the bathroom and reluctantly pulled them on.

Hetta followed his progress and made an unhappy sound when he reappeared half-clothed. "I suppose you're right." She raised her voice. "I'm coming, Marius!" She slipped out of the bed and hunted around for her dressing gown.

"Under the bed," Wyn said, voice still low enough that Marius wouldn't hear. "Do you want me to hide?" He would *not* use glamour on Marius. It would be a breach of trust, given their history. *Though I'm not sure Marius will understand the finer points of honour in this precise situation.*

Hetta paused, considering and then discarding the idea. She shook her head. "No. Either this is trivial enough that I can send him away without letting him in, or serious enough that you need to hear what he has to say too. And I'm tired of living my life worrying about offending my relatives' sensibilities."

Hetta retrieved her dressing gown while he found her pyjamas. Once dressed, she nodded decisively and strode to the door. Wyn slunk sideways, out of its line of sight, hoping that Hetta's first supposition was correct and that it was something trivial. Marius would be hurt if he found Wyn here at this hour in this state, hurt for more complicated reasons than worrying about his sister's reputation.

"Were you asleep?" Marius said when Hetta opened the door. Her expression must have spoken volumes. "Sorry," he said in a rush. "But the twins are back, and His Royal Featheriness said he could sense Wyn's presence! He's nearby!"

Wyn felt a sharp surge of irritation at his older brother. Damn Rake. He'd wager quite a lot that Rake knew exactly what he'd sent Marius to interrupt; he'd think it extremely funny. Wyn should've paid more attention in his early morning musings. He reached out now and found, sure enough, the blaze along the leylines that signified the presence of greater fae. Rakken and Catsmere had left their presence unmasked deliberately, for the blaze snapped out as he touched it.

"Why aren't you excited?" Marius said. Wyn heard him suck in a breath of intuition. "You already know he's back."

"Yes," Hetta said. She sent Wyn a resigned glance as her brother pushed his way into the room.

Marius was already dressed in his day clothes. A mass of tension fell from his shoulders as he caught sight of Wyn.

"Thank the gods. You're all right!" And he strode over and embraced him briefly, heedless of Wyn's bare-chested state. "You're all right," he repeated, pulling back and frowning at the fading scar on Wyn's abdomen. "What happened?"

Guilt and fondness fought for primacy. Marius had been worried about him, and Wyn had extended that worry longer than necessary. Stormwinds, but he'd been a terrible friend of late.

"A nightwyrm happened," he said. "But I am better now."

Marius's initial relief was fading, replaced by suspicion. He looked to Hetta, who had sunk down onto the edge of the bed. "How long, exactly, have you been here, Wyn?" he said slowly. A flush crept over his cheeks and made a bid for his ears as he took in the full scene: the rumpled bed, Wyn's bare chest, and Hetta's dishevelled hair. His horrified gaze caught on Hetta's neck, and Wyn realised with a thrill of shame that there was a very incriminating love-bite blooming just above her collarbone.

There was a long silence.

Marius screwed up his face as if in pain. "No," he said. "Please tell me what I think is happening is not happening."

"Honestly, Marius, don't be such a prude," Hetta said matter-of-factly, though her own colour was high. Should Wyn try to draw Marius's ire or was it better to let the siblings sort it out between them?

Marius opened his eyes but seemed unable to find anywhere to look that didn't increase his embarrassment and eventually settled on the ceiling. "Dash it, Hetta! We're in a hotel with spies outside looking for Wyn and half of Meridon already spreading malicious talk about you. And you're not married yet!"

"This may surprise you, but marriage isn't actually a mandatory prerequisite," Hetta said acerbically. "And you've only yourself to blame for barging in here at this hour!"

"Where are my siblings, Marius?" Wyn asked. But this only

reminded Marius of his presence, and he whirled on him, equal parts self-righteous fury, horror, and embarrassment.

"You! Are you going to try to pretend you don't know exactly how inappropriate this is?"

"I'm aware of mortal customs," Wyn said. "Though I don't always agree with them. Why does it matter if we're married or not? Particularly since I intend to marry Hetta eventually?" He shook his head. "But I fear no good can come of pursuing this line of conversation."

But Marius was not to be shifted. "What do you mean, eventually? There's no *eventually* about this; you'll marry her as soon as we can arrange it."

Hetta stood, sparkling with anger. "I'm not chattel to be married off at someone else's command! Especially hypocritical ones. If I was a man, you wouldn't give a damn what I did with who!" Marius went white, and Hetta made an impatient sound. "Oh for goodness' sake, I didn't mean it that way! Not everything is about you!"

"I actually can't marry her yet, Marius," Wyn said, hoping to distract him. He was so very sensitive about his proclivities. Understandable, in a mortal society that was so against them. There were few things Wyn preferred about the fae courts over the Mortal Realm, but that was definitely one of them. "I need the fae High King's permission to do so, since I am fae royalty, but I intend to seek it."

"Well, you should have bloody thought of that before!" Marius spluttered, still beet red.

Wyn sighed. "I'm prepared to accept a certain amount of recrimination from you, but do you mind if I fetch a clean shirt first? I would prefer to be dressed if either the queensguard appears to fetch me or my sister sends further monsters to kill me."

Marius folded his arms with a huff. "Oh, very well. But don't think this means I'm finished yelling at you."

Wyn had about five seconds' warning between hearing rapid footsteps approaching and Alexandra bowling into the room. Hetta's sister pulled up short, immediately absorbing the general atmosphere of awkwardness if not its specifics.

"Wyn?" Alexandra said. "You're back! Are you all right? What happened?" She took in his half-dressed state and blushed.

"He can explain later," Hetta said firmly. "And you can all show yourselves out while I get dressed. Wyn, go and find a shirt."

"As you wish, my Star," Wyn said, unable to stop from smiling, and slunk out of the room.

He met Aunt Sybil in the corridor on his way to his room and pulled up a glamour without compunction, struck with a strong urge to laugh. He met no other obstacles as he navigated the hotel, but his leysight told him trouble was waiting ahead.

He contemplated his door, noting that the wards he'd originally set up had been dismantled. A petty jab at him, or something more sinister? He took a deep breath, pulling cool air over his skin, and opened the door.

41

OBSIDIAN

RAKKEN LOUNGED IN the armchair next to the window in a position that declared he considered Wyn's quarters his to use as he wished. Wyn wasn't particularly attached to his hotel room, but the deliberate insolence irritated him nonetheless. It had probably been Rakken who'd dismantled his wards. An old but familiar feeling crept over him: that of being the youngest of six siblings who were constantly trying to get under his skin.

Still, he chose to take it as a good sign that Rakken was simply trying to irritate him rather than anything more sinister, since it was clear his brother was absolutely furious beneath his mask.

But it wasn't Rakken that concerned him the most. Catsmere stood next to the mantelpiece in the wide-legged stance she tended to fall into as a default—a position she could hold for hours, or, alternatively, from which she could attack with the speed of a peregrine falcon.

Both the twins were dressed in Spires fashion, though they were in their mortal forms. It had been a long time since Wyn had seen Cat with her softer human face, and for a moment it made it difficult to tell what she was thinking. His heart beat very fast as despite himself he looked for some sign that she was glad to see him. She wore an ensemble in dark green leather with a softer shade of over-tunic, which meant she thought violence was possible but not guaranteed; otherwise she would have worn black.

She took in his appearance, lingering a moment on the healing wound from the nightwyrm. Her stance did not change, but she eventually said, "Hello, little brother."

"Will you let me embrace you?" he asked, remembering Marius's greeting and wishing for a moment that his own family were more demonstrative.

She canted her head to the side, but a smile curved her lips. "Still so sentimental? But if you wish."

Rakken snorted, and Wyn ignored him as he strode forward and hugged his sister. It was strange not to feel feathers as he did so. She smelled very faintly of cinnamon, one of the signatures of her magic. The other was the salty tang of the sea in storm.

"You reek of sex," she said when he released her, wrinkling her nose. Amusement sparked in the depths of her green eyes.

Rakken plucked idly at the leather buttons on the armchair. "Yes, I hope you satisfied Lord Valstar, Hollow, given the relationship with FallingStar seems increasingly important in this new world we find ourselves in."

"Neither of you is as funny as you think you are," Wyn told them.

"Didn't you enjoy your welcome party this morning?" Rakken said, levering himself off the armchair in a single swift motion. His outfit was more ornate than Cat's, a pattern of twining serpents tracing their way from his high collar down his sleeves.

"Was that bit of pettiness truly necessary?"

Rakken's smile sharpened, but that was the only warning Wyn got before he attacked. Wyn had been living at human-speed for too long; he'd forgotten how fast fae could move. Old training kicked in, and he blocked the first blow, aimed at his head, but missed the second. Rakken's jab hit him just under his ribs. Pain exploded, and he stumbled backwards, but before he could try to retaliate, Rakken had him pressed against a wall, an obsidian knife to his throat.

Wyn went very still, the blade cold against his skin. Rakken wanted the Spires, badly. *And he's thought about killing me for it.* That knowledge sat between them as he met his brother's eyes, and a chill went down his spine. But there was no scent of magic in the air, and Catsmere had made no move to back her twin up, though Rakken was as furious as Wyn had ever seen him, emerald eyes ablaze with it.

He gambled. "Your move, brother. Are you going to cut my throat?"

The green fire in Rakken's eyes flared, and he snarled. "You can't even defend yourself. Pathetic."

Wyn's temper bristled. He knew what was behind Rakken's anger, if not his actions, but it was neither Wyn's fault nor his desire that ThousandSpire prefer him over his brother. And as for defending himself? Rakken was older and stronger than Wyn, a talented sorcerer, and regularly sparred with one of the Spires' greatest warriors. Wyn had spent the last decade as a human butler. What did Rakken expect, truly? But he did not care for the disdain in his brother's voice. His father's voice came back to him, telling him he was weak and sentimental, a disgrace to his court.

His power stirred. "Let me go, Rake."

"Make me," Rakken sneered.

Wyn only dared do it because Rakken was a stormdancer and, as such, largely resistant to elektrical charge. He drew the lines up like unspooling yarn until they writhed in anticipation.

Rakken laughed, a hint of citrus in the air. "Don't you dare bring magic into this, little Hollow."

The lightning cracked out in a whip. Rakken's magical shield was fast, but not quite fast enough. The shock threw him across the room, where he landed like a cat, spitting mad, his dark hair on end with static, charge crawling down the fine gold hairs threaded through it. Sparks of lightning danced in his eyes.

"Did you kill Father?" he snarled, his power abruptly vast, blanketing the room. *Was* Rakken more powerful than he should've been? Wyn was the youngest; his siblings had always been more powerful than him. *But I am more than what I was*, he thought, refusing to back down.

"Why do you care if I did or not? You were planning to kill him anyway!" he pointed out. "Father's death was always part of your plans!"

"How well will Lord Valstar like you with your teeth rearranged, do you think?" Rakken said.

Wyn increased the amount of charge in the air. Rakken growled. The air churned with magic, and despite Wyn's increasing trepidation, he'd never felt more *alive*.

Catsmere still stood to one side with a faintly chiding air, which was reassuring. She wouldn't let Rakken kill him, would she? And his brother might be furious, but his actions were never dictated by pure emotion. Wyn frantically tried to figure out what Rakken was trying to achieve here, but adrenaline made his thoughts thick and hard to sieve as Rakken prowled towards him.

Wyn jumped atop the bed, really the only direction he could go in the small room, and wondered if the higher ground would make Rakken relent. But his brother smiled, the expression without mirth. A knife glinted in his hand, and Wyn nearly missed the movement. He ducked and rolled away as the knife thunked into the wooden headboard. It quivered there, and Wyn gulped. Maybe Rakken *did* wish to kill him.

"Stariel killed Father," he said, a chill running through him.

This appeared to only enrage Rakken further. "Ah, yes. Weak little Hollow, still running to others for protection." Another knife appeared in his hand. That was a spell Wyn hadn't mastered before he left home—the trick of folding space to store small objects. Rakken had always been good at it. "Still running now."

"You requested Stariel's help to rid yourself of our father in the first place, so I don't see why you should object to the faeland's part in this."

"I," Rakken said, eyeing Wyn like a jaguar about to pounce, "own my dark deeds, brother. And I am not as defenceless as a lamb in the night."

Wyn didn't move fast enough this time, and the second blade nicked his bicep as he flung himself backward. The flesh wound stung, bleeding freely, though he knew it would heal within minutes. *If I survive that long.*

But Catsmere still hadn't joined Rakken. She leaned back against the wall nearest the door, expression cool.

"Neither am I," Wyn told his brother, and sent a whip of air to wrap around Rakken's feet. Rakken dodged it contemptuously, but Wyn followed it with a snake of elektricity arcing down the lampshade cord. Rakken winced as it snapped down from his body, discharging most of its power into the carpet. Ozone filled the room. Oh dear—the hotelier would not be pleased.

"Pitiful," Rakken taunted.

"Do you want me to truly try to fry you, Rake?" Wyn said, growing tired of this game, whatever it was about.

"Do you think you have the control or the power to do that?" He sounded genuinely curious.

Flick. Another knife. Wyn felt a chunk of hair shear off as he sidestepped. *How many knives does he have stored?* But even if Rakken's obsidian ones ran out, he could resort to air-blades if he wanted to keep this up.

"I've power enough to make you regret it if I try," Wyn said truthfully.

"Interesting." Rakken played with his current knife, throwing it from hand to hand without taking his eyes off Wyn. "But you must know that I'm toying with you, little brother. Cat and I could slit your throat in under ten seconds if we were minded to do it." Anger blazed up in his eyes again. "And Set is more powerful than both of us together, even now."

Understanding flashed through Wyn, confirmed by a second glance at Cat. Her gaze wasn't just cool but evaluating.

"You're testing me!" he said indignantly. "Is it truly necessary to keep throwing knives at me, Rake? I don't know what you're hoping will happen! Of course I'm out of practice. You already knew that!"

The words cost him, for this time the knife scored across the healing wound on his abdomen. He hissed in pain. The aim had been deliberate too, for Rakken's eyes gleamed with satisfaction.

"You've spent too much time playing human, brother." He tossed the next knife almost idly. "It won't help you survive in the Spires."

"I don't *wish* to return to the Spires," Wyn said, sensing that this was the heart of the issue. "I don't wish to rule, Rake, if that's what's driving this behaviour. There's no point raging at me because you couldn't hold the Spires against Set, or because you fear it might choose me over you."

"Wishes are for children," Rakken said, and his anger transformed into something hard and cold. There was so much bitterness in him, enough to freeze over the hottest day of summer, and Wyn saw a concerned echo cross Catsmere's expression, though she did not shift out of her watchful stance. "Are you a child, still?" He canted his head. "A human child? Or a royal stormdancer?"

"Fine," Wyn snapped, temper flaring. "Fine, if you must cling to your melodrama. I knew what would happen when I translocated Father to Stariel. I meant for it to kill him." Truth like acid. He changed forms. He wasn't a child, and Rakken was right; he ought to own his sins. Ice grew in his chest, suffocating his anger. Was that why ThousandSpire wanted him? "Does that satisfy you?"

Rakken stilled. Catsmere abandoned her post and closed the distance between them. She gestured for Wyn to spread his wings, and after a moment of inner debate, he obliged. It was cramped in the small room, and his primaries brushed the walls on one side.

"Does this mean you're going to stop throwing things at me?" he asked Rakken pointedly.

Rakken ignored him. Wyn hated how they still treated him like a younger sibling to be snubbed or praised depending on their moods.

"Your blood feathers have grown in," Catsmere noted, examining his back. "I would have thought you too young." Her attention made the skin between his shoulders itch, but Rakken was right. If the twins wanted to kill him, they could. Wyn had to trust that this wasn't just some elaborate prelude to another attack. Catsmere, at least, would be unlikely to choose such a roundabout approach.

"When did this happen?" Rakken asked, and Wyn narrowed his eyes.

"Are you going to continue throwing knives, brother?" he repeated. Rakken shrugged, showing empty palms, and Wyn thought about how much he was willing to reveal to his siblings. "Last winter. I don't know when the first signs began, but after the Maelstrom, the changes accelerated."

"Interesting," Catsmere said. "It didn't affect Mouse's wings."

Rakken raised a sardonic eyebrow in response to Wyn's incredulity. "Yes, brother, I survived the storm too. *Without* breaking my wings, I might add."

So Wyn's instincts had been right—Rakken's power *had* increased, though it was hard to tell how much. Both twins had better control than he did, the legacy of the years they'd spent in Faerie while he'd been in Mortal.

"Not you, though?" Wyn asked Catsmere.

She shrugged. "It was a calculated risk." He heard what she didn't say; that they'd thought whichever one of them entered the

Maelstrom might not come out again, but that Rakken at least had been desperate enough to chance it. Had Catsmere tried to argue him out of it? Had she even known what he was planning? Many people made the mistake of thinking the twins always acted as a unit—a perception they both took pains to encourage—but the truth was more complicated.

Rakken was still considering Wyn's wings. "Has it occurred to you that they look remarkably like Mother's?" He blinked, as if startled by his own words.

Did they? Obviously Wyn knew the colour of his own mother's wings. Didn't he? He reached for the memory, but it was strangely elusive. His mother...she'd had green, green eyes, Rakken and Catsmere's eyes, and her wings were blue, weren't they? But trying to remember was like struggling through thick, cloying fog that whispered that everything was fine. Everything *was* fine. There was no reason to be anxious.

Rakken frowned. What had he just asked? Wyn couldn't recall; it was gone like mist under sunlight. Rakken opened his mouth, shut it again, and shook his head, as if whatever he'd wanted to say had suffered the same fate.

They'd been talking about Wyn's wings, hadn't they? He flared his wings slightly, the motion a small challenge. "Blue is Stariel's colour—I've chosen to take this as an omen. Why are you both so sure the Spires wants me, anyway? What of Koi and Quil?"

"Koi was in the Spires when Father fell. If it had wanted him, it could have taken him then," Catsmere said.

"But where is he now? He said he was stuck." He told them about the astral projection Irokoi had sent. "And what did he mean, Cat, that there isn't another way?"

Catsmere's expression was closed, but she shook her head. "The High King knows. He's always liked being cryptic."

Rakken dropped back into the armchair with a sigh. "At least he's not dead, if he's sending you messages. At least Set hasn't killed him as well." He said it almost to himself, and a warning bell sang in Wyn's head, a sixth sense of imminent sorrow.

"Torquil Tempestren is dead," Catsmere said, and Wyn froze. A soft, sharp pain sliced into his chest.

"I didn't feel it," he protested. Torquil *couldn't* be dead. It had been a comfort, to think that at least one of his siblings had escaped the Spires.

"*We* did," Rakken bit out. "It was Set. She's determined to have the Spires. At any cost."

"And you're not?" he challenged.

Rakken smiled. "Don't think I wasn't tempted, Hollow. But Cat feels a degree of responsibility for your wellbeing. I suppose helpless things must have a certain hold on the conscience, else newborn babes would be abandoned before they drew their first breaths."

Wyn said nothing. He didn't much appreciate being likened to a newborn babe, but he didn't want any more knives thrown at him either.

Torquil was *dead*. The words echoed and echoed until the individual syllables ceased to have meaning.

Rakken's expression grew oddly pensive. "I've killed for the Spires before." Though he was outlined in sunlight from the window, Wyn had the sudden impression of a fin surfacing briefly from dark waters. Was Rakken thinking of DuskRose's golden prince? "I would prefer, on the whole, that no more of my kin died for it."

"Even Set?" Wyn asked, surprised. *Dead, dead, dead. My brother is dead.*

"It may be necessary," Rakken conceded. "But it seems a waste. These Valstars of yours make me wonder what we could've achieved if Father hadn't played us off against each other. Perhaps this was merely his way of preventing us from banding together to overthrow him. There are—were—six of us, little brother. Most of the other courts guard their offspring jealously and would spend greatly to preserve them, but we have been profligate. Father would have killed you merely for his own love of power. He encouraged Set to attack Koi, and now she's succeeded in killing Torquil. She'll kill us and anyone else who might oppose her if she can." He rubbed at the nape of his neck. If he'd had wings, they would've drooped. "You must return to the Spires."

How could he refuse, with Torquil's true name ringing in his ears? *Dead*, he thought. *Gone.* There was no brother between him and the twins now. He'd known Aroset was trying to kill him, but it was still shocking, somehow; in Faerie, death came rarely for greater fae and almost never for royal fae. King Aeros's death had shaken him; it seemed unfair that *another* of Wyn's family could be dead too. *And I am also responsible for this one.* If he'd accepted ThousandSpire's bond when the faeland had reached for him the first time, would Torquil still be alive?

"You say you and Cat could cut my throat if you wished, and yet together you're still not strong enough to overcome Set," Wyn said, mouth suddenly dry. "What do you expect me to do?" His heart beat too fast. *I don't wish for this*, he wanted to shout. But who would he shout it at? Faelands didn't care for mortal politics or mortal hearts.

"Don't be disingenuous, Hollow. You know it won't matter what your relative powers are if you bond to the faeland," Catsmere said, flicking one of his flight feathers. "We neither of us hoped to see you as king, but better that than Set."

"Or a lordless faeland," Rakken murmured. "The Spires grows... restless." His gaze grew distant. "I'll need to think where the best chance of achieving resonance will be in this realm, so we can cross the borders. Set will have found the one in Knoxbridge by now— she's been trying to block translocation, but her power is spread thinly, trying to ward the entire faeland without a bond to it." He grimaced. "Father's wards have begun to unravel."

Wyn pulled his wings hard against his body and changed back, as if he could deny his heritage as easily. "I know where there's a resonance between here and the Spires."

COFFEE AND CRUMPETS

ETTA SAW THE future in Wyn's expression when he and the twins entered the sitting room, and her heart dropped like a stone. Suddenly light-headed, she tightened her fingers around her coffee cup, grounding herself in its warm, comforting solidity. She'd asked a maid to bring up a carafe and a generous breakfast tray for her—or rather Wyn. She didn't know yet how they were going to solve the dual problems of Queen Matilda and ThousandSpire, but she *did* know that magic used energy and that Wyn would need to eat before he went running off to sacrifice himself for the greater good or whatever he was about to propose.

Of course, she'd imagined a *private* breakfast where they could discuss it. Her interfering relatives, however, were all squashed into the sitting room with them, and Aunt Sybil pounced on Wyn as soon as he came in, launching into an impressive lecture on all the reasons why his absence and lack of communication were unacceptable. Alexandra and Marius observed from the chesterfield, punctuating the lecture with vigorous nods. Wyn's siblings took up silent observation posts on either side of the door, though a faint hint of amusement stirred around Catsmere's mouth.

Hetta handed Wyn a cup of tea; she'd learnt he preferred it to coffee. He took it with a silent nod of thanks, not taking his polite attention from her aunt, who was now dwelling on the indignity of having her quarters searched by uncivilised ruffians before enumerating the various impertinent questions she'd had to endure from her acquaintances. The timepiece on the mantel showed it wasn't yet eight o'clock.

Eventually, the diatribe wound down into affronted silence.

"I'm sorry to have worried you, my lady," Wyn said sincerely. "And thank you for your forbearance."

Aunt Sybil sniffed. "Yes, well, such behaviour is not to be repeated!"

"Do you mean that he's not to run away from the queen again? Because technically he's *still* on the run," Marius pointed out helpfully. "And in just as much trouble as before."

Hetta glared at her brother.

"Well, he is," he said, unrepentant.

"Your mortal politics are not our primary concern," Catsmere said from beside the door. "This is pointless delay, brother. We should leave for the Spires now."

Marius made a garbled sound. "What do you mean *leave*? You can't just leave, not after—" His cheeks flushed, and he bit his tongue, glancing at Aunt Sybil, who fortunately misunderstood.

Aunt Sybil pulled herself straight. "No, you certainly cannot leave now! You must go to Her Majesty and explain yourself before you do anything else," she said firmly. "And I must say that though I'm *not* in favour of the match, it's unacceptable for you to embroil Henrietta in scandal and then not offer to marry her! Though I for one wouldn't blame her if she won't have you after this!"

Hetta met Wyn's eyes and wasn't reassured by the expression in them. She'd known this was coming. In her head, she even knew it was probably for the best. The King of Ten Thousand Spires might not be able to solve all the issues faced by Prydein now that Faerie was here to stay, but it would certainly help a great deal. And, as Marius had pointed out, they could probably use Stariel's ability to make its own treaties for leverage with the queen.

It didn't stop the scream building up in her lungs, a childish wail of unfairness. She pressed her lips together and held it in. She wasn't a child, and she'd *make* this work, she vowed, despite all the obstacles Wyn had listed last night. There had to still be space in this for her and Wyn as individuals.

The russet of Wyn's irises was very clear, the flecks of brandy-gold picked out by the pale sunshine filtering through the windows.

"I said I had things to do first, Cat," he said quietly. He smiled at Aunt Sybil. "I *do* intend to present myself to Queen Matilda, my lady. But first, I would also like to encourage the rest of you to return to Stariel. My sister is dangerous, and I can't guarantee she won't target anyone I care about. It would ease my mind to have you all safely inside its borders."

There was an immediate uproar. Rakken and Catsmere accused Wyn of procrastination; Marius of selfishness. Alexandra wrung her hands anxiously and tried to become as small as possible in the corner of the sofa.

Wyn made his way to Hetta where she still stood rooted to the floor by the window. He looked down at her, soft and sad, and she gave in to the urge to smooth the lapels of his coat. They didn't need smoothing, but she wanted to touch him. Marius squawked, and she shot him a look she hoped conveyed how silly she thought he was being. The barn doors were open, and the horses had well and truly fled.

"The queen told me not to leave the city," she said. "And even if she hadn't, I'm not running away and leaving you to sort out this mess by yourself."

"It's my mess," he said.

"No, it's very much *my* mess, if we must assign ownership. Queen Matilda wouldn't even know you existed if it weren't for me. I know you're hoping that turning yourself in voluntarily will soften the queen towards you," she said. His expression took on a sheepish edge that said her deduction was correct. "But what if it doesn't? And what if she was responsible for trying to frame you with those guards?"

"More to the point," Rakken said, "handing yourself over to this mortal queen doesn't get you any closer to the Spires, particularly if she has more dismae."

"I won't voluntarily wear dismae again," Wyn said with a hardness that told her just how much they'd affected him. "Nor am I proposing to remain a prisoner at Her Majesty's indefinite leisure. But I need to ensure Queen Matilda does not hold Hetta or Stariel to blame for my disappearance." He smiled. "She will, at least, have to admit that the feathers her guards found were *not* mine. Perhaps that will spur her to investigate her own court and remove some attention from Stariel and me."

Hetta put her cup down with a clink. "All right, enough." She glared at both her and Wyn's assorted relatives. "You can all go away now. Go and eat breakfast downstairs or something." She made a shooing motion. "I want to talk to Wyn without you all arguing at cross-purposes."

"It's not appropriate to leave the two of you alone—" Aunt Sybil began.

Hetta just managed to stop herself from saying she didn't care, instead reining in her temper. "Please, Aunt?" Hating the pleading note that had crept into her voice, she added: "It's not as if anyone else knows he's here. We just need to talk. *Alone.*"

Marius levered himself up off the sofa and gave both her and Wyn a narrow look. "It better be just talking, Hetta." She nearly rolled her eyes at him but refrained, since he seemed to be on her side in this. He narrowed his eyes at Wyn. "We'll see you after

breakfast. Come on, Alex." He shepherded his younger sister past
the twins. Aunt Sybil hesitated.

Rakken offered her an arm. "Might I escort you down, Lady
Langley-Valstar?"

✦❦✦

She went straight into Wyn's arms. He leaned his cheek against
her head as she breathed in the smell of clean linen and magic. It
was tempting just to stay there and let the rest of the world go hang,
but eventually she pulled away.

"You're leaving," she said flatly.

"Not this minute, but yes, once I have done what I can here."
He told her about Torquil, and it shook her, the careful way he
told her his brother was dead, the stunned denial he couldn't quite
hide. If something happened to one of her brothers or sisters, she
would—she couldn't *imagine* what she would do. And to imagine
them murdering each other? She felt sick. "I can't keep running
from the Spires."

She took the lid off the breakfast tray. "You *can* eat some toast,
though. And bacon."

He chuckled, considering the mountain of food. "What did you
tell the maid?"

"That I was ravenous but also indecisive." She helped herself to
a crumpet.

They sat together on the sofa, knees touching, eating in a silence
that wasn't so much companionable as charged. The space between
them had become an overlapping thing, as if her body had mem-
orised the shape of his and now adjusted for it unconsciously. And
yet she'd never been more aware of him, the brush of his arm against

hers as he leaned forward, the heat of him against her side. From prior experience, she knew sex and emotional connection weren't necessarily related, but she was forced to admit something *had* changed between them since last night. She didn't regret it. Did he?

"How exactly were you planning to approach the queen? I have to go and sign official paperwork tomorrow morning, if you want to smuggle yourself in as part of my entourage. I was planning to bring Marius with me to double-check Her Majesty hasn't slipped anything she shouldn't in."

He put down his cup. "I fear that may lead Her Majesty to think you knew my whereabouts. Or, at least, that you didn't hand me over as soon as I reappeared. I'd like to spare you that charge, at least."

"What are you proposing then? Drop out of the sky?" Hetta didn't like this suggestion, remembering the bristling hostility of the guards. "What if one of the guards shoots you?"

"Princess Evangeline told me that she and her mother walk alone in the queen's private garden before breakfast."

She looked at the timepiece and wrinkled her nose. "That's still tomorrow then." Thank the gods. She still had him for one more day at least. "But what if you can't talk her round? What if she summons her guard and tries to imprison you again?"

He sighed. "Then I become a fugitive in truth. And hope she'll change her stance at a later date if I become the ruler of a foreign nation." He smiled, attempting levity, but uncertainty flickered in his eyes.

She swallowed. "King."

He flinched as if she'd struck him and then immediately apologised. "Sorry—"

"Don't. I don't like it any more than you do, but we can't not talk about it. I of all people ought to understand that sometimes we have obligations bigger than just ourselves." *Even though I haven't been doing a good job of that lately.* She gave a weak smile. "But I do expect you to give Stariel very favourable trade terms for our sheep."

He didn't say anything for long moments, and then he forcibly pulled himself together. "You're right. If I am…king, then that will put me in a significantly better bargaining position with your queen. I—*we*—need to use that." He turned back to her, expression soft, and walked his fingers over to her hand, matching their palms together. "I should remind you of all the reasons why you'd do better to wash your hands of me, but I don't want to in case you listen," he admitted.

"Well, don't remind me then." She laced her fingers between his. "Plan with me, instead."

They talked. It steadied her, drawing lines around the future, even if the scale of it still daunted her. With his warm presence beside her, it didn't seem so outlandish, imagining a future in which fae and humans lived side by side. *Yes, but you won't be side by side, really, will you?* a small voice in the back of her mind pointed out. Hetta shushed it.

"Is the High King likely to make an appearance, if you're crowned King of ThousandSpire?" she asked. He hadn't turned up when she'd been chosen, but Stariel wasn't exactly a typical faeland. But then, he *had* turned up for the signing of the Northern Charter between Stariel and the Crown three hundred years ago. Quite aside from Wyn needing his permission to marry, Hetta had a large and ever-growing list of questions for the High King of Faerie. Questions that were starting to verge on demands.

Wyn considered the brightening light through the windows. "I don't know. I don't know if there's anyone who would remember my father's ascension. He is—was—the oldest faelord I know." A tightness came into his expression, and she squeezed his arm.

"Well, at least I won't be the only novice at this."

He smiled. "There is that. Perhaps you can give me pointers."

"It'll certainly make our practice sessions more interesting."

He smiled at the 'our', but his gaze flicked to his wrists, where the dismae had been. "They were already sufficiently interesting for me."

The respite from their respective relatives didn't last nearly long enough, of course. There was some very pointed and extended knocking before Marius returned to the room with the rest of the party in tow. He frowned at Wyn and Hetta's proximity to each other, and she rolled her eyes at him.

"Well, brother?" Catsmere said.

"Tomorrow," he told her.

43

THE OCTAGON GARDEN

EARLY THE NEXT morning, the seaward wind whipped Wyn's hair back from his face, and despite his worries, he revelled in the sensation. Below, the river stretched like a silver serpent through the city, curving around bright square-edged patches of green where parks interlaced with the urban fabric. He leaned on his air magic and banked into a tight turn over the palace, his attention going straight to the raw wound in the earth where the nightwyrm had come through. It steeled him. He would make sure Aroset set no more nightwyrms loose to wreak havoc in Mortal, at least. *Now I just have to convince Queen Matilda of that.*

Circling, he searched until he found the garden Princess Evangeline had mentioned, an accurately named green octagon. A fish pond of the same shape gleamed like an eye as he descended towards it in a rush of wind and wings. He made a neat landing of it—*I'm definitely improving*—stumbling only a little on the gravel edge of the pond. Whoever had designed the Octagon Garden had aimed for a carefully cultivated wilderness, softening the geometry with artful plantings.

"Prince Hallowyn!" Princess Evangeline said with satisfaction as he landed. She was perched on the edge of the fishpond, a paper bag of what was presumably fish food clutched in one small hand. The princess was again dressed in pale colours, this time a pattern of daisies embroidered on robins-egg blue, and the outfit was already somewhat the worse for wear.

"Good morning, Princess." He smiled, not letting his internal wince show at the use of part of his true name. But Aroset already knew he was in the city and that he'd been at the palace recently; a single mention of part of his true name here carried minimal risk. He hoped. "You may call me Wyn, if you'd like."

"They said the fairy monster killed you," she informed him, inspecting his appearance with interest. Wyn tightened his grip on his coat under one arm. He'd meant to change before confronting the queen—shirtsleeves didn't constitute proper dress for mortals—but now he reconsidered. There was nothing of horror in the princess's eyes, only curiosity.

"I am not killed, as you can see," he said, fanning out a wing for emphasis. "Though the nightwyrm did injure me."

A shaft of sunlight broke through the clouds at that moment and lit up the silver filigree edging his feathers, and Princess Evangeline made a fascinated sound and reached out longingly.

"You may touch," he told her.

"You can fly," she breathed, touching the tip of her finger to one of his primaries. She bit her lip, and Wyn had a very good notion of what she was about to say next: "Could you fly with me?"

"I think you should ask your mother for permission first," he said, turning to face Queen Matilda as she emerged hurriedly from a nearby path.

The queen must have heard his voice, judging from her rushed entrance, but she clearly hadn't been prepared for his appearance. She jerked to a halt, sketching the shape of his wings and horns with alarm. He repressed the urge to arch his wings up in challenge. It would be pointless, anyway, as well as childish; she wouldn't be familiar with the body language of stormdancers. Instead he clamped his wings tightly against his back.

"Your Majesty," he said with a nod.

"Evangeline," she said with quiet intensity, as if he were a wild animal she feared to startle. "Come here."

"I would not hurt a child. Particularly not Crown Princess Evangeline of the house of Allincourt. Even though she may or may not outrank me," he added, with a flicker of a smile, remembering how she'd introduced herself so pompously. Princess Evangeline grinned back at him, unaffected by her parent's anxiety.

"Mother, can Prince Wyn take me flying? He's not dangerous, and I haven't thanked him for saving me from the monster—what did you call it?"

"A nightwyrm," he murmured, not taking his attention from her parent.

"What are you talking about, Evangeline?" she asked, her gaze also fixed on him.

The princess scuffed her feet and blurted out: "I was in the kitchen when the monster came."

If Wyn had any doubts that Queen Matilda loved her child, the way her face went white quelled them. He knew she was remembering the vast bulk of the nightwyrm, the glint of razor teeth.

"That's why you were hurt, wasn't it?" the princess asked him. "Because you had to stop running and fight it after you pushed me out the door?"

"In part," he allowed. "But it needed to be dealt with regardless."

"Evangeline," the queen said firmly. "Go and find Kitty in the schoolroom. I shall see you at breakfast."

The princess's mouth grew mulish, but a glance between Wyn and her mother told her that the latter wasn't likely to relent. She went, with much dragging of feet and backward glances.

Queen Matilda watched her go. At least she no longer looked alarmed, though she didn't look pleased either. "Prince Hallowyn," she said when Evangeline was safely out of earshot. Her gaze lingered on the lines of his shirt, correctly concluding that he wore no dismae under his sleeves.

"Ah, I would prefer 'Wyn'—my name acts as a kind of beacon, and I don't wish to attract further attacks. I would also like it noted," he said, "that Lord Valstar had nothing to do with my disappearance, and that she did not know of my whereabouts when I left the palace. I was injured, and it took me some time to recover sufficiently to return." Queen Matilda didn't need to know about Gwendelfear. How had Sunnika dealt with the lesser fae? Despite everything, he still felt a measure of sympathy for her. *After all,* he thought fairly, *we are even now. I imprisoned her; she imprisoned me.*

He delved into the satchel he'd brought with him—he must get one properly fashioned for his fae form—and held out the dismae to the queen. Her eyebrows went up, and she refused to take them from him, so he leaned down and put them carefully on the ground, though he would've preferred to hurl them into the pond instead.

"I didn't want to be accused of theft. The damage was unintentional, Your Majesty, but I doubt they are salvageable." He was pleased at the lack of emotion in his tone.

Her lips pursed. "I take it you didn't use the key to remove them?"

"I did not." He waited to see if she would bring up the unconscious guards, the planted feathers. His wings shivered with the tension, ready to flare out if she called out to summon her guard.

"Will you tell me how, then?" she asked instead.

He searched for a diplomatic answer, and not only because he wasn't wholly sure himself how he'd broken the dismae, except perhaps for the cumulative effect of battering magic at them for so long. "While I'm in favour of peaceable fae-human relations, I don't wish to help you build more weapons aimed at my people. Besides, mortals already have so many advantages, and I've taken quite a personal dislike to this particular one." He nudged the dismae with his boot, where they clinked against the gravel.

"Do we?" She watched him closely; the question wasn't idle.

"Humans can lie; you are not bound by your oaths; iron has no effect on your magic; and you are more selfless than the fae. Yes, I'd say you have many advantages."

A muscle in Queen Matilda's cheek twitched, but she said levelly: "The damage to the palace is extensive."

"The nightwyrm's teeth and claws are made of diamond, which I imagine will help considerably with the repair bill." He swallowed. "Was anyone hurt?" That was something that couldn't be remedied with diamonds, if so. Hetta hadn't said anything, and she would have, if she'd heard otherwise, which meant probably no one had been badly injured, but he still needed to hear it confirmed. He thought of Mrs Lovelock and the guards he'd met, and a chill went through him.

Beyond the cultivated peace of the Octagon Garden, he could hear the muted sounds of the palace, but for the moment there was only him and this mortal queen, alone. He found her difficult to read, though he had the uneasy sense she wasn't having the same trouble. He'd never been so aware of his own feathers than under her measuring appraisal.

After a long silence, she spoke. "Some minor injuries, the worst being a broken arm—one of the maidservants. She'll recover, I'm told."

"I am sorry," he said, with perfect sincerity.

Her eyes narrowed. "And what assurances can you give that there will be no more such creatures? Have you come to return yourself to our custody again?"

He straightened. *I am a prince. I am the storm, and you cannot cage me.* "I am not your subject, Your Majesty. I have tried to allay your fears, but ultimately, I am of royal blood, and I owe a duty to my court to remember that. However, I didn't wish you to think I had simply fled your hospitality without taking my leave." There was no harm in maintaining the appearance of good manners. "As to ensuring there are no more such attacks—I would negotiate with you as an equal, on the relationship between the fae of ThousandSpire and the mortals of Prydein."

He met her eyes and tried to convey an authority he didn't feel. King Aeros wouldn't have negotiated like this, at least, but he could still feel his father's ghost beside him, his guinea-gold eyes mocking. *You are weak, Hallowyn.* The thought of assuming his father's throne... His stomach twisted.

I will burn it, he thought with sudden and irrational ferocity. *Perhaps my fate is sealed, but the throne itself need not be part of it.*

Childish, equating a symbol with the thing itself, but he couldn't seem to entirely quell the mindless panic churning in the back of his mind, even when he flattened his wings more tightly against his back. He took a deep breath. *I will keep Hetta and Stariel and my Valstars safe.* That, at least, was a rock he could cling to.

"I take it the succession war Lord Valstar referred to has resolved then?" she asked as the wind rattled the bullrushes at the edge of the pond.

"Not quite yet. But I intend to return to my home court as soon as possible, and I have reason to be sure of the outcome when I do." The words tasted cold and bitter, but he had no difficulty speaking them. "If I'm crowned King of ThousandSpire, Stariel is not the only entity I could negotiate with. I would look favourably upon *treaties* with my future spouse's home nation. Trade deals and such."

The queen's eyes narrowed at his emphasis; she'd known then, of the bit of archaic law that Marius and Rakken had found. He hated reducing Hetta to such terms, but that was, after all, the nature of politics. He hadn't missed it, in the years he'd been away from court. It was yet another thing he would need to re-accustom himself to.

"It isn't trade that most concerns me."

"I intend to try to prevent conflict between Faerie and Mortal."

She smiled faintly. "You're a poor negotiator, Prince Hallowyn. You are supposed to name your terms first before making such promises."

The tightness in his chest eased a little. "I said exactly what I meant."

Her smile widened for an instant, a bit of realness undamped by politics. "You also haven't tried to leverage the fact that you apparently saved my daughter's life," she said abruptly.

"She would not have been in danger if not for me." Or if he hadn't been wearing the dismae, but he chose not to remind the queen of this. Why undo the small amount of goodwill Princess Evangeline's revelation had bought him? "And I didn't do it to win your favour; I won't bargain with the lives of children."

The tiny aborted movements in her neck betrayed the fact that she was trying not to stare at his wings and horns. He appreciated the effort, nonetheless. Should he raise the subject of the drugged guards? If the queen had been responsible for it, doing so would hardly endear him to her, but he needed to know. But how to begin? He couldn't say Hetta had told him about it. But how to state that he'd seen them himself whilst making it clear he'd had nothing to do with the scene?

She could hardly have failed to notice his wing colour, but he still made a show of half-stretching his left wing, so that his primaries caught the light. One eyebrow rose, and he had the sense that he'd amused her, but the movement worked as he'd intended.

"An incriminating feather was found near the bodies of two unconscious guards outside the Treasury the night your 'nightwyrm' attacked," she said. "Though I see Lord Valstar was correct in saying it wasn't yours."

"No. I did not enchant your guards, nor attempt to break into your Treasury. How sure are you that it was enchantment and not mortal means that rendered them unconscious?"

Her blue eyes flashed, but there was no guilt in her, and some of the tension went out of him. It hadn't been her framing attempt, then. That boded well.

He waited, watching calculations turn furiously. "It appears there is someone in my court with a grudge against you," she admitted eventually.

"And possibly Lord Valstar also. *Lady Peregrine's Society News* has been threatening to publish damaging articles about both of us, though I am not sure exactly what that will entail."

"That gossip rag?" She frowned.

"I believe the Earl of Wolver owns an interest in the paper. Does he also have the power to command your guard?"

Her eyes narrowed. "I do not appreciate what you are insinuating." But he could see her reaching the same conclusions as him and Hetta.

In the growing silence between them came the distant crunch of approaching footsteps. Guards coming to investigate after the princess's tales? He tensed.

The queen came to a decision, a kind of cool resoluteness straightening her posture. "You may speak to Simon about it yourself, if you can delay your departure a few hours. I have already asked him to witness Lord Valstar's signature." A very dry humour circled her mouth. "Tell me, what was she intending to do if I set my guards on you this morning?"

"I have already stated that Lord Valstar was unaware—"

Queen Matilda waved his protest away. "Oh, you've an excellent poker face, Your Highness, and I do believe, incidentally, that Lord Valstar wasn't involved in your disappearance. But I do not believe in coincidence, and Lord Valstar is due at the palace this morning. Besides, you have not asked after her welfare, which seems uncharacteristically disinterested of you if you truly haven't seen her since that creature attacked."

He gambled. "I may have delayed speaking to you, a little, after

I recovered from my injuries. I wanted to assure myself that my enemies hadn't gotten to Lord Valstar in my absence."

She seemed amused rather than angry. "So the fae are just as foolish in love as humans then. I begin to see why she's put up with the complications you've caused her."

Must *everyone* comment on his love life in some way? He turned from the queen to face the set of guards who had just rounded the corner towards them. His wing muscles bunched in preparation for a rapid exit.

"Your Majesty!" the lead guard began, but the queen interrupted him, her manner as assured as that of any ruler in Faerie.

"I commend your caution, Captain, but there is no need for alarm. I do not require my guard at this moment." She considered Wyn thoughtfully. "Tell me, Prince Wyn, have you breakfasted?"

SIGNATURES

ETTA HADN'T PERSUADED Aunt Sybil and Alexandra to get on the day train back to Stariel. Instead, she and Marius left them at the hotel under Rakken and Catsmere's watch—which felt a bit too much like leaving foxes in charge of hens for her liking, even if Alexandra seemed much less concerned about the pair than she had previously. *Is it right to get my family mixed up in this business?* she couldn't help wondering, not for the first time, followed by, *but if I'm planning to marry the king of ThousandSpire, they'll only be more mixed up than ever.* She pressed her gloved hands together and swallowed.

Marius was doing a good impression of their aunt in her absence. His mouth didn't shift out of its hard, straight line as they caught a hackney to the palace, and the sounds of the city magnified in the silence between them, the clatter of hooves and cries of hawkers. He still hadn't looked at her when they neared the long approach to the palace.

Hetta huffed. "Honestly, Marius, this brotherly outrage is growing tiresome. My personal affairs are none of your business, and it's childish to refuse to speak to me because of them in any case."

"It's not—not *that*," he said, flushing. He screwed up his eyes. "Gods, don't remind me. I'm just…angry. At him, mostly, for planning to leave, even though I know he doesn't want to. At you, for not picking someone human, for starters."

"That's not—"

"I just want you to be happy, Hetta," he said, and then added, "And what's best for Stariel."

"I *am* happy!" she snapped back, but he just shrugged and looked away.

"Are you? Good, then."

"And this *will* be better for Stariel." Wouldn't it? Why, then, was she plagued by so much doubt? She pressed her palm against the ring under the collar of her dress; Stariel had no answers at this distance, though it wasn't exactly good at answers anyway.

He didn't answer, but his expression spoke for him. She felt very twelve years old and tempted to strangle him. Instead she took a deep breath and said: "We can argue about it later. Let's try to resolve Stariel's minor diplomatic incident first."

The stray reporters from two days prior had dispersed, and the polished stone columns and uniformed guards were as blankly composed as ever. Presumably there were still workmen scurrying madly behind the public facade to repair the nightwyrm's damage, but you wouldn't know it from looking. Hetta found it reassuring. After all, if there had been a confrontation between Wyn and the guards, there would've been some sign of it, surely?

He promised he wouldn't let himself be imprisoned again, she tried to reassure herself. Maybe he was already winging his way north, if the queen hadn't reacted well to his reappearance, although that thought was the very opposite of reassuring.

"I'm sure he's fine," Marius murmured, as the butler stiffly took their coats.

She didn't point out that he had no way of being sure about that as the butler took them on a path that carefully avoided the damaged parts of the palace. Hetta could still smell plaster and fresh paint, somewhere out of sight.

They were led to the same receiving room where they'd first met Queen Matilda, but this time the only person present was the Earl of Wolver, standing next to the window.

The earl turned when the butler announced them and replied civilly enough when Hetta introduced Marius, though he made no attempt at small talk. Could he really be the person behind the drugged guards? But why? Had it been on the queen's orders? Did he know about his paper's threat to publish further scandal about her and Wyn? She tried to read some sign of guilt in him and failed. He just looked haughty.

"The relevant papers are here for your inspection," he said, gesturing at an ornate writing desk. "Her Majesty asked me to witness."

"Where is Her Majesty? Doesn't she need to sign as well?"

The earl's lips pressed into a thin line, as if it had been rude of Hetta to point out that the queen was running late. Hetta's old schoolmistress would be disappointed in her. "We await her," he said quellingly.

"I heard you own *Lady Peregrine's*," she said, giving up on subtlety. The earl frowned slightly but didn't seem particularly discomposed.

"I own an interest in the *Times*, Lord Valstar. But yes, the magazine you refer to is a subsidiary." He said the word 'magazine' with distaste, and she had to admit it fit better with his rigid manner, the idea that he'd inherited *Lady Peregrine's* as an unfortunate side-effect of owning a 'proper' paper. What in Prydein had Brad seen in the man?

"And the article it published spreading gossip about me and my staff?" She watched him closely for a reaction.

His gaze was very cold. "I do not concern myself with the day-to-day running of nor contents of the magazine." He made a curt gesture at the papers on the writing desk. "Did you wish to inspect these, Lord Valstar?"

What had she been expecting? For him to spread his arms and announce to the room, "Yes, 'tis I who have been conspiring against you!". Oh well. It had been worth a shot.

She sat at the writing desk and began to read through the papers, handing each page to Marius as she finished. Her name was already printed on the last page, awaiting her signature: *Lord Henrietta Isadore Valstar.* She stared at the stark black letters, at the echo of her father's name. But that was her identity now, wasn't it, the Lord of Stariel? Why, then, did the sight of her name next to the queen's make her feel like an impostor?

What would happen if she refused to sign it? But that was just pigheadishness speaking. Even if Stariel was in any position to rebel against the Crown—*with our vast armies and resources and so on,* she thought wryly—her people wouldn't thank her for it. Oh, the Northern folk might grumble about the Southern monarchy, but when it came down to it, they'd all benefited from being one united Prydein for three hundred years.

But what if the queen had tried to imprison Wyn again? What if she'd *succeeded?* Wyn shouldn't count in this calculation, not against the weight of duty, and yet, he did. She thought of the oath-words she'd made to Stariel, when she'd become lord: *to protect this land from that which threatens it; to put its interests above my own.* She swallowed. She'd always clung firmly to a belief that that wouldn't be necessary, that she could be a good lord *and* achieve her own personal goals. But what if that had been only a convenient lie she'd told herself?

"They're as they should be," Marius said softly, handing her the last page of text. She started, but took it and laid it back on the desk.

The earl narrowed his eyes at Hetta's brother, and there was something stronger and more personal than disapproval in the expression. Marius sensed it too, and he blinked.

"Why do you hate me?" he blurted out, with typical disregard for tact. He sounded puzzled rather than hurt, but his eyes widened suddenly, and all the blood drained from his face.

The earl drew himself up, but before he could answer, the door opened, and the butler announced: "Her Majesty Queen Matilda and Prince Wyn."

They turned. *Apparently Her Majesty also has a penchant for dramatic entrances,* Hetta thought, though she couldn't help but admire the effect. Wyn was in human form, cool and collected, and his gaze swung to hers, clearly trying to radiate silent reassurance towards her. Relief nearly made her sag, and she gripped the desk for support. Whatever he'd said to the queen, it didn't seem to have gone badly.

The earl reeled back as if struck. "Your Majesty—" The protest died on his lips. *Is he going to point out that she's accompanying a fugitive?* she wondered, but the earl realised the absurdity of that and shook off his initial reaction. "I'm afraid I don't understand *his* presence here."

The queen raised blonde eyebrows. "Prince Wyn?" The combination hit Hetta's ears strangely, but it was a good sign that she was avoiding using his full name. "He has returned to take his leave of us after the regrettable incident with the—what did you call it?"

"A nightwyrm, Your Majesty," Wyn murmured.

"Yes, the nightwyrm. He has explained himself over breakfast. In any case, he wished to speak to you, Simon, so he seemed an expedient choice for a second witness."

Hetta nearly rolled her eyes at Wyn. Only he would manage to go from fugitive to breakfast companion in the space of a few hours.

"Your Majesty—" the earl hissed in a low tone as he caught up to her. "Is this wise?" The earl flushed in the face of the queen's cool sapphire gaze—how pleasing to know it worked on other people too—but persisted nonetheless. "What of the enchanted guards?"

"His Highness has persuaded me he was not involved in that."

Queen Matilda moved further into the room towards the writing desk in a swish of silk poplin. "Lord Valstar, are you satisfied that all is in order? This is your brother, I presume?" she asked, with a hint of irony, since Marius was still staring at the earl, apparently oblivious to the fact that he was ignoring their monarch in order to do so. His face had gone grey around the edges, and he looked like he might be sick.

"Yes, Your Majesty," Hetta said, putting a hand on his arm. "Mr Marius Valstar." He jerked back to the present company and cut a hasty bow.

She frowned at him. What was wrong? But he only shook his head, his jaw tight.

"Your Majesty, may I ask *why* you are persuaded Prince Hallowyn was not involved?" the earl said. "What of the feathers? And, forgive me, but there have been…certain questions raised as to his character."

A spurt of indignation went through Hetta. So he *did* know very well about the article!

The queen gave a bright smile. "Ah, yes, Simon. I have decided to issue a statement to reassure the public and to repair the damage to His Highness's reputation. I am trusting you to see that the requisite puff piece runs in *The Times*."

The earl stiffened and shot a poisonous look at Wyn. "Your Majesty, have you considered that *he* may have persuaded you using unnatural means?"

Wyn shrugged out of his coat and handed it to Hetta before she had time to protest. Blue feathers rustled into place, sparkling even in the weak sunlight filtering through the window. The queen didn't seem the least surprised. *Staged*, Hetta thought. *She suspects the earl was involved but isn't sure.*

Wyn fanned out a wing. "I hope this reassures you as to the colour of my feathers," he said mildly.

The earl reared back as if confronted by a snake, and his expression made Hetta curl her hands into fists. Strange Wyn might be in his fae form, but he wasn't a monster, and no one should look at him like that!

But it became apparent why the earl was one of the queen's advisors. He recovered swiftly, re-focusing on the queen. "Your Majesty," he objected. "You may be unaware, but one of the subsidiaries of *The Times* was planning to publish an account of certain allegations linked to His Highness."

"I am aware of the piece," Queen Matilda said. "I trust you can see that it does *not* run?"

"But what about the allegations?"

"Are you talking about the incident at the bank in Alverness?" Hetta asked. "We were attacked by fae creatures there, which was obviously upsetting for the staff, but Wyn certainly wasn't to blame for it."

"I am not," the earl said stiffly. "The informant's allegations involve a quite different incident."

"Well, it might be easier to refute it if you'd tell us what it is!"

"Compulsion. Enchanting people to do his bidding."

Hetta glared daggers at him. "Do you think he would've voluntarily put on those iron cuffs if he was inclined to casually compel people?" Though beneath her anger, she couldn't help remembering Rakken's compulsion unfurling in the train station. The earl wasn't wrong to worry about that magic in general, even if he was entirely wrong to worry about it in this specific instance.

"I have already assured Her Majesty that I have no compulsive magic spells active on any mortals," Wyn said. "And I have no desire to compel any mortals in the future."

"Perhaps *you* do not," the earl said in a tone dripping with disbelief, "but what of those around you? Are you saying you've never used compulsive magic at a friend's behest?" The earl looked straight at Marius, something sharp and vindictive in his expression. "That you never would?"

Oh no. There it was—the connection Hetta hadn't seen, that

Marius must have realised earlier. What had Bradfield said? That the earl had thrown him over for a fresh-faced young man? Mr John Tidwell, who Wyn had bound not to speak Marius's name, would certainly fit that description. Oh, of all the bad luck! *What a pity Wyn had that attack of conscience and undid the compulsion*, she thought, despite all her earlier misgivings about that magic. But the idea that John Tidwell had presented *himself* as a victim—oh, she wanted to hunt him down and give him a piece of her mind! Possibly with accompanying fireworks.

"Simon, if you have something specific to accuse His Highness of, please lay it out plainly," Queen Matilda said.

The earl's mouth tightened. He couldn't admit that his male lover had told him—what, exactly? From the way the earl was looking at Marius, John Tidwell had painted him in a very black light. Marius looked ghastly, like he might faint, and Hetta willed him not to. "I would like His Highness to answer my question, Your Majesty. Have you ever used compulsive magic in the past, on someone else's behalf?"

Wyn sighed, outwardly relaxed, though Hetta knew him well enough to spot the fine line of tension in his muscles. His feathers were flattened down against his spine, but they twitched in restless small movements, a sure sign that he was furious.

"I misled you before, Your Majesty. It's true that I have no compulsions binding any mortals. But I *have* used mild compulsive magic on Hetta's sister Alexandra, at her request, as she desired to practice resisting it." Marius swayed slightly, and Hetta squeezed his arm, faking a need for support. "At no other time have I used compulsion on a mortal only because a friend asked me to do so." Splitting hairs, but apparently that was acceptable. It was terrifying, really, the way Wyn could lie with truth. He took a deep breath, met Hetta's eyes.

The earl was narrow-eyed. "Perhaps my source was mistaken then." He didn't sound as if he believed this to be the case, but the queen beamed at him, her smile hard and cold as crystal.

"I'm glad that's resolved, then," she said. Something predatory gleamed in her eyes as she looked at the earl and added sweetly, "Remind me also, Simon, once we are done here, to discuss the procedures for who gives commands to my queensguard." She turned back to Hetta. "Now, Lord Valstar, I believe you have some paperwork to sign."

◦⊱✦⊰◦

IT WASN'T VERY SATISFYING, to have one's hands tied, but for Marius's sake, Hetta held her tongue as she signed the official documents. The only satisfaction was seeing the earl similarly hamstrung. He radiated disapproval throughout the ceremony and signed his name with a curtness that would've torn lower-quality paper. But he didn't object further, even when the queen informed him that he would be in charge of arranging a photographer to take "the requisite charming photo of Prince Hallowyn taking his leave of me at the end of his ambassadorial visit."

Maybe that will teach the earl to choose better bed-mates, she thought viciously as his eyes flashed in response. Marius was worryingly quiet, though this was better than him blurting out everything for all and sundry. How bad would it be if he did? Surely the queen couldn't be so unaware of her advisor's personal activities? But Hetta couldn't take that sort of risk with her brother's life, even as the unfairness of it burned at her.

After dismissing the earl, the queen sat down upon her throne-like chair, waving for Hetta to follow suit, and pierced Hetta with sapphire intensity.

"I dislike the haste in which this business was conducted, Lord

Valstar, Prince Wyn. It does not constitute a proper introduction to society, nor an adequate ambassadorial visit."

Hetta sank down upon the stiffly upholstered armchair opposite, while Wyn and Marius were directed to the sofa with another wave of Queen Matilda's hand. Wyn had re-assumed his human form.

"Er—" Was Hetta supposed to point out that they hadn't come here to do either of those things when she'd summoned them?

But the queen continued. "Do you still wish to marry him, Lord Valstar?"

"Well, yes, but also I'd like that to be a question between him and me," she couldn't help saying. Marius gave her a pained look. Wyn looked like he was trying very hard not to laugh, and Hetta felt an answering smile tug at her lips.

The queen's eyes narrowed. "Not if you want me to support your union." Wyn made a sound, and she waved her hand to stop him voicing his objection. "No, do not quibble with me about loopholes and treaties; you are not so foolish as that."

Hetta knew what she meant; it was the same thing she'd thought earlier, pen in hand, when she'd hesitated over her signature. Stariel was just one small estate. Angering the Southern monarchy wasn't a good management decision, no matter the legal technicalities. Or how much she wanted to rage at the queen's unfairness over the past few days. She took a deep breath, setting her complicated feelings aside. "You ought to support us, though, regardless of all that," she pointed out.

"And why is that, Lord Valstar?" To her relief, the queen seemed genuinely interested in her answer, despite the appalled look on poor Marius's face.

She laced her fingers together. "Well, I admit I'm still learning my way in terms of politics, but isn't a union between ranking members of two realms a traditional way to resolve differences? Which makes Wyn and me marrying good politics." She gave Wyn a sideways look to see how he took this. Did he mind being shuffled about like a chess piece? *She* certainly did, even though she was the one suggesting it. But there didn't seem to be any option other than to hold them up as a symbol of unity or some such thing.

The queen looked faintly amused, and Hetta had an insight then that would've done Marius proud. "And for that reason, you were never truly opposed to our relationship, were you?" she said indignantly.

The queen's laugh was slight but genuine, and she inclined her head. "It is, as you say, a traditional resolution. However, I do not approve of the scandal you are creating between the pair of you." She pinned Wyn with a look, her humour fading. "You have said it will take little time to resolve your succession. You will return here immediately afterwards, with Lord Valstar, to negotiate the details between Prydein and ThousandSpire—and I will announce your engagement."

Hetta exchanged a look with Wyn.

"Ah, there are…other complications," he said to the queen.

She pursed her lips. "*What* complications?"

In very bare terms, Wyn told her about the High King. "I see," she said at the end of it, looking displeased. "And how does one contact the High King? I know you have made assurances on behalf of your court, Your Highness, but you have also admitted that it does not represent all of Faerie."

Wyn paused. "Contacting the High King can be difficult, but I intend to try. And though it's true that there are other courts, I think you are unlikely to find a ruler among them who cares more for Mortal than I." He said it with careful neutrality, but the queen still looked between him and Hetta and raised an eyebrow.

"Yes, I can see that may be the case," she said dryly, and Hetta wondered if some version of the star-crossed romance story she'd told at the duchess's soiree had made it to her ears. A certain steeliness came into her expression. "You make a compelling couple, but I have a nation to think of. You are not king of Ten Thousand

Spires yet, Prince Wyn, and your ascension seems by no means guaranteed." Her gaze fell on Hetta. "Good intentions are not the same as actions, and Lord Valstar is far too valuable an addition to my Northern lords to waste on unfulfilled promises." In response to Hetta's astonishment, she added, with a brief, wry smile: "The Conclave could do with modernising."

"I mean to fulfil my promises," Wyn said, before Hetta could recover her balance. He and the queen locked gazes for several long moments, the tick of the grandfather clock the only sound. How did he manage to look so *certain*, when Hetta knew how much he dreaded going back to ThousandSpire? When who knew how that might change his priorities? Except that she suspected it wouldn't. Part of her rather liked that, but another part—the bit that knew what it was like to be soul-bonded to a faeland, with all the responsibilities that entailed—thought, *should he really be prioritising another faeland over his home court?*

Eventually, Queen Matilda gave a small, irritated sigh. "A compromise, then. In a few months' time, I host the annual Meridon Ball. At it, you will bring me some broader assurance on behalf of your people, Prince Wyn, and I will announce your engagement." *Or else*, she didn't say, but Hetta heard it anyway.

45

A QUIET DRINK

THE NEXT MORNING, Wyn sat with Marius in a café across from the railway station, watching the ordinary bustle of passengers streaming out of the entrance into the grey of the city. The train to Stariel didn't leave for another hour, and the journey would take most of the day. He tried not to think about what lay at the other end of it. *A day's grace, still.* His siblings had said they would meet them at the estate, choosing wingpower over being stuck within human iron technology again for so many hours. They hadn't been particularly impressed with his choosing otherwise.

A pointed clink recalled Wyn's attention. Across the table, Marius had dumped a small mountain of cream and sugar into his coffee and was stirring it with unnecessary force. "I know what you're doing," he said, not meeting Wyn's eyes.

"Having a refreshing drink before we get on the train?" Wyn suggested, lifting his own tea pointedly.

Marius's mouth tightened. "I'm not as fragile as you and Hetta seem to think."

Wyn put his cup down and canted his head, trying to judge his friend's mood. Marius had refused to discuss what had happened at the palace yesterday, shutting himself in his room and claiming he needed to catch up on the student marking he'd brought with him. "I don't think you're fragile," he said. "I think, on the contrary, that you show considerable strength of character."

"Then why," Marius demanded, pushing his drink away, "have you and Hetta set out to coddle me? I'm not an idiot!"

Wyn took a sip of his tea as he considered the complaint. "It's true that she wasn't very subtle, leaving us together. But I don't think wanting me to talk to you truly counts as coddling." Hetta had pointedly announced her intention to go for a walk about the block and stretch her legs before they got on the train, dragging Alexandra and Aunt Sybil with her before they could object. There were things Marius would never discuss with his sister, and Hetta knew it. "I hope I am still your friend, regardless of the tension between us these past few months."

"You mean since I found out you lied to me and you started tupping my sister?" Marius's cheeks bloomed red. Fortunately their corner of this café was deserted, and he'd spoken quietly enough despite his anger. He closed his eyes and pinched the bridge of his nose. "Sorry."

Wyn winced. "An accurate if vulgar summation."

Marius opened his eyes and narrowed them at Wyn. "And you're just going to leave her? You didn't truly promise Her Majesty you were going to marry her, and don't give me that talk of 'complications' and needing your High King's permission. You think it would be better for her if you parted, if you have to go be king of the Spires."

This was always the problem with Marius. When he saw things, he saw too much.

Marius stirred yet more sugar into his coffee and then said grimly into it, "I think you might be right to leave."

Oh, that hurt, despite having the same thought himself.

Marius looked up. "Not because I think you're not good enough for her, you idiot!" His shoulders went up. "You're probably the most genuinely good person I know. Look at yesterday! All this time I've been on my high horse about compulsion, but it—" There it was, the self-recrimination Wyn had known would lodge in Marius like a cancer, the reason he'd wanted to talk to him alone.

"Don't you dare blame yourself for this," Wyn said fiercely.

"How can I not? If I wasn't, wasn't—" he lowered his voice— "*deviant*, none of this would've happened!"

Wyn reached out and gripped his shoulder, forcing him to meet his eyes. "There is *nothing* wrong with you, Marius, nothing you should feel any shame for." He hated that Prydinian culture had done this to his friend, forced him into this position of self-loathing. A small, hard intention formed, to make the Prydinian legalities regarding that one of the matters he and Queen Matilda 'discussed', when he returned.

Marius shook him off. "Maybe not, but it's my fault John set the earl on you."

"John Tidwell had reason to hate me," Wyn said. "For the compulsion I placed upon him."

"Because of me," Marius pressed.

"If anyone is to blame for John Tidwell's actions, it is me. *I* chose to compel him. *I* chose to remove the compulsion, more concerned with my own conscience than with consequences. It was *my* error of judgement that caused this, not yours." All his mistakes coming home to roost, the cumulative weight of them forcing him to face the truth: *it is time I stopped running.*

"No," Marius said, shaking his head. "You're always ready to martyr yourself, Wyn, but this wasn't your fault. If I hadn't gotten involved with John, if I hadn't asked you for help when he tried to blackmail me, none of this would've happened."

"I will not cede the debt to you, Marius Rufus Valstar," Wyn said flatly.

Marius huffed, amusement softening the lines of his face. "I'm human, Wyn. You can't just go all fae on me and expect me to agree with you. I *don't* agree with you." Something else occurred to him. "Gods, your brother calling me 'Marius Valstar' all the time. It's some bizarre fae thing, isn't it?"

"Ah—there is power in names. Using someone's full name, or near to it, is used to denote"—Wyn spread his hands, reaching for the right word—"weight, in a conversation. But it can also be used because one is..." He trailed off, uneasy with where this was headed. "Engaging in a kind of dominance posturing."

Marius gave an incredulous laugh. "You mean: 'I'm more powerful than you because you can't stop me from flinging your name about as I like?' That style of thing?"

"Yes," Wyn agreed reluctantly. "Rake has a...peculiar sense of humour."

"He called me 'dangerous'," Marius said, twisting his cup around in its saucer. "Do you know why he'd say that?"

"Not without context, no. But you know how well we can bend truth to mislead."

The twisting of the cup continued, though Marius still hadn't managed to actually drink any.

"Does Rake...?" he began but trailed off.

"Does Rake what?" Wyn prompted.

But Marius shook his head, cheeks flaming. "Never mind. Forget it."

Understanding arced through Wyn, and he choked on his tea. Once he'd stopped spluttering, he said, low and incredulous: "Marius, are you asking me about my brother's bedmate preferences?"

Marius's shoulders hunched, and he refused to meet his eyes. "I said forget it. How much longer do you think Hetta will be?" he asked, desperately trying to change the subject.

Wyn wanted simultaneously to demand to know why Marius wanted the information and shout at him that any thoughts in that direction were a bad idea, but he took a firm grip on himself. Marius didn't need more shame right now. He took a deep breath.

"Ah—I'm not sure I can give you the answer you want. We don't... discriminate the way humans do, and I've always been deliberately incurious about my siblings' private activities."

"What do you mean you don't discriminate?" Marius asked, still examining the insides of his cup intently.

"I mean that gender is not usually the primary consideration of what we find attractive," he said helplessly. "Rake, as far as I know, is usual in that respect. But if you are asking if he would find—No." He shook his head. "No, I don't wish to speculate in that direction. Please tell me you are not."

A slight smile curved Marius's lips. "It's less fun when it's *your* sibling, isn't it?" He sighed. "Don't worry. I know he's dangerous, and I've no speculations in that direction, as you put it. I just—I just wanted to know."

"*Good,*" Wyn said, with an emphasis that made Marius laugh. But the awkwardness of the topic had eased the tension between them, and he considered Wyn with a kind of ironic amusement.

"Gods, I can be a bastard sometimes. What I said before, about maybe it being for the best if you left—I wasn't thinking of Hetta, though gods know you've made her life more complicated than I'd like." His gaze grew distant. "I was thinking of the fae, of your home court. What I've seen of other fae—" He coloured. "Well, they are somewhat amoral, aren't they? If I had to choose someone I trusted to change them for the better, it would be you. And, well, how could I *not* welcome you as my future brother, after all we've been through?" He hid behind his coffee.

There was a long silence, and eventually Marius risked a glance upwards and gave a bark of laughter. "I didn't think it was actually possible to shock you speechless."

"I am honoured by your faith in me," Wyn said when he'd found his voice again.

Marius shook away the words like a dog shedding water. "And that's quite enough of this cloying talk about feelings." He took a sip of coffee and grimaced, putting the cup down to glare at the liquid in indignation.

"Perhaps an eighth sugar will do the trick?" Wyn suggested mildly.

Marius rolled his eyes at him. "There's not enough sugar in the world to cover the taste of overbrewed coffee."

There was a single warm moment of camaraderie between them before all Wyn's senses flared to high alert: the scent of Spire magic, rolling towards the train station like an oncoming storm.

46

AROSET TEMPESTREN

"MARIUS," WYN SAID, pushing up from the table. "Princess Aroset Tempestren is here." He said his sister's name deliberately, hoping to draw her attention, because he knew with sickening certainty that if Aroset couldn't get to him, she'd target anyone he cared about.

Marius gulped and stood so hurriedly he knocked his cup out of its saucer and had to hurriedly right it. Rivulets of liquid ran across the table. "Where?" His face was ashen, and Wyn knew he was remembering his last encounter with Aroset, when she'd tried to compel him. Thank the High King Marius had natural mental shields that prevented such influence. *Alexandra doesn't*, he thought, on the heels of that. Heart of the Maelstrom, he had to make sure Aroset didn't get to her again.

"I don't know," Wyn said, moving towards the exit whilst scanning the leylines for a hint of his sister's location. Marius followed him out. The street between them and the station was relentlessly normal, bustling with traffic and pedestrians spilling out from the arched entryway. Footsteps, the whirr of kineticars, the clip-clop

of hooves, the *thunk* of baggage: nothing out of place. Wyn concentrated. All the iron warped his leysight, but his sister's magical
signature was faint but unmistakeable: copper and old-fashioned
roses, along with the tell-tale storm-scent. The metallic signature
was rare for a fae, but Father had had that same copper note as well.

Stretching his senses to their limits, he located Hetta a block away.
She blazed to his leysight almost like a greater fae, even though they
were outside Stariel. That was new. What had changed? Was it the
ring, or had sex connected them more than he'd anticipated? No
time for such questions. Regardless, he'd need to teach her how to
hide it if they survived this.

They crossed the road, the space between his shoulder blades
itching. Thinking of Rakken's trick with the knives, he pulled up
shields of air around Marius and himself. At least that would give
him some warning—but that raised the question of why his sister
had announced her presence. She had enough control to mask her
signature if she wished. Was she simply relishing the chance to
intimidate him in advance of her arrival? If so, it was working, and
he felt Cat and Rake's absence keenly. But how had Aroset known
where Wyn was in the first place?

They reached the bottom of the steps to the station entrance.
Should he leave Marius to join Hetta and the others? Should they
both go? He rapidly calculated risks and made a decision.

"Please go and get on the train without me. Any train. I'll fetch
Hetta and the others."

"The iron," Marius said, understanding at once.

"Yes," he said, casting out his leysight in a wide net but still failing
to pinpoint Aroset's location. Had she done that on purpose, or was
it the effect of the iron, tangling his leysight into incomprehensible
knots wherever it touched?

Marius didn't argue with Wyn's instruction, but he didn't look
happy about it. "I suppose I *am* just a helpless distraction otherwise,"
he said philosophically before striding up the steps into the station.

Wyn disliked sending him away, but the train station was one of the most uncomfortable human locations he'd ever visited. Full of iron and with criss-crossed supports giving a strong impression of a cage, the architect might have built it specifically to antagonise stormdancers. It was unlikely it would resonate with anywhere in Faerie, which meant that if Aroset had built a portal, she wouldn't come through there.

As soon as Marius disappeared through the entryway, Wyn turned and sprinted in the direction of Hetta's magic. Pedestrians squawked indignantly as he darted around them. He'd have to thank Rakken for the reminder that moving at human speed was an ingrained habit, not actually compulsory. He barrelled around the corner of the station and spotted Hetta arguing with her aunt next to a newspaper stand, with Alexandra standing awkwardly to one side. Hetta's head turned towards him even before he called out. Their eyes met, his alarm communicating itself to her, and she stiffened and spun around, searching for the danger.

He had a single heartbeat of warning, which he used to shove people away from him with a blast of air. Cries of outrage turned to fear as lightning struck from a clear sky. Out of sheer, mad reflex, he raised his arms and let it come, pouring down his arms. The power of it forced him into his fae form, wings tearing free of his clothing. Sparks sprayed from his spread primaries, but he managed to divert most of it into the pavement under his feet, cracking the surface and filling the street with the stench of ozone and burnt stone. His ears rang, and he could feel all his hair standing on end.

Thank the Maelstrom he'd had so much practice recently at channelling unexpected lightning, because if he'd paused to think about what he'd just done, the hesitation might have killed him. His low-charge elektrical strikes to irritate Rakken had been nothing to this; Aroset's lightning had been at full strength, meant to kill.

People were shouting and running away from him—thank the high wind's eddies. But where was Aroset? Hetta's presence burned even more brightly in the leylines, anger and shock fuelling her magic.

He sensed his sister's presence and blasted out with air as he spun towards it. Aroset diverted the currents effortlessly, landing with a laugh two wingspans away. Her silver hair was braided, but stray strands wafted in elektrical currents, creating an impression of swaying tentacles. Her golden eyes gleamed.

"Hallowyn Tempestren," she said with satisfaction, and his true name twanged in the air between them. Her wings fanned out in challenge, different from the pure red he remembered. Gold threads glittered in their depths, as if every feather had been inlaid with gold filigree. Aroset's smile widened as she noticed him take them in. "The gift of the Maelstrom."

Wyn felt faintly indignant. The Maelstrom had granted her even *more* power, as if she didn't hold entirely sufficient already? And she, like Rakken, hadn't broken her wings for the trouble—unlike him. He felt his youth and inexperience sharply, but he shoved the rising fear straight into his magic, the only useful place for it right now.

"What do you want, Aroset?" he asked. "I heard what you did to Torquil."

She didn't bother to answer, and charge hissed in the air. Somewhere close, thunder rumbled. He didn't dare glance up to check, but he could feel the storm forming above them. The day had darkened to the point of twilight, despite the early hour.

I have touched the Maelstrom too, he reminded himself. *My powers are also greater than they've ever been.* If only he understood them properly! When the next strike hit, he surrendered to instinct and moved within it, letting it curve smoothly around his body and back towards Aroset. She was more adept than him, and the lightning arced perfectly to discharge in a wide circle around her. Little flames flared as a stray newspaper caught, burning up in an instant. She laughed again.

"You've grown, little brother. But I think you don't fully

understand what you're doing." A spark of anger kindled in her eyes. "You do not deserve the throne."

He ignored her and drew the power of the building storm towards him, until he was bursting with the wild energy and he couldn't tell whether it was charge or magic itching under his feathers. Aroset shook her head chidingly as he leapt into the air and simultaneously threw a strike at her, redirecting it easily, but the diversion worked as he'd hoped, giving him time to wing his way past her.

He landed next to Hetta with barely a wobble. *Eventually I may even pull off elegance in my landings.* The street was empty now for a block, cracked pavement and smoke rising from the lightning strikes, newspapers flung into disarray. The stand owner had fled with the rest of the crowd, and Alexandra and Aunt Sybil huddled behind the stand. He caught a glimpse of Alexandra's pale face, her eyes wide and terrified.

"You're in charge of the lightning," Hetta said grimly, ducking past his wings and flinging out a hand in a very familiar gesture.

Love welled up in him, fierce and primitive. He pushed that emotion into his magic as well. One couldn't do that forever, not without cost, but if ever there was a time to take risks, this was it.

Taking a breath, he redirected another strike from Aroset as Hetta poured forth an inferno. Aroset hissed as flames hit her wings, but they winked out as she stole the breath from them, leaving her annoyed but uninjured. She threw another lightning strike at him, almost casually, and he grit his teeth and pulled it towards him as strongly as he could, curving it around himself and sending it back. Hetta gasped, her auburn hair sticking out in every direction from the static, but she was unhurt.

Aroset's attention swung behind them, and she said in a sing-song voice: "Come out, come out, little Valstar." Her magic pushed out, filling the air with copper and roses.

Alexandra took a lurching step forward, her eyes oddly blank, and then she sucked in a harsh breath, the blankness giving way to horror. Her hands balled into fists. "No! No, I won't!" she shouted at Aroset, shaking.

The magic in the air increased, but before Aroset could double-down on the compulsion, Hetta grabbed his hand. "Help me! Like we practised."

Understanding at once, he abandoned lightning for his more familiar air magic, wrapping air around the flames she poured forth. There was a still, silent heartbeat in which everything synchronised, as if they were casting magic as one rather than two, and then sound rushed back in as a vast, crackling wall rose to stand between them and Aroset.

Of course, he wasn't the only one with air magic. Sweat trickled down his spine as he panted, wrestling with his sister as she tried to snuff out the fire. He'd had more practice at this, but she had more power; the two forces counterbalanced. The wall of flames kept burning, but it didn't move any closer to Aroset even though he could see Hetta recklessly pushing her anger into it.

Stalemate. Aroset's eyes narrowed, considering the two of them. She didn't look tired, but already Wyn could feel his own fatigue threatening, the air currents slippery in his grasp. How long could Hetta keep the fire burning without Stariel to draw on? Would Aroset go for her weapons next? He quailed, knowing he wasn't fast enough, wasn't skilled enough—*damn you, Rake, for being right*— but instead the copper-and-rose of her magic strengthened and the air in front of her warped into a portal, pulled out of nothing.

Disbelief held him paralysed. Aroset had shown an uncanny knack with portals before, but this was different. You couldn't just— just *force* portals to open willy-nilly wherever you wished, with no regard for resonance! Aroset's lips stretched wide at his expression, and she stepped through her portal with a smirk. It winked out behind her, leaving only a haze of smoke and charred newspaper fragments spinning in the air above the cracked pavement. He stared, panting, at the empty space. How distinctly unfair that the Maelstrom had only made Aroset *better* at portals.

"Is she gone?" Alexandra asked shakily. Aunt Sybil was still frozen by the newspaper stand, staring at him as if she'd never seen him before.

"Are you all right, Alexandra?" he asked, feeling sick that he'd failed to protect her yet again.

She jerked her head, her eyes bright. "I'm fine." Her hands were still balled into tight fists, and she gave an angry, choked sob. "She didn't get me this time, did she? I stopped before—"

"You did."

"Where's Marius?" Hetta asked urgently, grasping his arm. There were dark hollows under her eyes; too much magic in too short a time.

"I sent him into the station." Surely Aroset couldn't make a portal into the station. But he no longer felt as confident in that as he had before, not after seeing what she'd just done, and he saw his fear mirrored in Hetta. "We need to find him before she does." He took hold of Hetta's hand, who took hold of Alexandra's, who tentatively tugged at Lady Sybil. Slower than he wanted, the four of them stumbled around the corner to the station's main entrance.

There were trains still pulling in and out of platforms, unaware of what had happened outside, though the crowds moved in an agitated way that suggested communication was starting to occur. Wyn scanned the station, but before he could spot Marius, the air warped and another portal opened at the top of the entry stairs, only a few yards from where he stood. Aroset stepped out, holding a struggling Marius by the neck and bonds of air both. Alexandra screamed.

Wyn took an instinctive step forward, flaring his wings to shield the mortals behind him, but Aroset tsked and tightened her grip. Marius made a choking sound. "So you care about this mortal *too*. How sentimental. But how much do you care, I wonder?"

"He has nothing to do with our quarrel. Let him go." His heart thundered in his ears, watching Marius's face redden as he struggled to breathe.

She smiled. "If you don't come here, I will kill the mortal." She looked down at Marius with a contemplative expression. "This is the one with the compulsive resistance. I wonder...how resistant?" Roses and copper saturated the air, and Marius whimpered. Aroset's approach to compulsive magic was force rather than subtlety, and if she couldn't bend Marius to her will, his mind would probably break under the strain. His back arched as she piled magical compulsion onto him, trying to fracture his natural shields.

"Stop!" Wyn cried, rushing towards her. "I surrender!"

But something broke with a wave of psychic force, and he stumbled under the backlash, ears ringing. Aroset reeled away from Marius, holding her head, and crashed against the nearest column. Marius crumpled, and Wyn caught him before he hit the ground, Hetta at his side a half-second later. Aroset had lost her balance, careening into the side of the building again as she tried to right herself. She propped herself against the wall, panting, her eyes flashing. Whatever had happened might have stunned her, but it had also made her furious, and he could feel her magic gathering for another attack, one he suspected would be all force and no finesse. How much longer could he keep diverting her lightning strikes, especially since unlike her, he had no margin for error, not surrounded by mortals.

"Really, Aroset, you should know better than to use compulsive magic on a telepath," Rakken drawled, and Wyn whirled to find him and Cat standing on the top of the steps behind them. The twins had clearly only just landed, their chests heaving with exertion. They must've flown like dervishes to get here so quickly. Wyn wasn't sure if they'd been shielding or if he'd simply missed their signatures amidst the cacophony of storm magic, but now they blazed up, a riot of cinnamon and tangerines.

Aroset's eyes narrowed, reassessing. Even with Cat and Rake backing them up, she showed no sign of fear, but her gaze fell on Marius and a ripple of unease washed over her expression. He saw the moment she decided to retreat, the portal forming behind her in the doorway. She leapt through and disappeared.

47

AFTEREFFECTS

WYN HALF-CARRIED A semiconscious Marius into the train station, his heart lurching every time his friend's weight stumbled against him. Alexandra fluttered around their path, her colour pale.

Hetta's face was drawn as well. "Shouldn't we be seeking medical attention rather than fleeing?" she asked in a low tone.

Wyn shook his head, holding Marius steady as he sagged. "I think Stariel will do him more good than any mortal doctor. He's suffering from magical backlash, not a mortal ailment."

Hetta's frown deepened, but she gave a reluctant nod.

Getting on the train to Stariel required glamour, illusion, and some compulsion.

"Rake," Wyn said warningly at the latter magic, but his brother ignored him and arranged matters without compunction so they had an entire compartment to themselves. Hetta shared a tired grimace with Wyn that said she couldn't muster the energy to object properly either. At least Alexandra barely seemed to notice, her attention wholly focused on Marius.

Wyn set Marius down on the padded bench inside the carriage, where he slid down onto the surface with a groan before curling into himself, eyes closed. Alexandra rolled up her coat and put it underneath his head. Aunt Sybil appeared to have been rendered mute, sinking into one of the seats in a daze.

The train pulled out of the station, the slow grind of iron reassuring. Wyn was fairly sure Aroset would need time to recover, but he could not help being glad of the protection of a moving iron box regardless.

"What did you call him before?" Hetta asked Rakken, who had perched in a seat next to the window, watching the outer suburbs of Meridon roll past. Catsmere had taken up position in the corner of the carriage, arms folded as she leaned against the wall.

"A telepath," Wyn answered in his brother's stead. Marius had gone eerily still, and Wyn tracked the rise and fall of his chest, trying and failing to reassure himself. *Stormwinds, Marius.*

"Did you truly not know?" Rakken pulled his attention back from the factories they were passing. "I'd assumed it was reasonably obvious. Interesting."

"Telepathy is the ability to read minds," Wyn explained to Hetta. "And no, we didn't," he answered his brother. "I knew he had strong natural shields against compulsion." Marius had always been intuitive, but telepathy wasn't a human magic. It wasn't a very common one in Faerie either, and it seemed a particular cruelty that the Valstars' distant fae blood might have inflicted such a curse.

But surely Wyn would have noticed, over the many years they'd been friends? Or was this a recent development? He hadn't spent as much time with Marius of late. A terrible suspicion bloomed. "Last year, Set tried to compel him." When Marius had been carrying out an errand outside Stariel's bounds—at Wyn's request.

Rakken raised an eyebrow. "You think that triggered a latent ability?" He frowned at Marius's still face. "Interesting," he said again. "Are you going to tell him?" He asked it casually, as if it were only a matter of academic curiosity, but Wyn caught the grimness beneath the question; Rakken knew the dangers of such magics as well as he did—probably better, in fact. Wyn exchanged a look with Catsmere, who grimaced.

"Of course we're going to tell him," Hetta burst out. "Why wouldn't we?" But she faltered in the face of Wyn's expression. "What is it?"

He rose and went to sit beside her, taking her hand in his. Alexandra watched silently, her face still very white.

"I don't know as much as I would like about telepaths," he said slowly, speaking to them both. "It is a rare magic, even in Faerie. But I know that one of the dangers is keeping your own thoughts separate from those of others. It's possible that if Marius has always had this ability, he has developed instinctive shielding mechanisms to cope with the, ah, 'noise'. Once he knows what he is, there's a risk that instinctive control may fail him."

"But you think your sister's meddling has changed him anyway?" Hetta bit her lip and looked down at her brother's still form. Marius's expression was taut with pain rather than the smooth composure of true sleep. "He's been getting more headaches in recent months," she murmured.

"I don't know if Set caused this or not," Wyn said, unhappy at uncovering yet another piece of ignorance. "Perhaps. Or perhaps it's another side-effect of the increase in Stariel's magic since the Iron Law came down." A futile anger burned in him—for Set, himself, or the High King of Faerie, he wasn't sure. The train rattled over the rails, swallowing the small sounds of Marius's breaths that Wyn couldn't help straining to hear.

"What happens if he can't control it? If it gets worse?" Hetta's grip on his hand tightened.

"It could be bad, depending on how powerful he is," Wyn said carefully. "But control is possible. There *do* exist functional telepaths in Faerie. And Marius's abilities could be quite mild if they've hidden for so long undetected. We won't know until he wakes what, if any, changes Set has wrought this time. He might be fine." He clung to that reassurance.

"Madness," Rakken said bluntly. "Or death. Or other people's madness or death, since today proves he can project as well as receive. No, I didn't know he was capable of that, brother," he added. He brought his legs up and crossed them, leaning his weight on his elbows as he peered across the carriage at Marius. "I assumed he'd always had some measure of mild psychic ability and that you chose not to tell him, either for his own good or to use as leverage." He smiled. "Or both."

Of course Rakken had assumed that; it was exactly what he would have done if their positions were reversed.

Hetta leaned against Wyn's side, and he put his arm around her without thinking how it would look. Aunt Sybil made a half-hearted clucking sound, which both of them ignored.

"And you're sure, are you?" she challenged Rakken. "That he's a… telepath?" She hesitated over the term.

"Your brother appears particularly sensitive to Mouse, Lord Valstar." Catsmere spoke suddenly. Rake narrowed his eyes at her, and she shrugged, unrepentant. "I assume that's why his abilities were more obvious to him."

Rake was an accomplished sorcerer—his mental shields should've been adamantine. Was it coincidence that Marius had asked about Rakken, earlier at the station? Wyn cut that thought off, uncomfortable with its direction.

Rakken pursed his lips, not entirely pleased with this revelation either. Then he shook himself back to composure. "Marius Valstar aside," he said, coolly assessing Wyn, "you acquitted yourself better than I feared, against our sister, Wyn."

The name caught Wyn by surprise. "Careful you don't inflate my ego with flattery," he said dryly.

"She'll be back, won't she?" Hetta asked quietly.

"Yes," said Rakken. "She would like all of us dead, but Wyn most particularly." He smiled, sharp and unamused. "Tell me, what sort of ruler do you think she'd be? Precisely how generous do you think she would be in her dealings with mortals?" His teeth caught viciously on the last word.

Hetta flared up in his defence, her body tense against his side. "You've already persuaded Wyn to go back to the Spires—there's no need to labour the point," she said. "And don't try to tell me you want Wyn as king out of some kind of altruistic motive; you're just trying to save your own skin."

Rakken met Wyn's eyes, the ice-cold accusation in them piercing straight to Wyn's core—because they both knew that hadn't been Rakken's point at all. The fate of mortals should not be what motivated the ruler of a fae people.

"I do care for those of the Spires," Wyn said. A weak truth. He cared what became of ThousandSpire's fae, yes—but it was as a candleflame to the sun compared to how he cared for those of Stariel, and he could not pretend otherwise, not with Marius lying deathly still only a wingspan away. But it only added further fuel to his determination; nothing like this could be allowed to happen to his Valstars again. "I have accepted my duty, brother." What did his reasons for doing so matter?

Rakken's mouth thinned into a hard line. "Just remember the cost of breaking your promises."

48

A MINOR CELEBRITY

HETTA DIDN'T REMEMBER the day-long journey to Stariel ever taking quite so long. The minutes stretched into hours, but still Marius didn't stir. She watched his chest rise and fall and tried to find it reassuring that the lines of pain on his face had smoothed into sleep. She dug her fingers into the stiff leather of the seats. *If I see Aroset again, I'm lighting an inferno with her at the centre.* Along the muted bond, Stariel pulsed in distant agreement.

Probably the murderous thought ought to horrify her, but there wasn't space in the hollow of her chest for anything but anger. Her mind kept flashing back to Aroset's face as the fae woman held Marius. As a child, she'd once seen a boy in the village pull the legs off a grasshopper and watch its disjointed attempts to escape with fascinated glee. He'd had the same expression as Aroset.

Her aunt hadn't said anything the entire journey so far, just sat silently watching Marius, but now she gave herself a shake and said, in an uncertain tone at odds with her normal authoritative way of speaking: "What about that fae girl, Miss Smith?" She looked at

Wyn. 'Miss Smith' was how Gwendelfear had styled herself when she'd originally come to Stariel.

Alexandra started from where she'd been slouched into her seat, knocking her untouched sketchbook from the seat onto the floor. She bent to pick it up with a murmured apology, her attention fixed on Wyn too. He and Hetta hadn't told them yet that Gwendelfear had been responsible for Wyn's recent imprisonment.

Wyn shook his head. "It isn't a physical injury," he murmured. The russet of his eyes was dulled. "Though we will try that, if it comes to it." He didn't suggest it wasn't a good idea to bargain with hostile fae, which told Hetta he was as worried as she was.

She shivered, and Wyn put an arm around her shoulders, ignoring Aunt Sybil's protest: "Henrietta!"

"There's no one here to see, Aunt." She leaned into him, trying to ignore the guilt prickling low in her stomach. This wasn't her fault. Was it? If she hadn't put her own desires above Stariel's best interests, would Marius be lying deathly still in a silent carriage? Would Alexandra still be staring at the blank page of her sketchbook as if she were reliving Aroset's attempt to compel her?

If Hetta had let the Spires have Wyn that first time, after King Aeros had died, this wouldn't have happened. The guilt sharpened, and she buried her face in Wyn's coat. He didn't object, and she breathed in the spice-scented comfort of him, the steady beat of his heart against her cheek.

Please let Marius be all right, she begged any gods that might be listening. She and Marius had been at odds so much recently. She hadn't wanted to hear his advice, that kernel of painful truth in it. It wasn't fair! If she was the one making selfish choices, why was it always everyone else who ended up hurt? Her hands clenched in the fabric of Wyn's shirt.

She looked up at the sound of movement some minutes later. Rakken was making his way over to Marius's still-unconscious form. He sat down next to him and closed his eyes as if he were meditating.

"What are you—?" But he shot her a look of pure impatience.

"I'm not going to hurt him, Lord Valstar. Of us all, *I* am the most qualified to understand magical injuries, and there is little else to occupy me on this train. You may thank me for my generosity later."

"I'm not going to thank you for trying to help Marius only because you're *bored!*" she said indignantly, but Rakken ignored her and closed his eyes. But only a few moments later he let out a hiss of pain and opened them. He rubbed at the nape of his neck and retreated to his earlier perch.

"His shields are…sharp," he said, as if that explained anything at all. His eyes narrowed. "But effective. If you want my advice, it is thus: *don't* tell him what he is, when he wakes."

"Why not, Rake?" Wyn asked before she could.

Rakken shrugged. "I'd rather not be here if that shield shatters."

"You think he'll wake, though?" she asked, latching on to the word 'when' with fierce hope. But Rakken spread his arms in an it's-anyone's-guess gesture and her heart sank.

He pondered the shifting countryside through the window, where the sun was curving towards late afternoon. "I am going to see if there is anything else to occupy me on this train," he announced, getting up to prowl towards the far end of the carriage.

"If you compel anyone, I'll burn every feather you've got," Hetta told him firmly, with a glance at her sister. Alexandra's shoulders straightened, and she glared at Rakken as well.

Rakken rolled his eyes at the pair of them. "Noted." He looked to Catsmere, and she raised an eyebrow.

"I'll look after them, Mouse. You need not fret."

He made a rude gesture at his twin that fortunately Aunt Sybil didn't see. It startled a burble of laughter from Hetta, and Wyn chuckled softly as well. Rakken shot them both a cold look and stalked out. Catsmere's expression was as unreadable as ever, but it occurred to Hetta that Wyn wasn't the only member of his family with a dry sense of humour.

After he left, Hetta reached along the bond, tried to judge the distance to Stariel, and couldn't. She sighed.

"We should pass Ulerain soon," Wyn murmured, drawing small circles on her back. Ulerain marked the last Southern city before they crossed into the North.

"Seven more hours then," she said. It felt like a lifetime.

WHEN THEY CROSSED THE border, Stariel washed over her in a wave of magic and familiarity, and the bond lit up like a firestorm. She sucked in a breath, suddenly alive in a way she hadn't felt since she'd left. But she didn't have time to savour the sensation, instead pushing it away impatiently.

<Yes, yes, I'm happy to see you too, but what about Marius?> She drew the faeland's attention to her brother. It was distracted, examining her like a dog inspecting new scents. It tried to tell her something, but she tugged it more forcefully. <Later! Marius needs our help now. *This* one.> She emphasised the spark of her brother. That was how Stariel saw the people it was connected to—like a web of tiny people-sparks spread across its land.

Previously, she'd tried to avoid examining the Valstar-sparks she was connected to in any detail. It felt too much like an invasion of privacy—and she'd rather not accidentally find out everything her relatives got up to in their spare time.

But now she knelt next to Marius and measured what she could see against the faeland's perception. His spark was…bruised, for lack of a better term, and Stariel coiled around him protectively.

<Can we help him?> she asked it, sending emotions along with

the words. For a long, awful moment, she couldn't communicate properly, but then, abruptly, she felt it understand what she was trying to convey. Knowledge unravelled in her mind, like the ghost of someone guiding her hands to the line of connection between her and her brother. It was thin as spider-silk, and she pulled it taut. A sense of Marius-ness hummed through her. To Stariel, he was a creature of growing things, old paper, and stubborn resistance to its influence.

The faeland plucked at his spark with something like satisfaction, and the line thickened with a zap that nearly made her drop it. Clinging on, she began to feed energy along the newly strengthened bond. She drew the land's energy up through her feet, tasting pine and new grass on her tongue, becoming more than herself, stretched all the way from the Indigoes into this tiny metal box running over her fields.

Marius's spark flared, an aura of shifting patterns slowly gaining speed, and the line between them narrowed as something sharp and defensive sprang into being between him and the faeland. *Shields*, she realised, jumping away from the slicing churn of them before the blades could catch her. *That's what Rakken was talking about.* Marius's land-sense had always been weak, and she wondered, suddenly, if this was why.

She blinked, coming back to her body. Marius groaned and curled in on himself, but he seemed to be waking. Oh, thank the gods. Wyn was crouched next to her, and he reached out and squeezed her hand. The movement made the faeland's interest shift to Wyn, agitated and possessive, and he staggered as it rubbed against him affectionately.

<Stop that!> she told it sharply, hauling its attention away. <What in Pyrania's name has gotten into you? What are you trying to tell me?> That's what it felt like—a string of exclamations in a foreign language, made of shapes and images and scent. It stopped trying

to—well, *nuzzle* Wyn, was the best verb she could come up with for its actions—but it still hovered, trying to convey a meaning she couldn't grasp.

"At least it's happy to see me," Wyn reflected, finding his balance again. "Marius?"

Her brother groaned again and opened his eyes. "Ow," he complained. He made an aborted attempt to sit and gave up, clutching his head. "Ow." He looked sideways at them blearily. "Where...?" He shut his eyes again. "Ow."

"You're not a lamb to bleat so, Marius Valstar." Rakken had returned to his previous seat a few hours ago, apparently un-entertained by the rest of the train's occupants.

Marius's eyes snapped open. "Fuck you, Rakken." It wasn't like him to swear, though Hetta broadly agreed with his sentiment.

Rakken chuckled. "Am I to take it your mind is intact, then?"

"Maybe it would be more intact if you stopped yelling at me to get up already," Marius complained and made a second, more successful, attempt. He leaned his elbows on his legs, panting, and flushed as he spotted Hetta, Aunt Sybil, and Alexandra clustering around him. "Sorry."

"I don't actually need my smelling salts to cope with strong language," Hetta said dryly before throwing her arms around him, dizzy with relief. He yelped, and she released him. "Sorry. How do you feel?"

"Terrible," he said. His expression crumpled at the edges as his land-sense kicked in. "We're in Stariel. How...?" He frowned around the empty compartment and winced. "What happened? I thought..." His gaze fixed on Wyn. "You told me to get on the train, but I don't remember getting on it."

"Aroset happened," she said, exchanging a glance with Wyn. "You don't remember?"

Marius paled but shook his head.

"Aroset tried to compel you and failed," Wyn said. "You've been unconscious since we left Meridon this morning." There was a warning in Rakken's eyes not to tell Marius the rest, though Hetta wasn't sure how he planned to enforce that if Marius could pluck the knowledge straight out of his brain.

But however Marius's telepathy worked, it clearly wasn't quite so simple.

"And everyone is all right?" he said, glancing around, his attention going to Alexandra. "Alex?"

"I'm fine," she said fiercely. "Why does everyone keep *asking* me? *You're* the one that was hurt!"

He frowned but rubbed at his head. "Where's Aroset? Sorry. I think I missed some steps in there somewhere. Can someone please explain? Gods, my head is killing me. How did Aroset find us?"

Rakken flung something at them, hard and so quick Hetta couldn't tell what it was until Wyn snatched it out of the air and frowned down at the rolled newspaper in his hand.

"*That*, I suspect," Rakken said. "Though on the brighter side, your name will now be useless as a trace, assuming this newspaper has a reasonably wide distribution and you remain a topic of interest. Congratulations on your new celebrity, Hallowyn."

Wyn unrolled the newspaper to reveal the front page of the *Meridon Times*. "The earl disobeyed the queen's instruction not to use my full name," he noted.

"Maybe that might finally make her punish him properly!" Hetta grumbled. It still rankled, leaving the earl and John Tidwell free to do what they liked back in Meridon—though at least the queen would be more suspicious of her advisor now.

She took the paper from Wyn, and Alexandra craned to see over her shoulder. In the photograph Wyn was in his fae form, wings slightly spread in front of a set of grand stone steps leading up to a terrace in the palace gardens. The photographer had caught him at an angle that emphasised the sharpness of his cheekbones and the pointed tips of his ears. Queen Matilda stood next to him. Their expressions were uncannily similar, warm and relaxed but ultimately false. Or perhaps it was only because she knew Wyn, knew that this wasn't what he looked like when he was actually enjoying himself.

"You look very dashing," she told him. "Very ambassadorial." She stared down at the picture, unsettled. The caption read: PRINCE HALLOWYN TEMPESTREN BIDS FAREWELL TO HER MAJESTY QUEEN MATILDA I IN THE PALACE GARDENS.

"I suppose this means I shan't be able to make any more dramatic reveals of my true self," he said, giving a deep, put-upon sigh. She laughed and reached instinctively to take his hand. Marius followed the motion with a frown but said nothing.

JACK WAS WAITING FOR them at Stariel Station, the station lamps a beacon of welcome in the evening. Marius still had difficulty with his balance, and he leaned heavily on Wyn for the transfer to the platform. Jack started forward in alarm before Marius waved them off.

"No, it's fine, I'm fine," he said.

"You have an unusual definition of fine," Wyn muttered, low enough that Hetta only caught it because she was standing just behind them in the carriage door.

"Says the person who was determined to climb every staircase in the house after we cut a bullet out of him," Marius retorted. It reassured Hetta—if Marius had the energy to make biting remarks, he must be feeling somewhat better.

The evening was cold and blustery, distinctly chillier than the milder weather of Meridon, where spring had taken a fuller hold. Hetta huddled into her coat as they were pelted with greetings, demands for explanations, and introductions. The station attendant

asked if they wanted help with their luggage. It was a far different reception to last time Hetta had returned home from Meridon.
Then, the platform had been empty, with only the wind in the
bracken and the baa-ing of sheep. *And this time I'm returning home
rather than leaving it.* The thought pinged a strangely neutral note.

"Yes, thank you, to the kineticar," she said to the attendant,
shaking off the memory and picking up her trunk. "You two are
welcome to help cart luggage," she said to Catsmere and Rakken.
"But you're going to have to fly to the House since you definitely
won't fit." Stariel swirled around the twins, respecting her permis-
sions but wary of the power they represented.

The two fae changed and took to the skies in a flurry of green
and bronze. The station attendant froze, mouth agape, and Jack was
only a little less startled.

"They're visiting fae ambassadors," Hetta said to the attendant,
who closed his mouth and swallowed. "Jack, be useful, will you?"
She waved at the remaining bags, and Jack shook himself back
into motion.

"Very good, my lord," the attendant said weakly.

What would the staff and the rest of her family think of Rakken
and Catsmere descending in a rush of wings? Or any of the villagers, who might look up and see them? *It didn't occur to them to hide
what they are.* She turned to find Wyn on the heels of that thought.
In contrast to his siblings, he looked entirely human as he helped
Marius gingerly lever himself into the front seat. Marius folded into
the space with a groan.

"Lady Philomena may have something that can help," Wyn told
him. "Marigold tea, maybe."

"We are going to have a long talk about magic and botany,"
Marius grumbled, and shut his eyes with a grimace. "Later."

Wyn closed the door and surveyed the view over the top of the
kineticar thoughtfully. "I wonder if they finished patching the roof?"
he mused. He met Hetta's eyes and smiled, but there was a heaviness

there. He knew it wasn't his role to care about such things—or at least, not for much longer. Her heart gave a single, painful squeeze.

Hetta went to check on the state of the Dower House, but Jack spoke before she could. "They have, and the linesmen came to look at wiring up the house. They want you to do some trenching work next week, Hetta." Her cousin waved a hand at the kineticar. "Pile in."

It was a very squashed trip. A cold, prickling guilt grew as they slowed to pass through the village of Stariel-on-Starwater. She hadn't thought much about Stariel while they'd been gone, hadn't thought about its people or its concerns; she'd been far more focused on her own interests. Wyn had thought about them, but Wyn was leaving. She needed to be *better* at this. Stariel's vast presence should've been reassuring after the muted connection of the last week, but instead she felt even more adrift.

<Why did you choose me?> she asked it, and then immediately felt foolish for it. There was no answer, of course, but its awareness curled around her, again trying to communicate something. It seemed…excited, for lack of a better word. How could she be a good lord if she couldn't even understand her own land-sense?

Jack parked the kineticar in the converted garage at the back of Stariel House. Marius was steadier on his feet, though he still complained of his head, and Hetta went in search of her grandmother for marigold tea while Wyn and Jack helped him up to his room. There was no sign of Rakken and Catsmere, and when Hetta reached, she found them up by the Standing Stones. Stariel watched them with interest as they examined the stone circle. Of course they'd be impatient to leave. *Well, they can jolly well wait*, she thought, fiercely.

49

HOME REMEDIES

"Marigold?" Grandmamma Philomena said when Hetta explained her errand. "Ah, yes, of course—it has spiritual healing properties." She nodded sagely. "I think I have some in the stillroom."

"How do you know so much about fae magic, anyway?" Hetta asked, following her grandmother through the house. Grandmamma was nearer ninety than eighty, but one wouldn't know it from the erect, energetic way she walked.

Grandmamma waggled her eyebrows. "At my age, m'dear, one knows many things." Hetta sighed, but the inexact answer didn't surprise her. Grandmamma loved to be mysterious. But to her surprise, Grandmamma paused and added: "Young Alexandra didn't get the Sight from the Valstar side."

The stillroom was on the second floor, and the layered scent of dried herbs always brought Hetta fond memories. Her grandmother strode decisively for the jar cupboard and began to rummage. She hummed to herself, steel-grey curls bouncing as she shook a jar and put it back, dissatisfied with the dry-rice sound. "Have you stitched things up with your young man yet?" she asked.

Hetta traced her fingers along the wooden table that ran down the centre of the room. "It's complicated."

Grandmamma made a dubious sound. "I can have a word with him if he needs to be brought up to scratch."

Hetta gave an involuntary giggle at the suggestion, wondering just what, exactly, Grandmamma would say to Wyn. But she shook her head. "Thank you, Grandmamma, but he's already asked. Sort of."

"Proposing is not a *sort of* question, Henrietta," Grandmamma said disapprovingly. "One proposes or one does not."

"Try telling him that," she said with a sigh.

"He must be nervous, then, about your answer." Grandmamma tsked.

Hetta opened her mouth to say something about the High King, but instead what came out was: "He's leaving."

Grandmamma paused with a jar in hand. "Well, have you asked him not to?"

"It's not that simple," she protested. How could she ask Wyn to put her above the Spires, above his family, above his people? And if she did and he agreed, how could she live with herself, being responsible for whatever further destruction Aroset wrought? She thought of Marius, lying deathly still in the carriage, and of the casual way Rakken had compelled an entire station's worth of people. "I have to put Stariel first, and he has to go home."

Grandmamma's expression was sympathetic rather than accusing, but Hetta felt the need to defend herself nonetheless.

"But he's going to come back and visit—or, well, we haven't worked it out yet, but we'll figure something out." A lump grew in her throat, as if she might burst suddenly into tears. She blinked them back, furious with herself. *I'm not going to turn into a weeping mess. Honestly, it's not as if I'll never see him again!*

Grandmamma put the jar down. "And that's putting Stariel first, is it? You having half a fiancé, bound to somewhere else?"

The words rocked Hetta back on her heels. "Yes!" she said. *No*, she thought. The negative slammed against her ribs, making them ache.

"Well, if that's what makes you happy," Grandmamma said slowly. She picked up a jar. "Here's the marigold. Let's see if it can help my grandson."

HETTA BROUGHT MARIUS THE tea, ignoring the doubt that Grandmamma's question had dragged to the surface. Marius was perched wanly on the edge of his bed with Jack and Alexandra hovering nearby. He accepted the tea with gruff thanks and threw them out. "I don't need you all standing about watching while I lie here and feel sorry for myself!" he said peevishly.

"Will he be all right?" Alexandra asked anxiously once they were out in the hallway. She lowered her voice and glanced at Jack. "Do you think Prince Rakken was right about"—she bit her lip—"the other thing?"

"I don't know, but I think it's a good sign that he's recovered enough to banish us from his side," Hetta said, trying to convince herself. She looked at Jack. "Do you know where Wyn is?"

"The housekeeper wanted him," he said. "Meanwhile, *you* need to talk to Councillor Talbot. The man's a pest! He doesn't approve of the linesmen coming from outside the district." He began to fill her in on what had gone on in her absence. She tried to listen, but it washed over her, drowned out by a mental ticking clock. They were at Stariel. The Standing Stones were ten minutes' walk from the house. Rakken and Catsmere were already there and probably expected Wyn to join them as soon as possible. And then—then they would build a portal to the Spires, and Wyn would be *gone*.

"Hetta, are you even listening?" Jack complained. Alexandra was watching her thoughtfully.

"No, no, I'm not," she said vaguely. "Excuse me." She shed the pair and went in search. She found Wyn mediating between the new housekeeper and her late father's valet, who'd been with the Valstars since before Hetta was born. She didn't intervene—that would only escalate the dispute. The servants' hierarchy was Wyn's business.

"What was that about?" she asked when she entered his office after she sensed its other occupants had left. It was all so very familiar, and for a moment the normality of it shook her.

Wyn's eyes danced. "The proper recipe for cleaning silver, if you'd believe it. And also…piskies."

"Oh. Are they all right?"

"The piskies or the staff?"

"Both. And the silver, I suppose."

He ran a hand through his hair. "I think I've persuaded them that the piskies aren't a danger, though it sounds as if there may be a war brewing between the piskies and the other housefae. You may need to assign the brownies house territory, but make it clear that you're only doing it as it affects your living quarters or you'll have wyldfae across the estate clamouring at you for favour."

"Right," she said. "And the silver?"

He smiled. "It wasn't really about that. My absence has created… certain tensions in the staff hierarchy. I attempted to remain neutral. They'll work it out between themselves." His expression darkened, but he didn't say the words *they'll have to* aloud. She heard them anyway, and she crossed the space between them to wrap her arms around him.

She'd wanted to talk to him about Marius, about Aroset, about when and how exactly he was proposing to go to the Spires, but the words washed away under the steady thump of his heart under her cheek, the familiar scent of him. She didn't want words, just now, and she tugged his head down to kiss him.

She kissed him desperately, as if just getting close enough would mean she could somehow keep him, and he answered with the same urgent need. How dare the Court of Ten Thousand Spires try to take him from her when they'd only just begun? How dare his sister be a murderous villain? She felt the back of her legs hit the desk as they pressed more tightly together, trying to eliminate all the spaces between them. His magic and hers thrummed in the air, combining in a riot of colour and scents. She wanted to drown in the taste until she forgot about responsibility and annoyingly cryptic grandmothers and the knowledge that two greater fae waited by the Standing Stones.

"Hetta," he said hoarsely. His eyes were black as night when he pulled back for a breath. Lust fought with sorrow in their depths, and it triggered her anger all over again. How dare *he* be sorry about this! She kissed him again.

How dare he be sorry when he'd been doing his level-best to convince her to let him go entirely? When he'd made her love him despite all the complications he brought with him? When she'd come to rely upon him being there? She poured her anger into the kiss, working his shirt loose of his belt so she could dig her fingers into the flat planes of his stomach. He groaned and pulled her closer, tangling his hands in her hair.

Distantly, she knew this was a delayed reaction to fear and uncertainty, and that this wasn't the wisest location in the world for such activities, but she didn't care, and she wasn't prepared to stop for even the few minutes it might take them to relocate. From his reaction, Wyn clearly agreed with this assessment.

Afterwards, his expression was as unguarded as she'd ever seen it, full of yearning uncertainty. Neither of them spoke as they righted themselves, stretching the intimacy as far as it would go. She helped him straighten his bowtie, and he smoothed her hair behind her ears.

"I am glad that Stariel has, ah, calmed down, as it were," he said, a slight roughness in his words.

He was right, though thinking of the faeland summoned its interest. It curled lazily around her for a moment, still trying to tell her something she couldn't quite catch. It subsided when she reassured it there was no need for its further involvement just now.

"I wonder what changed?"

Amusement flickered briefly around his mouth. "I think Stariel may have discerned its *encouragement* was no longer needed."

She let out an incredulous laugh. "Oh. *Oh.* Well, if it wanted me to successfully seduce you, it was going about it completely the wrong way." She sent an indignant thought in Stariel's direction. <Who I choose to seduce isn't your business, anyway!> It didn't respond.

"Faelands do not think in mortal—or even fae—terms," Wyn pointed out. His focus drifted towards the darkening view of Starwater through the narrow windows—which fortunately nothing overlooked, given recent activities. You couldn't see the Standing Stones from this angle, though Hetta could feel them. Rakken and Catsmere acted as a sort of beacon, pulling her own attention if she wasn't careful. "Do you remember showing me how to skim a stone, years ago?" he asked suddenly.

She blinked as the memory came tumbling out of the distant past. "Yes." At the time she'd been surprised no one else had taught him the trick already, but it made more sense now. Perhaps it wasn't a game young fae played—or, more likely, one played by young princes. "You weren't a very apt pupil. I think you sank nearly every stone in Stariel without a single skip before you got the hang of it, and even then, you never could get as many skips as me." She frowned. "Which, now I think about it, seems improbable." His lips curved, though he didn't turn from the window. "I can't believe you pretended you didn't know how to skim stones just to butter me up!" she accused.

"Oh, I wasn't pretending," he said. "You did teach me." He smiled, a hint of mischief in it. "But I may have learnt as slowly as I dared. I liked watching you demonstrate. You had a way of weighing each stone in your palm before you threw, as if you were measuring its worth." The great lake's surface was a dark blur in the dusk, but Hetta could see all the way back to that long-ago morning. The much-younger Wyn had shyly followed her instructions, all awkward angles and bones, height not yet fleshed out properly. And here he was now, more than a decade later, both of them grown into themselves, his profile achingly familiar and beloved.

"You have to go," she said, suddenly unable to bear the pretence of it, the ticking clock she was sure they could both hear. "We should go."

"Yes," he said, finally meeting her eyes.

"Would you stay, if I asked?" The question escaped before she could help it.

"*Are* you asking me?" He went very still.

She almost did, the words burning on the tip of her tongue, but then she shook her head. "No. No, I'm not. I won't ask you to put me before your people and everyone else Aroset might hurt, and you're being unfair, wanting me to." It didn't matter what either of them wanted; there wasn't a better alternative here. But Grandmamma had been right too—how could she build a life with someone as intimately tied to another faeland as she was to Stariel? She *knew* what it was like to share half your soul in that way.

To her surprise, for Stariel didn't often comment on her thoughts, it sent her a memory: ThousandSpire, reaching through the portal for Wyn, and Hetta and itself pushing the incursion back. There was a distinctly possessive edge to the image. <I know you're trying

to be reassuring, but that's exactly the problem,> she told it sternly. <He has a duty to ThousandSpire now, and that supersedes our claim on him. We have to let him go.>

Taking a deep breath, she said the words she didn't want to say. "And I'm being unfair to both of us." Her heart wasn't breaking. Hearts didn't break—that was just a stupid metaphor.

It only felt like it.

50

PAPERWORK

WYN'S HEART CRYSTALLISED. He knew Hetta was about to speak bitter truths, and he did not want to hear them. And yet, this too was part of why he loved her. He'd always known she wouldn't let him go too far, take too much, that he could trust her to hold her line in the sand. It had made it safe to love her. *As if I could have stopped myself.* But he didn't regret it, not even when he saw her swallow and draw that hard line between them now.

"I don't want it to matter, that you're fae, or this thing with the Spires. But it sort of does, doesn't it?" She drew herself up, each word becoming firmer. "You can't rule another faeland and still put me and Stariel first. You *can't,* Wyn, and I know that better than anyone. It's only going to hurt us both—*and* our respective faelands—to pretend that's not the case, isn't it?"

"I…" He trailed off, because he could not find a truth that wasn't jagged edges to counter her words with. He swallowed. "What of your mortal queen?"

Her smile was wan. "That's exactly the point, isn't it? She's using us and our respective positions as leverage against each other. It would be better for ThousandSpire if you could negotiate with her without that hanging over you." She paused and added reluctantly, "And better for Stariel if I wasn't tying myself to someone intimately bound to another faeland." *And better for me,* she didn't say, but he saw it in her eyes.

I won't go to the Spires! he wanted to cry, but he couldn't—not with the memory of the attack at the station still fresh. Aroset couldn't be allowed to hurt anyone else, and this was the only way to stop her. He'd known it was impossible, when Hetta had talked of finding a way to be together, but oh, how he'd wanted to be wrong. But there was no denying she would be better off without her loyalties divided, better out of fae politics. All the Valstars would be—as this morning's attack at the station had proved in painful detail.

"I'm sorry," he said, brokenly, because he could think of nothing else to say. He ran his hands through his hair, trying to flatten it, trying to rein in his magic. It fought him, and feathers itched under his skin, straining for release. *Another reason Hetta's better off without you,* he thought, viciously. *You can't even control your damned magic!*

"Don't be sorry," she said. "It's not your fault. It's unfair, and neither of our faults, but it doesn't change anything." She took a deep, shuddering breath, her composure cracking. "Gods, I thought it would be you that did this, that decided we were better apart."

Oh, he couldn't bear it, the desolation in her eyes. He moved to wrap his arms around her without conscious thought, but she shook her head sharply and stepped back, out of reach.

"No." She swallowed. "I'm not going to get over you if I keep letting you comfort me, am I?" It was like her, to act decisively once she'd made up her mind, but it didn't make it hurt any less. "I'll tell Queen Matilda she's not announcing any engagement." She fished below her neck and pulled out the ring he'd made, holding it out to him.

He stared down at the metal, finding it oddly hard to draw a full breath. "Ah—I appreciate the symbolic gesture, but I don't want you to lose the practical aspect of it, when you travel outside the estate again."

A heaviness crept into her posture. "Oh. Oh, yes, you're right." She tucked it into a pocket, and a tiny bit of him eased. At least he could give her that. "Shall we go, then?"

"I was actually going to suggest we wait until tomorrow morning," he said sheepishly. "It's growing dark, and while I hope my sister hasn't set guards on the point of resonance, if she has, I'd rather not encounter them at night." He paused and waved at his desk. "Also, I wanted to tidy my affairs up a little more." *And to see how Marius does.* Hetta and Stariel's healing had helped, enormously, but it still worried him.

Hetta stared at him and then she began to laugh. "You!" she spluttered in between giggles. They tinged towards hysteria, and he suppressed the urge to go to her again. "You can't just let me heroically decide to give you up and then announce that you have to do some paperwork first! How can you even think of paperwork at a time like this?!"

"Because this is something I can control, and I cannot bear to think of all the things I can't!" He tamped down the anger and sagged. "I'm sorry. You're right. I'm being foolish. What difference, after all, can a day make, in the context of a decade's service?"

"Well, probably quite a lot, knowing you," she said, the hysteria fading, leaving something old and sad in its wake. "I doubt it'll make much difference to the Spires if you arrive there tonight versus tomorrow morning. And since you've already spoiled my attempt at a dramatic clean break, we may as well bring practicality into the equation."

He smiled. It felt brittle as dry leaves. "Are we taking turns being reasonable?"

"What am I going to do without you?" she whispered.

"You'll carry on," he told her. "You've always been strong, and you do not need me to make you so."

"I just…" He felt her teeter on the precipice, but then she waved at his desk, beginning to back out of the room. "I'll tell your siblings. Do what you need to do."

51

TO THE SPIRES

THE NEXT MORNING, he stood beside Hetta at the Standing Stones. All around the hilltop, it was raining, a grey drizzle obscuring the wider landscape, though the Stones themselves stood in a bubble of dry space, thanks to Hetta. The soft background hiss was the only sound as Rakken made the portal between ThousandSpire and Stariel. It was as easy as Wyn had feared, and within moments, Stariel's rain-blurred mountains shimmered into the towering rock formations of Aerest. Dust, metal and storms rolled out, clashing with the damp greenness of springtime.

He recognised the location on the other side of the portal as the top of the prison spire where Hetta had been held last year. Probably not an accident that the portal resonated between these two points. No guards were visible, which meant Aroset hadn't been aware of the potential resonance point. That was promising. Now he just needed to make his feet move.

More than ten years, he'd been flying away from ThousandSpire, in one way or another, hoping that if he flew far and fiercely enough, he could escape who and what he was. And now here he was, about to return, and in such a way that would make escape truly impossible hereafter.

Stariel quivered. He'd never before been so conscious of Hetta as Stariel's lord, her presence magnifying the faeland's. That heightened sense of connection still stretched between them, despite her words last night. Did she feel it too? Her expression didn't show it—pale but steady, though her eyes were shadowed. Stariel was, ironically, much less composed than its lord, nosing at him with nearly tangible frustration.

Rakken glared at him. "What are you waiting for, brother?"

Catsmere's expression was similarly unsympathetic.

What was important here? What did he want? What was right? Hetta took his hand and squeezed it, briefly. "Go, Wyn," she said. Her mouth curved. "And don't forget about the favourable sheep-trading terms."

His heart thumped painfully. "I won't." *I love you*, he wanted to say, but he pressed his teeth together and held the words in. It would only hurt Hetta more, he knew.

It is for the best, he told himself. *It will be better this way; everyone will be safer.* Taking a deep breath, he stepped through the portal, Catsmere and Rakken following. He slipped a little on the smooth shell-rock as they emerged on top of the roof of the prison spire.

He'd expected the portal to snap shut behind them, but it continued to shimmer in the air. Perhaps Stariel didn't want to let the connection close. Or perhaps he was being unhelpfully sentimental. Focus!

The city would've been beautiful, in other circumstances. The sun was rising, painting the towers in shades of marigold and coral, the gemstones embedded into many of the walls dancing in ten thousand tiny, multihued flames—though there were actually somewhat less than ten thousand spires in the city. He had asked one of his tutors once, but the exact total escaped him now.

But any beauty in the view was outweighed by the sorrow

coating his feathers like icicles. ThousandSpire's grief was palpable through his connection with it, causing the leylines to tremble and rearrange with every breath. Dark flecks circled the city—draken—their piercing cries making the hair on the back of his neck stand on end. In the distance, above the salt plains, the Maelstrom churned, as violent as he'd ever seen it, bolts of lightning flashing through the deep, bruised purple of the permanent storm, a physical manifestation of the faeland's unrest.

Heart of the Maelstrom, how were the inhabitants of the Spires surviving under such an onslaught? Wyn had only been here for half a minute, but already he could feel his teeth aching from the wildness of the magic in the air. Stariel, for all that it was smaller and less powerful, was used to changing rulers, used to the short lifespans of mortals. The Spires had been bonded to King Aeros for a long, long time.

He wasn't surprised that the Spires didn't notice him immediately amidst such immense magical confusion. Steeling himself, he reached out along the bond. <I am here, ThousandSpire.>

That got its attention, and it fell on him with a roar, overwhelming his senses with metal and dust and the cold, clean taste of ozone. He didn't blame the faeland for his upbringing here, but its magic was so bound up with memories of his father that it was hard not to recoil from the assault. *But I won't be like my father.* If kingship was his fate, he would make the Court of Ten Thousand Spires into something new, find a way to weave Mortal and Faerie together. He held the thought close, a comforting talisman.

ThousandSpire, for all its power, was hesitant as it wound its way around him, like a feral cat unsure of its welcome. But he could feel its desperation, its incompleteness without a lord; faelands couldn't sustain themselves for long without a bond to a living soul. So it would take him, ambivalent as he was, rather than be alone.

He needed to relax. He knew, instinctively, that this was going to hurt if he didn't, if he resisted. *I should have asked Hetta for advice.*

Her bonding with Stariel had knocked her temporarily unconscious, but he didn't think it had hurt. Probably because deep down she'd embraced it, he thought wryly. He needed to embrace this.

Closing his eyes, he tried to think of all the good he could do as King of Ten Thousand Spires. He thought of the way sunset painted Aerest gold, of the cool shade of the eucalypts to the south, where he'd spent some of his happiest days as a child at the summer palace, before his mother had left. He thought of the lazy thermals above the plains and how Irokoi had patiently taught him the exhilarating flight path through the narrow canyons, before he'd been blinded.

But over these memories, newer, stronger ones kept intruding. Hetta's tear-filled eyes at seeing him whole and unharmed. The high-pitched shrieking of Valstar children as they scampered down hallways, giggling and trying to hide from their parents. The rich sweet-sour of sloe gin, and a sixteen-year-old Hetta laughing as he balanced atop a fence post to get to the hardest-to-reach berries on the hedgerows. Discussing thatching with cottagers and bridge repairs with stone masons. The solemn stillness of snow high on the Indigoes and the distant baa of sheep. Bare skin and honey-suckle-scented sheets. He pushed the images away, but they kept bubbling up. *Focus!*

He'd been right; his resistance hurt. Knives of charge sliced through to his bones, a hundred times worse than the recoil of the dismae, as the faeland tried to force its magic to merge with his.

Abruptly it wasn't just ThousandSpire clawing at him as another presence surged, foreign but familiar, flowing through the still-open portal. He hung suspended between the vying magics as the faelands clashed, the seam along which two great seas met, trying to keep his feet as the two faelands roared at each other. He flung out his wings, excess magic sparking off them like sea spray from colliding waves.

Stariel shouldn't have been able to reach here, not on the soil of a foreign faeland, but it was using Hetta as a magnifier, somehow finding the strengthened connection between them that he'd sensed earlier. The faeland flung out a thread towards him through the chaos of ThousandSpire, like a rope dropped to the bottom of a well.

A choice, he realised, in the sudden stillness at the eye of the storm. A person couldn't be tied to two faelands. But it changed nothing; he'd already made his choice, and his own selfish wants had no place in it. He would accept ThousandSpire's claim, let the threads of the Spires weave their way into his soul.

But rising up from his soul was a truth he could not extinguish, a denial as hard and unassailable as iron:

This is not my home.

Something inside him snapped loose and, oh, it hurt, hurt worse than anything had ever hurt before. He screamed. Pain and ecstasy tore through him, piercing down to his bones, and he lost all sense of who and what he was. The taste of Stariel flooded his senses, rolled over every shadow in his soul. He was unmade and reformed, new and shaking and vulnerable.

Smugness quivered through him, but it wasn't his own emotion, and he realised with a start that where his connection to ThousandSpire had been now lay…something else entirely.

Stariel.

He stood on ThousandSpire's lands and couldn't feel the faeland. It should've been disorienting, that loss of sensation, but replacing it was something that felt far more like home than his own court ever had. Stariel thrummed, very pleased with itself, its emotion intimate in a way he'd never before experienced. ThousandSpire, however, was *not* pleased. He didn't need a connection to it to taste the increased chaos in the air, the pressure of magic against his eardrums.

"What are you doing?" Rakken demanded while Wyn wobbled. "What have you *done?*"

Lightning flashed, and thunder rolled out, deafening.

"Look!" Catsmere directed. The churning mass of the Maelstrom was expanding. The Maelstrom wasn't a static entity, of course. That was part of what made it so terrifying. But Wyn had never seen it behave as it was doing now, its lightning clouds unfurling across the sky like a thousand fingers stretching towards the city. The rumble of thunder shook the world like a rockslide, and Wyn stumbled. It wasn't merely magical shaking; the ground had become suddenly unstable.

Rakken was pleading with the faeland to stop, but his words made no discernible impact. Eerie cold and magic flowed thick as water out from those clutching storm fingers. What would happen when they reached the city? Aerest was home to many fae, and the merest touch of the Maelstrom had nearly killed him, a royal storm-dancer. Most of the populace would not be so lucky.

"We have to stop it," he said, sick with horror. This was his fault, his moment of selfishness rippling outwards with catastrophic results.

"What did you do, Hallowyn? If it doesn't want you either, then who else is left?" Rakken stared at the oncoming storm, and Wyn saw something flicker in his expression he'd never seen there before: fear. The scent of his magic spooled out, and Wyn knew he was trying to reach the Spires, but he might as well have been shouting at the moon.

Catsmere looked from Wyn to Rakken and then back to the vast oncoming wrath of the Maelstrom. She sagged for a moment, her green eyes old and weary, before her shoulders lifted in sudden decision.

"Sleep is not death," she murmured, meeting Wyn's eyes. "Get to the portal. Make sure he goes too." And then she moved.

Catsmere had long been one of the most feared warriors of the Spires, but Wyn had forgotten the swift deadliness of her at full attack speed. Even if Rakken had been prepared, he would've been hard pressed to evade the strike—and he wasn't prepared. Not when it came from his twin.

Catsmere's sword struck with a thin whine of silk, and Rakken's primaries sheared away. Bronze and green fluttered to the ground as Rakken spun towards his sister, shock slowing him, but Cat was already aloft.

"Get to the portal, all of you. *Now*, Hallowyn!" she snarled at Wyn before winging away, her magic so potent that he could taste cinnamon even amidst the riot of ThousandSpire's turmoil. And he understood, as Rakken let out a roar of denial, that she'd grounded her twin deliberately, to prevent him from following her—because Rakken would never have let Catsmere fly into the heart of that nightmare storm alone.

For a moment she was brilliantly visible, a halo of lightning flashing around her, but then the wind whipped her away into the depths of the Maelstrom. The storm roared towards the city with renewed speed, and the ground shaking increased in intensity, cold and magic whipping around them in vicious snakes.

"Foolish godchild! You need to leave now!" a familiar but completely unexpected voice said from behind them.

They both whirled to confront Lamorkin, Wyn's godparent, who smiled brightly, showing teeth.

"You really ought not to let people sneak up on you unawares," they chided. They had wings at present—and they flexed them in a shooing motion. "Out! Out! Or you will be caught in it."

"Caught in what?" Wyn asked.

"We cannot leave our people to face the Maelstrom," Rakken said flatly, magic still pouring off him, thought it was barely noticeable against the background roar. "And I'm not leaving Cat."

To Wyn's surprise, Lamorkin straightened and said coldly: "Perhaps I wasn't clear, Prince Rakken Tempestren of the Court of Ten Thousand Spires. The High King accepts the bargain. The Spires will enter stasis, until the faeland bonds with its new ruler. Do you wish to sleep for a hundred years or more?"

Stasis. There was an old, old legend in Faerie about a faeland that the High King had put to sleep until a princess of the right blood-line had found the key to wake it. But it was a legend; something out of tales that no one could verify from having been there. Wyn had never considered that such a thing could happen in his lifetime, to his home court.

"*Sleep is not death.*" Rakken growled Catsmere's words, glaring at the sky. "What did you *do*, Cat?"

Whatever Catsmere had done, she hadn't shared it with Rakken, that much was clear.

"She's not dead," Wyn tried to reassure him. "We'd know if she was."

Rakken's gaze fixed on him, blazing with fury, and he launched himself at Wyn. "You!" But he was hampered by his crippled wings, and Wyn dodged, making a grab for him. Lamorkin took hold of Rakken's other arm, transforming into a bear-like creature to better manage the task.

"We have to leave, Rake," Wyn said, as his brother struggled. "We can't fight the High King himself." Together he and Lamorkin dragged Rakken back through the portal. Wyn could feel Stariel's anxiety. It wanted him back, and under his shock, something in him burned bright at the thought.

The portal snapped closed an instant after they were all through. Stariel vibrated with satisfaction, and Wyn lost his grip on Rakken, distracted by the overwhelming sensation of homecoming. He'd always been aware of Stariel, but it wasn't the same as being blood-bound to the faeland.

Rakken tore his way free of Lamorkin as well and snarled. "This is your fault!" But before he could reach Wyn, the earth sank beneath his feet, liquefying and re-solidifying in a heartbeat. Rakken swore and batted his wings, wrenching at his legs, but he was stuck fast in the earth up to his knees.

"Now, I know we're all having a very trying day, but I'm not letting you strangle Wyn," Hetta said firmly, folding her arms and looking down at Rakken. "What is—" But she broke off, staring at Wyn. He felt her pluck at the new connection between him and Stariel. All the colour drained from her face.

"Ah, I think you might be somewhat stuck with me now," he said sheepishly. "I'm not quite sure how that happened. I didn't know it was even possible." Was she angry with him? Stormwinds, of course she'd be angry with him. Hadn't she told him they needed to make a clean break of things, and he'd gone and done rather the opposite. But a surge of possessiveness washed over him suddenly, and he knew it wasn't just from Stariel.

"Our sister and the entire Court of Ten Thousand Spires is caught in stormwinds-bedamned *stasis* because of you, is what happened!" Rakken spat. "Are you happy now, Hallowyn, with what your selfishness has wrought?" He wrenched at his trapped legs again, but they didn't budge. His eyes narrowed. "Let me go," he demanded of Hetta.

"I will, if you stop trying to attack Wyn," she said. "What happened to your feathers?" She frowned at Lamorkin. "And who are you?"

52

CONSEQUENCES

IT TOOK SOME time to get Rakken to agree not to try to kill
Wyn upon release. Hetta was tempted to leave him stuck in the
earth till he calmed down completely, except that this would
probably mean waiting several lifetimes, judging from the way his
eyes glowed with rage, greener than emeralds.

Eventually Rakken bit out: "Fine. *Fine*, I won't rip his damned
feathers out. But this isn't over, brother. Not until we get Catsmere
out and free the Spires. You owe us that." His voice was a snarl. At
least he had the sense not to reach for his magic. Even if he had,
Stariel had grown used to dealing with unexpected lightning.

"Yes," Wyn agreed soberly. He went to say something else but
then closed his mouth instead. Hetta agreed with him—any other
commentary would just make Rakken angrier, and then they'd have
to start this over again.

Wyn didn't meet her eyes, and anxiety worried at her insides.
He'd explained what had happened in ThousandSpire in the carefully measured tones he used when he was trying to contain his
emotions, and she could tell he was still holding the leash tight.

What must it feel like, to have your land-sense torn out of you and replaced with another's? Even before she'd been Stariel's lord, her connection to the estate had been a fundamental part of her identity. *And it's my fault this happened. So much for letting him go.* The knowledge threatened to tilt her world on its axis, and she pushed it aside to consider Wyn's brother.

"Just remember I can re-quicksand you if I want." It had been instinctive, in the moment before he'd leapt for Wyn, but she mentally marked down the trick for future use next time her relatives were particularly irksome.

Rakken bared his teeth at her, and with a sigh, she let water seep into the earth around his legs, softening it. He pulled his legs free, flaring out his ruined wings for balance, and she had to put a hand over her mouth to stop a choke of laughter escaping, because he looked quite ridiculous, with his feathers shorn and mud up to his thighs. He glared at both Wyn and her, closed what was left of his wings with a snap, and stalked off without speaking, as if he didn't trust himself to keep his promise if he didn't immediately remove himself from the vicinity. His posture didn't change in the slightest as he crossed outside the bubble and into the rain, as if nothing as trivial as damp registered. She could feel his magic trembling with the force of his anger as he strode towards the distant Indigoes.

Lamorkin tilted their head at her. Wyn had explained that his godparent had no primary form, but it was still unsettling to watch Lamorkin's shape shift restlessly. The fae had emerged from the portal as a cross between a stormdancer and a bear, but now their wings had grown paper-thin, their limbs elongated and many-jointed as an insect, and their skin was covered with tiny glittering scales. They watched Hetta with unblinking beetle-black eyes.

"You want to speak to my godson alone," they said, their voice resonant in a way that wasn't exactly unpleasant, though it was disconcerting.

"Er, yes, if you wouldn't mind."

They smiled, their mouth stretching wider than it should as their flat features extended, growing into a muzzle. "I do not mind. I shall enjoy viewing this faeland." Their paper-thin wings buzzed suddenly against their spine.

"It might be better if you didn't let the locals see you," she said apologetically.

Lamorkin's eyes narrowed. "Very well." The buzzing of their wings increased, and they took flight like a dragonfly, hovering for a moment before zooming away over the landscape.

The sudden absence of other people echoed in their still cocoon. Around them, the rain began to increase in strength, the wind picking up and howling across the fields.

She rubbed at her head. She'd figure out how to introduce Lamorkin to the rest of her family later, after she'd dealt with the most important thing. Her heart in her throat, she turned back to Wyn.

He stretched out a hand, the physical gesture a manifestation of a more metaphysical one, because Hetta felt his new connection to Stariel flex in response. "I need to find Irokoi. He clearly knew what Cat was planning, so he may know how to undo the stasis." He took a careful breath, still staring down at his palm as if it were the most impossible thing in the universe. "And he might also know how to find the High King, since he is eldest. If, that is, you still want…"

"Are you angry?"

He looked up, surprise clear on his face. "Angry? No. I am… amazed." He tried out the word slowly. "I never dreamed—I don't know how this is possible, but angry is the very last thing I feel about it." There were shadows in his eyes, and a deep, yearning vulnerability. "Are *you* angry with me for it? I'm afraid I've added to rather than subtracted from my complications, but I cannot truthfully say I am sorry for this particular one, though I know I ought to be." Again, there came that metaphysical stretching sensation, as if he couldn't resist testing the connection. A warring mixture of delight and guilt flickered in his expression.

She wrapped her arms around him. "Stariel couldn't have grabbed for you if I didn't want you here," she said. He stiffened as if unsure he deserved this treatment before relaxing into it with a long sigh of relief that mirrored her own. It felt like coming home.

Stariel quivered in an expectant sort of way, like a dog that had successfully retrieved a wayward stick and would now quite like to be thanked for it. She ignored it, as panic tried to find gaps in the wall she'd built between herself and the knowledge she didn't particularly want.

"We can call it *our* fault, if you like," he offered softly, drawing a small circle on her lower back.

A burble of hysterical laughter threatened to choke its way out of her, and to her great annoyance, she started to tremble.

His embrace tightened, and he looked down at her in concern. "What's wrong?"

"It's just—that's a very apt phrasing. Our fault." She swallowed. "I think I know why Stariel was so enthusiastically trying to throw us together, before. In its own strange way, it was trying to give me what I wanted: a way to keep you. It wanted to create a connection between us, and then I think it used that to wrench you away from ThousandSpire."

She wasn't sure whether or not to be angry at Stariel for that. On the one hand, well, it had *worked*, worked in a way she hadn't dreamed possible. ThousandSpire couldn't steal him from her now no matter how many pragmatic political reasons there might be to let it do so, and part of her was fiercely, unrepentantly happy about that regardless of all the complications it would mean. On the other hand, to find her faeland was making extremely intimate decisions based on its idiosyncratic interpretation of her emotions rather than on *actual instructions* was troubling and probably another sign she wasn't doing this lording business right.

Wyn canted his head. "I *have* been sensing your energy along the leylines more strongly, since Meridon," he said thoughtfully. "I've never heard of that as a side effect of intimacy, though."

Hetta closed her eyes, briefly, still not quite believing it herself, but Stariel was only too happy to provide confirmation.

<I'll deal with you later,> she told it. <I know you were only trying to help, but this isn't something you should've interfered with. If you did interfere with it.> Stariel either couldn't or refused to understand the chastisement. Instead it bubbled at the back of her mind, a low hum of satisfaction.

She shook her head. "That's not why. I wouldn't have known— shouldn't have known yet—except Stariel's been trying to tell me ever since I crossed the border." The words came tumbling out unevenly, sticking in her throat and dislodging in bits. She was trying to be calm and sensible about this, so why was panic the only emotion she seemed to be able to feel, rising up in a slow, inevitable tide to drown her? *I didn't plan this, and I don't know what to do, Wyn. Help.*

"It took me a while to work out why. I mean, it's much too early to announce, really, and it might not, er, stick. And I know I said I'd taken precautions, but Stariel might've interfered with that, or it might've just been bad luck, or maybe I just didn't take into account our respective magics well enough, and I'm sorry for dropping this on you, but it's been dropped on *me*, and we're definitely going to need to find your High King sooner rather than later, and not just because of ThousandSpire and Queen Matilda—"

Wyn was frowning. "Forgive me, but I don't entirely follow—"

Hetta took a deep breath. "I'm pregnant."

TO BE CONTINUED...

AUTHOR'S NOTE

I hope you enjoyed *The Court of Mortals*! I am currently hard at work on the next book in the series, *The King of Faerie*. If you'd like to be emailed when it's released, you can subscribe to my mailing list on my website www.ajlancaster.com.

Please consider reviewing *The Court of Mortals* on Amazon or Goodreads, even if you only write a line or two. Reviews mean a lot to authors, and I appreciate every one!

ACKNOWLEDGEMENTS

Being a writer and indie publisher can be a lonely undertaking, and I owe thanks to the following people for making it a little less solitary:

My beta readers, Erin, Rem, Carla, Kirsten, and Cilla, for your enthusiasm, critiques, and occasional impassioned shipping debates. Any remaining plot holes are my own.

Steph, you are a fount of brilliant marketing and social media advice. One day I'm even going to manage to implement it! In the meantime, thank you for your unflagging moral support.

A shout out to Verve Café, who are under the impression I do Very Serious Professional Work on my laptop while I'm there (no one tell them!). Speaking of coffee, an extra thank you to Kirsten for all those Saturday morning latte offerings. You may keep coming to my house.

Carla, who has so far managed not to strangle me despite the ten thousand or so forgotten half-made cups of tea scattered around the flat. You are the best sister in the world.

And last but very much not least, a huge thank you to my readers, for reading and recommending my book, for leaving reviews, for sending me emails, for making and liking posts, for tweeting tweets. It wouldn't be nearly as fun without you!

ABOUT THE AUTHOR

Growing up on a farm in rural Aotearoa New Zealand, AJ Lancaster avoided chores by hiding up trees with a book. She wrote in the same way she breathed—constantly and without thinking much of it—so it took many years and accumulating a pile of manuscripts for her to realise that she might want to be a writer and, in fact, already was. On the way to this realisation she collected a degree in science, worked in environmental planning, and became an editor.

Now she lives in the windy coastal city of Wellington and writes romantic, whimsical fantasy books about fae, magic, and complicated families.

You can find her on the interwebs at:

- instagram.com/a.j.lancaster
- facebook.com/lancasterwrites
- twitter.com/lancasterwrites

CPSIA information can be obtained
at www.ICGtesting.com
Printed in the USA
LVHW011654150120
643721LV00001B/62